Robert Ornsby

Memoirs of James Robert Hope-Scott of Abbotsford

With Selections From His Correspondence. Second Edition, Vol. 2

Robert Ornsby

Memoirs of James Robert Hope-Scott of Abbotsford
With Selections From His Correspondence. Second Edition, Vol. 2

ISBN/EAN: 9783337005375

Printed in Europe, USA, Canada, Australia, Japan

Cover: Foto ©Raphael Reischuk / pixelio.de

More available books at **www.hansebooks.com**

MEMOIRS

OF

JAMES ROBERT HOPE-SCOTT

OF ABBOTSFORD, D.C.L., Q.C.

LATE FELLOW OF MERTON COLLEGE, OXFORD

WITH SELECTIONS FROM HIS CORRESPONDENCE

By ROBERT ORNSBY, M.A.

PROFESSOR OF GREEK AND LATIN LITERATURE IN THE CATHOLIC UNIVERSITY
OF IRELAND : FELLOW OF THE ROYAL UNIVERSITY OF IRELAND :
LATE FELLOW OF TRIN. COLL. OXFORD

IN TWO VOLUMES—VOL. II.

SECOND EDITION

LONDON

JOHN MURRAY, ALBEMARLE STREET

1884

CONTENTS

OF

THE SECOND VOLUME.

CHAPTER XVIII.

1841-1842.

CHAPTER XIX.

1842-1843.

CHAPTER XX.
1844–1845.

CHAPTER XXI.
1845–1851.

CHAPTER XXII.
1839–1869.

CHAPTER XXIII.

1847-1858.

CHAPTER XXIV.

1859-1870.

CHAPTER XXV.

1867-1869.

CHAPTER XXVI.

1851-1873.

CHAPTER XXVII.

1868-1873.

APPENDIX I.

APPENDIX II.

APPENDIX III.

APPENDIX IV.

MEMOIRS

OF

JAMES ROBERT HOPE-SCOTT.

CHAPTER XVIII.

1841–42.

Mr. Hope's Pamphlet on the Jerusalem Bishopric—IIis Value for the Canon Law—Continued Correspondence of Mr. Hope and Mr. Newman on the Jerusalem Bishopric—Mr. Newman's Idea of a Monastery—Mr. Newman writes from Littlemore, April 22, 1842—Dr. Pusey consults Mr. Hope on his Letter to the Archbishop of Canterbury—Dr. Pusey and the Jerusalem Bishopric—Letters of Archdeacon Manning, Mr. W. Palmer, Sir John T. Coleridge, Sir F. Palgrave, Bishop Philpotts, and Count Senfft, on Mr. Hope's Pamphlet.

Two days after the date of the letter to Lady Henry Kerr, given in the preceding chapter (Dec. 20, 1841), took place the publication of Mr. Hope's pamphlet on the Anglo-Prussian Bishopric of Jerusalem. It may be described as a learned and very closely reasoned argument against the measure; and a dry (even if correct) analysis of it would be of little biographical interest, especially as Mr. Hope's views on the question have already been abundantly illustrated from unpublished materials. I therefore refer those of my readers who wish for more extended information to the pamphlet itself, but shall quote from the Postscript to the second edition [1] an eloquent passage on Canon Law, which is as characteristic of the writer as anything I have yet been able to produce, and exhibits, I think, in a striking manner how singularly this austere subject constituted at the time the poetry of his life, and how largely the conflict between the principles of Catholic jurisprudence and Anglicanism must have influenced the reflections which ended in his conversion. Mr. Hope here refers to some remarks on his pamphlet which had appeared in one by the Rev. Frederick Denison Maurice, entitled 'Three Letters to the Rev. W. Palmer, &c.' (Rivington : 1842).

Value of the Science of Canon Law.

[Mr. Maurice] sets all lawyers at nought, and canonists he utterly despises. Hastily, indeed, I think, and for the purpose of the moment only, can he have given way to such feelings, for he needs not that I should tell him that the Church of Christ rests not upon speculative truth alone, but upon the positive institutions of our Lord and His Apostles. Surely, then, to trace these institutions from the lowest point at which they come in contact with human existence, whether in nations or individuals, up to the highest to which our eye can follow them, the point of union with the unseen world in which they take their rise, and from which they are the channels of grace and truth and authority to the souls of men—to trace, I say, the outward and the visible signs of sacraments, of polity, of discipline, up to the inward spiritual realities upon which they depend, which they impart and represent to faith, or shelter from profanation; to study the workings of the hidden life of the Church by those developments which, in all ages and countries, have been its

[1] *The Bishopric of the United Church of England and Ireland at Jerusalem*, considered in a Letter to a Friend, by James R. Hope, B.C.L., Scholar of Merton, and Chancellor of the Diocese of Salisbury. Second edition, revised, with a Postscript. London: C. J. Stewart. 1842.

necessary modes of access to human feeling and apprehension; to systematise the end gained; to learn what is universal, what partial, what temporary, what eternal, what presently obligatory, and wherefore; surely a science such as this, so noble in its subject, so important in its practical bearings upon the unity and purity of the Church, and upon her relations to the temporal power, is not one of which Mr. Maurice would deliberately speak evil. Yet this is the science of the canonist.[2]

There are still portions of his correspondence with Mr. Newman, belonging to the same period and subject, which must not be withheld :—

J. R. Hope, Esq. to the Rev. J. H. Newman.

6 Stone Buildings, Lincoln's Inn:
December 21, 1841.

Dear Newman,—Your speedy reply and return of my proofs was very kind. The *hard* passages I did not know how to make easy, as they are pure law, so have left them. . . . I hear that the Bishop of London refused a man orders last week on three points—Eucharistic sacrifice in *any sense*, real presence in elements, grace in orders. The second point (being also the Bishop of Winchester's) I have illustrated in a note to my pamphlet (very briefly) by reference to Augsburg Confession.

You see the young Prince is to have a R. Catholic sponsor on one hand, and the King of Prussia on the other. This is a good balance, though the Canon tolerates neither. . . .

Ever yours,
J. R. HOPE.

The Rev. J. H. Newman to J. R. Hope, Esq.

My dear Hope,— . . . You take the canons of 1603 as *legal authority*, I see. This has been a bone in my throat. I *wish* them to show the animus of our Church, but directly you make them authority, the unhappy Ward is *ipso facto* excommunicate for having been to Oscott, until he repent of his wicked error. But there is no resisting law.

[2] Mr. Hope's pamphlet on the *Jerusalem Bishopric*, 2nd ed., p. 55.

Palmer's 'Aids to Reflection' contain some very valuable documents.

What the Bishops are doing is most serious, as well as unjustifiable, as I think. Really one does not know but they may meet in council and bring out some tests which will have the effect forthwith of precipitating us, and leaving the Church clean Protestant. Pray, does a *majority* bind in such a council? I mean in the way of canons. Can a majority determine the doctrine of the Church? If so, we had need look out for cheap lodgings. . . .

Ever yours,
JOHN H. NEWMAN.

Oriel College: December 23, 1841.

J. R. Hope, Esq. to the Rev. J. H. Newman.

Palace, Salisbury: December 31, 1841.

Dear Newman,—I am again settled here for ten days or so. . . . As to the Bishops meeting and making tests, they can *in law* do nothing, except in Convocation, with the Presbyters and under licence of the Crown. They may, however, as heads of dioceses, agree to enforce particular things, but there is not, I think, sufficient unity amongst them at present to allow of this. The Jerusalem business I hope is yet to be of good service to us, by rallying men of various shades against it, and by making the Bishops stand up against what cannot be called otherwise than usurpation of their rights by the Archbishop and the Bishop of London. The Bishop of Exeter, in acknowledging (to Badeley) the receipt of my pamphlet, says :—

'Would that those who direct proceedings of this hazardous and most questionable character may take warning from the effects of their inconsiderateness on this occasion! I doubt whether any three Bishops were consulted, or even informed, before the measure was completed.' This looks, I think, like action. . . .

When I publish again, I should like to bring out more fully the bearing of the Augsburg Confession on the Thirty-nine Articles. I perhaps overrate the importance of this point, but it seems to me to put Tract 90 in great measure under the sanction of the Archbishop and Bishop of London. If you think of doing anything more about Tract 90, perhaps (which would be far better) you would take this up. If not, do you think you could get any one to collect for me the sense of Luther, Melanchthon, &c., as to the meaning of the chief articles of the Aug. Conf.? I have always understood consubstantiation to be properly held under that document, and, if so, the admission of it with our Articles will appear to many people very awkward. You must not think me unreasonable for thinking that you can get this done for me (as you did the search about canons) at Oxford. Were our colleges what they ought to be, there would be in each a concurrence of labour whenever required, and I believe that you have men about you who have the feeling from which this (if ever it does) must spring.

I am not without hope that some public move may be made about the bishopric. What say you to an address to the Crown, praying it to license the discussion of it in Convocation? I think some Bishops and many clergy would join in this, and it would, I suppose, be very 'constitutional.' I have not, however, looked up the formal part yet. Tell me what you think of the thing, and I will consider it further. . . .

(Signed)   J. R. HOPE.

The Rev. J. H. Newman to J. R. Hope, Esq.

January 3, 1842.

My dear Hope,—A happy new year to you and all of us— and, what is even more needed, to the English Church. I am afraid of moving about Convocation. Not that we should not be in safer hands than in those of the Bishops, but, though it restrained their acts, it would abridge our liberty. Or it might formally recognise our Protestantism. What can we hope from a body, the best members of which, as Hook and Palmer [of Worcester Coll.], defend and subscribe to the Jerusalem Fund . . . ? Therefore 1 do not like to be *responsible* for helping to call into existence a body which may embarrass us more than we are at present.

I think your τόπος about the Augsburg Confession a very important one, and directly more men come back will set a friend to work upon it.

I am almost in despair of keeping men together. The only possible way is a monastery. Men want an outlet for their devotional and penitential feelings, and if we do not grant it, to a dead certainty they will *go* where they can find it. This is the beginning and the end of the matter. Yet the clamour is so great, and will be so much greater, that if I persist, I expect (though I am not speaking from anything that has *occurred*) that I shall be stopped. Not that I have any intention of doing more at present than laying the foundation of what may be.

. . . Are we really to be beaten in this election [for the Poetry Professorship] ? I will tell you a secret (if you care to know it) which not above three or four persons know. We have 480 promises. Is it then hopeless ? . . . I don't think our enemies would beat 600; at least, it would be no *triumph*. . . .

The Bishop of Exeter has for these eight years, ever since the commencement of the Ecclesiastical Commission, been biding his time, and the Duke of Wellington last spring disgusted him much. This both makes it likely that he will now move, and also diminishes the force of the very words you quote, for peradventure they are ordinary with him. I have good hopes that he will.

Ever yours,
JOHN H. NEWMAN.

The experiment of offering to minds which had lost all sympathy with Protestantism, yet were unable to close with Rome, an imitation of the monastic life by way of shelter from the rude checks which their aspirations sustained in the world without, seems to have answered for a time, and possibly retarded for about three years that rush of conversion which made 1845 such an epoch in the history even of the Church. This may be inferred from the next letter, written shortly after Mr. Newman and his disciples were regularly settled at Littlemore.   I am not aware what the report was which he so emphatically denies.

The Rev. J. H. Newman to J. R. Hope, Esq.

April 22, 1842.   *Dabam è Domo S. M. V.*
apud Littlemore.

My dear Hope,—Does not this portentous date promise to outweigh any negative I can give to your question in the mind of the inquirer? for any one who could ask such a question would think such a dating equivalent to the answer.   However, if I must answer in form, I believe it to be one great absurdity and untruth from beginning to end, though it is hard I must answer for *every* hundred men in the *whole* kingdom. Negatives are dangerous : all I can say, however, is that I don't believe, or suspect, or fear any such occurrence, and look upon it as neither probable nor improbable, but simply untrue.

We are all much quieter and more resigned than we were, and are remarkably desirous of building up a position, and proving that the English theory is tenable, or rather, the English state of things.   If the Bishops let us alone, the fever will subside.

[After a few words on business] I wish you would say how you are.

Ever yours,

JOHN H. NEWMAN.

Early in 1842 came out Dr. Pusey's 'Letter to the Archbishop of Canterbury on some Circumstances connected with the Present Crisis in the Church.'   In the preparation of this important pamphlet Dr. Pusey sought the advice of Mr. Hope, and the letter in which he asked it must be placed before the reader as an evidence of the value attached to Mr. Hope's opinion in the counsels of the party.

The Rev. Dr. Pusey to J. R. Hope, Esq.

My dear Hope,—You will be surprised that I should consult you as a layman and a younger man as to a work on the religious state of things, but I do it on N.'s suggestion, as seeing and being able to judge of men's minds; and yᵉ question is not as to *what* is said, but whether it is expedient to say it, and for me, what will be its probable effect.

The origin of it was my visit to Addington last autumn: after my return Harrison wrote me some long letters, recommending that one shᵈ take occasion of yᵉ Bishops' charges, under wʰ people writhed so much, to make one's defence, show that one was not so unsound as one seemed, and plead for sympathy.[3] I was unwilling to leave what I was doing and put myself forward; but as H. told me that he had spoken on yᵉ subject with yᵉ Aᵇᵖ, it seemed to come with his authority, so I set myself to it. It has been delayed until now, waiting in part for unpublished charges, and for yᵉ documents about yᵉ Jerus. Bpric. It is now about finished, and wᵈ occupy about ten sheets; what I send is, then, not half. The object of yᵉ analysis of the Bishops' charges is to show that some do not object to our main principles, but to matters of detail; that others (as the Bᵖˢ of Chester, Winchester, Calcutta) do not object to our principles at all, but to certain principles which they conceive to be ours. The effect of both, I hoped, wᵈ be that our friends, who were fretted by these charges, wᵈ see that neither we nor (wʰ alone signifies) Catholic truth is condemned, that others mᵗ be better disposed towards us, and that the hint mᵗ be taken in some charges this year. Anyhow, that there wᵈ seem less of a consent of Bishops agˢᵗ us. I was rather sanguine about this part. Then there follows something about the Jerusalem Bishopric and the East and Lutheranism, my object being to say that things are safe so long as the

---

[3] This fondness for the use of the indefinite pronoun very much characterised the Puseyite dialect, as I have somewhere read that it did the Jansenist. The *phase* which it marked may be seen fully developed in the tract 'On Reserve,' by Isaac Williams.

Bishops do not make any organic changes in our Church, or she be committed to any wrong principle. I conclude with some pages meant incidentally to reassure persons about ourselves, and of our good hopes and confidence and love for our Church. This I have been urged to do in some way or other by several, *e.g.* E. Churton, confidence having been terribly shaken by Golightly's wild sayings, and by the version put upon my own visits to ye convents. This I c^d do by implication without any formal profession.

| Private. | | Private. |

Newman was agst it from the first; he thought H. wanted to commit me to say things w^h N. thought I c^d not say; in a word, to express H.'s own views. About this I did not feel any difficulty, for, having put forth doctrinal statements in my two last letters, I did not feel called upon to do it again, and so I went on. N. now likes it much in itself; indeed, he tells me he likes it the best of anything w^h I have written, but does not feel his former opinion removed; but he wished me to take another opinion. People seem to like the notion. The only part about w^h I have any misgiving is in these first slips, lest the picture of the temptations to Romanism sh^d seem too strong; and yet, unless our Bishops realise that this tendency has some deeper foundation than any writings of ours, what they will do will be in a wrong direction.

For myself, of course, I do not care what people think of me; and, on the other hand, one does not like to waste what one has employed time upon; but I am quite willing to give it up and be still, if it seems best; of course, one sh^d be very sorry to add to our confusions.

No one has suggested the mere omission of ye Romanist part. Jelf only (who had seen that part only without some additions w^h I have since made, that I m^t not seem gratuitously to exalt Rome to the disparagement of our own Church) suggested that it be printed only to send to ye B^{ps}. N. thinks this of no use. I have no other opinions. But I am entangling you with the opinions of others, when I meant to ask you yours simply. I know you will not mind y⁰ trouble.

Yours affectionately, E. B. PUSEY.

Christ Church: September 27.

The Romanist part, of course, has not y⁰ Aᵇᵖ's sanction, and it must be so expressed.

In the date of the above letter ' September ' is struck out ; ' January ' substituted, and ' '42 ' added in Mr. Hope-Scott's hand, I think. How this is to be explained I do not know, but Dr. Pusey can hardly have made such a clerical error. Mr. Hope-Scott has endorsed the letter : ' I recommended publication, with some alterations and additions.—J. R. H.'

Whatever influence Dr. Pusey may at an earlier period have exercised on the religious views of Mr. Hope must have been a good deal shaken by his inclination in the first instance to favour the Jerusalem Bishopric, followed, indeed, by a disapproval, but one far short of the energy with which Mr. Hope himself combated the measure.

The Rev. E. B. Pusey to J. R. Hope, Esq.

My dear Hope,—I thank you much for your ' letter ,' which I had been looking for anxiously, but which by some mistake was not forwarded to me, so that I only saw it two days ago. It is very satisfactory to me ; it seems quite to settle the point as to the duty of Bᵖ A. I was also very much cheered to see yʳ own more hopeful view of things in our Church.

I am a good deal discomforted by this visit of y⁰ Kg. of Pr. It seems so natural for persons to wish that Episcopacy shᵈ be bestowed upon those who desire to receive ; and people for y⁰ most part have very little or no notion as to y⁰ unsoundness even of the sounder part of y⁰ G. Divines. As far as I have heard of yᵉ progress of truth there the restoration of Xᵗʸ in some shape has been far more rapid than I anticipated or dared hope, the soundness of the restoration far less.

Yours affectionately,   E. B. Pusey.

116 Marine Parade, Brighton: January 7, 1842.

In another letter, dated Sexagesima Sunday [January 30], 1842, Dr. Pusey says:—

I do not know your τόπος about yᵉ Augsburg Conf. I have very little, next to nothing, about it. Do not leave anything for me. Each can do best what he feels most. I should be very sorry to take anything out of yʳ hands ; and altogether I can say yᵉ less about this because, wretched as it wᵈ be that we shᵈ appear in yᵉ E. connected with Lutherans, I do not feel that it wᵈ introduce any organic change in us, and so cannot anticipate that it wᵈ.

I see that the Conf. of Augs. does not express consubstantiation. Art. X. may express Catholic doctrine.

I subjoin a few more letters from Mr. Hope's correspondence relating to his pamphlet on the Jerusalem Bishopric question, interesting as it is in itself, and forming so great a crisis in his religious history.

The Ven. Archdeacon Manning [since Cardinal Archbishop of Westminster] to J. R. Hope, Esq.

December 30, 1841.

My dear Hope,—I have this moment ended your pamphlet, and will not wait for a cooler moment to thank you. I do so heartily. God grant we may be true and manly in affirming the broad rule of Catholic order. I add my thanks to you in another shape. In your last three or four pages you and I were nearing each other's thoughts. It is refreshing to find an answer at a distance. Forgive my long neglect of the enclosed paper, which after all bears only my name, and probably too late for use.

Ever yours, dear Hope, most sincerely,
H. E. Manning.

*The Rev. William Palmer (of Magdalen College, Oxford) to
J. R. Hope, Esq.*

Mixbury, near Brackley: December 29, 1841.

Dear Hope,—I am much obliged to you for sending me a
copy of your letter, which I have read with the greatest pleasure. . . . I see that in the statement just published by
authority, *no Prussian* documents are given. I think your
letter will be a puzzling one; but the spirit of practical Protestantism is subtle and versatile, and able to set aside everything
— laws, principles, rubrics, and canons. Else I do not see how
the mischief which I apprehend could be realised.

Ever yours sincerely,   W. PALMER.

P.S.—I am glad you think my pamphlet may be useful.
We have taken entirely different sides of the same subject; I
the theoretical (as it seemed to me), and you the practical view
of the question.

Sir John Taylor Coleridge to J. R. Hope, Esq.

My dear Hope,—Many thanks for your letter, which I have
read through with, I may say, a painful interest. Of course, in
a matter so difficult in itself, and so new, I must confess, to
me, I do not take on me at once to pronounce that you are
right, but I cannot at present find out where you are wrong;
and I am the more inclined to think that you may be right
because I see in the Act just words enough to satisfy people
rather precipitate that the Prussian scheme might be carried
through safely on them. ' Spiritual jurisdiction,' ' over other
Protestant congregations,' would seem to ordinary minds
enough—till it was further considered *how* the English Bishop
was to work out the scheme by virtue of these words, and yet
be consistent with his own engagements.

I shall not be sorry, however, to find that you are answered;
not that I wish to accomplish, or seem rather to accomplish
any end by a disorderly and indigested attempt at union; nor
do I think *this* thing of itself so important as many do: still

it is one which very much arrests the imagination, and excites strong devotional feeling; and I rather looked on it as leading to more important matters with Prussia itself. I cannot, too, help a little more personal feeling for the Bishop than it fell within our plan to express—a good and pious man, I believe, but not by intellect or previous habits fitted to meet such emergencies as you place before him.

Very truly yours,

J. T. COLERIDGE.

December 30, 1841.
Montague Place.

Sir Francis Palgrave, K.H. to J. R. Hope, Esq.

Rolls House: January 4, 1842.

My dear Sir,—I ought before this to have thanked you for your kindness in sending me your most able letter, but I did not like to do so until I had read it with that attention which it deserves.

It is difficult to understand how your arguments can possibly be shaken. The statute 25 Hen. VIII. c. 21 evidently relates only to such dispensations upon the suit or for the benefit of individuals as had been theretofore usually issued by the Roman Chancery, and to wrest it into the power of establishing an *uncanonical* see appears a most bold attempt.

Nothing would more clearly show the true relation of the Church of England to 'other Protestant churches' than a reprint of the *whole* proceedings of the Convocations from William and Mary to their extinction—adding proper notes.

Yours ever truly,

FRANCIS PALGRAVE.

The Right Rev. Dr. Philpotts, Bishop of Exeter, to J. R. Hope, Esq.

Bishopstowe, Torquay: November 10, 1842.

My dear Sir,—Permit me to ask you whether you can receive and answer a case of ecclesiastical law? That you an answer it better than any other man I have no doubt;

but can you receive the case *professionally,* so as to enable a Bishop to show your opinion as his authority for action ?

I have never thanked you for your kindness in sending me a copy of the second edition of ' The B^{pric} of the U. C., &c., at Jerusalem,' for I am ashamed to own I have never, till this day, read the new matter which it gives to us. Accept now my hearty thanks for your kindness to me in sending to me a copy, and my still heartier acknowledgments of your invaluable service to the Church in furnishing it with such a lesson.

You have, of course, seen the ' Alterius orbis Papa's ' letter of June 18 to the King of Prussia, and have, with me, wondered at the mixture of temerity and cowardice (which latter quality, by the way, is the rashest of all feelings) indicated in such a mode of escaping from the difficulties by which he was pressed.

I grieve for this marvellous indiscretion. But I am amused by the bolder defiance of all consistency which is exhibited by his prime Adviser, who, while he prompts his Chief to trample Rubrics, Canons, Statutes, under his feet, commands His own Clergy to observe them ' with Chinese exactness.'

I went to your second edition, in order that I might find your promised remarks on the need in which the Church stands of a Church Legislature. I have read them with great gratification, and implore your close attention to the subject. My Clergy are, I believe, about to meet and to address me to urge on the A^{bp} their earnest desire of leave from the Crown for Convocation to consider the best means of altering its own constitution, or otherwise devising a new Body empowered and fitted to act synodically.

This is, at present, somewhat of a secret, but it will in a few days, I believe, transpire.

From other quarters, I hear, similar proceedings may be expected. The B^p of Llandaff tells me that he makes the necessity of a Church Legislature one topic in his Charge.

Y^{rs}, my dear Sir,
Most faithfully,
H. Exeter.

[P.S.] Pray tell me whether you think the argument in my Charge on Escott v. Mastin is now tolerably effective?

What 'oath of obedience' is the ordained German to take to the Bishop? Not Canonical—that is plain. What oath can it be? Of course, it will hardly be an absolute promise on oath to obey all commands. All *lawful* commands w^d involve a question—what are lawful commands? Who is to judge? What law is to be the rule?

Somebody named by the King is to attest for the Candidates their qualification for the *Pastoral Office*; but the Bishop is 'to convince himself of their qualifications for the *especial* duties of their office, of the purity of their faith, and of their *desire to receive ordination* at his hands!'

What is meant by the Clergyman's prep^g Candidates for Confirmation in the *usual* manner? Usual *where?* in Prussia or in England?

Have the baptized Godfathers in Prussia? If they have not, how can they be conf^d acc^g to the Liturgy of the U.C. of E. and I.?

To these letters from such distinguished co-religionists of Mr. Hope's, all belonging, with various shades of difference, to his own religious party, I add a portion of one, bearing on the same subject, from a Catholic and foreign friend of his who has been mentioned in a previous chapter,[4] Count Senfft-Pilsach. The contrast will be interesting; and it is also interesting to record a specimen of an influence, no doubt beginning to be more and more felt, though years had to pass before the result was visible in action. Count Senfft, though an active diplomatist, a friend of Metternich's, and quite in the great European world, was an example of the union, so often found in the lives of the saints, of deep retirement and devotion in the very thick of affairs;

[4] Vol. i. chap. xiii. p. 246.

and we may be sure that his prayers for Mr. Hope were faithfully applied to assist his arguments.

Count Senfft-Pilsach to J. R. Hope, Esq.

La Haye: 21 Janvier 1842.

Mon cher Hope,— . . . J'ai lu avec un vif intérêt vos réflexions sur ce nouvel Evêché de Jérusalem, dont on paraît vouloir faire un lien entre l'Église anglicane et le Protestantisme Evangélique de Prusse, en cherchant à vivifier les ossemens arides de celui-ci par une sorte de greffe de votre Episcopat auquel nous contestons encore, comme question de fait, la continuité de la succession Apostolique. Si on réussiroit dans ce projet, une partie de vos objections pourroient se résoudre. Mais M. Bunsen, l'artisan de la complication de Cologne, n'a pas la main heureuse, et la fécondité de son génie, secondant son ardeur de courtisan, pourroit bien, en prétendant servir les tendances vagues de piété de son maître, embarquer celui-ci dans les plus graves difficultés en provoquant l'opposition des vieux protestans réunis aux rationalistes allemands. 'Quid foditis vobis cisternas dissipatas?' O mon ami! Comment s'arrêter à quelques abus plus apparens peut-être que réels, que l'Église supporte çà et là sans les autoriser, et ne pas reconnoître cette admirable unité de doctrine, cette continuité de la Tradition, qui caractérise la cité bâtie sur la montagne, figure de la véritable Église selon l'Évangile. Certes ce n'est pas sous la domination de César qu'on pourroit aller chercher l'Épouse légitime de J. C. Mais doit-on espérer la trouver dans la création combinée de la volonté tyrannique de Henri VIII. et de la politique d'Elisabeth, tandis que la Doctrine comme la Discipline du Concile de Trente ne vous laisse rien à désirer, et conquiert déjà vos suffrages? . . .

J'ose compter partant sur votre intérêt amical, et vous connoissez les sentimens sincères d'attachement et de respect avec lesquels je suis à jamais

Tout à vous,

SENFFT.

CHAPTER XIX.

1842-1843.

IT results in general from the documents furnished in
the preceding chapter, that Mr. Hope's confidence in
the Anglican Church had sustained a severe shock by
the Jerusalem Bishopric movement; and from about
the year 1842 he seems to have thrown himself with
increasing energy into his professional occupations, not
certainly as becoming less religious (for his was a mind
never tempted to the loss of faith), but as being deprived of that scope which his convictions had formerly
presented to him in the pursuit of ecclesiastical objects.
It seems probable, also, that the same cause was not
unconnected with his entering, some years later, into
the married life; the news of which step is known to
have fallen like a knell on the minds of those who looked
up to him and shared his religious feelings, as it appeared
a sign that he no longer thought the ideal perfection

presented by the celibate life—which he certainly contemplated in 1840–1—was congenial with the spirit of
the Church of England. That communion was now
losing her hold upon him, though he still could not
make up his mind to leave her, and might conceivably
never have done so but for events which forced the
change upon him at last. His professional career and
his habits in domestic life will require to be sepa-
rately described; for, though of course they proceeded
simultaneously with a large part of that phase of his
existence which is now before us, it would only con-
fuse the reader to pass continually from one to the
other. I propose, therefore, without any interruption
that can be avoided, to go on with the history of his
religious development up to the period of his conversion.

The year 1842, commencing, as we have seen, with
the storms of the Jerusalem Bishopric movement and
the Poetry Professorship contest, agitated also, towards
the end of May, by a movement for the repeal of the
Statute of Censure against Dr. Hampden, passed off, for
the rest, quietly enough—at least, Mr. Hope's correspondence shows little to the contrary; but 1843 was
marked by much disturbance, commencing early with
Mr. Newman's 'Retractation,' which the great leader
announced to Mr. Hope in the following letter a few
days before that document appeared in the 'Conservative Journal:'—

The Rev. J. H. Newman to J. R. Hope, Esq.

Littlemore : In fest. Conv. S. Pauli, 1843.

My dear Hope,—In return for your announcement of some change of purpose, I must tell you of one of my own, in a matter where I told you I was going to be very quiet.

My conscience goaded me some two months since to an act which comes into effect, I believe, in the *Conservative Journal* next Saturday, viz. to eat a few dirty words of mine. I had intended it for a time of peace, the beginning of December, but against my will and power the operation has been delayed, and now, unluckily, falls upon the state of irritation and suspicion in good Anglicans, which Bernard Smith's step [1] has occasioned. I had committed myself when all was quiet. The meeting of Parliament, will, I hope, divert attention.

Ever y^{rs},

JOHN H. NEWMAN.

P.S.—I am publishing my Univ. Sermons. You got a headache for *one*—it would be an act of gratitude to send you *all*. Shall I do so?

J. R. Hope, Esq. to the Rev. J. H. Newman.

6 Stone B$^{dg^s}$, Linc. Inn :
Feast of Purification [Feb. 2], '43.

Dear Newman,—You will think me ungracious for having so long delayed my answer to your last, but I did not get hold of the *Conservative Journal* till Monday, and have been very busy since.

Perhaps you will like to know what effect your article has produced on me. Simply this : it has convinced me that you are clearing your position of some popular protections which still surrounded it. Beyond this I do not see. I mean it does not show me that, esoterically, you have made any great move, nor yet that, to the world at large, you are disposed to do more than say, 'Do not cry me up as a champion against Popery; for the

---

[1] The conversion of the Rev. Bernard Smith, Fellow of Magdalen College, Oxford.

c 2

rest, you may judge of me as you please.' People whom I have heard speak of it (few, perhaps, but fair samples) are rather puzzled than anything else.

I give you this merely as gossip, and not as asking whether my construction is right, though if you think it material or useful to tell me, of course I shall be glad.

I need not say that I shall be very thankful for a copy of your sermons—that is, if you will write my name in it yourself; otherwise I will buy the book, for Rivington's ' from the author ' does not fix the stamp which I chiefly value.

Do you observe in the papers that Sir R. P. is designing *great* things for the Church? It gives me some hopes that they will also be *good*, to see that Gladstone is in his councils. We shall have much ado about the Eccl. Courts Bill, which, I believe, is certainly to come on. I am in some hopes we may make it an instrument for drawing a line between us and the Dissenters, but must not be sanguine.

Believe me, dear Newman, ever y^{rs} truly,

JAMES R. HOPE.

Rev. J. H. Newman.

Mr. Newman wrote in explanation as follows :—

The Rev. J. H. Newman to J. R. Hope, Esq.

Littlemore: February 3, 1843.

My dear Hope,—It is amusing in me to talk of being tired of giving explanations, when I have neither given nor mean to give any ; but so it is, whether my hand aches, or I am sick of the subject, I feel as if I have given a hundred. Since you ask me, I will say, as far as I can collect my thoughts on an instant, that my reason for writing and publishing that notice was (but first I will observe that I do not wish it talked about, though it is not worth while going into the reasons why I did it in the way I have. I did it thus after a good deal of thought and fidget, and not seeing any better way, *i.e.* clearer of objections)— but my reason for the *thing* was my long-continued feeling of the great inconsistency I was in of letting things stand in print against me which I did not hold, and which I could not but be contradicting by my acting every day of my life. And more especially (*i.e.* it came home to me most vividly in that particular way) I felt that I was *taking people* in; that they thought me what I was not, and were trusting me when they should not, and this has been at times a very painful feeling indeed. I don't want to be trusted (perhaps you may think my fear, even before this affair, somewhat amusing); but so it was and is; people *won't* believe I go as far as I do—they will cling to their hopes. And then, again, intimate friends have almost reproached me with ' paltering with them in a double sense, keeping the word of promise to their ear, to break it to their hope.' They have said that my words against Rome often, when narrowly examined, were only what *I* meant, but that the effect of them was what *others* meant. I am not aware that I have any great motive for this paper beyond this—setting myself right, and wishing to be seen in my proper colours, and not unwilling to do such penance for wrong words as lies in the necessary criticism which such a retractation will involve on the part of friends and enemies; though, since nothing one does is without a meaning [that is higher than one's own], things may come from it beyond my own meaning.

Thanks for . . . the information from newspapers, which you give me, of our hopes from Sir R. P., which 1 had not seen in them.

By-the-bye, in the paper, for ' person's respect ' near the end, read ' persons I respect ; ' and ' to the editor ' is fudge.

Ever y^rs,

J. H. NEWMAN.

P.S.—Thanks for your flattering answers about my book. It must go, however, from Rivington's with ' from the author,' and I will add my own writing when we meet. Since you have had a specimen of the book (dose ?), I may add, in opposition to you, that it will be the best, not the most perfect, book I have done. I mean there is more to develop in it, though it is *im*perfect.[2]

---

[2] A week later (February 10, 1843) he writes to Mr. Hope : ' My University Sermons are the least theological book I have published.'

The famous case of Macmullen *versus* Hampden was disturbing the University for most of the latter half of the same year 1843. I can only give a mere chronological outline of it, which may assist such readers as wish to pursue the subject in consulting other sources of information. The Regius Professor of Divinity, Dr. Hampden, had refused to act as Moderator in the Schools, to enable the Rev. R. G. Macmullen, Fellow of Corpus Christi College, to make his exercises for the degree of B.D. [Mr. Macmullen, it should be remarked, was a strong opponent of the project at that time before the University, mentioned a few pages back, to reverse the condemnation which had been passed on Dr. Hampden when he was first appointed Regius Professor of Divinity.] Mr. Macmullen, on his refusal, brought an action into the Vice-Chancellor's Court on May 26, 1843, where, on June 2, Dr. Kenyon of All Souls' presiding, Mr. Hope appeared for Mr. Macmullen, Dr. Twiss on the other side. Dr. Kenyon pronounced in his favour on certain amended articles. Dr. Twiss appealed to the Delegates of Congregation (none of them lawyers), who heard the appeal on November 29, sitting from ten in the morning till seven at night. Mr. Erle and Dr. Twiss both spoke against the articles, and were replied to by Mr. Hope. The Court ultimately gave judgment against the articles, reversing Dr. Kenyon's decision, and gave costs against Mr. Macmullen.[3] Mr. Badeley's bitter comment will amuse the reader:

---

[3] For this outline of the proceedings in Macmullen *v.* Hampden, I am indebted to accurate memoranda kindly furnished me by Mr. David Lewis, late Fellow of Jesus College, Oxford.

'Mischievous idiots! and so all the conclusive arguments you put before them are set at nought, and the
battle is to be fought again!'[4]   However, there was
no further litigation, and in the end Mr. Macmullen
succeeded in obtaining his degree, the old form of dis-
putations for that purpose being restored, which has
ever since been in force.   It should be added that Mr.
Hope's services in this case, undertaken amidst all the
pressure of his ordinary legal work, were gratuitous.

In the summer of 1843 took place another critical
moment of the strife in Dr. Pusey's suspension from
preaching, by sentence of the Vice-Chancellor's Court,
for his sermon 'On the Holy Eucharist a Comfort to
the Penitent.'   In the question of his appeal against
this, which was matter of anxiety for more than a
twelvemonth, it is almost needless to say that he sought
the advice of Mr. Hope.   The Everett affair, on Com-
memoration Day (June 28), will have its place in every
chronicle of the movement.   This was a protest on the
part of members of the Tractarian party against an
honorary degree conferred in the teeth of a demand for
scrutiny (which, however, it was asserted had not been
heard in the din), on the American Envoy, Mr. Everett,
who was a Unitarian.   Mr. Hope, however, was not
present; and I mention this only as one of the many
signs of the times which were then rapidly accumu-
lating.   Nor did he take any part in the opposition made
in the following year to Dr. Symonds' election as Vice-
Chancellor, though he was consulted, in the law of the
case, with Mr. Badeley and Dr. Bayford.   It ended in a

[4] Mr. Badeley to Mr. Hope, January 6, 1844.

crushing defeat of the Tractarians, who were beaten by a majority of 882 against 183.

In September 1843 Mr. Newman resigned the vicarage of St. Mary's. On this step Mr. Hope, writing to him on September 28, says that he had not differed from him about it, but, ' as to the general tendency of which you described the increase [Mr. Newman's expression (September 5) was : ' The movement is going on so fast that some of the wheels are catching fire '], all I can do is to sit still and wait the issue.'

The ' Lives of the English Saints ' were at this time in preparation, the importance of which in the history of the movement is too well known from Cardinal Newman's ' Apologia ' and from other sources to require me to enlarge upon it. At length there was no disguise or reservation, but sympathy was openly avowed by members of the Anglican Church for the whole spirit hitherto associated with the idea of ' the corruptions of Popery '—as monasticism, the continued exercise of miraculous power in the Church, finally, the supremacy of the Holy See. From a copious correspondence which followed between the two friends, I extract, as usual, such portions as will throw most light on the progressive change in Mr. Hope's religious convictions. His sense of prudence, and the bias derived from his particular legal studies, restrain, rather curiously, the inclination which his feelings in other directions show ; but it is best to let him speak for himself:—

The Rev. J. H. Newman to J. R. Hope, Esq.

Littlemore: Nov. 2, '43.

My dear Hope,—[After stating the perplexity he felt on the question of stopping the 'Lives,' which appeared to present itself in consequence of an objection expressed by Dr. Pusey, in conversation with Mr. Hope, against the Roman tone which had been manifested, Mr. Newman continues :] I did not explain to you sufficiently the state of mind of those who are in danger. I only spoke of those who are convinced that our Church was external to the Church Catholic, though they felt it unsafe to trust their own private convictions. And you seemed to put the dilemma, 'Either men are in doubt or not : if in doubt, they ought to be quiet ; if not in doubt, how is it that they stay with us?' But there are two other states of mind which might be mentioned. 1. Those who are unconsciously near Rome, and whose *despair* about our Church, if anyhow caused, would at once develop into a state of conscious approximation and *quasi*-resolution to go over. 2. Those who feel they can with a safe conscience remain with us, *while* they are allowed to testify in behalf of Catholicism, and to promote its interests ; *i.e.* as if by such acts they were putting our Church, or at least a portion of it, in which they are included, in the position of catechumens. They think they may stay, while they are moving themselves, others, nay, say the whole Church, towards Rome. Is not this an intelligible ground? I should like your opinion of it. . . .

Ever yours sincerely,

JOHN H. NEWMAN.

J. R. Hope, Esq. to the Rev. J. H. Newman.

6 Stone Buildings, Linc. Inn :
Nov. 4, '43.

Dear Newman,— . . . As to the Roman leaning, no doubt your 'Lives,' at least many of them, must evince it ; no doubt also that, unless carefully managed, it will give offence. But may not caution obviate the latter ? Is it not possible to *com-*

mence by lives which will not at once bring the whole set into popular disrepute? the less palatable ones being kept for a more advanced stage. May it not also be provided that in an historical work, a purely historical character shall be given to what as matter of fact cannot be denied, and which can only be objected to when it is adopted by the writers as a matter of principle in which they themselves concur? To the asceticism, devotion, and anti-secular spirits of the English saints we are, under every point of view, entitled to refer; and if any part of these virtues was displayed in necessary relation to Rome, or to Roman institutions, this in a portraiture of their lives cannot be omitted, but certainly need not be canonised as amongst their merits. It seems to me possible simply to take the Church of their times as *the* Church, without entering into the question whether any of the conditions under which it then existed are necessary for its existence now. And so their acts done in relation to the Church of their day may be dwelt upon, while the further question whether the Church of our day is capable of eliciting such acts may be left to the judgment of the reader.

I am not sure whether I have made myself intelligible in this, and still less whether it is worth your reading, but I fancied that you wished an opinion, and I give it, *valeat quantum.* . . .

Y^{rs} ever truly,

JAMES R. HOPE.

Rev. J. H. Newman.

The Rev. J. H. Newman to J. R. Hope, Esq.

Littlemore: Nov. 6, 1843.

My dear Hope,— . . . You have not gone to the bottom of the difficulty. It is very easy to say, Give facts without comment; but in the first place, what can be so dry as mere facts? the book won't sell, nor deserve to sell. It must be ethical; but to be ethical is merely to colour a narrative with one's own mind and to give a *tone* to it. Now this is the difficulty: altering this or that passage, leaving out this or that expression, will not alter the case. I will not answer for being aware

of the tone in myself.   Pusey put his finger on passages which
I had not thought about.   Is he to be ever marking passages?
if so, he has the real trouble of being editor, not I.

Naturam expellas furca, &c.   Is the Pope's supremacy
the only point on which no opinion is to be expressed? if so,
why?   It is not more against the Articles to *desire* it than to
desire monachism.   Will it offend more than others?   I will
not limit certainly the degree of disgust which some people
will feel towards it, but do they feel less towards the notion of
monks, or, again, of miracles?   Now Church history is made
up of these three elements—miracles, monkery, Popery.   If
any sympathetic feeling is expressed on behalf of the persons
and events of Church history, it is a feeling in favour of
miracles, or monkery, or Popery, one or all.   It is quite a
theory to talk of being ethical, yet not concur in these elements of the narrative—unless, indeed, one adopts Milner's or
Neander's device of dropping part of the history, praising what
one has a fancy for, and thus putting a theory and dream in
the place of facts.   But it is bad enough to be eclectic in
doctrine.

Next it must be recollected how very much depends on the
disposition, relative prominence, &c., of facts; it is quite impossible that a leaning to Rome, a strong offensive leaning,
should be hidden.

And then still more it must be recollected that a *vast*
number of questions, and most important ones, are decided
this way or that, on antecedent probabilities, according to a
person's views, *e.g.* the question between St. Augustine and
the British Bishops—of Easter—of King Lucius, &c. &c.
Opinion comes in at every step of the history.

From what I have said you will see that I consider it impossible to choose *easy* 'Lives' for the first of the series; there
are none such, or if there be a few, when can I promise to have
them ready?   I suppose Bede must be pretty easy.   Keble
has it.   I do not expect him to send it to me for several years,
with his engagements.   Take missions, take Bishops, the
Pope comes in everywhere.   Go to Aldhelm and his schools;

you have most strange miracles. Try to retire into the country, you do but meet with hermits. No; miracles, monkery, Popery, are too much for you, if you have any stomach. . . .

The life P. looked at, St. Stephen's, was taken as having hardly, if at all, any miracle in it. If he thinks it will give offence, doubtless the others will still more.

You see, in saying all this I am not deciding the question whether the work is to be done *at all*. On that point I have had great doubt since P.'s objection. Only to do it without offence is impossible, and the more so because, in parts at least, it is likely to be a very taking work. . . .

And then so many ' Lives ' are in progress or preparation, that it is most unlikely the work will be stopped; others will conduct it instead of me who will go further; and though this is a bad reason for doing oneself what one feels a misgiving in doing, it is a good reason when one feels none at all. . . .

If the plan is abandoned, this significant question will be, nay, is already asked—' What, then, cannot the Anglican Church bear the Lives of her Saints ? '

Ever y^{rs},
JOHN H. NEWMAN.

J. R. Hope, Esq. to the Rev. J. H. Newman.

6 Stone B^{dgs}, Linc. Inn:
Nov. 8, '43.

Dear Newman,—Your last shows me plainly what I had not before understood, that the question of the ' Lives ' depends immediately upon that larger one which your previous letter had mooted, and that to solve it one must know more than I do of the conclusions at which you have arrived as to the claims of Rome, and as to the mode, time, and circumstances in and under which those claims ought to be recognised. I feel therefore very incompetent to offer any further suggestion. When I last wrote I thought the questions separable, and meant that the Roman parts of your histories should be treated dramatically (if I may so say), being represented really and faithfully, but only as the scenery in which the actors stood.

Your letter shows me that this cannot be, unless your writers have more self-command, and more disposition to exercise it than men in earnest can be expected to have. I must therefore ask, what is your general view as to Rome ? Is union with it immediately *necessary*? or is it only *desirable*—under new circumstances and at some distant period ? If the former, then one would think that the question should be openly and professedly discussed, the arguments given and the authorities stated. If the latter, I should imagine that much remains to be done, in the way of raising the general tone of our Church in matters of faith and practice, before it can be fit to deal with such a question ; and though you think monachism, miracles, and Popery inseparably allied, yet I feel convinced that there are many minds prepared to consider the two former which have no disposition to the latter.

On either view, then, I think that a work which is addressed only or principally to men's feelings would be mistimed—it would not convince of the necessity, and it would find but a small number of men disposed at present to give it their sympathy.

There are, indeed, those other considerations which you mention respecting the minds which would find relief in being allowed to dwell upon the subject, and so might be the better persuaded to remain within our communion ; but, on the other hand, there is the risk of provoking such conduct on the part of the Bishops and others as would drive some out, and render the position of those who remained more difficult than ever. And surely it would be most unfair to take the measure of what the Church of England allows on this or any other difficult point in theology from what might happen to be the view of men such as our present rulers, upon whom the whole question has come unawares, and whose prejudices upon this point in particular, backed by the secular policy of the State for 300 years, would be pretty sure to lead them to some active, and probably united censure. I wish therefore, much, that minds of this class could be persuaded that it is not the Church of England which they are testing, but a disorderly body which ten years ago did not know what it was, and is now only gradually becoming conscious; and that if they can satisfy themselves that the views they entertain are compatible with what they deem the true theory of the Church of England, they would be content to hold them quietly for the present, and not risk themselves and others upon so doubtful a venture.

This, I think, is all that I can say—being confessedly in the dark upon the most material points; but if you should think it useful either to myself or to others to give me a full statement, you shall have my best judgment. Your confidence I have no other claim upon than that which arises from my disposition to put confidence in you—to think that you know better than any one else the real difficulties of our present position, and that you can look at the remedy, however painful, firmly and practically. Whatever, therefore, approves itself to you, I am anxious to know, as furnishing for myself, if not the best conclusion, yet the best hope of a conclusion—the best track into which to let my thoughts run. But beyond what you may think good for me in these respects I have no right to ask, and I do not ask for your thoughts. They probably would be above and beyond me, and the responsibility of knowing them would outweigh the use which I should be able to make of them.[5]

Y^{rs} ever truly,

JAMES R. HOPE.

Rev. J. H. Newman.

In a letter to Mr. Newman dated the following day, November 9, Mr. Hope criticises, on the side of caution,

---

[5] To this letter of Mr. Hope's I do not find a reply of Mr. Newman's until November 26, when he apologises for having kept him in suspense, adding: 'So far from your not having written to the purpose, you laid down one proposition in which I quite acquiesce; that the subject of the supremacy of Rome should be moved *argumentatively*, if at all. I felt I had gained something here, and rested upon it, and gave up answering you, as it turns out, selfishly.' At the end of the letter he says: 'As to myself, I don't like talking; when we meet we shall see how we feel about it.' His reserve may, I think, be safely accounted for by his great unwillingness that such a man as Mr. Hope should be swayed by him to an act to which, as yet, he himself did not feel himself called.

various passages in the 'Life of St. Stephen Harding' (by Mr. J. D. Dalgairns, afterwards so well known as Father Dalgairns, of the London Oratory), the first and most celebrated of the series, proofs of which Mr. Newman had sent to him for his opinion.   These criticisms chiefly relate to expressions which might offend ordinary Anglican eaders, and which Mr. Hope proposed to soften.   Mr. Newman in the end noted against almost all these expressions *stet*.   He remarks to Mr. Hope (December 11): 'It seemed to me that, considering the *tone* of the whole composition, an alteration of the word (*e.g.*) " merit " was like giving milk and water for a fit of the gout, while it destroyed its integrity, vigour — in a word, its go.'   Again : 'I am convinced that those passages are *not* flying in people's faces, but are parts of a whole, and express ideas which cannot *otherwise* be expressed.'

These points were rather matter of prudence as viewed by Mr. Hope; on two others, touching the questions of 'exemptions' and 'impropriations,' Mr. Hope appears to have been himself unable to go along with the view of the writer of the 'Life of St. Stephen,' whom he considered to defend the *principles* of exemption too far.   Mr. Newman here conceded some alterations, which, however, I am unable to state, not having the proof before me, which Mr. Hope does not quote, but, as finally given, the passages referred to may be found in the 'Life of St. Stephen Harding,' pp. 47–49 and 65.

In the same letter of December 11 Mr. Newman informs Mr. Hope that he had resolved on giving up the 'Lives' as a series, and publishing such as were in type, or were written, as separate works. His comment on the motives which had led him to this decision is of great interest:—

I assure you, to find that the English Church cannot bear the Lives of her Saints (for so I will maintain, in spite of Gladstone, is the fact) does not tend to increase my faith and confidence in her. Nor am I abandoning *publication* because I abandon this particular measure. Rather, I consider I have been silent now for several years on subjects of the day, and need not fear now to speak. . . . If these ['Lives,' as separate works] gradually mount up towards the fulness of such an idea as the 'Lives of the Saints' contemplated in process of time, well and good.

He had said in a letter to Mr. Hope of December 5: 'G.'s remarks have shown me the *hopelessness*, by delay or any other means, of escaping the disapprobation of a number of persons whom I very much respect.' This was in reply to a letter of Mr. Hope's of the same day, which I found it difficult to introduce in its chronological order, and which may conveniently be placed here, as Mr. Hope in it clearly shows that his sympathies, notwithstanding his difficulties, went with the 'Lives,' and, like himself, backs his moral support with open-handed liberality:—

J. R. Hope, Esq. to the Rev. J. H. Newman.

Dec. 5, '43.

Dear Newman,—I enclose the proofs and Gladstone's remarks. The great point made by him here, as elsewhere, at present, is non-estrangement from the exciting Ch. of E.; and in this many who are disposed to quarrel with the Reformation are yet heartily disposed to join. In fact, I suppose it will shortly become, if it be not already, the symbol of a party.   To that party I do not feel myself at all strongly drawn, and therefore do not sympathise in G.'s views about the *Life* ; but if his views be a fair representative of the best class of opinions such as I allude to, you may conclude that the high Anglicans will be against you.   Of the middle and low there never, I suppose, was a doubt.

For my own part, I read the sheets greedily, and felt that they took me back to subjects which were once much in my thoughts, and ought never to have got so far out of them as they have. Nor was I at all put out by the general tone which seems to me inseparable from the subject ; but here and there are passages which I think needlessly direct and pointed, so much so indeed as to appear, merely in point of composition, abrupt and wilful. These I think I could point out.   G., you see, thinks his objections separable from the main design, which seems to me hardly possible—perhaps you will think the same of mine, but they relate only to isolated passages, and rather to giving them *obliqueness* than to changing them altogether.

However, I do not mean to say that I could suggest anything which would obviate G[ladstone]'s difficulties, and these are, after all, your main subjects for consideration.   What effect they will have upon you I cannot certainly conclude, but in case they should incline you either to delay or to total giving up, I have only to say that I shall be glad to contribute one or two hundred pounds towards defraying the expenses. . . . . . In fact, if upon any public eccl. grounds the work is to be delayed or not to go on, I cannot see that my money could be more fitly bestowed than in facilitating the arrangement.

Y^{rs} ever truly,

JAMES R. HOPE.

Rev. J. H. Newman.

No need was eventually found for the liberal offer with which the above letter concludes.   The following letter, though rather a long one, is certainly not

likely to fatigue the reader, and seems almost necessary
to be given, in order to complete this part of my
subject:—

The Rev. J. H. Newman to J. R. Hope, Esq.

Oriel College: Dec. 16, 1843.

My dear Hope,—You have not understood me about Gladstone, doubtless through my own fault. The truth is, I am
making a great concession—not to him, but to my respectful
feelings towards him. I thought you could see it, and only
feared you would think it greater than it really was. So I tried
to put you on your guard.

1. I withdraw *my name* from *any plan*. This is no slight
thing. I have frequent letters from people I do not know on
the subject of the Lives of the Saints, and doubt not it is
raising much talk and interest. A name always gives point to
an undertaking—considering my connection with the Tracts of
the Times, it would especially to this. You yourself and Badeley (whom, please, thank for some kind trouble he has been at
about a book for me) said, 'Delay the plan, *for* you will be
putting *yourself* at the head of the extreme party—the
B[ritish] C[ritic] having stopped:' now, I am more than
delaying, I am withdrawing my name. I am sure this is a
great thing, even though my initials occurred to this or
that life.

2. I have given up continuity, and that certain and promised. 128 pp. were to come out every month, and the work
was to go on to the end, except as unforeseen accidents interfered (as they have). Now we know how difficult it is to keep
people up to their work. The work is now left to the un-
pledged zeal of individuals. And there will be nothing metho-
dical or periodical in it to force itself upon people.

I do consider, then, I have given up a very great deal. But
what I have *not* given up is the *wish* that the work should be
done ; only I have put it under great disadvantages—so great
that I do not think it ever will be done—at the utmost frag-

ments will be done—and that without method, precision, unity, and a name.

And why have I done this? 1. Sincerely because I thought both by heading it and by giving it system I should be administering a continual blister to the kind feelings towards me, and the conscientious views of persons I respect as I do G. I assure you it is no pleasant thing to me to lose their good opinion, tho' I can't expect much to keep it. 2. I fear to put up something the Bishops may aim at. I may be charged at, as the Tracts have been. Then I should be in a very false position. I must move forward or backward, and I dread compulsory moves. 3. What is the most immediate and practical point, I don't think I could get a publisher to take on him the *expense* of a *series*, but few people would dread the risk of a single life of one or two hundred pages. Accordingly, I think I shall publish the one of which you saw a bit at once, to see whether it sells. That I shall to a certain extent be connected with it, and that I shall aim at making it a series, is certain; and this, as I said, was my reason for warning you that I was not giving way to G. so fully as I appeared to be.

. . . .

Ever y^rs aff^ly,

J. H. NEWMAN.

P.S.— . . . What set me most urgently on my present notice was that *I could not help it*. Though I gave up my series, which I wished to do, *Lives remained*, written or printed, or promised, *which would appear anyhow*, or scarcely could not.

There are two or three letters of this period in the Gladstone correspondence which shew an effort (subsequently renewed) on the part of Mr. Gladstone to draw off the mind of his friend from the gathering storms of controversy to objects like those in which his earliest zeal had found its scope.

The Right Hon. W. E. Gladstone, M.P. to J. R. Hope, Esq.

13 Carlton II. Terrace: Nov. 23, '43.

My dear Hope,—I do not doubt that you have looked to what has appeared in the public prints respecting a receptacle for the Destitute: and it is remarkable that an impulse of this kind should appear to have begun to operate in overt forms just at the time of your conception, and further, that it should have taken the direction of μηδὲν χωρὶς ἐπισκόπου. The Bishop must, I should think, have received before this time, some application. It will be difficult for him on the ground of authority alone to impress on the movement, or on the resulting institution, a thoroughly and specifically religious character. Can you consider whether it could be possible for you to throw yourself in at this juncture with the tender of personal aid, *i.e.* of yourself and those whom you may have consulted or on whom you can reckon ? It seems to me as if this might have a great effect and might be taking the tide at the flood. I am ready to concur in any act in which I could be useful, and have only this motive to keep back, that after fair professions I might find or think it necessary to place my practice under shabby limitations.

Ever your attached friend,

W. E. GLADSTONE.

In another note, dated, 'Whitehall, December 14, 1843,' Mr. Gladstone invites Mr. Hope to look at an article on the same subject in the 'Times' of that day, and especially to a letter of Mr. Arber's, on whom he suggests his calling. To this Mr. Hope replied a few days later :—

J. R. Hope, Esq. to the Right Hon. W. E. Gladstone, M.P.

Dec. 18, 1843.

Dear Gladstone,—[After proposing to meet Mr. Gladstone, Mr. Dyce, and Mr. Badeley in committee on the subject of a drawing of Trinity Coll., which the Scotch Committee wished lithographed] I received your note about Arber, but have not had strength or energy enough to do anything. To-day, I am still a rag.

Have you seen Newman's *new* Volume of Sermons? It is, I suppose, only just out, but Badeley got a copy on Saturday, and I read several yesterday. In those on the question of allegiance to the Church of England, there is much which is to me very cheering, and will to you, I think, be satisfactory.

Yours affectionately,
JAMES R. HOPE.

The *Ecclesiastical Courts Bill* is the subject of the first letter I find in the same correspondence of the next year (1844). The following note, of no great importance in itself, will still serve to illustrate the languid interest Mr. Hope now took in Anglican church affairs:—

J. R. Hope, Esq. to the Right Hon. W. E. Gladstone, M.P.

Private.   Lincoln's Inn: Feb. 5, 1844.

Dear Gladstone,—I return with thanks the Eccl. Courts Bill. It has, I think, a fair chance of passing, though the main inconveniences of the old Testamentary law remain unaltered. These, however, are points in which the public will suffer more than the County Registrars, and, unless their clients, the attornies, push them on, I do not anticipate much resistance from them.

From the Church side I see no great reason for opposition, though there are many points of detail, and forms of enactment, which I think are unecclesiastical, and likely to do mischief. However, it would require a good deal of attention to be positive upon these questions, and I suppose the measure will not be hurried through the Lords, so that we may, if necessary, get them well considered.

Yours ever truly,
JAMES R. HOPE.

The Right Hon. W. E. Gladstone.

The Parliamentary session causes a break in the correspondence, but the subject is resumed in a letter to Mr. Hope, dated 'Fasque, Aug. 12, '44,' in which Mr. Gladstone says :—

I should like to say a good deal, upon a review of the Session, about the Eccl. Courts Bill and other matters. I cannot but think there is a special Providence manifest in the impediments which have beset the measure in its different and conflicting forms. It seems as if the surrender of the temporal jurisdiction were reserved, and not by man's counsel, until it can be made part of a larger plan.

A highly interesting exchange of letters follows, on which I am tempted largely to draw, though only indirectly bearing on this biography, which, however, would hardly be complete, without the evidence they afford of a confidence extending even outside of that ecclesiastical sphere which was attracting everything towards it.

J. R. Hope, Esq. to the Right Hon. W. E. Gladstone, M.P.

Manchester : August 16, '44.

Dear Gladstone,— . . . I went on Wednesday to Leamington in order to commune with Mr. Lynch, the Master in Chancery, under whom I act in the office of Receiver of the rents and profits of divers estates.

He is, as you probably know, an Irish R. Catholic, and we often discuss together the claims and prospects of his Church. On this occasion we fell upon the question of Maynooth, and in discussing the probability of Peel's doing anything for it, he said that it would be impossible for you to remain in office if any such course were pursued. On the other hand, he did not think Peel would part with you, if he could possibly avoid it, and so concluded that you were Peel's chief difficulty in the matter. He seemed to think, however, that you had made a

' gulf ' of the Dissenters' Chapel Bill, on which point I did my best to undeceive him, and stated the un-religious view which you had taken of that question—adding that I had no doubt you valued place too cheaply to force your conscience in order to retain it, &c. &c.

This conversation I retail to you, in order that you may see how closely other people's minds have followed your own upon this question, and how well you have done in adopting the position in which you stand.

Lynch, if I mistake not, said he thought Peel would have done something this year, but for you.

Your review of the Session I should be glad to have. As to the Eccl. Courts Bill, I am much of your mind, but still I fear that the question cannot be staved off long enough to allow of the action of sound principles upon it. The Bishops might indeed still effect a good settlement, but, I wish I could add that they have the *united* wish to do so. . . .

By the 15th of Sept. I have arranged (D.V.) to be at Munich.

Y^r affectionate friend,

J. R. HOPE.

The Right Hon. W. E. Gladstone.

The Right Hon. W. E. Gladstone, M.P. to J. R. Hope, Esq.

Fasque: August 20, '44.

My dear Hope,—. . . . I must thank you for your communication about Lynch's discourse, which I have some notion of making known, with or without your name, at head-quarters. It is confirmation strong, as the testimony of an intelligent and disinterested witness ; and he is singularly true throughout in his conjectural delineation.

I am very well content to look forward and pack up my things. If there were any reasons which made it desirable with reference to the future, or the *paulo-post* future, that I should be in office under the present Government, I think they are now satisfied and exhausted. As connected with trade, I am certainly a cause of weakness and not of strength to Sir Robert Peel in the *two* houses of Parliament. It is not my opinion that on this score he will readily part with me : but it removes a cause of regret that I should have had, if the case had stood otherwise. And I do not think that another Session or two would pass without my exciting more mistrust. I am strongly and painfully impressed with recent disclosures concerning the physical state of the peasantry: for whose sake mainly, as my notion has been, we have maintained the Corn Laws. Last Session I had to answer a speech of Cobden's on this subject, five-sixths of which I should have been glad to have spoken. My conviction is, that our course in these matters has been generally right—but it involves progression, and it is a high probability that one bad harvest, or at all events two, would break up the Corn Law and with it the party. Hitherto, it has worked better than could have been hoped, but I cannot deny that it is a law mainly dependent on the weather. I have not in office spoken so much free trade as Sir Robert Peel. On the contrary, scarcely anything of dogma is to be gathered from *my* effusions, but people will naturally and properly bear from him a great deal which they will not take from a whipper-snapper.

The purpose of Parliamentary life resolves itself with me simply and wholly into one question—Will it ever afford the means under God of rectifying the relations between the Church and the State, and give me the opportunity of setting forward such a work ? There must be *either* such a readjustment, or a violent crisis. The present state of discipline cannot be borne for very many years ; and here lies the pinch. Towards the settlement of money questions something has been done by the Church Commission and the Government, and I think they may do more.

As to the general objects of political life, they are not my objects. Upon the whole, I do not expect from the good sense of the English people, the force of the principle of property, and the conservative influence of the Church, less than the maintenance of our present monarchical and parliamentary constitution under all ordinary circumstances : and I do not flatter myself with the notion that this will be better done by my remaining to take part in it. But the real renovation of the

country does not depend upon law and government: and those
who desire to take part in the work, except so far as it is connected with the specific readjustments to which I have referred,
must, I think, seek their province elsewhere.

Here is a very slight and naked sketch. If I were to fill
it up, I should break the back of a ricketty postman who daily
carries the Fettercairn letters at two miles an hour towards
Montrose.

> Believe me always
> Your obliged and attached friend,
> W. E. GLADSTONE.

J. R. Hope, Esq.

The great event connected with the movement in
1844 was the publication of Ward's 'Ideal of a
Christian Church,' which at first caused less excitement
than might have been expected, at least in London.
Thus Mr. Badeley writes to Mr. Hope (October 26),
'Ward's book passes very quietly here at present;'
and again (November 8), 'The book here makes very
little noise.' But meanwhile the heads of Houses were
moving at Oxford, and on February 13, 1845, a memorable day, the book was condemned, and its author
deprived of his degrees by the House of Convocation.
Mr. Hope was absent on the Continent at the beginning
of the strife, to which his letters do not contain much
allusion. Perhaps the same motives of caution upon
which he objected to the 'strong meat' of the 'Lives
of the English Saints' would have led him to similar
views as to the extreme un-reserve of the 'Ideal.'
When, however, the question of Mr. Ward's condemnation came on, he voted against it, as he was sure to
have done if he voted at all. It is hardly necessary to

remind the reader that on the same occasion it was proposed to pass a censure on No. 90 ; but this was vetoed
by the proctors, and consequently never came to the
vote.   I find the following draft of an address of thanks
to the proctors in Mr. Gladstone's hand, and with the
subjoined signatures and date in Mr. Hope's, among the
Hope-Scott papers :—

> We the u.s. M. of C., understanding that you have resolved
> to put your negative upon the Proposal relating to the Nine-
> tieth Tract in Convocation on Thursday, the 13th instant, beg
> leave to tender to you our cordial thanks for a determination
> which we consider to have been demanded by the principles of
> our Academical Constit".
>
> W. E. G.
> Manning and self. Feby. 11, '45.   J. R. H.

As far as regards Mr. Gladstone, this ought to be
compared with a correspondence in the Oakeley case,
which will be found cited *infra*, p. 66.

To the earlier part of the period now before us
belongs some very kind service rendered by Mr. Hope
to his dear friend the Rev. W. Adams, Fellow of Merton,
and Perpetual Curate of St. Peter's-in-the-East, Oxford,
in seeing through the press his celebrated allegory, ' The
Shadow of the Cross,' on which there is a rather full
correspondence extant (1842–43), but of more special
interest as connected with Mr. Adams' biography than
his own, except so far as it proves the affectionate intimacy which subsisted between them.   One letter of
later date (December 15, 1846) is endorsed in Mr.
Hope-Scott's handwriting :—' William Adams, R. I. P.
sub umbra crucis. J. R. H. S. 1871.' The work was pub-

lished for the Christian Knowledge Society, of the committee of which Mr. Hope at the time was still a member. In connection with the same society Mr. Hope undertook a serial work, already alluded to (which was in course of publication in 1844), consisting of engravings from Scripture subjects, in a high style of art, from the cartoons of Raphael in the Loggia of the Vatican. Mr. Hope was strongly impressed with the utility of such a work for directing and elevating the taste of the humbler classes and of schools generally, and he expended large sums of money in bringing this out. It was published in numbers containing six plates each, under the superintendence of Professor Gruner, afterwards Director of the Department of Engravings at the Royal Museum at Dresden, and prepared by Signor Corsini, a distinguished Roman draughtsman. Mr. Hope-Scott, indeed, did not carry on the work after the first five numbers (a large and costly business, however), and it was completed by Mr. Gruner alone, who published it under the title of 'Scripture Prints from the Frescoes of Raphael in the Vatican,' edited by Louis Gruner, &c. (London : Houlston and Wright, 1866). Mr. Hope-Scott continued his benefactions to the Society for the Propagation of the Gospel for several years later than the time now before us. I find a donation of 210*l.* under his name in the year 1847. He had given 200*l.* in November 1846 to the College Chapel at Harrow Weald.

Another undertaking of some importance in which he took great interest in those days, relating both to literature and religion, was the 'Anglia Christiana,' a

series of the monuments of English history, which was
publishing in 1844-45. Only three volumes of it came
out—' Chronicon Monasterii de Bello ' (Battle Abbey),
Giraldus Cambrensis 'De Institutione Principis,' and
' Liber Eliensis.' Mr. Hope much wished to have had
included in the list the work called ' Pupilla Oculi,' a
treatise on moral theology by John de Burgh, Chancellor
of the University of Cambridge about the year 1385,
which was much in use among the clergy before the
Reformation. Mr. David Lewis, of Jesus College (as a
Catholic so well known for his admirable translations of
the works of St. John of the Cross and of St. Teresa),
collated the text for him, but I believe it was never
published. I find in the Badeley correspondence a
very interesting letter of Mr. Hope's dated February
28, 1843, about the ' Pupilla Oculi,' its history and
authority. The book had been cited by Mr. Badeley
in the Court of Queen's Bench, and by others in the
House of Lords, in the case of the Queen v. Willis. Lord
Lyndhurst and some of the judges objected to its value
as evidence on the ground of its contradicting the common law on the question of legitimation by subsequent
marriage. Mr. Hope discusses the subject in a masterly
style : I must refrain from quoting such merely anti-
quarian or legal matter for its own sake, yet will subjoin
some paragraphs of the letter which illustrate the line
taken by him as a lawyer at that time on the important
point of the relations of Church and State :—

There can be, I think, very little doubt that in old times the
distinction between Church and State was one of *jurisdictions*
rather than of *laws*. I mean that each was supposed to have

its proper subject-matter of legislation as well as of judicial
inquiry. Where the subject-matter was conceded to the Church
altogether, there the Church law prevailed absolutely; where
the subject-matter was of mixed cognizance, there the Church
law was modified by the common or statute law; where the
subject was altogether lay, there both the laws and the tribunals of the Church were silenced. When, therefore, we would
ascertain whether the law of the Church is to govern a given
subject, we must first ascertain how far it was of the exclusive
cognizance of the Church; and, if we find that it was principally but not exclusively of ecclesiastical cognizance, how far
the common law interfered to modify the ecclesiastical laws by
which it was to be determined.

Now, in the case before us, this much, I think, must be
admitted, viz. that marriage, *as a sacrament*, was exclusively
subject to the ecclesiastical jurisdiction; and, therefore, that
whatever view the common law might entertain as to the consequence to be attached to this or that form of it, the essence of
the sacrament itself was determinable by the doctrine of the
Church, and by that alone.

But if this was so, then whatever was accepted by the
Church of England as to the *essence* of marriage must necessarily be allowed to have been the common law upon that
point, i.e. there could be no other law by which it could be
decided.

Granting, therefore, that J. de Burgh, or any other ecclesiastical writer, has laid down rules upon subjects of mixed
jurisdiction which the common law disallows, it by no means
follows that his authority is to be slighted where he speaks of
matters which were exclusively ecclesiastical. Indeed, the opposition of the common law upon given points, e.g. the legitimation by subsequent marriage, gives a pregnant meaning to
its silence upon others.

I find that in the autumn of that year (1843) Mr.
Hope spent some time in making researches into the
records at York connected with the law of marriage.

In a letter to Mr. Badeley (September 28) he says, ' At
York I was successful in finding a variety of matri-
monial causes, from A.D. 1301 downwards, which I think
illustrate the *right* view of the question.   The records
there abound in well-preserved forms of proceeding,
and it was with regret that I gave up further investi-
gations. The labour, however, of reading and transcrib-
ing extracts was occasionally harder than suits holiday
work.' In the same letter he speaks with much pleasure
of a day spent at Burton Agnes with Archdeacons R.
Wilberforce, Manning, &c., and as particularly indebted
to the Archbishop of York and his family for the reception they gave him. The correspondence, indeed, affords
a gracious epistle from the Archbishop himself (then
nearly eighty-six years of age) to Mr. Hope, dated
Trentham, September 30, 1843, in which, after expressing his high satisfaction at some legal advice which he
had received from him, he goes on to say :—

I have only to add that nothing could gratify us more than
your having occasion—and the sooner the better—to refer again
to the York archives for any purpose whatever; ' provided
always, and be it hereby enacted, that such reference be had
during the period of the Archbishop's annual residence at
Bishopthorpe.'

Ever truly y^{rs},
E. EBOR.

It may here be permitted me to quote a few lines
from memoranda about Mr. Hope, kindly written at the
request of one of his nearest relatives by a lady whose
genius as well as catholic feeling especially fitted her to
preserve those traces which I am sure no reader would

wish should be allowed to fade away. They afford at once a proof that when doubts as to his religious position were approaching their most painful stage, he never allowed them to interfere with those duties of religion which are binding on all intellectual states alike, and they present a glimpse both of his appearance and manner at that date which will greatly assist the reader in forming an idea of him.

I think it was in 1843 that I first saw your dear brother in Margaret Street Chapel, the favourite place of worship of the Puseyites in those days, and noticed him and his friend Mr. Badeley walking away together, and was more struck with his appearance than with that of any other person I have ever seen before or since. . . . It is only in pictures that I have ever seen anything equalling, and never anything surpassing, what was, at the time I am speaking of, the ideal beauty of his face and figure.

During the next two years I used often to see him at Margaret Street Chapel, and I may say that his recollection in prayer and unaffected devotion made a strong impression upon me. Having been very little in England since my childhood, it was quite a new thing to me to see a layman in the Anglican Church so devout, but without a tinge of fanaticism or apparent excitement. In 1844 I made acquaintance with Mr. Hope, and met him occasionally in society. He was all that his appearance would have led one to expect; the charm of his manner enhanced the effect of his conversational powers.[6]

I have not found any record of Mr. Hope's personal religious state about that time, like the diaries of his earlier manhood. He writes, however, to Mr. Newman on March 1, 1844 (from Lincoln's Inn): 'If I can manage it, I should much like to spend Passion Week at

---

[6] Lady Georgiana Fullerton to Lady Henry Kerr, May 5 (1881).

or *near* Oxford. Could you let me into the guest-chamber at Littlemore ? ' Mr. Newman (March 14) writes in reply that the guest-chamber was quite at his service, but adds : ' Pray do not fancy us in such a state that we can profess a retreat, or any one here able to conduct one.' In another letter Mr. Newman acknowledges ' a splendid benefaction ' of Mr. Hope's to the house of Littlemore.

49

CHAPTER XX.

1844-1845.

AT the end of August or beginning of September 1844
Mr. Hope set out for a tour on the Continent, accompanied by Mr. Badeley. Of the earlier days of it I have
no information, but they parted at Heidelberg about
September 12, Mr. Badeley for the Rhine country and
Belgium, Mr. Hope for Munich. By this time, as has
already been evident, he was deeply engaged in professional pursuits, and his health had begun to suffer from
his unremitting labours. Several passages might be
quoted from the letters of his intimate friends, showing
the anxiety they felt on the subject. Some real relaxation, however, had at last become necessary; and it
would appear that he rather wished to leave the turmoil of the movement, as well as business, behind him.
In a letter of Mr. Badeley's to him, dated Brussels, Sep-

tember 22, the following sentence occurs :—' If you like
to see what is going on in this [the affair of opposing
Dr. Symonds' election as Vice-Chancellor at Oxford] and
in Church matters, I will send you the " English Church-
man ; " but as you said " No," when we parted, I forbear
to forward any papers till further orders.' Afterwards,
however, ' after all,' he asks Mr. Badeley to send it. On
his way to Munich, Mr. Hope stopped at Augsburg,
where ' of course he visited Butsch the bookseller,' buys
a copy of the ' Summa Divi Thomæ Aquinatis,' and sees
some good books which he did not want. At Munich,
where he arrived on September 14, rooms were provided
for him at the Austrian Legation by the kindness of his
friend Count Senfft. These particulars I take from a
letter of his to Mr. Badeley, dated Munich, September
18, and subjoin some further details in full :—

D[öllinger] is, I think, remarkably well, and I am more
struck with him than ever.   I found him already deep in
Ward's book, with which he is much struck.   I have already
had some interesting conversations with him, and anticipate
more.   He is Rector elect of the University, and highly
spoken of by all I see.   My new acquaintances consist of the
Papal Nuntius Viale, a very striking person, Professor Walther,
the canonist, and some intelligent Bavarians.   I am to visit
Görres this evening. . . .   There is an English service here
very decently and nicely performed by Mr. de Coetlogon, a
man in Scotch orders, and the chapel is a modest but respectable room. . . . I ask hard questions about marriage, and
receive very doubtful answers ; but I am resolved, if possible, to
get some definite information from the best sources in Germany.

The following letter, connected with this tour of Mr.
Hope's, is also very instructive as to a particular phase
of the movement :—

The Rev. Dr. Pusey to J. R. Hope, Esq.

My dear Hope,—I have no news as yet to communicate to you except that some few are taking up ye matter of ye V. C. in r^t earnest, and so I suppose it will be a pitched battle, and we shall win at last, even if but a handful as yet.

I have 2 or 3 commissions for you, w^h will not occupy your time, and w^h will, I hope, be a subject of interest to you. It is for my little library of R. C. works. The perplexity is to find out y^e best books upon $diff^t$ subjects, for I cannot read all. The general class is, as you know, ascetic books, books of guidance, w^h shall give people knowledge of self, enable us to guide consciences, build people up in y^e higher life, force them to mental prayer, or give them subjects of meditation in it, the spiritual life, X^{tian} perfection, holy performance of ordinary actions, love of God, or any X^{tian} graces in detail, devotions, books on holy seasons—in a word, anything in practical theology in its widest range, or, again, cases of conscience.

I have learnt more or less as to French & Spanish, & some Latin works, but of Italian I know those only of Scupoli, and of German absolutely nothing. The only books I have seen are some sermons by Sailer, w^h, altho' clear and energetic, contain nothing w^h one did not know before; they have nothing to build people up with.

I sh^d be glad also of any information on a subject w^h I know drew y^r thoughts when you were last abroad—the system as to retreats. I saw a book, 'Manuale dell' Esercitatori,' but I sh^d be very glad of any information or any guidance.

If it w^d not occupy you too much, I sh^d be much obliged to you to procure on my account any practical works w^h m^t be recommended.

Perhaps also Dr. Döllinger could give you some information as to S. Ignatius Loyola's ' Exercitia Spiritualia,' for they seem to have been so often re-moulded that there is some difficulty to ascertain (1) what is ye genuine form, or at least to obtain a copy, (2) whether any other re-casting of it be found easier to use.

I trust these inquiries will not be so much an encumbrance to you, as lead you to happy subjects and more acquaintance with happy-making books.   God bless you ever.

Y^{rs} affectionately,

E. B. PUSEY.

Christ Church: September 9, 1844.

[P.S.] There is yet a subject on w^h I sh^d like to know more, if you fall in with persons who have ye guidance of consciences,—what penances they employ for persons whose temptations are almost entirely spiritual, of delicate frames often, and who wish to be led on to perfection.   I see in a spiritual writer that even for such, corporal severities are not to be neglected, but so many of them are unsafe.   I suspect y^e 'discipline' to be one of ye safest and with internal humiliation the best. . . . C^d you procure and send me one by B. ?   What was described to me was of a ve~y sacred character ; 5 cords, each with 5 knots, in memory of ye 5 Wounds of our Lord. . . . I sh^d be glad to know also whether there were any cases in w^h it is unsafe, e.g. in a nervous person.

On October 1 Mr. Hope left Munich to pay a visit at Tetschen, the seat of his friends the Thun family (described vol. i. p. 42), taking Ratisbon and other places in his way.   At Tetschen, where he stayed from October 5 to 12, he found a sad blank in the recent death of the Countess Thun.   From an interesting letter to Lady Hope (dated Vienna, October 26, 1844) which furnishes these dates, I transcribe also the following particulars :—

Countess Anna is still in very uncertain health. . . . The Count himself seems to have rallied lately, but it will be long before he gets over his loss.   The second daughter, Countess Juza, seems to be now the stay of the family.   Of the sons, only Francis, the eldest, was at home.   He is devoted to art, and has besides abundance of business in the management of

the estates which his father has made over to him, and with
various charitable societies at Prague, in which he and his
family are interested. From Tetschen I went to Prague, with
Count Joseph Thun, a cousin, with his wife and two sons. At
Prague I spent Sunday, Monday, and Tuesday, in constant
admiration of the town, to which I did not do justice when I
was last there. It is really beautiful, and, out of Italy, I think
Edinburgh alone equal to it, of all the towns which I have
seen. With Tetschen for summer, and Prague for winter, I
think the Thuns have two as charming residences as could be
found.

On Tuesday evening [Oct. 15] I left for Königsgrätz, a provincial town, where Leo Thun, the youngest, is officially
employed. He is a noble fellow, and has devoted himself for
years to the details of business, with a view to becoming useful
to Bohemia, to which he is very much attached. He is also
prominent among the revivers of the Bohemian language and
literature, which is Sclavonic, and has thus become well known
in Germany, as well as in Hungary and other countries where
there are Sclavonic tribes. The movement is in a political
sense important, as well as influential upon manners and modes
of thinking, and it has already excited a good deal of discussion
and some animosity. It would take too much time, however,
to explain what I have learnt of its bearings. With Leo I spent
two very agreeable days, and have had much to talk about, as I
had not seen him since I was last in Bohemia. I was introduced to the *notables* of the place, his *chef* and the commander
of the garrison (an old Irish officer of the name of Fitzgerald),
and saw his mode of life, which to a man with plenty of employment must be convenient, though not very amusing.

From Königsgrätz I started on Thursday night, and arrived
here [Vienna] on Saturday week, the 19th [Oct.], and took up my
abode at the same inn with Fritz Thun, the diplomat, who was
here on his way from Turin, which he has now left for Prague.
You will remember how pleasant a person he is, and will be glad
to hear that his professional prospects are excellent, as he is in
high favour with Prince Metternich, to whom he was strongly

recommended by Schwartzenberg, his last *chef*. One of my first acts was to call on Sir R. Gordon [the British Ambassador], who has been *most* kind, giving me dinner as often as I can go to him, and assisting me in everything. On the evening of my arrival he took me to Prince Metternich, when I had the honour of a conversation with the great man. George was remembered by him and his daughter, and by the Countess Zichy, the Princess's mother, and I was very kindly received by them all. Palmerston was expected here, and the Prince told Sir R. Gordon that, if he came, I should be invited to meet him at dinner; but unluckily he has changed his plans, so that I shall not see him and Metternich together, which would have been a great sight. I gave Sir Robert your good accounts of Lady Alicia,[1] and beg that you will in return tell her that Sir R. is very flourishing, and that in my opinion he is a very magnificent ambassador, and, what is better, a very kind one. His establishment is admirably *monté*, and I found in François a friend of the Hope family in general. George's letters of introduction I duly received. Schwartzenberg is not here, but I have seen Esterhazy, who has asked me to his country place, about three hours' drive from Vienna. . . . Besides the people I have named, I have seen others, to whom I get access through Count Senfft, among whom is the Dowager Duchess of Anhalt-Cöthen, a natural sister of the King of Prussia, and a clever woman. . . .

Your affect. Son,
JAMES R. HOPE.

Mr. Hope was unable to accept the invitation of Prince Esterhazy, in consequence of an engagement to visit another Hungarian magnate, Prince Palffy. The latter visit, with various other interesting details, is recorded in the following letter:—

---

[1] Sister of the Earl of Aberdeen and of Sir R. Gordon, died 1847.

J. R. Hope, Esq. to Edward L. Badeley, Esq.

Vienna: Nov. 7, 1844.

Dear Badeley,—[After giving some account of his visit at Tetschen, Mr. Hope goes on to mention his interview with Prince Metternich.] Prince Metternich honoured me with a conversation of some ten minutes or so, and which would pro- bably have been both longer and more interesting but for the intrusion of a German who chose to thrust himself upon us. He spoke of some points of commercial and manufacturing in- terest with great clearness and precision, and pleased me very much by the simplicity of his manner. By means of letters which Count Senfft gave me I have also become acquainted with several of the persons who are known as active friends of the R. C. *high* Church party; but I do not know very much of them, and of the Vienna clergy nothing at all. . . .

On Monday, the 28th [Oct.], I started for my promised visit to Prince Palffy at Malatzka, and arrived there in a few hours. The house resembles most of those one sees abroad, built round a court, with long passages, white exterior, &c., and, as the country round it is very flat and sandy, it cannot be called a very interesting place. It was, however, my first resting-place in Hungary, and, as such, an object of curiosity to me. Besides which, I found in it a hearty welcome, and a large family party, which gave me a good idea of the society of the upper class. The Prince is an extensive landowner, holding it all in his own hands (as is generally if not universally the case, both in Bohemia and Hungary), and working it by the tributary labour of the peasants, who, besides a small money payment, contribute labour for a certain number of days in each year. With the obligation of this quittance, the latter class hold in fee the cottages and plots of land which they occupy, and ap- pear to be a thriving and comfortable race. They are, how- ever, exclusively the tax-payers, as the nobles are still free from all imposts. An effort has indeed been made lately, which has partially succeeded, to tax the nobles; and it is probable that amid the numerous reforms of the Hungarian

Diet, this will eventually be fully carried out. Our mode of life at Malatzka was to rise when we chose, breakfast in our own rooms, to meet at half-past twelve for luncheon, then to go out, and to dine at six, and to spend the evening in the drawing-room. Coursing, a badger-hunt, and an expedition to a property of the Prince's at the foot of the Carpathians, constituted my out-of-door amusements ; and of these, the last at least was very interesting. I saw an immense tract of wood and pasture, a herd of wild oxen, sheep innumerable, a curious stalactite grotto, and an Hungarian farmhouse.

From Malatzka I went, furnished with letters, to the seat of Prince Liechtenstein in Moravia—Eisgrüb. He is one of the richest men in the Austrian dominions, having possessions in Moravia, Bohemia, and Hungary, and several houses in Vienna. A great sportsman, and in this point, at least, a great imitator of English manners. The house at which I was is a summer residence, with very fine pleasure-grounds, park, &c.; but he has an autumn château not far off, which I also visited, and which is a fine specimen of foreign country architecture. Everything about him seemed to teem with expense and luxury, which, although probably not greater than what is to be found in the residences of English noblemen, appears greater from its contrast with the rudeness and simplicity of the general condition of the country. These great nobles seem, in fact, to combine the most striking points of barbarism and civilisation, and to turn them both to their enjoyment. I stayed only one day at Eisgrüb, though I had pressing invitations to remain longer ; but I was anxious to go to Presburg to see the Diet, and so returned to Malatzka, which I left again the next morning, Saturday, 2nd Nov., for the seat of the Hungarian Parliament.

At Presburg I spent four days. The place itself is uninteresting, though there are points of beauty about it ; but it contains at this moment some of the most turbulent politicians in the world ; and their movements are of considerable importance as well to the twelve million souls who constitute the population of Hungary, as to the integrity of the Austrian Empire.

I should write a book were I to tell you all I have heard from
different quarters upon this question; but this much seems
certain—that Hungary is in a state of violent transition, and
that in a few years its internal condition and perhaps its relations to the Austrian monarchy will have undergone a complete revolution. Sir R. Gordon gave me a letter to an
Englishman, who is employed by the British Embassy to attend the sittings of the Diet; and by his kindness I was
enabled to make acquaintance with many of the most distinguished men. I was also present at several debates in the two
Chambers of the Diet, and though (the language being Hungarian) I could not understand a word, yet it was most interesting to watch the proceedings of this Magyar Parliament,
in which freedom of speech exists as fully as in any assemblage
in the world. The members all attend in Hungarian costume,
which, on common occasions, consists of a laced surtout coat,
a cap, and a sword. They speak from their places and without
notes. Each member may speak as often as he pleases, and
some take advantage of the privilege to a somewhat formidable
extent. There seemed to be much fluency and not a little
action ; but the management of the voice was bad, and energy
seemed to pass at once into violence. Though party runs
high, organisation is very little understood, and business is
transacted both slowly and with very uncertain results. They
have the misfortune of all foreign constitutional states, that of
desiring to imitate England, i.e. to do in a few years, and
designedly, what the accidents of centuries have produced with
us. There is, however, no lack either of talent or courage, and
one governing mind might make Hungary a nation. It is immensely rich in natural productions, and wants only a market
to have a great trade. This they are well disposed to establish
with England, and I hope they may succeed; but Austria has
interests which I fear may render this difficult. In both
Chambers the clergy are represented : in that of the magnates
by the Bishops; in the Lower House by deputies of the
chapters. To the Primate I was introduced at one of his
public entertainments. He is said to have 40 or 60,000*l.* per

ann., and his personal carriage as well as his establishment are quite becoming his station.   I made acquaintance also with the Archbishop of Erlau, a poet and a man of taste and learning, but victim to the tic douloureux.   Lastly, with the Bishop of Csanad (Mgr. Lonowics), who has charmed me.   He is well read, in English as well as other literature and history, and is as kind-hearted and Christian a man as I ever met with.   Indeed, I shall be tempted to visit Hungary again, if it is only to spend a day or two with him.   In the meantime we have established a mutual book-relation.   He is to send me works on Hungarian Ecclesiastical Law, addressed to Stewart, and I have promised to send him some things which I beg you will at once see to.   [Mr. Hope mentions Winkle's ' Cathedrals;' Ward's ' Ideal ; ' Newman's last vol. of ' Sermons ; ' the ' Life of St. Stephen ; ' Oakeley's ' Life of St. Austin ; ' and his own pamphlet ' On the Jerusalem Bishopric.']

Yours ever truly,

JAMES R. HOPE.

On November 25 we find Mr. Hope at Milan, where he mentions having seen his old acquaintances, Manzoni and Vitali.   The following letter will show how much he had impressed the former, brief as their communications had been :—

Alessandro Manzoni to J. R. Hope, Esq.

Milan : 8 Mai, 1845.

Monsieur et respectable ami,—Je profite de l'occasion que me présente mon ancien et intime ami, M. le Baron Trechi, pour me rappeler à votre bon souvenir. . . .

Agréez mes remercîments bien vifs et bien sincères pour les *Scripture Prints* que Mr. Lewis Gruner a bien voulu me remettre de votre part.   Si le nom du peintre n'y était pas, je suis sûr qu'en les voyant, je me serais écrié : Ah !   Raphael. C'est tout ce qu'un homme n'ayant, malheureusement, aucune connaissance de l'art, peut vous dire pour vous rendre compte de l'impression que lui a faite la copie.   Je ne vous charge de rien pour Mr. Gladstone, parce que je me donne la satisfaction de lui écrire par cette même occasion. J'espère que nous le reverrons bientôt au ministère. N'allez pas me demander si je suis anglais pour dire : nous ; car je vous répondrais que *homo sum ; humani nihil a me alienum puto* ; et qu'il n'y a rien d'*humanius* que d'aimer à voir le pouvoir uni à la confiance ; je ne dis pas : à de hautes facultés ; car, malheureusement, le cas est moins rare. [After giving his friend an account of a great family affliction he had sustained in the loss of a beloved daughter, the writer goes on to say :]

Je ne crains pas de vous importuner en vous parlant ainsi de ce qui me touche si profondément : je sais la part que vous prenez à tout ce qui est douleur et confiance en Dieu, par Jésus Christ. Je n'ai pas craint non plus de vous choquer en vous écrivant avec un ton si familier, et comme il conviendrait à une ancienne connaissance ; car il me semble que nous le sommes ; l'affection et l'estime de ma part et une grande bonté de la vôtre, ont bien pu suppléer le temps. Permettez-moi d'espérer que le bonheur que j'ai de vous connaître n'aura pas été un accident dans une vie, et que des causes plus heureuses que d'autrefois vous ramèneront bientôt encore dans ce pays ; et, en attendant, veuillez me garder une petite place dans votre souvenir, comme vous êtes toujours vivant dans le mien. Je suis, avec la plus affectueuse considération,

Votre dévoué serviteur et ami,

ALEXANDRE MANZONI.

Mr. Hope proceeded from Milan to Florence and Rome. Almost the only letter referring to this visit to Rome that has come before me is the following written to Mr. Badeley on December 19. It contains comparatively little of importance. Much of it is taken up with an account, with which many readers will be interested, of Sir William Follett, then at Rome, and verging towards his end, of whom Mr. Hope had seen a great deal.

J. R. Hope, Esq. to E. Badeley, Esq.

Rome: December 19, 1844.

Dear Badeley,— . . . My time here has been spent some-what idly, partly owing to the variable weather, partly to English society, partly to that vacant feeling which the climate of Rome usually produces in me. I have, however, enjoyed my stay on the whole, and feel very little disposed to face a winter journey through France, though I should not be sorry to find myself in England at once, could it be accomplished without effort. Follett is the person about whom you will probably be most anxious to hear. I see him constantly, and have endeavoured to assist him in sight-seeing, which my acquaintance with some well-informed people has enabled me in some measure to do. He takes a lively interest in everything he sees—ecclesiastical and tem-poral. Ancient Rome, however, seems to have most attractions for him, and under the guidance of Messrs. Colyar and Pfyffer (both friends of Rogers) we have *done*, and propose to do more of the Imperial city. We have also been to some monasteries, and at the Irish Franciscans (where he could talk English) he seemed to be very much amused. I believe he understands sufficiently to read and to catch part of what is said, but not enough to enjoy, as he otherwise might, the society of the Friars. To-morrow we are to visit our English cardinal, Acton, and in the evening I hope to introduce him to one of the first advocates in Rome, with whom we may talk law. His party consists of Lady F., two daughters, and his sister-in-law, Miss Giffard, all nice people, but with whom I have got into bad repute by carrying off Sir W. into a separate course of sight-seeing. He proposes to leave Rome after Christmas, and to go by Naples to Malta, whence he will return in a Government steamer for the meeting of Parliament. As to his health, I really am not in condition to form a definite opinion, and I do not like to write home an account which I am not sure is correct. *To you*, however, I may say that I wish much he would remain abroad at least till next summer. That he is better there can, I think, be no doubt, but that he is not thoroughly restored is also certain, and I dread his return to the excitement of his political and professional position. Pray do not tell others more of what I write about him, than that he is going on well, and is interested by his journey. Among the other English here are some very nice people. Those of whom I see most are Mr. and Mrs. Vivian. He is learned in architecture and painting, and joins F. in his expeditions sometimes, and we go about a good deal together. . . . Among old acquaintances here, I found Waterton the traveller and naturalist, who is a very amusing person, and a very strict Catholic. In the latter character, he gave me an interesting account of Tickell's reception into the Church of Rome at Bruges. He was himself present, and was very much struck by T.'s devout and humble behaviour. To him and to another English R. C. I gave your 'English Church-man' with Oakeley's letter—Waterton is furious about it. . . . Of the Roman clergy I have seen little, and have indeed almost given up my inquiries among them. Books too I look but little after, so you may judge of my indolence.

According to my present plan, I propose to leave Rome on January 1 or 2, and to speed homewards viâ Leghorn, Genoa, Marseilles, and Paris. . . .

This is not a long letter, but I have little to say. I am on the whole well. Colds indeed attack me here as elsewhere. Though occasionally very wet, the weather has not been severe here, and some days perfectly delightful.

Ever yours truly
JAMES R. HOPE.

The following note, endorsed in Mr. Hope-Scott's hand, ' q' 1845,' supplies additional proof that in the list of the many friends who felt there was something in his character which powerfully drew them towards him, Sir William Follett must also be numbered :—

Sir William Follett to J. R. Hope, Esq.

Park Street: March 31.

Dear Hope,—. . . I have had a terrible attack of cold and cough, which has put me much out of spirits, but it is now leaving me, and I hope, as the weather improves, I shall get round again.

If no one else, I shall always be happy to see you, whenever you can find time to call. I gave orders indeed for your admittance at all times.

Ever, dear Hope,

Most truly yours,

W. W. FOLLETT.

Notwithstanding all apparent coldness, and in spite of all the expressions of disappointment with Rome that have appeared in the Roman correspondence,[2] it is clear that the secret influence and spirit of the place were working their effect on his mind. A great proof of this will be given further on, in a letter of the Père Root-haan's to a friend relative to Mr. Hope's conversion.

A sentence from a letter of Mr. Hope's about two years afterwards is here in point. 'Your impression of Rome (he writes to Mr. Badeley, October 16, 1847) appears to be similar to that of most who see it for the first time; but it grows upon one, and the recollection will be deeper than the present feeling.'

There is a pleasing note to Mr. Hope, dated December 20, 1844, from Mgr. Grant, then Rector of the

---

[2] On the cause of this dissatisfaction an intimate friend of his has observed: 'For myself I think the real and sufficient reason of his disappointment with Rome was, that the Roman authorities naturally and reasonably would not open to a Protestant. They would fear their information would be used against them. They could not know his honesty of purpose.'

English College at Rome, and afterwards the well-known
Bishop of Southwark, one of the most beloved and
venerated friends of his Catholic period. It merely
gives information to assist him in visiting St. John
Lateran's, and promises to send an order for St. Peter's.
It concludes characteristically : ' I shall be too happy
to serve you whenever I can be useful. Although you
do not think so, you will find that *little people* are not
without some use ; and, in the hope that you will allow
me an opportunity of proving that I am in the right, I
remain, with many thanks for your kindness, &c.,—
THOMAS GRANT.' I may here also give a short letter of
Bishop Grant's, of later date, illustrating their friendship, and including some traces of its beginning at
Rome :—

> *The Right Rev. Dr. Grant, Bishop of Southwark, to*
> *J. R. Hope-Scott, Esq. Q.C.*
>
> June 23, 1853.

My dear Mr. Hope-Scott,—The *frescoes* have arrived, and I
hasten to thank you for a gift, valuable in itself, but most dear
to me, because it will ever remind me of the beginning of that
friendship which has always been so pleasing to me, and which
forms one of the consolations that are allowed to me in the
midst of the weighty duties of my present state—duties which
I little expected when we quarrelled peacefully about Swiss
guards and troops of soldiers lining St. Peter's on grand days.

When you next visit the churches and antiquities of Rome
Mary Monica will catch up the ardour that will then probably
have gone by for you and myself, and will wonder why you care
so little for them ; and if I am with you I fear I shall be more
tempted to tell her of the quiet rooms in Via della Croce,
where I first knew her father, than of the Arch of Drusus, or
other pagan monuments that once entertained our attention.

> Yours very sincerely,
> †THOMAS GRANT.

Mr. Hope-Scott had a high admiration for this saintly Bishop, and used to speak of him as ' *the* Bishop,' always meaning by that Bishop Grant.

Early in 1845, and not many weeks after his return to England, Mr. Hope resigned his chancellorship of Salisbury. It can scarcely be doubted that misgivings as to his religious position, more apparent perhaps to us now than they then were even to himself, were among his leading motives for taking this important step; although the immense accumulation of his business before the Parliamentary committees must have rendered it difficult for him, even with his talents, to hold with it an appointment like that in such times ; and feelings of friendship for his successor, the present Sir Robert Phillimore, may also have influenced him. The date of the resignation was Feb. 10.

The judgment of Sir Herbert Jenner Fust in the celebrated ' Stone Altar Case,' by which wooden altars only were permitted, was a severe discouragement to the Tractarian party, being felt to interfere with the idea of sacrifice. From the following passage of a letter (undated) of Dr. Pusey's to Mr. Hope, it appears that he (Mr. Hope) had endeavoured to take a more favourable view. The letter probably belongs to Feb. or March 1845.

I do not know whether the opinion you give is as to law previous to Sir H. J. F.'s decision, and as a ground of appeal agst it, or as to what w^d still be allowed. W^d his judgment preclude our having a stone slab, either upon stone pedestals or a wooden panelled altar ? I have comforted others with the same topic you mention, that wooden tables are altars by virtue of ye sacrifice, and so that this decision really alters nothing. Still, it does seemingly, and was intended to discountenance the doctrine. . . . It must be confessed, too, that this decision of Sir H. J. F. is a defeat—only an outward one, and availing nothing while truth spreads within. Still it is well to neutralise the sentence as much as we can.

Ever y^{rs} affect^{ly},

E. B. PUSEY.

Notwithstanding this, Mr. Hope is remembered, after the adverse decision, to have despondingly asked, 'Where is the use of fighting for the shell when we have lost the kernel?'

Among the other agitations of that time was the prosecution instituted in the Court of Arches by Dr. Blomfield, Bishop of London, against the Rev. Frederick Oakeley (the late Canon) for views which he had expressed about the Blessed Sacrament. Canon Oakeley, in a conversation I had with him in 1878, gave me the following information as to the part taken by Mr. Hope as his friend and adviser in this case, and general recollections of him. He had resolved to let the case go by default, partly because he felt convinced that it was sure to be decided in favour of the bishop, as those cases always were; partly because he disliked a subject like the Blessed Sacrament to be bandied about by the lawyers in that way. Mr. Hope, on the other hand, urged him to place himself in the hands of counsel, and thought a good case might be made by reference to books on canon law and Roman writers of the moderate school (Gallican), showing that, in point of fact, the holding of ' all Roman doctrine ' (thus interpreted) was compatible with the doctrine of the Church of England.[3]

---

[3] *Thus interpreted*, observe. Mr. Newman himself, in a letter to Mr. Hope, dated Littlemore, May 14, 1845, says: ' You are quite right in saying

The principle on which he went was the approximation made out by Sancta Clara and in Tract 90. Mr. Hope had more hopes of the House of Lords than of the Court of Arches, and wished Mr. Oakeley to appeal to the former. If he was afraid of the expenses, he said they would manage all that for him.[4] He added, however, 'But I think you are inclined to go over to the Church of Rome; and if that is the case, it is useless to proceed.' Mr. Hope at that time (said the Canon) was a staunch Anglican. He did not, however, see more of him than of any other member of his congregation—perhaps once in three months. After Mr. Oakeley had become a Catholic, Mr. Hope once asked him to breakfast, which he accepted rather hesitatingly. At that time he (Mr. Oakeley) thought less favourably of Protestants than he did now, and hinted that he must take a line in conversation that might not be acceptable. Mr. Hope said they need not talk of that, let him come. At this break-

---

l do not take Ward and Oakeley's grounds that all Roman doctrine may be held in our Church, and that *as* Roman I have always and everywhere resisted it.'

[4] Mr. Hope had formed a committee (in conjunction with Serjeant Bellasis, Mr. Badeley, and Mr. J. D. Chambers) in order to raise contributions to meet Mr. Oakeley's expenses. I find an exchange of notes dated March 10, 1845, between Mr. Hope and Mr. Gladstone on this matter. Mr. Hope encloses a circular, and invites Mr. Gladstone to contribute, remarking: 'As the process must throw light upon many collateral points, I amongst others am much interested in its being well conducted. I am, moreover, as a friend of O.'s, anxious that he should have fair play. . . . This looks like the beginning of the end.' Mr. Gladstone, in reply, alludes to doubts he had had whether he could subscribe *in re* Ward. 'Although I am far from having (upon a slight consideration as yet, for I have been very busy with other matters) found them conclusive; for I think we are going to try questions of academical right, and even of general justice.' He therefore declines subscribing in Mr. Oakeley's case, promising to give Mr. Hope his reasons whenever they should meet.

fast Mr. Hope mentioned that he had been lately at
Rome (he could allude to no other visit than that of
1844–5), where he had seen a procession of the Pope
in the *sedia gestatoria,* and thought how much better
it would have been if he had walked in the procession
like any other Bishop—that was the line he took.   [I
ought to add that, later in my conversation with him,
Canon Oakeley seemed rather to hesitate whether it
was Mr. Hope or some one else who made this observation about the Pope's procession, but in the end he
appeared to feel satisfied that it was Mr. Hope.]

In the same troubled spring of 1845 a movement
was going on to assimilate the office of the Scottish
Episcopalian Church to that of the English.   Dean
Ramsay of Edinburgh had asked Mr. Hope for a legal
opinion on a case in which he was concerned bearing
on this.   Mr. Hope, in a letter to him dated April 8,
declines to meddle with the question, and adds :—

> I can hardly tell you how much I deprecate any steps
> which may tend to diminish the authority of the *native* office ;
> how entirely I dissent from any plans of further assimilation
> to the foreign English Church.   Indeed, the consequences of
> such schemes at this moment would in my opinion be most
> disastrous.

Some letters of great interest with reference to Mr.
Hope's religious position at this period occur in the
Gladstone correspondence.   Mr. Gladstone, being now
thoroughly aware that his friend was entertaining serious
doubts as to the Catholicity of the Church of England,
writes him a very long and deeply considered letter,
appealing in the first place to a promise of co-operation

which Mr. Hope had made him in the earlier days of their friendship, and placing before him, with all the power and eloquence of which he is so great a master, what he regarded as the most unanswerable arguments for remaining in the Anglican communion. From this letter I quote the following passages as strictly bio-graphical :—

The Right Hon. W. E. Gladstone, M.P. to J. R. Hope, Esq.

(*Private.*)

13 Carlton House Terrace:
Thursday night, May 15, '45.

My dear Hope,—In 1838 you lent me that generous and powerful aid in the preparation of my book for the press, to which I owe it that the defects and faults of the work fell short of absolutely disqualifying it for its purpose. From that time I began to form not only high but definite anticipations of the services which you would render to the Church in the deep and searching processes through which she has had and yet has to pass. These anticipations, however, did not rest only upon my own wishes, or on the hopes which benefits already received might have led me to form. In the commencement of 1840, in the very room where we talked to-night, you voluntarily and somewhat solemnly tendered to me the assurance that you would at all times be ready to co-operate with me in further-ance of the welfare of the Church, and you placed no limit upon the extent of such co-operation. I had no title to expect and had not expected a promise so heart-stirring, but I set upon it a value scarcely to be described, and it ever after entered as an element of the first importance into all my views of the future course of public affairs in their bearing upon religion.[5]

.   .   .   .

If the time shall ever come (which I look upon as extremely uncertain, but I think if it comes at all it will be before the

---

[5] With this may be compared Mr. Hope's letter to Mr. Gladstone of October 11, 1838, given in chapter ix. (vol. i. pp. 172-3). ·

lapse of many years) when I am called upon to use any of those opportunities [the writer had just spoken of 'the great opportunities, the gigantic opportunities of good or evil to the Church which the course of events seems (humanly speaking) certain to open up '], it would be my duty to look to you for aid, under the promise to which I have referred, unless in the meantime you shall as deliberately and solemnly withdraw that promise as you first made it. I will not describe at length how your withdrawal of it would increase that sense of desolation which, as matters now stand, often approaches to being intolerable : I only speak of it as a matter of fact, and J am anxious you should know that I look to it as one of the very weightiest kind, under a title which you have given me. You would of course cancel it upon the conviction that it involved sin on your part : with anything less than that conviction I do not expect that you will cancel it ; and I am, on the contrary, persuaded that you will struggle against pain, depression, disgust, and even against doubt touching the very root of our position, for the fulfilment of any actual *duties* which the post you actually occupy in the Church of God, taken in connection with your faculties and attainments, may assign to you.

. . . .

You have given me lessons that I have taken thankfully: believe I do it in the payment of a debt, if I tell you that your mind and intellect, to which I look up with reverence under a consciousness of immense inferiority, are much under the dominion, whether it be known or not known to yourself, of an agency lower than their own, more blind, more variable, more difficult to call inwardly to account and make to answer for itself—the agency, I mean, of painful and disheartening impressions—impressions which have an unhappy and powerful tendency to realise the very worst of what they picture. Of this fact I have repeatedly noted the signs in you.

. . . .

I should have been glad to have got your advice on some points connected with the Maynooth question on Monday next, but I will not introduce here any demand upon your kindness; the claims of this letter on your attention, be they great or small, and you are their only judge, rest upon wholly different grounds.

God bless and guide you, and prosper the work of your hands.

Ever your aff^te friend,

W. E. GLADSTONE.

J. R. Hope, Esq.

The friends both being in London at the time, the correspondence gives no further light at this point. In July Mr. Gladstone proposed to Mr. Hope that they two should go on a tour in Ireland together. The invitation must be given in his own words:—

The Right Hon. W. E. Gladstone, M.P. to J. R. Hope, Esq.

13 C. H. Terrace: July 23, 1845.

My dear Hope,—Ireland is likely to find this country and Parliament so much employment for years to come, that I feel rather oppressively an obligation to try and see it with my own eyes instead of using those of other people, according to the limited measure of my means.

Now your company would be so very valuable as well as agreeable to me, that I am desirous to know whether you are at all inclined to entertain the idea of devoting the month of September, after the meeting in Edinburgh, to a working tour in Ireland with me—eschewing all grandeur, and taking little account even of scenery, compared with the purpose of looking from close quarters at the institutions for religion and education of the country, and at the character of the people. It seems ridiculous to talk of supplying the defects of second-hand information by so short a trip; but though a longer time would be much better, yet even a very contracted one does much when it is added to an habitual though indirect knowledge.

Believe me

Your attached friend,

W. E. GLADSTONE.

It is much to be regretted that this tour was not accomplished, but various engagements prevented Mr. Hope's accepting the invitation : he spent that part of the vacation in Scotland, and Mr. Gladstone on the Continent. Shortly after the date of the preceding letter Mr. Gladstone appears to have suggested to Mr. Hope the idea of his joining some association for active charity, which is partly illustrated by a correspondence which I shall presently quote ; but Mr. Hope (August 6) writes :—

As to the guild or confraternity, I am not at this moment prepared to join it. My reasons are various, but I have not had leisure to think them out. When I have revolved the matter further, perhaps I may trouble you again upon it.

On October 9, 1845, Mr. Newman was received into the Catholic Church, and Mr. Hope writes to him on the 20th :—

I was so fully prepared that the event fell lightly on my mind, but the feeling of separation has since grown upon me painfully. The effect which, I think I told you, it would have upon my conduct, is that of forcing me to a deliberate inquiry ; but I feel most unfit for it, and look with anxiety to your book as my guide. I hope to be at Oxford early next week, and trust to see you. Meantime, if it be anything to you to know that all my personal feelings towards you remain unaltered, or rather, are deepened, that much I can sincerely say.

On December 1 he speaks of his own joining the Roman Catholic Church as ' what may eventually happen,' adding : ' But I feel that I have yet much before me, both in moral and intellectual exertion, ere I can hope for a conclusion. Meantime I beg your prayers.'

On December 22 he gives his impressions of Newman's ' Essay on Development,' so eagerly expected:—

I have read your book *once* through.   To apprehend it fully
will require one, if not two more perusals.   The effect produced
upon me as yet is that of perplexity at seeing how wide a
range of thought appears to be required for the discussion.   I
had thought that the principles which I already acknowledge
would, upon a careful application, suffice for the solution of the
difficulties ; but you have taken me into a region less familiar
to me, and the extent of which makes me feel helpless and
discouraged.

It may be worth mentioning that soon after the
' Essay on Development' came out, Mr. Hope asked a
friend at dinner across the table (the anecdote was
given me by the latter), ' Have you read the " Extravagant of John " ? '   To understand this, the unlearned
reader must be told that certain celebrated constitu-
tions, decreed by Pope John XXII., are called by
canonists the ' Extravagantes Joannis.'   The play on
the word was one which would be relished by Mr.
Hope's friend, who was almost as great a student of
the canon law as himself.   His meaning, however, may
have been that he thought Mr. Newman had taken up
a view outside of the received system.

In the two letters I have just quoted Mr. Hope
enters, like a kind friend and adviser, into Mr. Newman's plans in the early days of his conversion, but
an interruption of the correspondence seems to have
followed on Mr. Newman's going to Rome, where he
was from autumn, 1846, to nearly the end of 1847.   It
is probable, indeed, that it was the consciousness of his
own affection for Mr. Newman, and of Mr. Newman's

influence over him, that led Mr. Hope to abstain, during that long interval, from intercourse with a friend whom he regarded with such deep respect and admiration. There is, however, a letter of Mr. Newman's from Rome in the interval, which will be read with great interest, both for his own history and for the light, yet thrilling touch of spiritual kindness which it conveys towards the end. It contains, too, a line explaining his own silence.

The Rev. J. H. Newman to J. R. Hope, Esq.

(*Private.*)   Collegio di Prop.: Feb. 23, '47.

My dear Hope,—I have been writing so very, very much lately, that now that I want to tell you something my hand is so tired that I can hardly write a word. We are to be Oratorians. Mgr. Brunelli went to the Pope about it the day before yesterday, my birthday. The Pope took up the plan most warmly, as had Mgr. B., to whom we had mentioned it a month back. Mgr. had returned my paper, in which I drew out my plan, saying, ' Mi piace immensamente,' and repeated several times that the plan was ' ben ideata.' They have from the first been as kind to us as possible, and are now willing to do anything for us. I have ever been thinking of you, and you must have thought my silence almost unkind, but I waited to tell you something which would be real news. It is *no* secret that we are to be Oratorians, but matters of detail being uncertain, you had better keep it to yourself. The Pope wishes us to come here, as many as can, form a house under an experienced Oratorian Father, go through a novitiate, and return. Of course they will hasten us back as soon as [they] can, but that will depend on our progress. I *suppose* we shall set up in Birmingham. . . . You are not likely to know the very Jesuits of Propaganda. We are very fortunate in them. The Rector (Padre Bresciani) is a man of great delicacy and real kindness; our confessor, Father Ripetti, is one of the most excellent persons we have fallen in with, tho' I can't describe him to you in a few words. Another person we got on uncommonly with was Ghianda at Milan. Bellasis will have told you about him. We owed a great deal to you there, and did not forget you, my dear Hope. Let me say it, O that God would give you the gift of faith! Forgive me for this. I know you will. It is of no use my plaguing you with many words. I want you for the Church in England, and the Church for you. But I must do my own work in my own place, and leave everything else to that inscrutable Will which we can but adore; . . . Well, our lot is fixed. What will come to it I know not. Don't think me ambitious. I am not. I have no views. It will be enough for me if I get into some active work, and save my own soul. . . . My affectionate remembrances to Badeley. . . .

Ever y^{rs} affectionately,

JOHN H. NEWMAN.

I find, towards the end of 1850, a very interesting exchange of letters between Dr. Newman and Mr. Hope, which may conveniently be given here, though chronologically they ought to come later. I first give a letter needed to explain them :—

J. R. Hope, Esq. Q.C. to the Rev. Stuart Bathurst.

Abbotsford: Nov. 4, '50.

Dear Bathurst,—Your kind letter needed no apologies ; and for your prayers and good thoughts for me I thank you much May they of God be blessed to me in clearer light as well as in a purer conscience ! As yet I do not see my way as you have done yours, but I pray that I may not long remain in such doubt as I now have.

From your address I conclude that you are with Newman. Tell him with my kind regards that I hope he has not forgotten me. I have very often thought of him, and have sometimes been near writing to him, but have had nothing definite to say. I have read his last lectures, and wish they were extended to a review of doctrine, and the difficulties which beset it to an Anglican.

Let me hear from you when you have time, and believe me, my dear Bathurst,   Yours ever aff^{tly},

JAMES R. HOPE.

The Rev. S. Bathurst.

The Very Rev. Dr. Newman to J. R. Hope, Esq. Q.C.

Oratory, Birmingham: Nov. 20, 1850.

My dear Hope,—It is with the greatest pleasure I have just read the letter which you wrote to Bathurst, and which he has forwarded to me. . . . I now fully see . . . that your silence has arisen merely from the difficulty of writing to one in another communion, and the irksomeness and indolence (if you will let me so speak) we all feel in doing what is difficult, what may be misconceived, and what can scarcely have object or use.

I know perfectly well, my dear Hope, your great moral and intellectual qualities, and will not cease to pray that the grace of God may give you the obedience of faith, and use them as His instruments. For myself, I say it from my heart, I have not had a single doubt, or temptation to doubt, ever since I became a Catholic. I believe this to be the case with most men—it certainly is so with those with whom I am in habits of intimacy. My great temptation is to be at *peace*, and let things go on as they will, and not trouble myself about others. This being the case, your recommendation that I should ' take a review of doctrine, and of the difficulties which beset it to an Anglican,' is anything but welcome, and makes me smile. Surely, enough has been written—all the writing in the world would not destroy the necessity of faith. If all were now made clear to reason, where would be the exercise of faith? The single question is, whether *enough* has not been done to *reduce* the difficulties so far as to hinder them absolutely blocking up the way, or excluding those direct and large arguments on which the reasonableness of faith is built.

Ever yours affectionately,

JOHN H. NEWMAN.

J. R. Hope, Esq. Q.C. to the Very Rev. Dr. Newman.

Abbotsford: Nov. 27, '50.

Dear Newman,—The receipt of your letter gave me sincere pleasure. It renews a correspondence which I value very highly, and which my own stupidity had interrupted. Offence I had never taken, but causes such as you describe much better than I could have done were the occasion of my silence.

You may now find that you have brought more trouble on yourself, for there are many things on which I should like to ask you questions, and I know that your time is already much engaged. However, at present my chief object is to assure you how very glad I am again to write to you, as the friend whom I almost feared I had thrown away. Whatever occurs, do not let us be again estranged. It is not easy, as one gets older, to form new friendships of any kind, and least of all such as I have always considered yours. . . .

Ever, dear Newman,

Y^{rs} aff^{tly},

JAMES R. HOPE.

The Very Rev. Dr. Newman to J. R. Hope, Esq. Q.C.

Oratory, Birmingham: November 20, 1850.

My dear Hope,—I write a line to thank you for your letter, and to say how glad I shall be to hear from you, as you half propose, whether or not I am able to say anything to your satisfaction, which would be a greater and different pleasure.

It makes me smile to hear you talk of getting older. What must I feel, whose life is gone ere it is well begun?

Ever yours affectionately,

JOHN H. NEWMAN,

Congr. Orat.

CHAPTER XXI.

1845-1851.

To return to the Gladstone correspondence which we
quitted some pages back. In a letter dated Baden-
Baden, October 30, 1845, Mr. Gladstone, after mentioning his having been at Munich, where, through an
introduction from Mr. Hope, he had made the acquaintance of Dr. Döllinger, criticises at some length
Möhler's 'Symbolik,' which he had been reading on
Mr. Hope's recommendation. I must quote the conclusion of the letter in his own words :—

No religion and no politics until we meet, and that more
than ever uncertain. Hard terms, my dear Hope; do not
complain if I devote to them the scraps or ends of my fourth
page. But now let me rebuke myself, and say, no levity about
great and solemn things. There are degrees of pressure from
within that it is impossible to resist. The Church in which
our lot has been cast has come to the birth, and the question
is, will she have strength to bring forth ? I am persuaded it is

written in God's decrees that she shall; and that after deep
repentance and deep suffering a high and peculiar part remains
for her in healing the wounds of Christendom. [Nor] is there
any man, I cannot be silent, whose portion in her work is
more clearly marked out for him than yours. But you have, if
not your revenge, your security. I must keep my word. God
bless and guide you.

Yours affectionately,
W. E. G.

The following letter is deeply interesting :—

J. R. Hope, Esq. to the Right Hon. W. E. Gladstone, M.P.

35 Charles Street, Mayfair :
December 5, 1845.

Dear Gladstone,—I return Döllinger's letter, which I had
intended to give you last night.

The debate has cost me a headache, besides the regrets I
almost always feel after having engaged in theological discussions. A sense of my own ignorance and prejudices should
teach me to be more moderate in expressing, as well as more
cautious in forming opinions; but it is my nature to require
some broad view for my guidance, and since Anglicanism has
lost this aspect to me, I am restless and ill at ease.

I know well, however, that I have not deserved by my life
that I should be without great struggle in my belief, and this
ought to teach me to do more and say less.

I must therefore try more and more to be fit for the truth,
wherever it may lie, and in this I hope for your prayers.

Yours aff^{ly},
JAMES R. HOPE.

The Right Hon. W. E. Gladstone, M.P. to J. R. Hope, Esq.

13 C. II. Terrace :
Dec. 7, 2nd Sunday in Advent, 1845.

My dear Hope,—I need hardly tell you I am deeply moved
by your note, and your asking my prayers. I trust you give
what you ask. As for them you have long had them; in

CHAP. XXI. MR. GLADSTONE ADVISES ACTIVE WORKS. 79

private and in public, and in the hour of Holy Communion. But you must not look for anything from them; only they cannot do any harm. Under the merciful dispensation of the Gospel, while the prayer of the righteous availeth much, the petition of the unworthy does not return in evils on the head of those for whom it is offered.

Your speaking of yourself in low terms is the greatest kindness to me. It is with such things before my eyes that I learn in some measure by comparison my own true position. . . . [Mr. Gladstone goes on to controvert his friend's desire for 'broad views,' on the principles of Butler, and proceeds] Now let me use a friend's liberty on a point of practice. Do you not so far place yourself in rather a false position by withdrawing in so considerable a degree from those active external duties in which you were so conspicuous? Is rest in that department really favourable to religious inquiry? You said to me you preferred at this time selecting temporal works: are we not in this difficulty, that temporal works, so far as mere money is concerned, are nowadays relatively overdone? But if you mean temporal works otherwise than in money, I would to God we could join hands upon a subject of the kind which interested you much two years ago. And now I am going to speak of what concerns myself more than you, as needing it more.

The desire we then both felt passed off, so far as I am concerned, into a plan of asking only a donation and subscription. Now it is very difficult to satisfy the demands of duty to the poor by money alone. On the other hand, it is extremely hard for me (and I suppose possibly for you) to give them much in the shape of time and thought. For both with me are already tasked up to and beyond their powers, and by matters which I cannot displace. I much wish we could execute some plan which, without demanding much time, would entail the discharge of some humble and humbling offices. . . . If you thought with me—and I do not know why you should not, except that to assume the reverse is paying myself a compliment—let us go to work: as in the young days of the college plan, but with a more direct and less ambitious purpose. . . . In answer give me advice and help if you can; and when we meet to talk of such things, it will be more refreshing than metaphysical or semi-metaphysical argument. All that part of my note which refers to questions internal to yourself is not meant to be answered except in your own breast.

And now may the Lord grant that, as heretofore, so ever we may walk in His holy house as friends, and know how good a thing it is to dwell together in unity! But at all events may He, as He surely will, compass you about with His presence and by His holy angels, and cause you to awake up after His likeness, and to be satisfied with it! . . . .

Ever your aff^te^ friend,
W. E. GLADSTONE.

J. R. Hope, Esq.

The above letter appears to throw a light upon Mr. Hope's views of action at that time (it was a year of approaching the acme of his professional energies) which I have not met with elsewhere. Those views he did not see his way to give up, notwithstanding the representations so kindly urged by his friend. It will have been remarked that Mr. Gladstone did not expect any answer, in the ordinary sense of the word, to the most serious part of his letter, and in his reply (December 8), which is merely a note, Mr. Hope simply says:—

Many, many thanks for your letter, which I received this morning. I will think it over, and particularly as regards the engagement in some temporal almsdeed. I see, however, many obstacles in my own way, both from health and occupation.

After this, though the two friends continued still to correspond, yet the letters are of comparatively little moment, the subject nearest to the hearts of both being of necessity suppressed, or almost so; topics once

of common interest, such as Trinity College (now near
its opening) [1] and Church legislation, having of course
lost their attractions for Mr. Hope. In the autumn of
1846 there was an interchange of visits between Rankeillour [2] and Fasque, and kind and friendly offices and
family sympathies went on as of old. Yet, if the *idem
sentire de republicâ* was long ago recognised as a condition of intimate friendship, how much more is the
observation true of the *idem sentire de ecclesiâ*! The
following letter, addressed to Mr. Hope early in 1846
by Dr. Philpotts, will show what powerful influences
were still at work to gain or recover Mr. Hope's
services to Anglicanism in political life :—

> *The Right Rev. Dr. Philpotts, Bishop of Exeter, to
> J. R. Hope, Esq.*
>
> Bishopstowe: 16 Feb., 1846.

My dear Sir,— . . . The miserable state of political matters
makes me earnestly wish (which I fear you do not) that you
may soon be in Parliament. It is manifest that we are approaching a most important crisis. To give any rational ground of
hope (humanly speaking) of a favourable issue, it is most necessary that there should be an accession of high-principled
talent and power of speaking to the honest Party. You would
carry this, and, forgive my adding, *ought* to carry it if a fit
opportunity be presented to you.

I say not this with any imagination that the objects of
political ambition have any attraction to you, but because I

---

[1] See vol. i. (ch. xiv. p. 284).

[2] Rankeillour, a family seat near Cupar, in Fifeshire, which Mr. Hope
with his sister-in-law, Lady Frances Hope, had rented the previous year,
1845, from his brother, Mr. G. W. Hope, of Luffness, and which was theirs
and Lady Hope's joint home when in Scotland, until Mr. Hope's marriage in
1847.

think you would (with God's Blessing) be a tower of strength
to all the best institutions and interests of the country.

Hactenùs hæc.

Yours most faithfully,

H. EXETER.

'Henry of Exeter,' in a conversation with Lady
Henry Kerr in those days, once said that he considered
three men as those to whom the country had chiefly
to look in the coming time : Manning in the Church,
Gladstone in the State, and Mr. Hope in the Law. The
Bishop was, I believe, thought rather apt to indulge in
what were called ' Philpottic flourishes,' but the above
letter shows his deliberate opinion of Mr. Hope, which
is quite borne out by the rest of his correspondence.
He constantly asks his counsel on Church affairs and
Church legislation, till his conversion was approaching ;
and even long after it, I find him in 1862, when about
to appeal to the House of Lords from a decision in the
courts below, asking Mr. Hope-Scott's assistance in these
terms : ' I venture to have recourse to you—as one
whose skill and ability, knowledge—as well as your
kindness often experienced—makes me estimate more
highly than any other. . . . I am *very anxious* to obtain
your powerful advocacy before the Lords. Is this contrary to your usage ? ' [3] In a letter, now before me,
from a member of the legal profession and a Protestant,
the writer, referring to some occasion in early days on
which he had met Mr. Hope and Mr. Gladstone together in society, remarks : ' They were constantly
discussing important questions. I am sure that, if a

Right Rev. Dr. Philpotts to J. R. Hope-Scott, February 22, 1862.

stranger had come in, and heard that one of them would be Premier, he would have selected [Mr. Hope] as the superior of the two. And I always thought that his abilities and character fitted him for the highest positions in the country. But his aims were for eminence in a still higher sphere, and he readily abandoned the road to worldly distinctions when he thought that his duty towards God required the sacrifice.' Of course I only quote this as evidence of the impression which Mr. Hope had made on an individual observer,[4] not as instituting any comparison, which would be wholly out of place.

The following letter is more of ecclesiastical and legal than personal interest. It is in reply to a line from Mr. Gladstone, asking his advice:—

J. R. Hope, Esq. to the Right Hon. W. E. Gladstone, M.P.

35 Charles Street :
Wednesday evening, March 18, '46.

Dear Gladstone,—I had some hopes of being able to call on you this morning, but was disappointed.

With regard to the Canadian Archbishopric, if you have seen what I wrote about a bishopric in the same colony you will have got the historical view which I was then induced to take. I am convinced that the parties to the Treaty of Paris and the framers of the first Act contemplated a Roman Church with an Anglican supremacy of the Crown. Their successors did not understand this, and proceeded upon the theory of toleration—thereby at once yielding the power of direct interference and refusing direct establishment. But in fact the R. C. Church is established, and consequently Rome has the advantage both of establishment and complete independence. I am not the man to say that the latter ought to be infringed, but I think it right to draw your attention to the departure

---

[4] 'It is perfectly just.'—*W. E. G.*

from the original idea of the position of the R. C. Church in
Canada. As matters now stand I think Lord Stanley had no
option, and could only be neutral; but the original theory of
royal supremacy having failed (as was natural), a concordat
alone can decide the relations of Church and State in that
quarter. The question of precedence is certainly not in itself
sufficient to decide the conduct of Government, but it presents
a difficulty; and the more difficulties there are, the more needs
of a complete solution.

It seems to me, therefore, that you must either follow
Lord Stanley in his neutrality, and leave the consequences to
chance, or at once originate a communication with the Holy
See; and for the latter purposes I think Canada affords as fair
an occasion as it is possible to find.

Yours ever truly,
JAMES R. HOPE.

Right Hon. W. E. Gladstone, M.P.

In the same year, 1846, the appointment of Dr.
Hampden to the see of Hereford was ' a heavy blow
and great discouragement' to the Tractarian party;
but the correspondence does not throw much light on
the subject as far as regards Mr. Hope. He must
have felt his profession sucking him in like a vortex,
from which it is wonderful how he could grasp the
Catholic faith in the end. Many of his friends were
now doing so, but he still held back. The following sen-
tences from a letter he wrote to Father Newman, then
(April 23, 1846) contemplating his departure for Rome,
will show something of Mr. Hope's then position—
Anglican ideas not so vanished that they might not
possibly have been, at least in imagination, renewed—
Catholic ideas not yet distinctly written in their place.

I can construe the obscure wish with which your letter

concludes. I join heartily in desiring *some* termination to my present doubts ; but whether in the direction you would think right, or by a return to Anglicanism, is the question. I am astonished to find how resolute Keble is in maintaining his present position. Others, also, of more earnestness and better knowledge than myself, are recoiling—and this troubles me, for I cannot but look around for authority.

To his own family he became more and more reserved on the subject, and showed unwillingness that difficulties should be touched ; for, great as was his wish that the Church of England should assert herself Catholic, he dreaded, on good grounds, that if awakened from her slumbers, the only effect would be that she would use her giant strength against her friends as well as enemies, hit them knocks, and then relapse into repose. Unable even yet to make up his mind whether those of his friends who had joined the Church of Rome had done right or wrong, materially, at all events, he remained an Anglican. Such a state of mind necessarily varied, if not from day to day, at least at longer intervals. At the close of 1846 came the troubles at St. Saviour's, Leeds, a stronghold of the section peculiarly under Dr. Pusey's influence, which encountered the opposition of the old Tractarianism, or rather Church-of-Englandism of Dr. Hook. They ended in some important conversions, but, as affecting Mr. Hope, seem scarcely to require to be dwelt on. In May 1847 I find him exerting himself in favour of Mr. Gladstone's candidature for the University of Oxford. On December 9 he writes (from Rankeillour) to Mr. Gladstone on the question of Jewish emancipation as follows :—

On the Jewish question my bigotry makes me liberal. To symbolise the Christianity of the House of Commons in its present form is to substitute a new Church and creed for the old Catholic one ; and as this is delusive, I would do nothing to countenance it. Better have the Legislature declared what it really is—not professedly, Christian, and then let the Church claim those rights and that independence which nothing but the pretence of Christianity can entitle the Legislature to with-hold from it. In this view the emancipation of the Jews must tend to that of the Church, and at any rate a ' sham' will be discarded. However, I am not disposed to press my views on this or similar points. I have withdrawn from Church politics, and never had to do with any others. How long this peaceful disposition may last I know not, but my station in life does not seem to me to require that I should meddle. For this reason if for no other, you may be sure I do not regret having lost the honour of being armour-bearer to the Bishop of Exeter in the Hampden strife. That appointment, however, is certainly bad enough.

Mr. Hope was now, in the ordinary sense of the word, ' settled in life ' (he married in August of that year, 1847) ; but the great happiness he found in this change of condition was no talisman that could ward off the question which still imperiously demanded a solution ; and perhaps scarce a month passed in these times without some new event arising to bring it more forcibly upon minds that had once been fairly within its influence. Mr. Hope's style in writing to Mr. Badeley on the Hampden affair, under date January 16, 1848, shows in some degree a renewed interest, but with symptoms, like the passage last quoted, of passing off into Liberalism.

I am right glad that you have got your Rule, and have good hopes that you will make it absolute. . . . When the argument is resumed pray remember my favourite plan of establishing the old Ecclesiastical Law as the Common Law of England before the Reformation, and requiring evidence of a direct statutory repeal. Reid writes me that there is a fund for the expenses of the opposition. If so I shall be happy to contribute, for I feel very strongly (not about Dr. Hampden, though I *do* feel as to him, but) about this violent piece of Erastianism, such as no Christian community ought to endure.

Following this, for about two years, the Church of England was convulsed with the Gorham case. This, too, has passed into the history of Anglicanism. It will be sufficient to remind the reader that Dr. Philpotts, the Bishop of Exeter, had refused to institute the Rev. G. C. Gorham to the vicarage of Brampford Speke, because he denied the doctrine of baptismal regeneration. Mr. Gorham sued the Bishop in the Court of Arches, but judgment was given by Sir H. J. Fust against the plaintiff, who then appealed to the Crown, and the result was that the Judicial Committee of the Privy Council, on March 8, 1850, reversed Sir H. J. Fust's judgment, and held that Mr. Gorham's doctrine was not repugnant to that of the Church of England. On March 12 a meeting was held at Mr. Hope's house in Curzon Street by several leading men of the Tractarian party—the number, I believe, was fourteen—including Mr. Hope himself, Archdeacon Manning, Archdeacon Robert Wilberforce, and Mr. Badeley— to consider the effect of this sentence on the Church of England. Certain resolutions were passed and signed, and afterwards circulated in a somewhat modified form The document, as finally issued, is to be found in more publications than one, and may be referred to in Mr. Kirwan Browne's 'Annals of the Tractarian Movement,' 3rd edition, p. 191. Its main significance is contained in Resolutions 5 and 6, which are given as follows, in a printed copy now before me :—

5. That inasmuch as the Faith is one, and rests upon one principle of authority, the conscious, deliberate, and wilful abandonment of the essential meaning of an Article of the Creed destroys the Divine Foundation upon which alone the entire Faith is propounded by the Church.

6. That any portion of the Church which does so abandon the essential meaning of an Article of the Creed, forfeits not only the Catholic doctrine in that Article, but also the office and authority to witness and teach as a Member of the Universal Church.

It is easy to see that these apparently strong declarations afforded a loophole for the escape of moderates ; but Mr. Manning and his friends, as the result proved, were prepared to act upon them in their original and unqualified form ; for all the four I have named, with two others, eventually became Catholics. The rest of those present at the Curzon Street meeting remained Protestants. As for Mr. Hope, the year rolled round, and he was still externally where he was ; but the following allusion, in a letter of his to Mr. Gladstone, dated Abbotsford, September 6, 1850, to some recent conversions, must have made it evident that his own was drawing very near :—

I have heard a good deal on the ——'s change : it is attributed more immediately to her—but however brought about, I cannot think hardly of it. Rather, I feel as if those were to be congratulated who have already done that which *intellectually*, and to a great extent *morally*, I feel persuaded should be done.

Yrs. ever affect^{ly},

JAMES R. HOPE.

The memorable 'Papal Aggression' excitement which arose in England in November 1850, is believed to have been what finally brought Mr. Hope to the conclusion, or rather, to action upon the conclusion, to which he had been so long tending. Some time after this, when in conversation, Mr. Lockhart asked him how it was possible he could have attributed such weight to so slight a reason, Mr. Hope replied to the effect that Mr. Lockhart would easily understand that the last link in a chain of argument on which actions depend, needs not in appearance be the strongest. He spoke of his conversion as of a veil falling from his eyes.[5] The same influence is visible in the letter in which Mr. Manning (since the Cardinal Archbishop of Westminster) announced to Mr. Hope his resignation of the Archdeaconry of Chichester.

The Rev. H. E. Manning to J. R. Hope, Esq. Q.C.

Lavington: Nov. 23, 1850.

My dear Hope,—Your last letter was a help to me, for I began to feel as if every man had gone to his own house and left the whole matter. . . . Since then events have driven me to a decision. This anti-Popery cry has seized my brethren, and they asked to be convened. I must either resign at once, or convene them ministerially and express my dissent, the reasons of which would involve my resignation. I went to the

---

[5] A correspondence of this period of Mr. Hope's with the present Cardinal Newman (very important as far as it goes) has been given in some previous pages (pp. 75–76).

Bishop and said this, and tendered my resignation. He was
very kind, and wished me to take time, but I have written
and made it final. . . . I should be glad if we might keep
together; and whatever must be done, do it with a calm and
deliberateness which shall give testimony that it is not done
in lightness.

Ever affect^{ly} yr^s,

H. E. M.

Mr. Manning was considerably Mr. Hope's senior,[6]
but they had been brother-Fellows of Merton College,
and were now intimate friends, passing through the
same stages of conversion, each having great confidence
in the logical powers and in the earnestness of the
other in applying them. Either at that time, or very
soon afterwards, Mr. Manning became the guest of Mr.
Hope at his house in Curzon Street; and here he used
to receive the many converts and half-converts who
flocked to consult him in their difficulties during that
period of transition, when such an unexampled rush
seemed to be making into the net of the Fisherman.
Mr. Hope's letters to Cardinal Manning were unfortunately destroyed about three years ago, but the other
side of the correspondence is still represented by a small
collection of letters of great interest. Mr. Hope, I
think, had made up his mind at Abbotsford, and on his
arrival in London announced it to his mother; but it is
certain that immediately before taking the final step he
and Mr. Manning went over the whole ground again
together, to satisfy themselves that there was no flaw or
mistake in the argument and conclusion.

---

[6] Four years exactly. He was born July 15, 1808. The same also was
Mr. Hope's birthday.

The Rev. Henry E. Manning to J. R. Hope, Esq. Q.C.

Private.   44 Cadogan Place : December 11, 1850.

My dear Hope,—I feel with you that the argument is complete. For a long time I nevertheless felt a fear lest I should be doing an act morally wrong.

This fear has passed away, because the Church of England has revealed itself in a way to make me fear more on the other side. It remains, therefore, as an act of the will. But this I suppose it must be. And in making it I am helped by the fact that to remain under our changed or revealed circumstances would also be an act of the will. And that not in conformity with, but in opposition to intellectual convictions : and the intellect is God's gift, and our instrument in attaining to a knowledge of His will. . . . It would be to me a very great happiness if we could act together, and our names go together in the first publication of the fact. . . The subject which has brought me to my present convictions is the perpetual office of the Church under Divine guidance, in expounding the Faith and deciding controversies. And the book which forced this on me was Melchior Canus' 'Loci Theologici.' It is a long book, but so orderly that you may get the whole outline with ease. Möhler's *Symbolik* you know.

But, after all, Holy Scripture comes to me in a new light, as Ephes. iv. 4–17, which seems to preclude the notion of a divisible unity : which is, in fact, Arianism in the matter of the Church.

I entirely feel what you say of the alternative. It is either Rome or licence of thought and will. . . .

Believe me always affect^{ly} yours,

H. E. MANNING.

The following extract from a letter of Mr. Hope's to the Rev. Robert Campbell [since also a Catholic], dated 'Abbotsford, September 15, 1851,' affords additional and important light on the motives of his own conversion :—

You seem to think that the present condition of the Church
of England has been the cause of my conversion. That it has
contributed thereto I am far from denying, but it has done so
by way of evidence only; of evidence, the chain of which
reaches up to the Reformation, and confirms by outward proofs
those conclusions which H. Scripture and reason forced upon
me as to the character of the original act of separation. This
distinction I am anxious should be observed, for the neglect of
it has led some to suppose that recent converts have, from
disgust or other causes, deserted a true Church in her time of
need, whereas, for one, I can safely say that I left her because
I was convinced that she never, from the Reformation downwards, had been a true Church. Pray excuse this digression,
which I do not mean by way of controversy, but merely of explanation.

                                                        J. R. H.

On *Passion Sunday*, April 6, 1851, Mr. Hope, and at
the same time with him Mr. Manning, were received
into the Catholic Church at Farm Street by the Rev.
Father J. Brownbill, S.J.

I must not withhold from the reader a note, written
the next day, and one or two passages from later letters
of Mr. Manning's referring to the same subject.

The Rev. Henry E. Manning to J. R. Hope. Esq. Q.C.

14 Queen Street: April 7, 1851.

My dear Hope,—Will you accept this copy of the book you
saw in my room yesterday [the ' Paradisus Animæ '] in
memory of Passion Sunday, and its gift of grace to us ? It is
the most perfect book of devotion I know. Let me ask one
thing. I read it through, one page at least a day, between
Jan. 26 and Aug. 22, 1846, marking where I left off with the
date. It seemed to give me a new science, with order and
harmony and details : as of devotion issuing from and returning
into dogma. Could you burden yourself with the same reso-

lution? If so, do it for my sake, and remember me when you do it. . . I feel as if I had no desire unfulfilled, but to persevere in what God has given me for His Son's sake.

Believe me, my dear Hope,

Always aff^ly yours,

H. E. M.

14 *Queen St.: Oct.* 21, 1851.—. . . I am once more in my old quarters. They bring back strange remembrances. What revolutions have passed since we started from this room that Saturday morning! And how blessed an end! as the soul in Paradise said to Dante. ' E da martirio venni a questa pace.' . . . You do not need that I should say how sensibly I remember all your sympathy, which was the only human help in the time when we two went together through the trial, which to be known must be endured.

Rome: March 17, 1852. . .—How this time reminds me of last year! On Passion Sunday I shall be in Retreat. 'Stantes erant pedes nostri,'[7] and we made no mistake in our long reckoning, though we feared it up to the last opening of Fr. B.'s door.   H. E. M.

The superficial impression which many of his friends had of Mr. Hope's conversion at the time will be illustrated by the following remarks, one of them made to me in conversation with a view to this memoir : ' Mr. Hope was a man with two lives : one, that of a lawyer ; the other, that of a pious Christian, who said his prayers, and did not give much thought to controversy. He would be rather influenced by patent facts. He was not at all moving with the stream, and rather laughed at X. with his " narrow views." He was a strong Anglican, an adherent of *learned* Anglicanism. His conversion

---

[7] These words were written in a copy of the *Speculum Vitæ Sacerdotalis*, given by J. R. Hope to H. E. Manning in April 1851. [Note by his Eminence Cardinal Manning.]

took *Catholics* by surprise, who were not aware how far he went.' The feeling in society as to his change was marked by a tone of much greater consideration than was commonly displayed in such cases, of which proof is given in an interesting letter which I have quoted in a former page. 'As far as I know' (writes Lady Georgiana Fullerton) 'there was no attempt made, in Mr. Hope's case, to trace that act to any of the causes which, in almost every other instance, were supposed to account for conversions to Catholicism. The frankness of his nature, his well-known good sense, the sound clearness of his judgment, so unmistakably evinced in his profession, precluded the possibility of attributing his adoption of the Catholic faith to weakness of mind, duplicity, sentiment, eccentricity, or excitability.'

I reserve what may be called the domestic side of this crowning event of Mr. Hope's religious life to a future chapter. The following is the letter alluded to by Mr. Gladstone in his letter to Miss Hope-Scott, given in Appendix III., and on which he wrote the words ' *Quis desiderio.*'[8]

[8] Let me balance Mr. Gladstone's *Quis desiderio* with a note written by Père Roothaan, Father-General of the Jesuits, to Count Senfft, on hearing of Mr. Hope's conversion:—

'Plurimam salutem nostro C. de Senfft, qui procul dubio maxima cum congratulatione accepit notitiam de conversione ad rel. cath. præclari Dni. Hope, Anglicani, quem ipse comes Monachio Romam venientem mihi commendaverat. Ipsum tunc et iterum et tertio Romam intra hos tres annos venientem videram sæpius, et semper vicinior mihi visus fuerat regno Dei. Nuper tandem cessit gratiæ. Alleluja!'—Given in a letter of Count Senfft's to Mr. Hope-Scott, dated Innsbruck: 1 Juin, 1851.

J. R. Hope, Esq. Q.C. to the Right Hon. W. E. Gladstone, M.P.

14 Curzon Street: June 18, '51.

My dear Gladstone,—I am very much obliged for the book which you have sent me, but still more for the few words and figures which you have placed upon the title-page. The day of the month in your own handwriting will be a record between us that the words of affection which you have written were used by you after the period at which the great change of my life took place. To grudge any sacrifice which that change entails would be to undervalue its paramount blessedness, but, as far as regrets are compatible with extreme thankfulness, I do and must regret any estrangement from you—you with whom I have trod so large a portion of the way which has led me to peace ; you, who are ' ex voto ' at least in that Catholic Church which to me has become a practical reality, admitting of no doubt ; you, who have so many better claims to the merciful guidance of Almighty God than myself.

It is most comforting, then, to me to know by your own hand that on the 17th June, 1851, the personal feelings so long cherished have been, not only acknowledged by yourself, but expressed to me—I do not ask more just now—it would be painful to you ; nay, it would be hardly possible for either of us to attempt (except under one condition, for which I daily pray) the restoration of entire intimacy at present ; but neither do I despair under any circumstances that it will yet be restored. Remember me most kindly to Mrs. Gladstone, and believe me,

Y^{rs} as ever most aff^{ly},

JAMES R. HOPE.

The Right Hon. W. E. Gladstone, &c. &c.

The subjoined reply of Mr. Gladstone to this beautiful letter, which he has mournfully called ' the epitaph of our friendship,' is certainly a noble and a tender one. The very depth of feeling which he shows at his friend's refusal of what he considers ' the high vocation ' before

him, is, however, only a proof of that spiritual chasm
which Mr. Hope more unflinchingly surveyed. After
this date the correspondence soon flags, and at length
sustains an interruption of years. It was practically
resumed towards the close of Mr. Hope's life, and affords
one more letter of great interest, in which Mr. Hope
explains his own political views. This I shall give as we
proceed.

The Right Hon. W. E. Gladstone, M.P. to J. R. Hope, Esq. Q.C.

6 Carlton Gardens: June 22, 1851.

My dear Hope,—Upon the point most prominently put in
your welcome letter I will only say you have not misconstrued
me. Affection which is fed by intercourse, and above all by
co-operation for sacred ends, has little need of verbal expression, but such expression is deeply ennobling when active relations have changed. It is no matter of merit to me to feel
strongly on the subject of that change. It may be little better
than pure selfishness. I have too good reason to know what
this year has cost me ; and so little hope have I that the places
now vacant ever can be filled up for me, that the marked character
of these events in reference to myself rather teaches me this
lesson—the work to which I had aspired is reserved for other
and better men. And if that be the Divine will, I so entirely
recognise its fitness that the grief would so far be small to
me were I alone concerned. The pain, the wonder, and the
mystery is this—that you should have refused the higher vocation you had before you. The same words, and all the same
words, I should use of Manning too. Forgive me for giving
utterance to what I believe myself to see and know ; I will
not proceed a step further in that direction.

There is one word, and one only in your letter that I do
not interpret closely. Separated we are, but I hope and think
not yet estranged. Were I more estranged I should bear the
separation better. If estrangement is to come I know not : but

it will only be, I think, from causes the operation of which is still in its infancy—causes not affecting me. Why should I be estranged from you? I honour you even in what I think your error; why, then, should my feelings to you alter in anything else? It seems to me as though, in these fearful times, events were more and more growing too large for our puny grasp, and that we should the more look for and trust the Divine purpose in them when we find they have wholly passed beyond the reach and measure of our own. 'The Lord is in His holy temple: let all the earth keep silence before Him.' The very afflictions of the present time are a sign of joy to follow. Thy kingdom come, Thy will be done, is still our prayer in common: the same prayer, in the same sense; and a prayer which absorbs every other. That is for the future: for the present we have to endure, to trust, and to pray that each day may bring its strength with its burden, and its lamp for its gloom.

Ever yours with unaltered affection,

W. E. GLADSTONE.

J. R. Hope, Esq.

The following letter, written on the same occasion by another celebrated person, will be read with a very painful interest :—

The Rev. Dr. Döllinger to J. R. Hope, Esq. Q.C.

Munich: April 22, 1851.

My dear Sir,—Allow me to express the sincere delight which I have felt and am still feeling at the intelligence which has reached me of your having entered the pale of the Church. This is indeed 'a consummation devoutly wished' ever since I had the good luck of making your acquaintance. How often, when with you, did the words rise to my lips: *Talis cum sis, utinam noster esses!* I knew well enough that *in voto* you belonged already to the one true Church, but I could not but feel some anxiety in reflecting that in a matter of such paramount importance those who don't move forward must needs

after a certain time go backward. Then came the news of
your marriage, and I don't know what put the foolish idea
into my head that you would probably get connected with the
' Quarterly Review ' and its principles, and that thereby a new
barrier would interpose itself between you and the Church,
and that perhaps your feelings for your friends in Germany
would not remain the same. Happily these *umbræ pallentes*
have now vanished, and I trust we will make the ties of friendship closer and stronger by establishing between us a community and exchange of prayers.

I can but too well imagine how severe the trials must be
to which you are now exposed—especially in the present
ferment, when a vein of bitterness has been opened in
England which will not close so soon, and when the hoarse
voice of religious acrimony is filling the atmosphere with
its dismal sounds. With the peculiar gentleness of your disposition you will have to encounter the fierce attacks of the
"Ελληνες, as well as of the 'Ιουδαῖοι, I mean of those to whom
the Church is σκάνδαλον, as well as of those to whom it is
μωρία. I can only pray for you, and trust that He who has
given you the first victory of faith will also give you *robur et
æs triplex circa pectus*, for less will scarcely do. . . .

Yours entirely and unalterably,

J. DOELLINGER.

Mr. James R. Hope, Queen's Counsel.

I have not met with any later correspondence of Dr.
Döllinger's with Mr. Hope-Scott than this, excepting a
mere note. He visited Abbotsford in 1852. There is
a letter of Count Leo Thun's to Mr. Hope (dated Wien,
den 7. Juli 1851), in which, after expressing the joy he
had felt at the news of his having become a Catholic, he
remarks : ' I know how slowly, and on what sure founda-
tions the decision came to maturity in your soul.' Two
letters of Mr. Hope's to Mr. Badeley, though not
coincident in point of time with the event before us,

contain passages so closely connected with it as to find their place here. Though Mr. Badeley's Anglicanism was scarce hanging by a thread, he held out for a time, but became a Catholic previously to July 15, 1852.

J. R. Hope, Esq. Q.C. to E. Badeley, Esq.

Abbotsford : Oct. 25, '51.

Dear B.,— . . . As for you, I hold your intellect to be Catholic. You cannot help it, but your habits of feeling will give you, as they gave me, more trouble than your reason. How can it be otherwise, considering how many years of training in one posture we both of us underwent ? But I pray and hope for you, and that speedily, that freedom of life and limb which has been vouchsafed to me. Freedom indeed it is, for it is to breathe in all its fulness the grace and mercy of God's kingdom, instead of tasting it through the narrow lattices of texts and controversies. To believe Christ present in the Eucharist, and not adore Him—not pray Him to tarry with us and bless us. To hold the communion of saints, and yet refuse to call upon all saints—living and departed, to intercede for us with the great Head of the body in which we all are members. To accept a primacy in St. Peter, and yet hold it immaterial to the organisation of the Church. To acknowledge one Church, and then divide the Unity into fragments. To attribute to the Church the power of the keys, and then deny the force of her indulgences while admitting her absolutions. To approve confession, and practically set it aside. To do and hold these and many other contradictions—what is it but to submit the mind to the fetters of a tradition which, if once made to reason, must destroy itself ? . . .

Y^{rs} ever aff^{ly},

JAMES R. HOPE.

Abbotsford : July 16, 1852.

Dear Badeley,—I received your most kind letter yesterday. I well knew that I should hear from you, for you are an accurate observer of my birthdays—not one for many years having escaped you. This one does indeed deserve notice in one sense, as being the first on which you and I could salute each other as Catholics. May God grant that this His great gift may be fruitful to us both! Forty years of my life are already gone—of yours, more. Let us try to make the best of what may still remain. We have now all the helps which Christ's death provided for us, and all the responsibilities which come with them. 'Deus, in adjutorium meum intende. Domine, ad adjuvandum me festina! . . .

Y^{rs} most aff^{ly},

JAMES R. HOPE.

E. Badeley, Esq.

To the above correspondence, the following scrap from a letter of Mr. David Lewis, congratulating Mr. Hope on his conversion, may form an appropriate *pendant*, as showing Mr. Hope's influence in the Catholic direction previously to that event : ' I may add that I owe in part my own conversion to conversation with you, which turned me to a course of reading the end of which I did not then suspect. It is therefore no small joy to me to see you in the same harbour of refuge ' (May 15, 1851). Some years later (in spring, 1855) it was a subject of intense joy to Mr. Hope-Scott when the news came from Rome that William Palmer had been received into the Church by Father Passaglia.

CHAPTER XXII.

1839-1869.

Review of Mr. Hope's Professional Career—His View of Secular Pursuits—Advice from Archdeacon Manning against Overwork—Early Professional Services to Government—J. R. Hope adopts the Parliamentary Bar—His Elements of Success—Is made Q.C.—Difficulty about Supremacy Oath—Mr. Venables on Mr. Hope-Scott as a Pleader—Recollections of Mr. Cameron—Mr. Hope-Scott on his own Profession—Mr. Hope-Scott's Professional Day—Regular History of Practice not Feasible—Specimens of Cases: 1. The Caledonian Railway interposing a Tunnel. 2. Award by Mr. Hope-Scott and R. Stephenson. 3. Mersey Conservancy and Docks Bill, · Parliamentary Hunting-day,' Liverpool and Manchester compared. 4. London, Brighton, and South Coast and the Beckenham Line. 5. Scottish Railways—an Amalgamation Case—Mr. Hope-Scott and Mr. Denison ; Honourable Conduct of Mr. Hope-Scott as a Pleader. 6. Dublin Trunk Connecting Railway. 7. Professional Services of Mr. Hope-Scott to Eton—Claims of Clients on Time—Value of Ten Minutes—Conscientiousness—Professional Income—Extra Occupations—Affection of Mr. Hope-Scott for Father Newman—Spirit in which he laboured.

On taking the step of which I have just related the history, Mr. Hope had not to encounter the usual array of external ills that assail the convert's life. Although he was now a Catholic, his eloquence had lost none of its magic, and railway directors were not very likely to indulge their bigotry at the expense of their dividends. He lost not, I suppose, a single retainer, and his practice at the bar went on as before. His conversion, however, affords us a convenient point at which to turn aside and review his professional career, contrasting so singularly with what the ordinary observer would have anticipated for him under such a condition. We are so much accustomed to associate religious doubts or convictions with an unworldliness which is rarely visible where great worldly success is attained, that on leaving the cloisters of Oxford, and entering with him the committee-rooms of the Houses of Parliament, we seem to behold the curtain raised all at once, and the same actor appearing in a totally new character, with hardly a feature left that can identify him with the previous representation.

He was, indeed, himself not insensible to this contrast, and had early marked off from purely secular pursuits that choice and precious portion of his time which could be reserved for higher objects. An interesting passage in a letter of his to Mr. Gladstone (dated from Lincoln's Inn, June 25, 1841) will illustrate this feeling by a phrase which I italicise, as I believe he was fond of using it: ' My reason for staying in town is to read ecclesiastical law, and to prepare (if so be) for election committees. *The former branch I reckon my flower-garden, the latter my cabbage-field.*' [1] When Anglicanism and its institutions had broken down under him, and others not as yet come in their place, he sought in the purely temporal works of his calling perhaps a refuge from doubts, certainly a means of sanctification ; and either alternative explains the issue. A religious mind could never succeed in silencing religious difficulty by earthly pursuits, but in whatever measure it sought to sanctify the latter, would be led onwards to the faith. The following passage from a letter of the then Archdeacon Manning (now Cardinal Archbishop of Westminster) to

---

[1] See letter of Mr. Gladstone to Miss Hope-Scott, Appendix III.

Mr. Hope (dated Dec. 9, 1842) will show that this ardent and restless application to his profession was watched at the time by Mr. Hope's friends with some degree of anxiety and surprise. The kind and wise admonitions it conveys, only distantly indeed bearing on the religious side of the question, many may read with much profit :—

> As a bystander I see you working too much, and looking at times overwrought; and I ask myself, what is this man's aim ? It must needs be something very high and far off to need all this unremitting tension of mind. I do much wish to see you more relaxed, and with more play. I know it is a more difficult attainment to be able both to work intensely and to relax thoroughly. But without it a man deteriorates. He becomes a keen, case-hardened tool, and no man. Our friends the Germans are not far wrong when they talk about developing what is universal in man, i.e. his humanity, which is a whole, and must be unfolded as a whole to be perfect, or even to approximate perfection. You will burn this if I go on, so I will leave you to Lancilotti.
>
> > Believe me ever yours affect^ly,
> >
> > H. E. MANNING.

The field finally adopted by Mr. Hope was the *Parliamentary Bar*, at which, as we have seen, he had practised to a certain extent from the first, though with considerable interruption from the legal and financial affairs of his college and the Sarum Chancery, as well as other weighty business, including in 1839 services rendered as Counsel to the Government in the preparation of the Foreign Marriages Bill; in 1843 of the Consular Jurisdiction Bill, the report which he furnished on which, to be seen in the Parliamentary Records, would alone have been sufficient to have made a great

reputation in that particular line; and in 1843–44 he
was engaged by Government in the matter of the
Franco-Mexican arbitration to prepare a report on
some points in dispute between France and Mexico,
which had been submitted to the arbitration of Great
Britain. I presume that his retainers in these cases
would be principally due to the fact that his brother,
Mr. George W. Hope, was now a member of the Government as Under-Secretary of State for the Colonies
in Sir Robert Peel's administration. But the 'fame'
that had already gone abroad regarding him, particularly for his learning in all matters that touched
ecclesiastical law, would have been sure, independently
of private interest, to have brought him early into prominence. The Ecclesiastical Courts Bill in 1843
engaged much of his attention, and his share in the
legal business connected with troubles of that year at
Oxford has been noticed in its place. On October 26,
1843, he took his degree of D.C.L. at Oxford. In 1844,
at the suggestion of the Bishop of London (Right Rev.
Dr. Blomfield), he was accepted by the Lord Chancellor
as one of the persons to consider the chapter on
offences against religion and the Church in the proposed Code of Criminal Law.

In a short time, however, his practice seems to have
merged in the department with which his name is
principally connected, that of railway pleading. This
branch of the profession, though affording little or no
scope for those powers of oratory which his first speech
before the Lords showed that he possessed, nor yet
opening those avenues to power and fame which usually

tempt minds of his class, was undoubtedly highly lucrative, and by this time Mr. Hope's charities must have nearly exhausted his modest patrimony. It had also one great advantage, in its business being principally confined to the Parliamentary session, thus leaving him free to travel six months in the year. I have seen it stated that in conversation with a friend he gave this as his chief reason for adopting it. He may have said so half in jest; but there can, I believe, be little doubt that a far deeper reason was that the Parliamentary bar was likely to present fewer cases of difficulty in point of conscience than he would have had to encounter in the Common Law courts.

It is needless to mention, except for the sake of the few persons who may not happen to have even that superficial acquaintance with the subject which newspaper reading can supply, that advocates practising at the Parliamentary bar are engaged in pleading for or against the private bills referred to committees of Parliament, relating, for example, to railways, canals, docks, gas-works, and the like. These are each referred to a committee of five, supposed to represent the whole House; witnesses of course are examined, and counsel heard on behalf of the companies or individuals concerned. To plead before a tribunal of such a nature and on such interests evidently demands qualifications of a special kind. Mr. Hope possessed some external ones which are by no means unimportant. His noble presence, in the first place, gave him a great advantage; and a known name and known antecedents like his were also additional recommendations of great value. Then came his tact, clearness of intellect, memory for names and details, his moral qualities, especially his perfect sense of honour, which gained him the ear of the committees, and, what is still more difficult, enabled him to keep it.

Mr. Hope then very early attained to the front rank in his profession, and on the retirement of Mr. Charles Austin, Q.C. (1848), and the death of Serjeant Wrangham (*d.* March 1869) and of the Hon. John C. Talbot, Q.C. (*d.* 1852), may be said to have had no rival in reputation or practice until the present Sir E. B. Denison 'gradually began to compete with him on not unequal terms.' Mr. St. George Burke, Q.C., Mr. Merewether, Q.C., and Mr. Rodwell, Q.C., were other contemporaries of his, who all had a large practice and great reputation, but were, I believe, as seldom as possible pitted against Mr. Hope-Scott.

The following letters illustrate in an interesting manner the particulars just given.

Charles Austin, Esq. Q.C. to Edw. Stanley Hope, Esq.

Brandeston Hall, Wickham Market :
May 6, 1873.

Dear Sir,—Mr. Carter has just shown me a letter from you, in which you give him an account of your uncle's last sickness and death.

I cannot help giving some expression to my feelings of sympathy with yourself and all who loved and lament him.

During several years Hope-Scott was, with Mr. John Talbot, Mr. Serjt. Wrangham and myself, amongst the leading members of the Parliamentary Bar, and on my retirement in 1848 he succeeded to the leadership of that Bar. I was therefore brought into almost daily and familiar intercourse with him, and was able to appreciate all that was excellent and high-minded in him, and to value his great intellectual qualities at their just worth. Accept this tribute of respect and regard, and allow me to express my sincere sympathy with all who mourn his loss.

I am, yours faithfully,
CHARLES AUSTIN.

P.S.—The state of my health must be my apology for, I fear, an illegible letter.

The Lord Elcho to Edw. Stanley Hope, Esq.

23 St. James's Place, S.W.:
May 2, '73.

My dear Edward,—I can well understand what a loss your uncle must be to you all—to you especially. . . . Years ago, when I used to see something of him on committees and else-where, I used to think him the best-looking, most intelligent, and brightest of beings. No man was thought more able, none was more popular. What surprises me, is the short notice there is of him in the *Times*. He had, however, been long in retirement, and those who die in harness monopolise too often public notice to the neglect of more deserving men. . . .

Believe me,
Very sincerely y^{rs},
ELCHO.

Early in 1849 Mr. Hope received a patent of precedence, entitling him to rank with her Majesty's counsel; and in April of that year attended the levée as Q.C. It was at his own request that the dignity of the silk gown was conferred upon him in this form; and his reason was a conscientious difficulty about taking the oath of supremacy so far as it denied the papal authority, ecclesiastical or civil, as existing *de facto et de jure* in the realm. He states his difficulty in a letter to Mr. Badeley (February 23, 1849), as follows :—

That the Pope *does* exercise jurisdiction in this country is notorious; and that he ought to do so over R. Catholics seems to be admitted by the present state of the law as to that church. The oath, then, cannot be taken as it was originally meant, and the only sense in which I think it can be accepted is, that the Pope has not, nor without consent of the Legislature ought to have, an external coercive power over the Queen's subjects.

But this compromise did not satisfy him, and he therefore refused the silk gown, except under the conditions previously stated, which did not require him to take the oath of supremacy at all. His request for the patent of precedence, and his reasons for wishing it, were conveyed through a legal friend to the then Lord Chancellor, Lord Cottenham, who made no difficulty whatever in granting it. The following anecdote will amuse the reader. When the Chancellor had to report to the Premier (Lord John Russell) the various appointments he had made, Lord John asked Lord Cottenham why he had given Mr. Hope-Scott a patent of precedence instead of making him a Q.C. On the Chancellor's replying that he had done it because of Mr. Hope-Scott's scruples about the oath, Lord John exclaimed, ' That's more than I would have done.'

Such illustrations of Mr. Hope-Scott's professional success as I have been able to collect, either from oral sources or correspondence, may fitly be introduced by a valuable paper on his characteristics as an advocate by Mr. G. S. Venables, Q.C. It is obviously drawn up

with great care and reflection by a skilled observer,
who had the best opportunities for arriving at a correct
judgment. I omit the two opening paragraphs, the
principal facts contained in which have been given in
a former page.

CRITICISM ON MR. HOPE-SCOTT'S CHARACTERISTICS AS A PLEADER. BY G. S. VENABLES, ESQ. Q.C.

The Bar is exempt from envy of merited success, and
Mr. Hope-Scott's undisputed pre-eminence never provoked a
feeling of personal jealousy. Though he cultivated little
intimacy with his professional associates, his courtesy and
good humour never failed ; and he showed due appreciation of
the services a leader requires from his junior colleagues.

His singularly attractive appearance produced its natural
effect in conciliating those around him, and the pleasant and
cheerful manner which nevertheless repelled familiarity tended
to make him generally popular.

The most remarkable forensic qualities of Mr. Hope-Scott
were facility, prudence, and grace of language and manner.
The subtlety of his intellect, if it had been ostentatiously displayed, might perhaps have impaired the confidence which he
had the art of inspiring. Inexperienced members of the
tribunals before which he practised were tempted to forget
that he was an advocate, while they listened to perspicuous
statements which led up with apparent absence of design to a
carefully premeditated conclusion. It could never be suspected
from his manner that he was constantly supporting a paradox,
or that he anticipated defeat.

When he had occasion in successive contests to maintain
opposite propositions, it seemed that the circumstances of the
case, not the position of the advocate, had been changed.

In Parliamentary practice there is no room for the more
ambitious kinds of eloquence, nor can it be known whether
Mr. Hope-Scott would have been capable of pathetic or elevated

declamation.[2]   In dealing with questions of fact, of expediency, of equitable policy, and of complicated agreements, he has probably never been excelled.   His lucid arrangement of topics, his pure polished style, and his appearance of dispassionate conviction secured the pleased attention of his audience. The more tedious parts of his argument or narrative were from time to time relieved by touches of the playfulness which is more popular than humour; but the colleagues and opponents who thoroughly understood his object, knew that it was pursued with undeviating constancy of purpose.

In the lightest of his speeches there was neither carelessness nor vacillation.   Less finished advocates turn aside to indulge themselves in playing with an illustration or a favourite proposition, at the risk of betraying the distinction between their own natural train of thought and their immediate argument. Mr. Hope-Scott was too consummate an artist to be tempted into irrelevance or digression.

His success would not have been less complete if his practice had required him to trace the fine analogies and close deductions of law.   His intellect was admirably adapted to the comparison of precedents and to the application of legal principles.   His acuteness was at the same time comprehensive and minute, and he delighted in finding appropriate expressions for the nicest distinctions.   When he had sometimes occasion to spend hours in contesting the clauses of a bill, he had a surprising faculty of averting the weariness which is ordinarily inseparable from the prolonged discussion of details.   Professional associates, who willingly recognised his general superiority, sometimes confessed that in the most irksome of their contests they were placed at an exceptional disadvantage in comparison of Mr. Hope-Scott's felicitous adroitness.   He excelled in dealing with skilled witnesses, who were themselves from the nature of the case supplementary advocates.   The object of cross-examination, where there is little serious dispute as to the facts, is to draw from the mouth of a hostile witness

[2 Of the latter, however, two or three specimens are given in this memoir. See vol. i. (pp. 204-207), vol. ii. (pp. 124-127).]

the other half of the story. An accurate memory, stored by abundant experience, enabled Mr. Hope-Scott to recall the history of every railway company, the expressed opinions of general managers, and the characteristics and theories of engineers. The wariest veterans needed all their caution to anticipate the design of the friendly conversation which gradually tempted them to damaging admissions. He was slow to resort to harder modes of attack, of which he was at the same time fully capable. Every facility was offered to a candid and confiding witness, and there was still greater satisfaction in baffling the vigilance of an adversary who was on his guard against an attack from a different quarter. A hostile witness, after an encounter with Mr. Hope-Scott, sometimes found that his answers formed a plausible argument in favour of the proposition he had intended to confute. His perplexity must have been increased when he afterwards heard his own statements reproduced in the speech of the opposing counsel. Almost the only point in which Mr. Hope-Scott could be charged with a want of caution consisted in his frequent affirmation of certain general opinions, such as the common and questionable doctrine that competition cannot last where combination is possible. An advocate who is changing his clients is ill-advised in hampering himself with the enumeration of maxims which may from time to time be quoted against him. In such cases Mr. Hope-Scott almost converted a self-imposed difficulty into an additional resource. With marvellous ingenuity he proved that any competition scheme which he happened to support formed an exception to the rule which he carefully reasserted; and unsophisticated hearers admired the consistency with general principles which was found not to be incompatible with immediate expediency.

It is almost superfluous to say that Mr. Hope-Scott never exceeded the legitimate bounds of forensic debate. All litigated questions, and especially this species of private legislation, have two sides, and it is the business of an advocate to present in the most favourable light the cause which he is retained to defend. Deliberate sophistry is as culpable as false relations of fact; but completeness or judicial impartiality belongs to the tribunal, and not to the representative of the litigant. When all moral scruples have been allowed their full weight, the qualifications of a great advocate are almost exclusively intellectual. It is to this part of Mr. Hope-Scott's character that I have strictly to confine myself. It is probable that an attempt to analyse a distinct personal impression may have produced but a vague result. I have little doubt that, although Mr. Hope-Scott was almost unequalled in professional ability, his real life lay outside his occupation as an advocate. The grounds of the affection and admiration with which he is remembered by his family and his nearest friends have but a remote connection with the faculties and accomplishments which I have endeavoured to describe.

Another friend (Mr. H. L. Cameron), who had continual opportunities, from about the year 1859, of observing Mr. Hope-Scott's character in its professional aspect, furnishes some very interesting reminiscences, on a part of which, however, it may be worth while to observe that the versatility and pliability of intellect which the writer so well describes in Mr. Hope-Scott is no doubt more or less common to every great barrister, and is a habit to which all who are actively engaged in the profession are obliged to train their minds as they can. Still, it is equally certain that Mr. Hope-Scott possessed this faculty in an uncommon degree; and, in order to form a complete idea of him as he appeared in the eyes of his contemporaries, as well as to understand the relations of one part of his character to another, it is necessary to draw these features in considerable detail. After noticing particularly a very pleasing trait in Mr. Hope-Scott's demeanour as a leading counsel, shown in the kindness and tact with which, in consultation, he took care to prevent the inexperience or ignorance of his juniors being made apparent, and sought rather to ask them questions on points which they were likely to know something about, Mr. Cameron continues as follows :—

RECOLLECTIONS OF MR. H. L. CAMERON.

What made Mr. Hope-Scott so much loved by all who were brought into contact with him was his great amiability, thorough kindness of heart: his care was always not to hurt or wound another's feelings; and even in the heat of debate, and under great provocation, I never heard him utter an unkind word, or put a harsh construction on the conduct of any one, even an adversary.

As regards his talents, they are so universally known and admitted, that I can say very little you have not heard already. Westminster has rarely—never certainly in later years—heard such an advocate. The secret of his great success at the bar, beyond his intellectual power, lay, I think, in a peculiar charm and fascination of manner—a manner which could invest the driest and most technical matters with interest, and compelled the attention of the hearers to the subject under discussion. The melody of his voice was, to me, one of his greatest attractions. Then, again, what a noble presence! and that goes a long way at the Bar. I can look back, and see him now, as he used to walk into this room to attend some consultation, how vigorous, handsome, and stately he always appeared, bringing the force of his powerful intellect at once to bear upon the subject under consideration, doing all in such a genial manner, without any attempt at showing his mental superiority to those around him.

In those busy times he would perhaps be engaged in twenty different cases on the same day; the competition to engage him was most keen: it was almost the first thing one thought about when clients came to consult upon a new scheme. He would go from one committee to another, by some extraordinary means always being at the place where he was most needed. It was marvellous how he kept all these matters distinct in his brain; he was never in confusion or at fault. In one room he would open a case, say for an Improvement Bill, with a brilliant speech setting forth all its merits, a speech which would probably immediately impress the committee and carry the case, whatever after arguments might be urged against it, or speeches made by other counsel. Then he would go into another room, and cross-examine a skilled witness in a railway case, showing his intimate knowledge of engineering, and beating the witness perhaps on his own ground. Then he would take an Irish case, or a Gas and Water Bill, or landowner's case, whose property was about to be intersected, a ratepayer's, a carrier's, each case being thoroughly gone into, and thoroughly mastered and understood. After all this, and late in the day, when any one else would have felt fatigued and exhausted, in mind at any rate, if not in body, he would go into a room where an inquiry had been going on perhaps for weeks, and reply on the whole evidence. Those who know what labour this entails can alone appreciate such a capability.

No one at the bar whom I have ever heard reasoned with such perfect lucidity. He would explain a case which his client the solicitor would have wrapped up in fifty or sixty brief sheets, and involved in as much obscurity as it were well possible, to a committee in a few minutes; and I have often thought his clients never understood their own cases until he had explained them. It was wonderful how he could make a committee (sometimes composed of by no means the brightest specimens of mankind) understand a case; and his persuasive power with those tribunals was also marvellous.

One word more on his character in his business life, and that is as to his entire conscientiousness. No case did he ever consider insignificant or beneath his notice. He gave the same attention to the humblest client that he would to a duke. He never left anything he had to do *half* done: his work was *thorough*, complete, good. Time, which he considered his client's, was never wasted; and to enable him to get through his work he would rise at four or five o'clock in the morning, and he would be engaged either getting up a case, attending consultations, or in committee until five or six o'clock in the evening. His life was an exact fulfilment of that precept, 'Whatsoever thy hand findeth to do, do it with thy might.'[3]

To what has now been expressed by critics so competent, I shall add the only passage which I have been able to discover, in which Mr. Hope-Scott has left on record any opinion relating to himself in connection with his professional experience in an intellectual point of view. In pleading before the Select Committee of the Lords, on behalf of Eton College, on the Public School Bill of 1865, after stating his objection to the notion of such subjects as natural philosophy playing so very large a part in early education as some persons would have them do, he goes on to say :—

I, if I may venture here to speak of myself, have observed enough in a life which has been tolerably devoted to business to know this, that the possession of knowledge upon any one subject is worthless compared to the possession of a power of using knowledge when you have got it. My Lords, in my profession, though not in my part of it, there are many men who will take up a patent case, or a mining case, without the slightest previous knowledge of the natural sciences relating to it, and who will make statements to a jury which the scientific men at hand will stand aghast at ; what does that mean ? It means that they have been so trained in the acquisition of knowledge when presented to them, that it becomes to them a mere matter of get-up, in many instances, to acquire an amount of knowledge which would absolutely electrify many a learned society.[4]

[3] Mr. H. L. Cameron. Letter to Miss Hope, October 28, 1877.
[4] *Min. Evid. Sel. Com. Public Sch. B. (H. L.)*, p. 209.

Notwithstanding the qualification under which Mr. Hope-Scott here speaks, it will be seen from a case I shall presently cite (the 'Caledonian Railway,' p. 119) that he describes a faculty he was of course aware that he himself possessed. He said, I believe, in conversation, that there was hardly any subject which he had not had occasion to look up in his profession, and this was one of the reasons which made him so fond of it.

It will perhaps give pleasure to those whose affection for Mr. Hope-Scott's memory has suggested this record, if I note down some particulars of his daily round of occupations during the most active period of his life, principally supplied me (with other interesting details) by the kindness of Mr. John Q. Dunn, who, from the year 1859 until the end, was Mr. Hope-Scott's confidential clerk, continually about him in the most unreserved trust, made out his daily *agenda*, and was intimately acquainted with all his habits and ways.

Mr. Hope-Scott rose early, between five and six o'clock, made his coffee, and then went through his devotions, a black ebony crucifix, with the figure of our Lord in brass, on the table before him. Wherever he went he had this carried with him.[5] His next employment was his brief, which he read with great rapidity,[6] making notes as he went on. This lasted till about eight, when he dressed and breakfasted. He then

---

[5] This particular crucifix, however, was only used by Mr. Hope-Scott after his first wife's death. It was the one which she held in her hands when dying.

[6] 'Bellasis says you never read even a brief, but divine its contents in half the time required.'—Bishop Grant to Mr. Hope-Scott, November 19, 1852.

drove from his private residence, or from Norfolk House, to attend consultations in Chambers at 9.30. Each consultation lasted five or ten minutes, sometimes fifteen, never more, until eleven o'clock, not a minute being wasted. Public business then commenced, in the Lords at eleven, in the Commons at twelve. His papers having been taken over to the various committee-rooms, he would go from room to room, making a speech here, or cross-examining witnesses there, as the occasion might require, throughout the day. He was always cool and business-like, never in the slightest degree flurried. This, which was only due to his immense self-control, made people *imagine* that the work was excessively easy to him. Business before the committees lasted till four, when the bags were collected (which were a porter's load) ; and in Chambers another series of cases ensued, from four to five or six. In the intervals of business he would dictate, with surprising exactness and calmness, letters on his private affairs, such as the management of his Highland estate—minute directions for painting outhouses it might be, or the like small matters. At six he went home in a cab, tired and exhausted ; dinner followed, after which he invariably went to sleep for two hours, waking up about ten, when he read his prayers. He commonly slept sound, and got up next morning bright and fresh. Clients sometimes came as early as six or seven, and had undivided attention for three-quarters of an hour : these audiences amounted, in fact, to fresh verbal briefs, but were never charged for, as the arrangement was made for his own convenience.

On first undertaking to write this memoir, the idea
naturally suggested itself whether it might not be possible to give something like a connected history of Mr.
Hope-Scott's practice at the bar, especially considering
the great social interest of the whole subject of railway
construction in these countries, of which it really forms
part. But I was assured by those thoroughly conver-
sant with the matter, that such a task was not to be
thought of. Legal arguments, occupying many hours
for days together, however extraordinary they no doubt
were as efforts of talent, and however important to
those concerned at the time, who, perhaps, might be
seen expecting, with white faces, the long-pending decision of committees for or against them, cannot, after
the lapse of a generation, nay, after a far shorter interval than that, be even understood without an amount
of labour which few would be inclined to devote to
them. It may, indeed, be said that railway law is the
creation of such great advocates as Mr. Hope-Scott,
who reigned supreme in their own province at the time
of its formation ; and no doubt suggestions of counsel
may have been adopted into law. But how to assign
to each his share in the mighty structure? or guess to
whom any particular change may have been due? It
would at all events be the office, not of the biographer,
but of the historian of jurisprudence. I shall nevertheless so far venture to deviate from the advice to
which I have referred as to notice five or six cases, not
as being in every instance of special and remembered
celebrity, but merely as specimens of the kind of practice in which Mr. Hope was engaged. Two of these

will also give me the opportunity of quoting some
clever articles from the contemporary newspaper press,
serving to show what the opinion about Mr. Hope-Scott
was at the time, as the criticisms of his professional
friends already given convey to us a distinct idea of the
impression which he produced on his brethren of the
Bar. I take first a case in which the Caledonian Railway Company were concerned, as it is very clearly and
concisely explained by Mr. Hercules Robertson (better
known as Lord Benholme, his title as Lord of Session),
one of the counsel associated in it with Mr. Hope-Scott,
in a letter which has been kindly communicated to
me :—

1. *The Caledonian Railway.*—' We were associated
together as counsel for the Caledonian Railway Company in supporting several important bills upon Parliamentary committees, involving difficulties of no ordinary
magnitude. One very important object that Company
had to attain was leave to alter their entrance into
Glasgow by lowering their access by many feet of per-
pendicular elevation. Their bill proposed to effect this
by a tunnel which had to be interposed between the
canal above, on the surface, and the Edinburgh and
Glasgow Railway beneath. Our tunnel had to pass between these hostile undertakings just at the point where
the former of these lay above the other with a very
scanty space between. The difficulty was to induce
the committee to believe that the thing was possible—
that it was in the power of engineering to thread a way
for the Caledonian Railway so as not to bring down the
water of the canal on the one hand, or to break into

the other railway by destroying its roof on the other.
Mr. Hope-Scott had a power of persuasion that owed
its efficacy not more to his commanding talents than to
his straightforward ways and his honest and candid
manner, which seemed to afford a satisfactory pledge
that he would not seriously and anxiously advocate anything that was not true and possible. By his powerful
assistance the Caledonian Company carried their bill,
and in the course of the proceedings I had a full
opportunity of estimating the elements of success
in Mr. Hope-Scott's career which made him one of
the most popular of Parliamentary counsel. I need
hardly say that his kindness and courtesy to myself
were all that I could expect or wish from one with
whom I was otherwise so closely connected.—H. J.
ROBERTSON.'

2. *Award by Mr. Hope-Scott and Mr. R. Stephenson.*
—In 1852 Mr. Hope-Scott was associated with Mr.
Robert Stephenson, the celebrated engineer, in making
an important award upon certain questions in difference
between the London and North-Western and North
Staffordshire Railway Companies. This document, dated
October 6, 1852, appears in the newspapers of the day;
but either to quote from or analyse it would not be of
the slightest interest to my readers. A letter of Mr.
R. Stephenson's to Mr. Hope-Scott on some private
business of later date is of more value for our purposes
as showing the opinion which this great engineer had
formed of Mr. Hope-Scott in his own field, and also that
these two remarkable men were by that time on the
terms of intimacy that might be expected where minds

of such calibre, and so capable of understanding each other, met in the conduct of affairs.

Robert Stephenson, Esq. C.E. to J. R. Hope-Scott, Esq. Q.C.

24 Great George Street: 2 Feb. 1855.

My dear Hope-Scott,—I have a sketch in hand for your bridge. Your specification is excellent. I know what you want exactly. If I had not finished my engineering career, I should certainly have been jealous of your powers of specification. I do not know that it is sufficient to base a contract upon that would hold water in law; nevertheless, it is sufficient for me. I cannot offhand state the cost; but when the sketch and estimate are made, you shall see them; and if the cost exceeds your views, there will be no harm done; on the contrary, I shall have had the pleasure of scheming a little for you by way of pastime.

Yours faithfully,
ROBERT STEPHENSON.

James Hope-Scott, Esq.

3. *The Mersey Conservancy and Docks Bill.*—The speeches delivered by Mr. Hope-Scott in this case (June 23 and 24, 1857) on behalf of the Corporation of Liverpool against the Mersey Docks and Conservancy Bill, were considered as among his greatest forensic efforts. His engagement in it was originally due to an accident, the brief having been given in the first instance to Mr. Plunkett, in whose chambers, as already mentioned, Mr. Hope had been a pupil. Mr. Plunkett having been prevented by illness from taking the brief, it was placed in the hands of Mr. Hope-Scott, who made a brilliant use of the opportunity. To place the reader in possession of the main question, it may be sufficient to state that the object of the Bill was to consolidate the Liver-

pool and Birkenhead Docks into one estate, so as to
vest the whole superintendence of the Mersey in one
body, principally elected by the Docks Ratepayers for
the time being. This was felt by the Corporation of
Liverpool as an unjust interference with their local
rights, and the case was argued by Mr. Hope-Scott (when
he comes upon general grounds) as one in which the
commercial was being sacrificed to the jealousy of the
manufacturing interest, and the principle of local government to that of centralisation. The reasonings as to
matters of fact and business which make up the great
bulk of these speeches are quite outside of our range,
which can only deal with that which is more popular
and rhetorical. Two specimens in the latter style I
venture to quote—one of them appearing an excellent
example of the genial humour he knew so well how to
throw around the driest of arguments ; the other a
highly coloured view of the history and position of
Liverpool in the commercial world, and of the danger
of disturbing it in obedience to the clamour of its manufacturing rivals. The treatment of the subject rather
reminds us of Burke's manner, and it is easy to see that
Mr. Hope-Scott's own political feelings, always constitu-
tionally conservative, would here assist his eloquence,
as, in a far higher degree, the same sympathies had
added splendour to his early display before the House
of Lords. In the case before us it is hardly necessary
to say that millions of money were concerned. An
exciting scene is remembered in connection with it, the
secretary of the Birkenhead Docks fainting away during
the proceedings. Mr. Hope-Scott is *said* to have re-

ceived a fee of 10,000l.; but a friend, likely to be well informed, thinks this is a fable.

THE PARLIAMENTARY HUNTING-DAY: A CHANGE OF MOUNT.

[After describing the provisions of an earlier centralising scheme proposed by Government in 1856, Mr. Hope-Scott proceeds:]

Well, sir, all this set the game fairly afoot; and such a day's sport could hardly have been anticipated since the days when—

> Earl Percy of Northumberland
> A vow to God did make,
> His pleasure in the Scottish woods
> Three summers' days to take.

The Queen herself had not indeed made a vow, but had announced the hunting from the throne. The Royal Commissioners had driven the whole country for game, and there was a large field, nearly all the counties of England being interested spectators; the hounds in good condition—very skilful whips—everything seemed to promise a fine day's sport: and what would have been the issue is not very easy to foresee, had it not been for what I may be allowed to term (pursuing the metaphor) the very unfortunate riding of the gentleman who, upon that occasion, acted as huntsman. It appears from his own statement at the outset that he had very little previous acquaintance with the country; but he went off with very considerable confidence upon 'the shipping interest,' and there seemed to be every prospect of his having a pleasant ride; but as he got along, he seems to have found the ground deeper and the fences stiffer than he had reckoned upon, and, moreover, that 'the shipping interest' had been a good deal exhausted in the service of the department before.

So about the middle of the day (it is more easy to give a description of personal events in the form of analogy than from direct representation)—about the middle of the day he seems to have changed his mount; and when he was next seen

he was going at a tremendous rate across country, firmly
seated upon the ' natural rights of man.' As you may suppose,
he very soon made up for lost ground upon so splendid a crea-
ture. But the difficulties began when he came up with the
hunt; for the horse in question is a desperate puller, very
awkward to manage in old enclosures, and not at all accustomed to hunt with any regular pack, least of all with her
Majesty's hounds. The consequence was what might have
been expected. He was hardly up with the hounds when he
was in the middle of them, rode over half the pack, and
headed the whole; and so there was nothing for it but for the
master of the hounds to call them off, and declare he would
not hunt that country again until he had had a further survey
made of it.

Now I have endeavoured to give, in as gentle a manner as
I can, an account of that which caused the principal disaster
on this famous sporting day. It was stated that further information was necessary. But another member of the
Government described the difficulty in a good deal broader
terms. Mr. Labouchere declared that 'the sons of Zeruiah
had been too strong for them.' However that may be, a select
committee was appointed.[7]

COMPARISON OF LIVERPOOL WITH MANCHESTER.

What has made Liverpool? Manchester says it has made
Liverpool. Sir, the East and West Indies, America and Africa
and Australia have made Liverpool, just as they have made
Manchester. We know that for a long time that western side
of the kingdom was far behind the eastern portions of it; that
it had no wool trade, which was the old staple of the country;
that South Lancashire was covered with forests; that in
Edward the Second's time there was but one poor fulling-mill
in Manchester: and what has been the eventual result?
After long waiting, after long delays, a new continent in the
far west, and a new British Empire founded in the far east,

---

[7] *Report: Mersey Conservancy and Docks*, Westminster, 1857, p. 46.

have come to the relief of that portion of the country; that, concurrently with the development of that system, a Brindley, a Watt, an Arkwright, a George Stephenson arose. And so it is that Liverpool became what it is; and so it is that Manchester became what it is. But who was watching this great design of Providence in its small beginnings? Who was fostering the trade? Who was promoting the internal communications with Manchester? Who was spending money and giving land for the benefit of the infant trade? It was the corporation of Liverpool. . . . Where was representation and taxation then, sir? . . . You cannot have it till the port is made. You cannot have it till the risk has been run, till the ratepayers have been created. Then, no doubt, you may turn round upon the body who have made the port, made the ratepayers, made them what they are; and you may insist upon dethroning them from that position which they have occupied, at so much risk and so much labour, up to the time when the full development of the trade takes place. Now, sir, that is the case with Liverpool. It is the case with nearly all the remarkable ports of this kingdom. And then, forsooth, when all this has been done, and when Liverpool has nursed from its infancy the rising trade of the Mersey, watched it, developed it into a system which is unequalled, I venture to say, in the habitable world, we are to have gentlemen from Manchester coming down upon us to tell us that the true nostrum to make a port is taxation and representation, and to turn out those who, before there was any trade to tax, taxed themselves in order to create it.

. . . .

Apart from the Great Western Company's intervention this is a case of Manchester against Liverpool; in other words, it is a struggle between a manufacturing and a commercial interest. Now, sir, what is called the balance of power in the British Constitution, meaning as it does the equipoise caused by conflicting interests and passions, is a principle which is not confined to constitutional forms, but works out throughout the whole body of society; and we find a gradual tendency in latter

days to conflicts between classes, and classes which were before
allied together against other classes. We know the distinctions between land and trade, speaking generally, and the
conflicts which have ensued. In these latter days we have
had trade subdivided into manufactures and commerce. . . .
What you are asked to do now is to humble a commercial
interest at the instance of a manufacturing interest. . . .
There can be no doubt, sir, that if we contrast the habits of
mind of different classes, commercial pursuits give a different
tone and a different feeling. I am not saying it is better,
I am not saying it is worse—that is not my question—but
a different tone and feeling from what manufacturing pursuits do. I will not even analyse the cause of it; but I may
state this much, that commerce has that which manufacture
has not. It has its traditions and its history upon a higher
and very different footing : it has even its romance and its
poetry. A profession exercised within a port which is associated with such names as those of Tyre, of Byzantium, of
Venice, of Genoa, of the Hanse Towns, and many of the chief
cities of history may be said to have some liberal features
which I do not say are beneficial; I am merely saying that
they are different from those which arise out of the associations
of manufacture. Images of greatness and of splendour are
connected with the one much more than with the other, and
the term 'merchant princes' is a term which neither historians
nor orators would treat as otherwise than properly applied to
many of the chief men of the cities which I have named in
former days, and many of the chief men of the cities with
which we are now dealing. Moreover, commerce brings the
parties engaged in it into connection and contact with almost
the whole known world. Liverpool is not the Liverpool of
Lancashire only, or of Cheshire only, or of England only;
Liverpool is the Liverpool of India, of China, of Africa, of
North and South America, of Australia—the Liverpool of the
whole habitable globe ; and she has her features of distinction ;
she has her habits of thought and feeling, her traditions of
mind fostered by influences such as these. There she sits upon

the Mersey, a sort of queen of the seas; and Manchester, her sister, looks at her and loves her not. *She* too is great, and *she* too is powerful—but she is not Liverpool, and she cannot become Liverpool. At Liverpool she is lost in the throng of nations and the multitude of commerce; she is merely one of the many customers of the port. Well, as she cannot equal Liverpool, what is the next thing? It is to pull down Liverpool; to make Liverpool, forsooth, the Piræus of such an Athens as Manchester! That, sir, will suit her purpose, but would it suit yours? . . . No commercial interests can act, sir, more than any other interests, without some local association, without some united home, such as is afforded in the constitution of our own port. . . . To found upon injustice, and to proceed by agitation, to put down a rival whom they cannot help admiring though they cannot love—that, sir, is a process neither worthy of them nor likely to accord with the views of the constitutional politician, who is willing indeed that, according to the natural force of circumstances and the development of time, every interest should acquire its legitimate position in the balance of power under the constitution, but who certainly would not lend his aid to destroy by anticipation and violently any of those great commercial landmarks which remain—and long may they remain—in this country, standing monuments of the past, and affording in the present working of different political passions and interests a counterpoise, the loss of which would soon be felt, and would lead every one to regret the legislation which had converted this Bill into an Act. (Pp. 213, 214, 221-4.)

4. *The L. B. & S. C. Company—the Beckenham Line.* —In this great case Mr. Hope-Scott was retained by the London, Brighton, and South Coast Railway Company to oppose a bill by which it had been sought to construct a new and rival line by Beckenham, and, with his usual address, succeeded in turning it out. The question was one of considerable local importance, and

on its decision a clever article appeared in the 'West
Sussex Gazette,' written by the editor of that paper, the
late Mr. William Woods Mitchell, in whose sudden
death in 1880 the public press of England lost a most
able and talented journalist, who (I may remark in
passing) had as considerable a share as any one in carrying the principle of unstamped newspapers. His description of Mr. Hope-Scott's style of pleading is interesting, as conveying the impressions of a very sharp-
sighted spectator, and, so to speak, placing before our
bodily vision what such refined criticism as that of Mr.
Venables has addressed rather to the eye of the mind.

To one of an impulsive temperament Mr. Hope-Scott's
unconcern and *sang-froid* is perfectly irritating. It is amazing
how he remembers minute points and names. From the
highest questions of policy down to Mr. Ellis's cow and ladder
case he was 'up' in detail, never lost for a word, and not to be
astonished at anything. If the House of Commons were on
fire he would ask the committee simply if he should continue
until the fire had reached the room, or adjourn on the arrival
of the engines. Whilst he delivers his speech he is keeping
up a little cross-fire with the clerks behind, who scratch out
the evidences and papers as he requires them. Now he will
drink from the water-glass, now take a pinch of snuff, then
look at his notes, or make an observation to some one; but
still the smooth thread of his speech goes on to the committee:
but it is smooth, and says as plainly as possible, 'My dear
friend, I am not to be hurried, understand that, if you please.'
When, however, Mr. Scott has a joke against his learned friend
he looks round, and his dark eyes twinkle out the joke most
expressively. . . . There was a slight twinkle as he said to
the committee, 'Now I come to the question of gradients.'
It was amusing to see the five M.P.'s twist in their chairs,
and how readily the chairman told Mr. Scott the committee

required to hear nothing further about gradients. Had the question of gradients been entered upon, one might have travelled to Brighton and back ere it was concluded. Mr. Hope-Scott had the advantage of a good case, and he 'improved the occasion.' He further had the advantage of the three shrewd gentlemen at his elbow, Messrs. Faithfull, Slight, and Hawkins, who allowed no point to slumber. The great features in favour of the Brighton Company were—first, that their line was acknowledged by all to be well conducted; secondly, that Parliament had never granted a competing line of as palpable a character as the Beckenham; thirdly, that it had been shown by a committee of inquiry that competing lines invariably combine to the detriment of the public; and lastly, that the opposition line was not a *bonâ fide* scheme, and not required for the traffic of the district. Mr. Denison replied at a disadvantage. [The chairman announced:] ' The committee are unanimous in their decision that the preamble of the bill has *not* been proved.' The B. and S.C. has won the race. Another victory for *Scott's lot!*[8] The Beckenham project thrown out.[9]

The same writer (I have been told) also remarked that Mr. Hope-Scott succeeded with the committee by making an exceedingly clear *statement* of the case, thereby making them think that they knew something about it—and that was half the battle. When it was over, Mr. Hope-Scott observed to a friend, ' It is very likely I shall hear of that again : and very probably I shall be on the other side.' In fact, the affair got mixed up with the South-Eastern, from which company Mr. Hope-Scott received a prior retainer, and carried the Beckenham line against the L. and B. On that occasion he met

---

[8] *Scott's lot !* There was a celebrated trainer of the day, named Scott; and this expression was very familiar in the records of the turf.

[9] *West Sussex Gazette,* June 18, 1863.

the probable production by the opposing counsel of the
statement from his previous speech by showing that circumstances alter cases, and that two or three years make
a great difference. These latter particulars, however, I
only give as conversational. To prevent any adverse
impressions which might be given by such random talk,
I would remark in passing, that a case like the foregoing is not a question of right or wrong, truth or false-
hood, but of a balance of *expediency*, which it is a counsel's
business in each instance to state, though certainly not
to *over*state. Further on (p. 133) the reader will find
evidence of Mr. Hope-Scott's resolute conscientiousness
in the matter of fees.

5. *Scottish Railways: an Amalgamation Case.*—A
bill for the amalgamation of certain Scottish railways
was one of the great cases in which Mr. Hope-Scott was
concerned in the Parliamentary Session of 1866. A
correspondent of the 'Dundee Advertiser' takes occasion from it to contribute to that journal a sketch of
Mr. Hope-Scott's personal history and professional career,
with sundry comments on his style as an advocate.
From this article I shall quote so much as refers in
general to the Scottish part of his practice, and particularly to the case above mentioned. It will be perceived
that the writer takes a comparatively disparaging view
of Mr. Hope-Scott's manner of pleading; but this only
shows the coarse drawing which those who write for the
people often fall into, like artists whose pictures are to
be seen from a great distance. For convenience of
arrangement I make a transposition in the passage
which I now place before the reader.

Mr. Hope-Scott in pleading his cases has a peculiarly easy
style of speech, which can hardly be called oratory, because it
would be ridiculous to waste high oratory on a Railway or a
Waterworks Bill.   But he has an apparently inexhaustible flow
of language in every case he takes up, and every point of every
case.   He has little gesture, but is graceful in all his movements.   He fastens on every point, however small—not a single
feature escapes him ; and he covers it up so completely with a
cloud of specious but clever words, that a Parliamentary committee, composed as it is of private gentlemen, are almost
necessarily led captive, and compelled to view the point as
represented by him.   It was eminently so in the Amalgamation
case.   The specious excuses for unmitigated selfishness there
put forth were poured into the ears of the committee with such
an air of innocent candour, and with such a clever copiousness,
that the committee was, as it were, flooded and overwhelmed
by his quiet eloquence ; and though Mr. Denison with the
keen two-edged sword of his logic cut through and through
the watery flood in every case, it was just like cutting water,
which immediately closed the moment the instrument was
withdrawn.   I am not doing Mr. Scott injustice when I say
that in the Amalgamation case his tact was at least in as much
demand as his ability, and that for downright argument his
speeches could not for one moment be compared to those of
Mr. Denison.   But having a bad case to begin with, and
having to make a selfish arrangement between two railway
companies appear a great public advantage, he certainly, by his
quiet skilful touches, turned black into white before the committee with remarkable neatness.   His reply on the whole case
was another flood of rose-water eloquence, which rose gently
over all the points in Mr. Denison's speech, and concealed if
it did not remove them.   It was like the tide rising and cover-
ing a rock which could only be removed by blasting.   Mr.
Denison has the keen logical faculty which enables him to bore
his way through the hardest argument, and blast it remorse-
lessly and effectually as the gunpowder the rock.   Mr. Scott,
again, prefers to chip the face of the rock, to trim it into

K 2

shape, to cover it over with soil, and to conceal its hard and rocky appearance under the guise of a flower-garden, through which any one may walk. And with ordinary men this style of thing is very popular. I do not mean that Mr. Scott is incapable of higher things. Far from it. I believe that had he to plead before a judge few could be more logical and powerful than he ; but it is a remarkable evidence of the ' Scottishness ' of his character, if I may coin a phrase, that when he has to plead before a committee of private gentlemen who have to be 'managed,' he should deliberately select a lower style of treatment for his subjects.

From his birth and social position, his mixing with the noblest and best society in the land, and his versatility and quick perceptive powers, Mr. Hope-Scott is so thoroughly master of the art of pleasing that a committee cannot fail to be ingratiated by him ; and is certainly never offended, as he is gentlemanly and amiable to a fault. His temper is unruffled, and his speeches brimful of quick wit and humour ; and when a strong-minded committee has to decide against him, so much has he succeeded in ingratiating himself with them that it is almost with a feeling of personal pain the decision is given. I remember seeing the chairman of one of the committees look distinctly sheepish as he gave his decision against Mr. Scott, and could not help thinking how much humbug there was in this system of Parliamentary committees altogether.

Mr. Hope-Scott has had a great deal to do in regard to Dundee and district business in Parliament. He represented the Harbour Trustees when they obtained their original Act, and he has had a hand in forwarding or opposing most of the railways in the district. He was employed by Mr. Kerr at the formation of the Scottish Midland ; and I may mention that he was also employed in regard to the original Forfar and Laurence-kirk line. In his conduct of the latter case a characteristic incident occurred which shows the highly honourable nature

of the man.   It was at the time of the railway mania, when
fancy fees were being given to counsel, and when some counsel
were altogether exorbitant in their demands.   Mr. Hope-Scott
was to have replied on behalf of the Forfar and Laurencekirk
line, but intimated that he would not have time to do so, he
being engaged on some other case.   It was supposed, as fancy
fees were being freely offered to secure attendance, that Mr.
Scott was dissatisfied with his, and accordingly an extra fee of
150 guineas was sent to him along with a brief and a request
that he would appear and make the reply.   Mr. Scott sent
back the brief and the cheque to the agents, with a note stating
his regret that they should have supposed him capable of such
a thing, also stating that he feared he would not have time to
make the reply ; but requesting that Mr. Kerr, of Dundee,
should be asked to visit him and prepare him for the case, that
he might be able to plead it if he did find time.   This was done ;
he did find the time, he pleaded the case, but would not finger
the extra fee !   How different this conduct from that of some
of the notorious counsel of those days, who, after being engaged
in a case, sometimes stood out for their 1,000-guinea fees being
doubled before they would go on with it ![1] (' Dundee Advertiser,' July 2, 1866.)

6. *Dublin Trunk Connecting Railway.*—This was a
case of some interest in 1868 or 1869, when schemes
were in agitation for the connection of lines and the
construction of one great central station for Dublin.
Seven bills had been proposed, two of which their supporters had great hopes of carrying : the Dublin Trunk
Connecting line few had thought would pass, when Mr.
Hope-Scott went into the committee-room one afternoon, examined some witnesses, and made a speech

---

[1] I have heard of even a stronger case at that period than those alluded
to by this writer—of a brief of 300*l.* being returned by the counsel and agents
backwards and forwards till it reached 3,000*l.*

which carried all before it; and, to the astonishment of
all, the bill passed. The project, indeed, was never
realised, but all agreed that Mr. Hope-Scott's single
speech before the committee had snatched the affair
from the hands of all the other competing parties.

7. His professional services to his old College of
Eton in one important case (the *Public Schools Bill* of
1865) have already been more than once referred to.[2]
But he similarly assisted Eton on other occasions also.
One of these was a contest it had with the *Great Western
Railway Company* in 1848, and which did not termi-
nate in complete success; but his exertions (which were
gratuitous) called forth a most emphatic expression of
thanks in an address to him from the head-master (Dr.
Hawtrey) and from the whole body of the masters.
They say :—

> It would indeed have been impossible by any such payment
> to have diminished our debt. For we feel that you spoke as if
> you had a common interest in our cause, and the advocate was
> lost in the friend. Nothing was wanting in our defence which
> the most judicious eloquence, combined with the sincerest re-
> gard for Eton, could supply :—

> Si Pergama dextrâ
> Defendi possent, etiam hâc defensa fuissent.

> But if the great object of our wishes could not be obtained
> against opposition so powerful, restrictions have been imposed
> on the direction of the Great Western line, which would not
> have been granted but for the earnestness of your address to
> the committee; and whatever alleviations there may be to the
> evils which we expected, we shall owe them entirely to your
> advocacy.

---

[2] See vol. i. p. 17, and the present vol. ii. p. 115.

I have little to add to what has now been brought together, yet a few scraps may still interest the reader.

Mr. Hope's first general retainers (as already stated) date in 1844; but by the time he retired he was standing counsel to nearly every system of railways in the United Kingdom (*not*, however, to the Great Western, though he pleaded for them whenever he could—that is, when not opposed by other railways for which he was retained). With the London and North-Western he was an especial favourite. It is believed that on his retirement his general retainers amounted to nearly one hundred—an extraordinary number; among which are included those given by the Corporations of London, Edinburgh, Dublin, Liverpool, and others. There was, in fact, during his last years, constant wrangling among clients to secure his services. The cry always was 'Get Hope-Scott.' That there may have been jealousy on the part of some as to the distribution of time so precious, may easily be supposed. I find a hint of this in a book of much local interest, but which probably few of my readers have met with, 'The Larchfield Diary : Extracts from the Diary of the late Mr. Mewburn, First Railway Solicitor. London: Simpkin, Marshall, and Co. [1876].' Under the year 1861 Mr. Mewburn says (adding a tart comment) :—

The London and North-Western Railway Company had, in the session of 1860, twenty-five bills in Parliament, all which they gave to Hope-Scott as their leader, and he was paid fees amounting to 20,000*l.*, although he was rarely in the committee-room during the progress of the bills.—'Larchfield Diary,' p. 170.

As to this, it must be observed that the companies engaged Mr. Hope-Scott's services with the perfect knowledge beforehand that the demands on his time were such as to render it extremely doubtful whether he could afford more than a very small share of it to the given case. They wished for his name if nothing else could be had ; and, above all, to hinder its appearing on the opposite side. It was also felt that his powers were such, that a very little interference or suggestion on his part was very likely to effect all they wished. People said, 'If he can only give us ten minutes, it will *direct* us. We don't want the chief to draw his sword—he will win the battle with the glance of his eye.' In reference to one case I have described (No. 6) a client exclaimed, ' Even in ten minutes he put all to rights. We should have gone to pieces but for those ten minutes.' One is reminded of the exclamation of the old Highlander who had survived Killiecrankie : ' Oh, for one hour of Dundee ! ' With these facts before us, and the astonishing unanimity of the best informed witnesses, as to Mr. Hope-Scott's straightforwardness and high sense of honour, I think Mr. Mewburn's objection is sufficiently answered. A remark, however, may be added, which I find in an able article in the ' Scotsman ' (May 1, 1873): ' Often unable to attend the examination of minor witnesses, Mr. Hope-Scott nevertheless took care to possess himself of everything material in their evidence by careful reading of the short-hand writers' notes, and he always contrived to be at hand when the examination of an important witness might be expected to prove the turning-point in his case.'

The same writer goes on to say :—

Mr. Hope-Scott was not classed as a legal scholar, nor did his branch of the profession, which was the making, not the interpreting of laws, demand that accomplishment. His power lay, first, in a strong common sense and in a practical mind; next, in a degree of tact amounting to instinct, by which he seemed to read the minds of those before whom he was pleading, and steered his course and pitched his tone accordingly ; and lastly, in being in all respects a thorough gentleman, knowing how to deal with gentlemen. . . Though sincere and zealous in [religious] matters, Mr. Hope-Scott never, in his intercourse with the world and with men of hostile beliefs, showed the least drop of bitterness, or fell away in the smallest degree from that geniality of spirit which marked his whole character, and that courtesy of manner which made all intercourse with him, even in hard and anxious matters of business, a pleasure, not only for the moment, but for memory.

The following anecdote will serve to show that Mr. Hope-Scott was not a man to abuse the power which of course he well knew that he possessed, of ' making the worst seem the better cause.' Once when engaged in consultation with a certain great advocate, they both agreed that they had not a leg to stand upon. —— said that he would speak, and did deliver a speech which was anything but law. Mr. Hope-Scott being then called, bowed, and said that he had nothing to add to the speech of his learned friend. ' How could you leave me like that ? ' asked the other. ' You had already said,' replied Mr. Hope-Scott, ' that you had no case.'

In his latter years Mr. Hope-Scott was thought to have become rather imperious in his style of pleading before the Parliamentary committees : I mention this, not to pass over an impression which probably was but incidental.   Of an opposite and very beautiful trait see an example in Mr. Gladstone's 'Letter' (Appendix III.).

It is obvious that Mr. Hope-Scott's professional emoluments must have been, as I have already said in general, very great.   Notwithstanding his generosity and forbearance, it was no more possible for him, with his talents and surroundings, to avoid earning a splendid income than (as Clarendon says of the Duke of Buckingham) for a healthy man to sit in the sun and not grow warm.   Into the details of his professional success in this point of view I must refrain from entering. Although, considering the great historical interest of the era of ' the railway mania,' the question of the fees earned by a great advocate of that period can hardly be considered one of merely trivial curiosity, still, the etiquette and let me add the just etiquette, of the profession would forbid the use of information, without which no really satisfactory outline of this branch of my subject could be placed before the reader, least of all by a writer not himself a member of the profession. The popular notion of it must, I suppose, have appeared not infrequently in the newspapers of the day—an example may be found at p. 214 of this volume—and but very recently a similar guess appeared in a literary organ of more permanent character.   But to correct or to criticise such vague statements on more certain knowledge, even if I possessed it, is what can hardly be here expected.   Indeed, I ought rather to ask pardon for mistakes almost certainly incident to what I have already attempted.

In concluding the present subject I may remark that Mr. Hope-Scott's professional labours by no means represent the whole work of his life. Nominally, he was supposed to be free for about half the year, but in reality this vacant time was almost filled up by other work of a business nature undertaken out of kindness to friends or relations—precisely what the old Romans called *officia.* Such was the charge of the great Norfolk estates, and of the long-contested Shrewsbury property ;[3] such was another trust, on a considerable scale, for connections of his family in Yorkshire, involving, like the former, a great deal of travelling, for he was not satisfied with merely looking at things through other people's eyes. Such, too, his guardianship of his elder brother's eight children[4] for about ten years before his death ; and again, that of the eight children of his father-in-law the Duke of Norfolk. He discharged the same office for the family of Mr. Laing, solicitor at Jedburgh, a convert who died young,

[3] Bertram Talbot, last Earl of Shrewsbury of the Catholic branch, had bequeathed considerable property to Lord Edmund Howard (brother-in-law to Mr. Hope-Scott), on condition of his assuming the name of Talbot. His right to make this bequest was disputed by his successor, and a protracted litigation ensued in 1857 and the next few years, throughout which Mr. Hope-Scott acted as friend and adviser of the Howards, to whom he was guardian. The importance of this *cause célèbre* here consists chiefly in the self-sacrificing labours by which Mr. Hope-Scott succeeded in saving something for his relative out of the wreck, when to rescue the whole proved to be hopeless. I am not aware that it need be concealed that he had a very strong opinion against the justice of the decision.

[4] Mr. George W. Hope died on October 18, 1863—a great sorrow to Mr. Hope-Scott, to whom for years, in the earlier part of his career, his house had been a home, and who regarded him throughout with deep affection.

requesting Mr. Hope to protect the interest of his seven
children. The guardianship of the children of his old
legal tutor, Mr. Plunkett, may be added to the list.
And, on the top of all this, add a most voluminous
correspondence, in which his advice was required on
important subjects by important persons—and often on
subjects which were to them of importance, by very
much humbler persons too.

Of the spirit in which he laboured, the following
passage of a letter of his to Father (now Cardinal) Newman gives an idea. Like some other letters I have
quoted, it almost supplies the absence of a religious
diary of the period. It is an answer to a letter of Dr.
Newman's, presently to be given (p. 153).

J. R. Hope-Scott, Esq. Q.C. to the Very Rev. Dr. Newman.

Abbotsford, Melrose, N.B.: Dec. 30, 1857.

Dear Father Newman,— . . . And now a word about yourself. I do not like your croaking. You have done more in
your time than most men, and have never been idle. As to
the way in which you have done it I shall say nothing. You
may think you might have done it better. I remember that
you once told me that 'there was nothing we might not have
done better'—and this was to comfort me; and it did, for it
brought each particular failure under a general law of infirmity,
and so quieted while it humbled me. And then as to the
future : what is appointed for you to do you will have time
for—what is not, you need have no concern about. There! I
have written a sermon. Very impudent I know it is; but
when the mind gets out of joint a child may sometimes restore
it by telling us some simple thing which we perhaps have
taught it. Pat your child then on the head, and bid him go
to play, while you brace yourself up and work on, not as if you
must do some particular work *before* you die, but as if you

must do your best *till* you die. Alas! alas! how much could I say of my past, were I to compare it with yours! And my future—how shall I secure it better than you can yours? But I must not abuse the opportunity you have given me. We are all well here, D.G. My wife better than she has been for years . . . The little boy thriving to a wish. Next, Badeley —for he is of the family—in good health and heart. With all good wishes of this and every season.

Yours very aff^{ly},
JAMES R. HOPE-SCOTT.

The Very Rev. Dr. Newman, Birmingham.

CHAPTER XXIII.

1847-1858.

Mr. Hope's Engagement to Charlotte Lockhart—Memorial of Charlotte Lockhart—Their Marriage—Mr. Lockhart's Letter to Mr. J. R. Hope on his Conversion—Filial Piety of Mr. Hope—Conversion of Lord and Lady Henry Kerr—Domestic Life at Abbotsford—Visit of Dr. Newman to Abbotsford in 1852—Birth of Mary Monica Hope-Scott—Bishop Grant on Early Education—Mr. Lockhart's Home Correspondence—Death of Walter Lockhart Scott—Mr. Hope takes the Name of Hope-Scott—Last Illness and Death of Mr. Lockhart—Death of Lady Hope—Letter of Lord Dalhousie—Mr. Hope-Scott purchases a Highland Estate—Death of Mrs. Hope-Scott and her Two Infants—Letters of Mr. Hope-Scott, in his Affliction, to Dr. Newman and Mr. Gladstone—Verses in 1858—Letter of Dr. Newman on receiving them.

THIS biography here reaches the point where the history of Mr. Hope's marriage may fitly be placed before the reader. It was an event which, as I have already hinted, may very probably have been connected, like his eager pursuit of the Bar, with the break-down of his early ideas as to the Church of England. Yet, viewed merely in its worldly aspects, the step was one which could have caused no surprise, the time for it having fully arrived, as he was now thirty-five, in a conspicuous position in society, and making a splendid income. The lady of his choice was Charlotte Harriet Jane Lockhart, daughter of John Gibson Lockhart, and granddaughter of Sir Walter Scott. It was through Lady Davy that Mr. Hope had made Mr. Lockhart's acquaintance ; and thus what appeared a very meaningless episode in his juvenile years materially affected his destiny in life. In a letter of July 23, 1847, to his sister, Lady Henry Kerr, he speaks as follows of the important step in life he had decided upon, and of the character of his betrothed :—

I have for a long time contemplated the possibility of marrying, and had resolved that, all things considered, it might, under God's blessing, be the best course which I could pursue. It was not, however, till I had made acquaintance with Charlotte Lockhart that I was satisfied I should find a person who in all respects would suit me. This a general knowledge of her character (which is easily known) convinced me of, and I then proceeded rapidly, and, as far as I can judge, am not mistaken in my choice.

She is not yet twenty, but has lived much alone ; much also with people older than herself, and people of high mental cultivation. She has also had the discipline of depending on those habits of her father which are inseparable from a literary and, in some degree, secluded life. In short, she has had much to form her, and with great simplicity of character, and unbounded cheerfulness, she combines far more thought than is usual at her age. Having no mother and few connections, she is the more likely to become entirely one of us ; which I value, not only on my own account, but for the sake of my mother, to whom I am sure she will be a very daughter.

I have said more to you about her than I have written to any one else, for I distrust marriage puffs, and desire that people may judge for themselves. . . . You may be assured that I look upon marriage in a very serious light ; and I pray God heartily that it may be to us, whether in joy or sorrow, the means of mutual improvement, so that, when the account is rendered, each may show some good work done for the other.

Y^{rs} aff^{ly},

JAMES R. HOPE.

A little expedition which ensued on the engagement was long remembered as affording a very bright passage

in their lives. With Lady Davy as kind chaperon, Mr.
Hope and his betrothed visited his brother-in-law and
sister, Lord and Lady Henry Kerr, at the Rectory of
Dittisham, near Dartmouth, that the future sisters might
become acquainted. The exquisite beauty of the scenery
about the Dart, the splendour of the weather, and the
charm of the moment, altogether made this a time of
happiness not to be forgotten by any of those who
shared in it. To the outline conveyed in Mr. Hope's
letter I shall add a few traits obtained from other
sources, and thus complete, as far as possible, the image
they present. Charlotte Lockhart is described as a very
attractive person, with a graceful figure, a sweet and
expressive face, brown eyes of great brilliance, and a
beautifully shaped head : the chin indeed was heavy,
but even this added to the interest of the face by its
striking resemblance to the same feature in her great
ancestor, Sir Walter Scott. A dearly cherished portrait
of her at Abbotsford shows all that sweetness we should
expect, yet it is at the same time full of character and
decision. Her style of dress was marked by singular
simplicity ; and, unless to please her husband, or when
society required it, she rarely wore ornaments. She was
of a bright and cheerful nature, at first sight extremely
open, but with that reserve which so often shows itself,
on further acquaintance, in minds of unusual thoughtfulness and depth. There was something especially interesting in her manner—a mixture of shyness and diffi-
dence with self-reliance and decisiveness, quite peculiar
to herself. Her look, ' brimful of everything,' seemed
to win sympathy and to command respect. Without

marked accomplishments, unless that of singing most
sweetly, with a good taste and natural power that were
always evident, she had a passion for books, about
which, however, she was particularly silent, as she
dreaded anything like pretensions to literature. Her
talent and quickness made everything easy to her, and
she seemed to get through all she had to do with great
facility. But this was much assisted by an extraordinary gift of order and method, which enabled her,
without consulting her watch, to fix the instant when
the time had arrived, for example, for prayers, so that her
friends would say they felt sure she carried a clock in her
head. Punctual to a minute, she seemed never to lose
a moment. She governed herself by a rule of life,
drawn up for her by Bishop Grant (and afterwards by
Cardinal Manning), memoranda of which were found
in her Prayer-book. Notwithstanding ill-health, she almost always commenced her devotions, even if unable
to rise early, at six in the morning, and observed a perfect system in the round of her daily duties. She was
never idle, and nothing that might be called her recre-
ations was allowed to be decided by the wish of the
moment, but was all settled beforehand—the time to be
allotted, for instance, to a carriage drive, or to visiting.
Mr. Hope-Scott himself said of her, that if she lay down
on the sofa in the afternoon to enjoy a few hours of
Dante or Tasso, you might be sure that every note had
been answered, every account set down and carefully
backed up, every domestic matter thoroughly arranged.
As Lady Davy expressed it, 'she was a very busy
little housewife, putting order into every department.'

Of the usual lady's industry of needlework, plain or fancy, she got through an amazing quantity; but she was also, in her early years, of great use to her father, whose companion she had been in a literary life of great loneliness, by relieving him of much of his correspondence. The same diligent and endearing aid she afterwards rendered to her husband in all his harassing overwork. Her great love and admiration for him, combined with her own natural reserve, made her somewhat disinclined to go into society; and in his compulsory absences, at which she was never heard to murmur, she could be happy for weeks together, with her child, in a comparatively solitary life at Abbotsford. Yet she was also quite able to appreciate society, and is described by her friends as a delightful companion, hardly ever talking of herself, and always charitable in talking of others. Though placed in the state of riches, and having unlimited permission from her husband to spend as much as she pleased, she was notwithstanding never wasteful, but governed her household expenditure with the prudence of an upright and well-regulated mind, taking the greatest pains that all around her should have strict justice. She spent nothing needlessly upon herself, but gave largely, and in the most self-denying manner, for charitable purposes, especially the Orphanage under the Sisters at Norwood, which she appears to have constantly endeavoured to follow in spirit, making her inner life, as far as possible, that of a religious. She is remembered to have disposed of, for the sake of the Norwood Orphanage, a precious ornament, given her by her husband, which had belonged to the Empress Jose-

phine ; but a portion was reserved for a Lady altar in
the Church of St. Mary and St. Andrew, Galashiels.
When in London, it was her delight to visit St. George's
Hospital, where her attendance was efficient and regular,
so long as she was able to render it.

Mr. Hope and Charlotte Lockhart were married at
the parish church of Marylebone on August 19, 1847,
his brother-in-law, Lord Henry Kerr, officiating; and
after the wedding he took his bride to the Duke of
Buccleuch's house at Richmond, which had been lent to
them for the honeymoon. The autumn was spent at
Rankeillour, and the winter at Lady Hope's in Charles
Street.   In 1848 Mr. Hope rented Abbotsford from his
brother-in-law, Walter Lockhart Scott, and removed
thither in August of that year.   On the death of the
latter, in 1853, he became its possessor in right of his
wife, and for the remainder of his days made it his
principal residence.

Mr. Hope's conversion, as we have seen, took place
before Easter in 1851.   To his wife, the surrender of
united prayer (of all trials the severest on both sides)
was a sore distress : but the perception of truth is
always aided by consistency, at whatever sacrifice ; she
had read and thought much on the controversy, and by
Whitsuntide had followed her husband into the True
Fold.   Mr. Lockhart regarded his son-in-law's conversion as a grief and a humiliation ; but, nevertheless, the
nobleness of his nature, and the deep regard he always
felt for his virtue, prevailed without an effort.   His
letter on that occasion does himself as much honour as
it does to Mr. Hope.

J. G. Lockhart, Esq. to J. R. Hope, Esq. Q.C.

S[ussex] P[lace]: April 8, 1851.

My dear Hope,—I thank you sincerely for your kind letter. I had clung to the hope that you would not finally leave the Church of England; but am not so presumptuous as to say a word more on that step as respects yourself, who have not certainly assumed so heavy a responsibility without much study and reflection. As concerns others, I am thoroughly aware that they may count upon any mitigation which the purest intentions and the most generous and tender feelings on your part can bring. And I trust that this, the only part of your conduct that has given me pain, need not, now or ever, disturb the confidence in which it has of late been a principal consolation to me to live with my son-in-law.

Ever affectionately yours,

J. G. LOCKHART.

That incipient leaning to Catholicity which is so observable among the literary men of the later Georgian era, especially of the school of Sir Walter Scott, was probably not wanting in Mr. Lockhart. At Rome he seems to have chiefly lived among Catholics ; and quite in keeping with this view is an anecdote I have heard, of his observing to Mr. Hope, when once at Mayence they were watching the crowd streaming out of the cathedral, 'I must say this looks very like reality.' This was in the course of a visit they made to Germany in 1850, when Mrs. Hope was staying at Kreuznach for her health. As for Lady Hope, her decidedly Protestant principles caused her to feel profound distress when her son became a Catholic. She anxiously sought to know what Roman Catholics really believed, and whether they worshipped the Blessed Virgin or not.

Her son wrote her the following beautiful letter the Christmas Eve after his conversion:—

J. R. Hope, Esq. Q.C. to his Mother, the Hon. Lady Hope.

Abbotsford: Dec. 24, '51.

Dearest Mamma,— . . . Writing on Christmas Eve, I cannot forbear, dearest mamma, from wishing you the blessings of this season, although I feel that in doing so I must necessarily cause painful thoughts ; but amongst these, I trust, you will never admit any which imply that my love for you has diminished, or that I profess a religion which does not enforce and cherish the feelings of duty and affection which I owe to you. That I have often been wanting in my conduct towards you I well know and sincerely regret ; but I can safely say that you have been throughout my life, to me, as you are still, an object of love, respect, and gratitude such as I scarcely have elsewhere in the world. Take then, dearest mamma, your son's Christmas prayers. They are addressed to the God who gave you to me, and whom I thank heartily for the gift ; and if I believe that His will has been manifested otherwise than you see it in some things, remember that this does not extend to the precepts of love and charity, or alter one tittle of my obligation and desire to be and to show myself to be

Your most affect° Son,

JAMES R. HOPE.

In the course of 1853 Mr. Hope's brother-in-law and sister, Lord and Lady Henry Kerr, were received into the Catholic Church. They ultimately settled near Abbotsford, at Huntley-Burn, a name familiar to all who have read Lockhart's ' Life of Scott,' which afforded more frequent opportunities for the intimate and affectionate intercourse which existed between the families. Mr. Hope's other immediate relatives, however unable they might be to sympathise with his change, retained their love and admiration for him undiminished. Writing from Luffness to Mr. Badeley (Jan. 21, 1852), he says : 'Here there has been no controversy, it being agreed that we shall not *talk*. . . . We meet everywhere so much kindness now, that we can make no pretence to confessorship.' His life as a Catholic, now that he had once found anchorage in the faith, passed in unbroken peace of mind, in wonderful contrast to the storms of which we have been so long telling, that swept over him before he reached this haven.

The years immediately succeeding Mr. Hope's marriage with Charlotte Lockhart were probably the happiest of his life. He was then most buoyant, most in health, most himself, and at the height of his intellectual powers. His improving and practical hand was soon felt wherever he resided. He did much for Rankeillour, but for Abbotsford wonders. The place had been greatly neglected, the trees unthinned, and everything needing a restoration. He added a new wing to the house, formed a terrace, and constructed an ingenious arrangement of access by which the tourists might be admitted to satisfy their curiosity, while some sort of protection was afforded to the domestic privacy of the inmates.[1] What he did for the church I shall tell by-and-by.[2] At both Rankeillour and Abbotsford Mr. Hope maintained a graceful hospitality, in every way befitting his position. A letter which has been communicated to me from a lady (now a nun) who was on a

[1] Particulars of some of the improvements will be given later on. The new house at Abbotsford was begun about 1855, and completed and furnished in 1857.

[2] See chapter xxvi.

visit at Abbotsford during the autumn and winter of
1854, gives a very pleasing and distinct idea of the domestic life there during that brief period of happiness,
which, however (as we shall see presently), was already
chequered by sorrow destined in the Divine providence
to become yet deeper and sadder.   To this letter I am
indebted for the following particulars, which I have
ventured slightly to rearrange, yet keeping as closely as
possible to the words of the writer :—

The impression left by that most interesting and charming
family could never be effaced from my mind. It always
seemed to me the most perfect type of a really Christian
household, such as I never saw in the world before or since.
A religious atmosphere pervaded the whole house, and not only
the guests, but the servants must, it seems to me, have felt its
influence.   But, apart from that, there was so much genial hospitality, and every one was made to feel so completely at his ease.
Mr. Hope-Scott was the *beau idéal* of an English gentleman, and
a model Catholic devoted to the service of the Church, doing
all the good that lay in his power, far and near.   There was a
quiet dignity about him, and at the same time he was full of
gentle mirth, full of kindness and consideration for others;
and for every one with whom he came in contact, high and
low, rich and poor, there was a kind word or a generous act.

Among all the guests of this happy interval,[3] none
were more joyfully welcome than Dr. Newman, who
spent above five weeks at Abbotsford during the winter
of 1852–3, though a much longer visit had earnestly
been wished for by his kind host.   It was a visit memorable in many ways, and at a memorable time of
the Cardinal's life, the year of the first Achilli trial

---

[3] Lord and Lady Arundel and Surrey, Count Thun, Lady Davy,
Dowager Lady Lothian, Lord Traquair, Bishop Carruthers, Mr. Badeley, &c.

(this took place June 21–24), in which Mr. Hope, though not one of his advocates, had rendered the most efficient help to the illustrious defendant by his counsel and support. The Catholic University of Ireland, as will be seen from the following letter, was also then preparing, for which its first legislator had turned to Mr. Hope as among the most trusted of his advisers.

J. R. Hope, Esq. Q.C. to the Very Rev. Dr. Newman.

> 5 Calverly Terrace, Tunbridge Wells:
> October 23, '52.

Dear Newman,—I am much grieved by the account of your health which you send. Do, I entreat you, take *rest* at once—and by rest I understand, and I suspect your doctor means total removal from work and change of scene. We hope to go to Abbotsford early next month. We have a chapel in the house, but no chaplain. You would confer on us the GREATEST pleasure, and would at the same time secure your doctor's object, if you would come down there and spend with us the three or four months which will elapse before our return to town. You can say mass at your own hour, observe your own ways in everything, and feel all the time, I hope, perfectly at home. Do, pray, seriously think of this.

As to the University question which you put to me, I can give no references here; and I suspect my view is rather historical than in the way of strict definition. In England public teaching in the schools preceded all the colleges, and the latter provided the training which the university did not undertake. In Scotland and in most places abroad there are no colleges in our English sense, and public teaching is the essence of their systems. Perhaps by looking into A^{thy} Wood you may find passages to refer to, but I would rather rest upon the general statement of their origin. There are some derivations ascribed to the word *universitas* as relating to universal knowledge, but I doubt them. Wife and child well.

> Y^{rs} aff^{ly},
> JAMES R. HOPE.

I subjoin a few lines from Dr. Newman's answer to
this invitation (which at first he was unable to accept) :—

It would be a great pleasure to spend some time with you,
and then I have ever had the extremest sympathy for Walter—
Scott, that it would delight me to see his place. When he was
dying I was saying prayers (whatever they were worth) for
him continually, thinking of Keble's words, ' Think on the
minstrel as ye kneel.' (Dr. Newman to J. R. H. from Edg-
baston, Birmingham, Oct. 29, '52.)

Not less interesting is a letter in which he recalls this
visit, years after. Writing to Mr. Hope-Scott on Christmas Eve, 1857 [compare p. 140], Dr. Newman says :—

I am glad to call to mind and commemorate by a letter the
pleasant days I passed in the North this time five years. Five
years has a melancholy sound to me now, for it is like a passing
bell, knolling away time. I hope it is not wrong to say that
the passage of time is now sad to me as well as awful, because
it brings before me how much I ought to have done, how much
I have to do, and how little time I have to do it in. . . . I
wonder whether Badeley is with you ? What a strange thing
life is ! We see each other as through the peep-holes of a
show. When had I last a peep at him or you ?

At Abbotsford one blessing was still wanting to the
completion of domestic happiness. It may be assumed
that, after successes so brilliant, Mr. Hope could not but
desire to found a family which should continue, in his
own line, names so famous as those which he inherited
and represented ; but this was long withheld. His first
child, a boy, was still-born (1848) ; the next, after an
interval of four years (October 2, 1852, Feast of the
Guardian Angels), was a daughter, Mary Monica (now
the Hon. Mrs. Maxwell-Scott), named after a favourite

saint of his ; and several years more elapsed before the birth of another son. A passage from one of Bishop Grant's letters to Mr. Hope will be read with interest at this point, both for the characteristic piety and for the intimacy of their friendship to which it witnesses :—

The Right Rev. Dr. Grant, Bishop of Southwark, to
J. R. Hope, Esq. Q.C.

Dec. 10, 1852.

My dear Mr. Hope,— . . . As you will have more opportunities at Abbotsford than you will perhaps find in London, it may be well to tell you that the Italian nurses begin, almost before children know how to use their eyes, to make them notice prints or statues of Our Dear Mother and of the Saints. This helps their imagination, such as it is ; and, after all, when we know how some babes notice their parents and nurses, there is every reason why we should accustom them to notice holy things. And, as they begin to talk, it is right to follow the rule which St. Augustine says his mother had, of constantly letting the Sacred Names drop, so that the great Doctor says she completely destroyed his relish for all oratory from which those sweet names were absent.

May the blessings of Christmas fall abundantly on all at Abbotsford !

Yours very affectionately,

†THOMAS GRANT.

Mr. Hope's domestic circle at this time included Mr. Lockhart, who, though not yet a very old man, was verging towards the close of a literary life of great toil. He was much with his son-in-law and daughter in Scotland and in London, and they sometimes stayed with him in Sussex Place. At length he had his books taken down to Abbotsford, where they still are, in a room called the Lockhart Library. When absent, he wrote almost daily either to his daughter or to Mr. Hope ; and the collection of his letters, still preserved, affords a most amusing record, sparkling with genial sarcasm, of whatever was going on around him in London society. There is endless talk and incident, floating in that society, which never finds its way into print, or not till after the lapse of many years ; and such is precisely the material of this home correspondence of Mr. Lockhart's. It would be perhaps difficult to name letters with which they can be accurately classed. I do not forget Horace Walpole, and Swift's 'Journal to Stella.' But Lockhart's wit was more playful and more natural. The great charm of his letters is, that he thought, so far, of nothing but simply to relate what was likely to amuse his daughter, whether the matter in itself was of the least consequence or not. Such, however, were not the only topics of which he had to tell. Mr. Lockhart, who, with his somewhat haughty self-possession, might have been described, as the late Lord Aberdeen was, by one who knew him well, as ' possessing a heart of fire in a form of ice,' had yet a deeply felt but secret sorrow, with which even his resolution could hardly cope. If I do not disguise that for years he had much to vex him in the wild ways of a son whom he yet never ceased to love, it is only because otherwise I could convey little idea of the unreserved manner in which that lofty spirit could turn for consolation, in letter after letter, to Mr. Hope, or to his daughter, never failing to find all the comfort with which a wise head and a kind heart can reward a confidence so pathetic.

M^r. Hope's conduct, all through these trials, was indeed forbearing and generous to such a degree as would make it a great example to all who have to sustain crosses of that kind. But enough, perhaps, has been said on the subject. In 1848 a severe illness of his brother-in-law at Norwich afforded another of those occasions in which he displayed that zeal and helpful ness in ministering to the sick, of which there are so many instances in his life, Walter Lockhart Scott died at Versailles on January 10, 1853.[4] Mr. Hope then assumed the name of Hope-Scott, by which I shall henceforth speak of him. It was on the occasion of her brother's death that Bishop Grant addressed the follow ing beautiful letter to Mrs. Hope-Scott :—

The Right Rev. Dr. Grant, Bishop of Southwark, to Mrs. Hope-Scott.

January 20 [1853].

My dear Mrs. Hope,—Although there is no artistic merit in the enclosed, I hope you will allow me to send it on account of the meditation which it suggests, how Our dear Lord had the thought of His sufferings present to His mind in early child-hood—indeed, from the first moment of His earthly existence. This thought may help to strengthen us when we reflect that He has not given us the foretaste of our sorrow, but has allowed us to grow up without any anticipation of distinct sorrow and suffering ; and, for the first years, without any thought of their coming at all. When affliction comes at last in all its real bitterness, we can lighten it by uniting it to His sorrow, and by asking Him to remember His promise of making it easy to us.

---

[4] Walter Lockhart Scott and Charlotte (wife of Mr. Hope-Scott) were the last survivors of the children of Mr. Lockhart and Sophia, daughter of Sir Walter Scott. The eldest son, though very short-lived, is well remembered as ' Hugh Littlejohn,' to whom the *Tales of a Grandfather* were dedicated.

I should not have troubled you so soon if it had not occurred to me that the days which follow the announcement of a
cause of grief are often more trying than the commencement
of them, and that during them the need of consolation may be
more felt.

I do not know why I should intrude my poor sympathy
upon you, but when we have shared in joy it seems ungrateful
not to be willing to have a part in sadness, and therefore I
hope you will excuse me. . . .

Yours very respectfully,

† THOMAS GRANT.

Mr. Lockhart never got over the death of his last-
remaining son. His health began to fail; he went to
Rome for change of climate; came back worse, and soon
after went down to his half-brother's at Milton-Lock-
hart. Thither Mr. and Mrs. Hope-Scott went to see
him, and entreated him to come to Abbotsford. He at
first decidedly refused, and his will was a strong one;
but some time after, when the house was full of Catholic
guests, he suddenly announced that he wished to go immediately to Abbotsford. He arrived there, hardly able
to get out of his carriage, and it was at once perceived
that he was a dying man. He desired to drive about
and take leave of various places, displaying, however,
a sort of stoical fortitude, and never making a direct
allusion to what was impending. To save him fatigue,
it was important he should have his room near the
library, but he shrank from accepting the dining-room
(where Sir Walter Scott had died), and it required all
Mr. Hope-Scott's peculiar tact and kindness to induce
him to establish himself in the breakfast-room close by.
There he remained until the end. Yet he would not

suffer any one to nurse him, till, one night, he fell down
on the floor, and, after that, offered no further opposition.   Father Lockhart, a distant cousin, was now
telegraphed for, from whom, during Mr. Lockhart's stay
in Rome, he had received much kind attention, for
which he was always grateful. He did not object to
his kinsman's presence, though a priest; and yielded
also when asked to allow his daughter to say a few
prayers by his bedside.   Mr. Hope-Scott, in the meantime, was absent on business, but returned home one or
two days before the end, which came suddenly.   He
and Mrs. Hope-Scott were quickly called in, and found
Miss   Lockhart   (affectionately   called   in   the   family
'Cousin Kate') reading the prayers for the dying.   Mr.
Lockhart died on November 25, 1854, and was buried
at Dryburgh Abbey, beside his father-in-law, Sir Walter
Scott.   The insertion of these particulars, which are of
personal interest to many of my readers, will perhaps
be justified by their close association with the subject of
this memoir.

After little more than a twelvemonth Mr. Hope-
Scott had the sorrow to lose his mother.   Lady Hope
died rather suddenly on December 1, 1855, in consequence, it was thought, of injuries she had sustained
from an accidental fall in the Crystal Palace a few days
before.   In writing to acquaint Mr. Gladstone with this
sad event (December 4)[5] Mr. Hope-Scott says :—

To you and Mrs. Gladstone, who knew her, I may confi-
dently say that I believe a kinder, more generous and self-

[5] Lady Frances Hope also died within a week after, on December 6,
1855.

denying nature has seldom existed. To us, her children, her life has been one of overflowing affection and care; but many, many besides her immediate relations have known her almost as a mother, and will feel the closing of her house as if they had lost a home.

The following letter, written from India on the same occasion, is in every way deeply interesting :—

The Marquis of Dalhousie to G. W. Hope, Esq.

Gov^t House : Feb. 6, 1856.

It was very kind of you, my dear George, to think of me, far away, when your heart must have been so sore. But, indeed, your kindness was not thrown away, or your considerate thoughtfulness misplaced.

Even Jim and yourself have not grieved with more heartfelt sorrow for that dear life that has been lost than I have in my banishment.

Thirty years have gone since your mother began to show to me the tenderness of an *own* mother. I loved her dearly—she loved me, and loved what I loved. In the prospect of a return which has few charms for me, the thought of finding Lady Hope good, kind, gracious, motherly, as she always was for me, was one of the few thoughts on which I dwelt, and to which I returned with real pleasure, and now it is all gone; and you would think it exaggerated if I said how deeply it depresses me to feel that it is so.

Give my love to Jim, and to your sister too. I see her boy goes to Madras. I had hoped to see him here, if only for a week.

In three weeks I am deposed. I have no wish to see England; but nevertheless I am, dear George,

Yours most sincerely,

DALHOUSIE.

The winter which followed Mr. Lockhart's death at Abbotsford was a mournful one. Mrs. Hope-Scott had been deeply attached to her father. She had shared his griefs, as we have seen. Her earlier years had been somewhat lonely; her disposition, with all its reserve, was excessively sensitive and excitable, and a change of scene had doubtless begun to be felt necessary, when Mr. Hope-Scott bought a Highland estate, situated at Lochshiel, on the west coast of Inverness-shire, north of Loch Sunart, and nearly opposite Skye. The history of the purchase of this property, and of all that Mr. Hope-Scott did for it as a Catholic proprietor, is very interesting and curious, but involves so much detail, that I reserve most of it for a future chapter. He built a residence there, Dorlin House, a massive, com·fortable mansion, practically of his own designing, abounding in long corridors, to enable the ladies and children to have exercise under shelter in the rainy Highland climate, and various little contrivances showing that few things were too minute for his attention. Here, as everywhere, he used a kindly and noble hospitality. Much of the charm of the place consisted in its remoteness and solitude, which caused just sufficient difficulty in obtaining supplies to afford matter of amusement. The post also came in and out only three times a week, and the nearest doctor was twelve miles off. All this, however, is now considerably changed by the greater vicinity of railways. A few lines from a letter of Mr. Hope-Scott's to Dr. Newman, dated 'Lochshiel, Strontian, N B., September 25, 1856,' will give a better notion of its surroundings than I can offer:—

We are here on the sea-shore, with wild rocks, lakes, and rivers near us, an aboriginal Catholic population, a priest in the house, and a chapel within 100 yards. We hope Badeley may turn up to-day, but are in doubt whether he will be as happy here as in Paper Buildings. The first necessaries of life sometimes threaten to fail us, and we have to lay in stores as if we were going on a voyage. At this moment we are in doubt about a cargo of flour from Glasgow, and our coal-ship has been long due. What Badeley will say to oat-cakes and turf fires remains to be seen.

On Christmas Eve of the following year (1857) Dr. Newman writes to Mr. Hope-Scott, in a letter I have already quoted from (p. 153) :—

I was rejoiced to hear so good an account of your health, and of all your party. I suppose you are full of plans about your new property and your old. Your sister tells me you have got into your new wing at Abbotsford. As for the far-away region of which I have not yet learned the name, I suppose you are building there either a fortress against evil times, or a new town and port for happy times. Have you yet found gold on your estate? for that seems the fashion.

Mr. Hope-Scott did not indeed find gold at Dorlin, but he spent a great deal over it, which he was some-times tempted to regret; but, on the whole, thought that the outlay had been devoted to legitimate objects, and that, as an experiment, it had succeeded. He built two chapels on this property, at Mingarry (Our Lady of the Angels) and at Glenuig (St. Agnes); and his letters are full of unconscious proof how the interests of Catho-licity were always in his mind. A long wished-for event had lately thrown a bright gleam of sunshine over the house. On June 2, 1857, Mrs. Hope-Scott gave birth to a son and heir, Walter Michael, which was cause of rejoicing, not only to the whole Scottish nation, but wherever the English language is spoken, as promise of the continuance of the name and the line of Scotland's

greatest literary glory. And, to complete the circle of
happiness, on September 17 of the following year, 1858,
was born also a daughter, Margaret Anne. Three
months after this had scarcely passed, when the mother
and both her infants were no more.

Mrs. Hope-Scott had never really recovered from
her first confinement. In the spring of 1858 she had
had a severe attack of influenza, and consumptive
symptoms, though not called by that name, came on.
Towards the end of October arrangements had been
made to take her to the Isle of Wight for the winter,
but she never got further on her journey than Edinburgh. When she called, a day or two after her arrival
there, on the Bishop, Dr. Gillis, he said to himself,
' Ah ! *you* have been travelling by express train ! ' Very
soon after this, bronchitis set in, and rapidly became
acute, and the case was pronounced hopeless. To herself, indeed, it was perhaps more or less sudden, though
she had virtually made a retreat of preparation during
the preceding six months, and left everything in the most
perfect order at Abbotsford. She had said to ' Cousin
Kate ' (Miss Lockhart) that God had been very merciful
to her in sending her a lingering illness ; yet, on the last
night, was heard to say, ' Hard to part—Jim—Mamo [6]—
God's will be done.' She accepted her death as God's
will. On being told of its approach, and after receiving
the last sacraments, she said, ' I have no fear now.'
Bishop Gillis gave her the last absolution, Fr. Noble,
one of the Oblate Fathers from Galashiels, assisting. Her
husband's disposition never allowed him to believe in
misfortune till it had really come, and, almost up to the

[6] Mamo: an affectionate abbreviation for Mary Monica.

last hour, he had failed to see what was plain to all other eyes; the parting, therefore, with him and with her little daughter Mamo (who could scarcely be torn from her) was sad beyond expression. The end came rapidly. She died on Tuesday, October 26, and on December 3 her baby daughter, Margaret Anne; and on December 11 the little boy, whose birth had caused such gladness. All three were buried in the vault of St. Margaret's Convent, Edinburgh; the mother on November 2 (All Souls' Day), her two children on December 10 and 17, 1858. Bishop Gillis spoke on November 2 and December 10, but his addresses were unwritten; Dr. Grant, Bishop of Southwark, on December 17. His address, and a beautiful one indeed it is, has fortunately been preserved.

Of three short letters, in which Mr. Hope-Scott had told Dr. Newman of each sorrow as it came, I transcribe the last :—

J. R. Hope-Scott, Esq. Q.C. to the Very Rev. Dr. Newman.

14 Curzon S^t, London, W.:
Dec. 11, 1858.

Dear Father Newman,—My intention, for which you so kindly said mass, has been fulfilled, for it was, as well as I could form it, that God should deal with my child as would be most for His honour and its happiness, and this afternoon He has answered my prayer by calling little Walter to Himself.

I rely upon you to pray much for me. It may yet be that other sacrifices will be required, and I may need more strength; but what I chiefly fear is that I may not profit as I ought by that wonderful union of trial and consolation which God has of late vouchsafed me.

Y^{rs} most aff^{ly},
JAMES R. HOPE-SCOTT.

The Very Rev. Dr. Newman.

On his wife's death Mr. Hope-Scott had written the following letter to Mr. Gladstone:—

J. R. Hope-Scott, Esq. Q.C. to the Right Hon.
W. E. Gladstone, M.P.

Abbotsford: Nov. 3, 1858.

My dear Gladstone,—I was uneasy at not having written to you, and hoped you would write—which you have done, and I thank you much for it. An occasion like this passed by is a loss to friendship, but it was not, nor is, easy for me to write to you. You will remember that the root of our friendship, which I trust [was] the deepest, was fed by a common interest in religion, and I cannot write to you of her whom it has pleased God to take from me without reference to that Church whose doctrines and promises she had embraced with a faith which made them like objects of sense to her; whose teaching had moulded her mind and heart; whose spiritual blessings surrounded and still surround her, and which has shed upon her death a sweetness which makes me linger upon it more dearly than upon any part of our united and happy life.

These things I could not pass over without ignoring the foundation of our friendship; but still I feel that to mention them has something intrusive, something which it may be painful for you to read, as though it required an answer which you had rather not give. So I will say only one thing more, and it is this: If ever, in the strife of politics and religious controversy, you are tempted to think or speak hardly of that Church—if she should appear to you arrogant, or exclusive, or formal, for my dear Charlotte's sake and mine check that thought, if only for an instant, and remember with what exceeding care and love she tends her children. . . .

And now good-bye, my dear Gladstone. Forgive me every word which you had rather I had not said. May God long preserve to you and your wife that happiness which you now have in each other! and when it pleases Him that either

of you should have to mourn the other, may He be as merciful
to you as He has been to me!

Y^{rs} affect^{ly},

JAMES R. HOPE-SCOTT.

And now Mr. Hope-Scott was left alone in Abbotsford, with his only surviving child, a very fragile and
delicate flower too, such as to make a father tremble
while he kissed it. We have already seen[7] that he
could resort sometimes to poetry as that comfort for the
over-burdened mind, in which Keble's theory would
place even the principal source of the poetical spirit.[8]
As every reader will sympathise with such expressions
of feeling, I do not hesitate to transcribe some touching
verses which he wrote at this season of sorrow, and
which, with a few others, he had privately printed, and
given in his lifetime to two or three of his very closest
friends. These others will be found in the appendix.[9]

Sancta Mater, istud agas,
Crucifixi fige plagas,
Cordi meo validè.

CHRISTMAS, 1858.

MY babes, why were you born,
Since in life's early morn
Death overtook you, and, before
I could half love you, you were mine no more?

Walter, my own bright boy,
Hailed as the hope and joy
Of those who told thy grandsire's fame,
And looking, loved thee, even for thy name;

[7] See pp. 44, 45, ch. ii. in vol. i.
[8] Keble, *Prælectiones Academicæ*, Oxon. 1844. Præl. i. t. i. p. 10.
[9] Appendix IV.

And thou, my Margaret dear,
Come as if sent to cheer
A widowed heart, ye both have fled,
And, life scarce tasted, lie among the dead !

Then, oh ! why were you born ?
Was it to make forlorn
A father who had happier been
If your sweet infant smiles he ne'er had seen ?

Was it for this you came ?
Dare I for you to blame
The God who gave and took again,
As though my joy was sent but to increase my pain ?

Oh no ! of Christmas bells
The cheerful music tells
Why you were born, and why you died,
And for my doubting doth me gently chide.

The infant Christ, who lay
On Mary's breast to-day,
Was He not born for you to die,
And you to bear your Saviour company ?

Then stay not by the grave,
My heart, but up, and crave
Leave to rejoice, and hear the song
Of infant Jesus and His happy throng.

That wondrous throng, on earth
So feeble from its birth,
Which little thought, and little knew,
Now hath both God and man within its view !

Yes, you were born to die ;
Then shall I grudging sigh
Because to you are sooner given
The crown, the palm, the angel joy of heaven ?

Rather, O Lord, bestow
On me the grace to bow,
Childlike, to Thee, and since above
Thou keep'st my treasures, there to keep my love.

It is scarcely necessary to say that one of the friends to whom Mr. Hope-Scott sent these verses on his family losses of 1858 was Dr. Newman. The note in which his friend acknowledged the precious gift witnesses to the intimacy of their friendship in as striking a manner as any I have been enabled to make use of :—

The Very Rev. Dr. Newman to J. R. Hope-Scott, Esq. Q.C.

The Oratory, Birmingham :
October 1, 1860.

My dear Hope-Scott,—I value extremely the present you have made me ; first of all for its own sake, as deepening, by the view which it gives me of yourself, the affection and the reverence which I feel towards you.

And next I feel your kindness in thus letting me see your intimate thoughts ; and I rejoice to know that, in spite of our being so divided one from another, as I certainly do not forget you, so you are not unmindful of me.

The march of time is very solemn now—the year seems strewn with losses ; and to hear from you is like hearing the voice of a friend on a field of battle.

I am surprised to find you in London now. For myself, I have not quitted this place, or seen London, since last May year, when I was there for a few hours, and called on Badeley.

If he is in town, say to him everything kind from me when you see him.

Ever yours affect.^{ly},
JOHN H. NEWMAN,
Of the Oratory.

James R. Hope-Scott, Esq.

CHAPTER XXIV.

1859–1870.

Mr. Hope-Scott's Return to his Profession — Second Marriage — Lady Victoria Howard—Mr. Hope-Scott at Hyères—Portraits of Mr. Hope-Scott—Miscellaneous Recollections—Mr. Hope-Scott in the Highlands—Ways of Building--Story of Second-sight at Lochshiel.

THE last of the poems in the little collection which is elsewhere given, evidently belongs to a time when Mr. Hope-Scott had regained his tranquillity, and was about to resume, like a wise and brave man, the ordinary duties of his profession. After his great affliction he had interrupted them for a whole year, first staying for some time at Arundel Castle, and then residing at Tours with his brother-in-law and sister, Lord and Lady Henry Kerr. To those readers who expect that every life which approaches in any way an exalted and ideal type must necessarily conform to the rules of romance, it may appear strange that Mr. Hope-Scott did not remain a widower for any great length of time. But in truth the same motives which led him to return to the Bar, notwithstanding the overwhelming calamity he had sustained, might also have led him again to enter the married state ; or rather, if under other circumstances he would have thought it right to do so, would not have interposed any insuperable obstacle against it now.

Mr. Hope-Scott, soon after his conversion, had become acquainted with Henry Granville, Earl of Arundel and Surrey, afterwards Duke of Norfolk. They were much in each other's society at Tunbridge Wells, where, on October 2, 1852, was born Mr. Hope-Scott's daughter Mary Monica (now the Hon. Mrs. Maxwell-Scott), at whose baptism Lady Arundel and Surrey acted as proxy for the Dowager Lady Lothian. But the acquaintance had developed into a most intimate and confidential friendship at a much earlier date, and this had now become still closer, from the fear which was beginning to be felt that the Duke's life, so precious to his family and to the Catholic world in general, was fast drawing to its early termination. To the Duke, therefore, and to his family, it was but natural for Mr. Hope-Scott to turn for comfort in his extreme need. In such times sympathy soon deepens into affection, and thus it was that an attachment sprang up between Mr. Hope-Scott and the Duke's eldest daughter, Lady Victoria Fitzalan Howard. This was towards the end of 1860. The Duke was then in his last illness, and on November 12 in that year the betrothed pair knelt at his bedside to receive his blessing. He died on November 25.

Although a notice of great interest might be drawn up from materials before me of Lady Victoria herself, and of the sweetness of character and holiness of life which so much endeared her to all with whom she was connected; yet the time of her departure is still so recent, that I shall better consult the feelings and the wishes of surviving friends by merely placing before my readers one passage from a letter relating to her. The writer was a nun intimately acquainted with her, and describes with great truth and simplicity the graces which especially adorned her: 'She was a person to be observed and studied ; and I do not think . . . I ever saw her without studying her, and consequently without my admiration for her increasing. She was so unworldly, so forgetful of self, and, what always struck me most, so humble, and striving to screen herself from praise ; and humility and self-forgetfulness like what she practised, these are the virtues of saints, and not of ordinary people.'

The marriage of Mr. Hope-Scott and Lady Victoria Howard was solemnised at Arundel on January 7, 1861, and this too, it is needless to add, proved a very happy union, though on the side of affliction, in the loss of two infants, and in Lady Victoria's early death, it strangely resembled the first marriage. Of twin daughters born June 6, 1862, Catherine and Minna-Margaret, the first lived for but a few hours.[1] There are, however, many days of sunshine still to record. Abbotsford and Dorlin, as before, were the chief retreats in which Mr. Hope-Scott found repose from the toil and harass of his professional life. At Arundel Castle and Norfolk House he and his family were, of course, frequent guests. From 1859 it was thought necessary that the surviving child of his first marriage should spend every winter in a warm climate. Hyères, in the south of France, was selected for this purpose, which

---

[1] Two more daughters, Josephine Mary (born May 1864) and Theresa Anne (born September 14, 1865), were born before (again, as it were, but for an instant) a son was granted ; this was Philip James (born April 8, 1868), but who lived only till the next day. He was placed beside his sister Catherine in the castle vault at Arundel. Mr. Hope-Scott's last and only surviving son is James Fitzalan Hope, born December 11, 1870.

led to Mr. Hope-Scott's purchasing a property there, the Villa Madoña, on a beautiful spot near the Boulevard d'Orient. Here he spent several winters with his family, in the years 1863–70. He added to the property very gradually, bit by bit; first a vineyard, and then an oliveyard, as opportunities offered, and indulged over it the same passion for improvement which he had displayed at Abbotsford and Dorlin. He took the most practical interest in all the culture that makes up a Provençal farm, the wine, the oil, the almonds, the figs, not forgetting the fowls and the rabbits. He laid out the ground and made a road, set a plantation of pines, and adorned the bank of his boulevard with aloes and yuccas and eucalyptus—in short, astonished his French neighbours by his perfection of taste and regardlessness of expense. He did not, however, build more than a bailiff's cottage in the first instance, but rented the Villa Favart in the neighbourhood, and amused himself with his estate, intending it for his daughter's residence in future years. At his death, however, the French law requiring the estate to be shared, it was found necessary to sell it. He greatly enjoyed the repose of Hyères, the strolls on the boulevard, and the occasional excursions that charming watering-place affords—Pierrefeu, for example, and all the beautiful belt of coast region extending between Hyères and the Presqu'île. He was also able to enter more into society at Hyères than latterly his health and business had permitted in London. One of his oldest and most valued friends, the late Mr. Serjeant Bellasis, had taken the Villa Sainte-Cécile in his neighbourhood, and there was a circle of the best French families in and around Hyères, whose names must not be omitted when we speak of Mr. Hope-Scott's and Lady Victoria's annual sojourn in the little capital of the Hesperides. Among these was the late Duc de Luynes, so well known for his researches into the hydrography of the Dead Sea, Count Poniatowski, Madame Du Quesne, M. de Boutiny, Maire of Hyères, M. and Madame de Walmer, and others. Cardinal Newman has noticed, what appears also in the correspondence, to how surprising a degree Mr. Hope-Scott was consulted by his French neighbours, even in affairs belonging to their own law. Whenever there was a difficulty, a sort of instinct led people to turn to him for counsel.

As it was at Hyères that I first became acquainted with Mr. Hope-Scott, I may introduce into this chapter, perhaps as conveniently as anywhere, such personal recollections of him as I can call to mind. They are much more scanty than I could wish ; still, where the memorials to be collected from any sources are but few, and rapidly passing away, surviving friends may be glad of the preservation of even these slight notices.

In 1864–5 I had the honour of being entrusted with the tuition of Henry, Duke of Norfolk, and, as the Duke spent that winter with his relatives at Hyères, I had several opportunities of conversing with Mr. Hope-Scott in his domestic circle, as on other occasions afterwards.

Mr. Hope-Scott was then in his fifty-third year. He was tall, largely built, with massive head, dark hair beginning to turn grey, sanguine, embrowned complexion, very dark eyes, fine, soft, yet penetrating. ' *Quel bel homme! quel homme magnifique!*' the French would exclaim in talking of him. In his features might be remarked that indefinable expression which belongs to the practised advocate. He had an exceedingly winning smile, an harmonious voice, and deliberate utterance. His manners, I need hardly say, showed all that simplicity and perfection of good breeding which art may simulate, but can never completely attain to.

I am not aware that there is any likeness of Mr. Hope-Scott in his later years. There is an excellent one of him about the age of thirty-two, a head, life-size, drawn in crayon by Richmond for Lady Davy, and now at Abbotsford, of which an engraving was published by Colnaghi. It is supposed to represent his expression when pleading. Mr. Lockhart, writing to Mrs. Hope-Scott on August 29, 1850, says : ' I called yesterday at Mr. Richmond's to inspect his picture of J. R. H., and was extremely pleased—a capital likeness, and a most graceful one. . . . I am at a loss to say whether I think Grant or he has been most lucky—and they are very different too.' Mr. Richmond drew in crayon, previously to 1847, one for Lady Frances Hope, subsequently given to the Hon. Mrs. G. W. Hope, and another in water-colours, a small half-length, for Mr. Badeley, after whose decease it was given by Mr. Hope to the Dowager Duchess of Norfolk. There was also a small life-portrait, done after his marriage by Mr. Frank Grant, but not thought so pleasing a likeness as Richmond's. There

is a good bust by Noble at Abbotsford, but this was
made after his death, by study of casts, &c.   It might
express the age of about thirty-five or forty.

In his hospitality Mr. Hope-Scott showed great kindness and thoughtfulness.   One day, for example, he
would invite to dinner the curé of Hyères and his
clergy ; on another occasion, a young lady having become engaged, a party must be given in her honour ;
or an English prelate passes Hyères on his way home,
and must be entertained.   He was very attentive to
guests, took pains to make people feel at their ease, and
dispensed with unnecessary formality, but not with such
usages as have their motive in a courteous consideration
for others.   Thus, when there were French guests, he
was particular in exacting the observance of the rule
that the English present should talk to each other, as
well as to the strangers, in French.   He had a thorough
colloquial knowledge of the French language, marked
not so much by any French mannerism, of which there
was little, as by a ready command of the vocabulary of
special subjects—for instance, agriculture.

In society Mr. Hope-Scott's table-talk was highly
agreeable.   There was, however, a certain air of languor
about him, caused partly by failing health, but far
more, no doubt, by that ' softened remembrance of
sorrow and pain ' which my readers can by this time
understand better than any of those who then surrounded him.   His conversation, therefore, when the
duty of entertaining his guests did not require him to
exert himself, was liable to lapse into silence.   Some
people seem to think it a duty to break a dead silence

at any price ; but this, in Mr. Hope Scott's opinion, was not always to be followed as a rule of etiquette ; so, at least, I have heard.

I cannot remember that he showed any great interest in politics. He told me that he seldom read the leading articles of the 'Times,' which he thought had little influence on public events. I can, however, recall an interesting conversation on the social state of France, of which he took a very melancholy view ; and again, in 1870, when he pronounced decisively against the chances of the permanent establishment of the Commune, on the ground of the total change in the condition of Europe since the Middle Ages—the old Italian republics having been alleged in favour of the former.

His conversation seldom turned upon general literature, and at the time I knew him he had given up the 'bibliomania.' His favourite line of reading, for his own amusement, seemed to be glossaries, such as those of the Provençal dialect, and the archæology of Hyères, on which a friend of his, the late M. Denis, had written an interesting volume. Le Play's elaborate treatise, 'La Réforme Sociale,' strongly attracted his attention. He was fond of statistical works, such as the 'Annuaire du Bureau des Longitudes,' a little compilation bristling with facts. He greatly cherished, as might be expected, the memory of Sir Walter Scott ; and, had his life been prolonged, would probably have done more for it than the republication of the abridgment of Lockhart's Life. I recollect his mentioning that there were in his hands unpublished MSS. of Sir Walter's which would

furnish materials for a volume.[2] 'What he chiefly
valued in the character of Sir Walter Scott (remarks a
correspondent) was his *manliness*. I noticed that when
Sir Walter was praised, Mr. Hope-Scott always spoke of
his manliness.' These observations may somewhat
qualify the impression of an intimate friend of his
later years, by whom I have been told that Mr. Hope-
Scott ' hardly opened a book, read scarcely at all,
though he seemed to know about books.' He certainly
could not, in the ordinary sense of the word, be called
a literary man; but the active part of his life was far
too busy for study, unless study had been a passion
with him; and towards its close the state of his health
made reading impossible.

Mr. Hope-Scott very rarely made mention of himself, and his conversation accordingly supplied little or
no biographical incident. Yet I have heard him allude,
more than once, to his intimacy with Mr. Gladstone.
' They had been,' he said, ' like brothers; ' and he spoke
also with pleasure of visits to the house of Sir John
Gladstone, from whom he thought the Premier had
derived much of his *back*.

Everything that I saw or heard of Mr. Hope-Scott
conveyed the impression that he always acted on a plan
and an idea; but this is so evident from what I have

---

[2] In a letter to Lord Henry Kerr, dated 'Norfolk House, London, S.W.,
July 6, 1867,' Mr. Hope-Scott says:—

'I have, because everybody seemed to think I must, become a purchaser
to-day of some of Sir Walter's MSS., viz. *Rokeby, Lord of the Isles, Anne of
Geierstein*, and a volume of fragments of *Waverley, Ivanhoe*, &c. I am
ashamed to say what they cost, but the *Lady of the Lake* alone cost *another*
purchaser more than half what I paid for the four, and I can hardly say
that it was to please myself that I bought at all.'

already related of him, that I am unwilling to add trivial anecdotes in its illustration. That tenderness of heart of which such ample proof has also been given, I recollect once coming curiously out in a chance expression. 'If a man wants to cry,' said Mr. Hope-Scott, ' let him read the Police Reports, or (checking himself with that humour by which deep feeling is often veiled) take a cup of coffee ! '

He was a thoroughly kind friend in this way, that, unasked, he thought of openings which might be available, and, without offering direct advice, threw out, as if incidentally, useful hints. In giving advice, he applied his mind to the subject ; and a small matter, such as the interpretation of a route in Bradshaw, received as complete consideration, as far as was needed, as he could have given to the most difficult case submitted by a client.

As to his religious habits, I only had the opportunity of remarking his regularity in attending mass. I recollect, too, that he was anxious that one in whom he took an interest should not leave Hyères without visiting a favourite place of pilgrimage in the vicinity called L'Ermitage, and heard with pleasure that St. Paul's, in the upper town, had not been forgotten—a church where St. Louis heard mass before setting out on his crusade, and which rivals the Hermitage as a resort of popular devotion.

I now throw together a few scattered recollections communicated to me by friends, for which I have not been able to find a place elsewhere.

Mr. Hope-Scott often talked of Merton College ; he

used to compare his affection for it to that felt for a wife.

In his professional habits of mind he was a contrast in one respect to his friend Mr. John Talbot. The latter (as he himself once remarked) was always anxious about a case, and a failure was a great blow to him ; but Mr. Hope-Scott, on the other hand, did the best he could, and if he failed, he failed ; but he did not allow *that* to wear him out. He always met the thing in the face, never *mourned* over it.

He never gave way to small troubles ; yet he was not a calm person by nature, but by self-command.

The only occasion on which I ever knew Mr. Hope put out (said a friend who knew him well) was when one of his fellow-counsel, whom he had endeavoured to supply with a complete answer to the whole difficulty in an important case, made a mess of it. 'How hard it is,' said Mr. Hope, ' to sit by and listen to a man speaking on one's side, and *always* missing the point ! '

Mr. Hope-Scott was a man *run away with by good sense.* He had great playfulness of character (by no means inconsistent with the last trait), and was especially addicted to punning. A constant fire of puns was kept up when he, Bishop Grant, and Mr. Badeley were together, though the Bishop always sought a moral purpose in his jesting.

After having heard Mr. Hope-Scott's and Mr. Serjeant Wrangham's arguments on the Thames Watermen and Lightermen's Bill (1859), the chairman of the committee said : 'Mr. Hope-Scott, the committee have three courses—either to throw the bill out, to pass it in its entirety, or to pass it with alterations. Therefore we shall be glad if counsel will retire.' After waiting for half an hour, the door opened. Mr. Hope-Scott said to Serjeant Wrangham : ' Come along, Serjeant ; now that they have disposed of their three courses, we shall have our *dessert.'*

A speech of his at the Galashiels Mechanics' Institute gave great amusement at the time : ' I am a worker like you,' he said ; ' my head is the *mill,* my tongue is the *clapper,* and I *spin long yarns.'*

Once, after signing a good many cheques in charity matters, he said, ' They talk of hewers of wood and drawers of water ; but I think I must be called a *drawer of cheques.'*

He was highly genial with everybody, and even in reproving his servants would mingle it with humour.

The last of Sir Walter Scott's old servants, John Swanston the forester (often mentioned in *Lockhart*), seemed rather shocked when Mr. Hope-Scott's son and heir was named Michael ; upon which Mr. Hope-Scott said to him playfully : ' Ye mauna forget, John, that there was an Archangel before there was a Wizard ; and besides, the Michael called the Wizard was, in truth, a very good and holy Divine.'

With servants Mr. Hope-Scott was very popular. He took great interest in people, taking them up, forwarding their views, advising, protecting, even interfering.

He was very fond of children, and they of him. The presence of ' Uncle Jim ' was the signal for fun with his little nephews and nieces : but the case was different with young people; they rather stood in awe of him (but another informant thinks these were the exceptions).

He abhorred gossip and spreading of tittle-tattle; avoided speaking before servants, or any one who would retail what was said. When there was any danger of this, he relapsed into total silence; and was, indeed, on some occasions over-cautious. He especially avoided talking of his good deeds, or of himself generally. He was singularly reserved; not by nature, but from his long habituation to be the depositary of important secrets. Sir Thomas Acland worked a good deal with him in Puseyite days. 'Tell me what my brother is about,' asked Lady H. K. 'I cannot tell,' was the reply; 'he is a well too deep to get at.'

He had a determined will, though affectionate and kind-hearted. When entertaining guests, he made all the plans day by day; used to lay out the day for them, seeing what could be done, though he might not himself be well enough to join the party.

He was extremely systematic in his habits, paid for everything by cheques; and used to preserve even notes of invitation, cards of visitors, and the envelopes of letters.[3]

Yet he had not punctuality naturally; he *drilled* himself to it. Nor was he naturally particular, but, when married, became over-particular.

He had great kindness and tact, and was always kind in the right way. He was once seen, as a lad,

---

[3] I recollect the great importance he attached to them as dates, and his regret at the change from the old method of folded sheets.— *W. E. G.*

flying to open a gate for perhaps the most disgusting person in the parish.

It was a feature in his life's history to keep up intimacies for a certain number of years; the intercourse ceased, but not friendliness.

'In giving me an explanation of the mass before I was received into the Church, I remember' (said a near relative of his) 'his saying that he delighted especially in the *Domine, non sum dignus*. "It is to me [he remarked] the most beautiful adaptation of Scripture."'

In discussing religion with Presbyterians, he was fond of asserting the truth, 'I, too, am a *Bible Christian.*'

In conversation once chancing to turn on the subject of one's being able to judge of character and conduct by looking at people in the street, Mr. Hope-Scott remarked : ' Yes, if you saw a novice of the Jesuits taking a walk, you would see what that means.'

The following more detailed recollections appear to deserve a place by themselves :—

When residing on his Highland property at Lochshiel, Mr. Hope-Scott personally acquainted himself with his smaller tenantry, and entered into all their history, going about with a keeper known by the name of ' Black John,' who acted as his Gaelic interpreter. His frank and kindly manners quite won their hearts. Sometimes he would ask his guests to accompany him on such visits, and make them observe the peculiarities of the Celtic character. On one of these occasions he and the late Duke of Norfolk went to visit an old peasant who was blind and bedridden. After the

usual greetings, they were both considerably astonished
to hear the old man exclaim, in great excitement:
'But tell me, how is Schamyl getting on?' It was long
after the Circassian chief had been captured; but his
exploits were still clinging to the old Highlander's
imagination, full of sympathy for warfare and politics.
The natural ease and politeness of the Highland manners in this class, as contrasted with the rougher type
of the Lowlands, used always to delight Mr. Hope-Scott.
Over and over again, after the ladies had withdrawn
from the dinner-table, he would send for a keeper, or a
gillie, or a boatman, and ply them with plausible questions, that his guests might have the opportunity of
witnessing the good breeding of the Highlands. John,
or Ronald, or Duncan, or whoever it might be, would
stand a few yards away from the table, and, bonnet in
hand, reply with perfect deference and self-possession,
his whole behaviour free, on the one hand, from servility,
and on the other, from the slightest forwardness. As
will readily be supposed, the interview commonly ended
with a dram from the laird's own hand.

In one respect he was very strict with his people.
He never would tolerate the slightest interference on
their part with the rights of property. Some of them
were in the habit of presuming on the laird's permission,
and helping themselves—no leave asked—to an oar, or
a rope, or any implement which they chanced to stand
in need of, belonging to the home farm. They indeed
brought back these articles when done with; but Mr.
Hope-Scott ever insisted they should be *asked for*, and
would not accept the excuse that the things were taken

without leave in order to save him the trouble of being asked. He was very severe in repressing drunkenness and dissipation, though no one was readier to make allowance for a little extra merriment on market days and festive gatherings.

Mr. Hope-Scott's chief source of relaxation and pleasure, when he could escape from his professional duties, was building. In this amusement he followed his own ideas, sifting the plans of architects with the most rigid scrutiny, and never hesitating to alter, and sometimes to pull to pieces, what it had cost hours of hard brain-work to devise. No amount of entreaty could extort his consent to what did not commend itself as clear and faultless to his understanding. It might not be a very agreeable process to some of those concerned, but the result was generally satisfactory to the one who had a right to be the most interested. As for contractors, he latterly abjured them altogether ; and Dorlin House was commenced and brought to completion under the management of a clerk of the works in whom he had great confidence. In the kindred pursuit of planting (as has already been noticed) Mr. Hope-Scott also took great interest, and the young plantations which now adorn the neighbourhood of Dorlin are the result of his care.

Strong-minded lawyer as he was, he had a firm belief in second-sight. One case in particular, which occurred in his immediate vicinity, is remembered to have made a deep impression on his mind. The facts were these : One Sunday, shortly before Mr. Hope-Scott came to Lochshiel, it happened, during service in a small country chapel close to the present site of Dorlin House, that one of the congregation fainted, and had to be carried out. After the service was over, the late Mr. Stewart, proprietor of Glenuig, asked this man what was the cause of his illness. For a long time he refused to tell, but at length, being pressed more urgently, declared that, of the four men who were sitting on the bench before him, three suddenly appeared to alter in every feature, and to be transported to other places. One seemed to float, face upwards, on the surface of the sea; another lay entangled among the long loose seaweed of the shore; and the third lay stretched on the beach, completely covered with a white sheet. This sight brought on the fainting fit. Somehow the story got abroad, and the consequence was, that the fourth individual, who did not enter into the vision at all, passed, in the course of the next four months, into a state verging on helpless idiocy, from the fear that he was among the doomed. But, strange to tell, the three men who were the subjects of the warning were drowned together, a few months later on, when crossing an arm of the sea not far from the hamlet in which they dwelt. One of the bodies was found floating, as described above. Another was washed ashore on a sandy part of the coast, and, on being found, was covered with a sheet supplied by a farmer's family living close to the spot. The third was discovered at low water, half buried under a mass of seaweed and shingle. The fourth, who had survived to lose his senses, as we have said, died only two years ago.

CHAPTER XXV.

1867-1869.

Visit of Queen Victoria to Abbotsford in 1867—Mr. Hope-Scott's Improvements at Abbotsford—Mr. Hope-Scott's Politics—Toryism in Early Life
—Constitutional Conservatism—Mr. Hope-Scott as an Irish and a Highland Proprietor—Correspondence on Politics with Mr. Gladstone, and
with Lord Henry Kerr in 1868—Speech at Arundel in 1869.

Towards the end of August 1867, her Majesty Queen
Victoria, visiting the Duke and Duchess of Roxburghe,
at Floors Castle, was received with great rejoicings at
the various Scottish border towns on the Waverley
route from Carlisle to Kelso. On this occasion her
Majesty honoured Mr. and Lady Victoria Hope-Scott
by calling at Abbotsford. The newspapers of the day
contain copious narratives of the tour, otherwise unimportant for our present purpose. The following
account is taken from the 'Daily Telegraph' of August
24, with a few additional particulars introduced from
the 'Border Advertiser' of August 23, 1867, the former
journal supplying details of much interest relating to
Mr. Hope-Scott's improvements at Abbotsford. I have
shortened the original, and made some slight alterations in it :—

Her Majesty visited Melrose and Abbotsford on Thursday,
August 22, with Princess Louise, Prince and Princess Christian,
the Duke and Duchess of Roxburghe, and the Duke of
Buccleuch. The Queen having viewed Melrose Abbey, Mr.
Hope-Scott and his family were honoured, later in the day,

by her Majesty's presence at Abbotsford, which was reached shortly after six o'clock. In the fields in front of the lodge, and for a great distance along the road, was a great concourse of people, many of whom had waited for hours, and vehement cheering rang through the Abbotsford woods.

Many alterations and additions had been made to the Abbotsford of Sir Walter during Mr. Hope-Scott's nineteen years' possession of the place. In the lifetime of the Great Magician, the ground on which he fixed his abode was nearly on a level with the highway running along the south front; and wayfarers could survey the whole domain by looking over the hedge. Mr. Hope-Scott, twelve years ago or more (1855), threw up a high embankment on the road front of Abbotsford, and it is from this steep grassy mound that one of the best views may be had. The long, regular slope, steep near the level top where laurels are planted, is a beautiful bank from end to end, being well timbered with a rich variety of trees, among others the silver birch, the oak, the elm, the beech, the plane, and the good old Scotch fir; and being, moreover, naturally favourable to the wild flora of the district, especially to the bluebell and forget-me-not. The wild strawberry also is in great abundance, with its sweet, round little beads of fruit dotting the green. The square courtyard of the house is planned as a garden, with clipped yews at the corners of the ornamental plots of grass, and with beds all ablaze with summer flowers, a brilliant pink annual making a peculiarly fine appearance by well-arranged contrast with the sober greys of an edging of foliage plants. On one side of the courtyard is a postern, which was thrown open when the royal cavalcade had entered the grounds by the lodge gate. The opposite flank of the quadrangle is a kind of ornamental palisade, or open screen of Gothic stonework, the spaces of which are filled up by iron railings. This palisade divides the courtyard from the pleasure-gardens, which are well laid out, and bordered with greenhouses. The porch was beautifully decorated with rows of ferns along the margins of the passage, and behind the ferns were magnificent fuchsias rising to the roof, and mingled with other choice and rare flowers. The floors of the porch and other rooms were covered with crimson cloth, but beyond that, and the addition of vases of flowers, ' Sir Walter's Rooms ' were in the same condition in which they have been witnessed by the many thousands drawn thither from every civilised country in the world.

Her Majesty was received by Mr. Hope-Scott, Lady Victoria Hope-Scott, and Miss Hope-Scott, the Duke of Norfolk, Lord and Lady Henry Kerr, Miss Kerr, and Miss Mackenzie. Mr. Hope-Scott bowed to the Queen, and led the way to the drawing-room, where a few minutes were passed. Her Majesty then in succession passed through Sir Walter's library, study, hall, and armoury, and viewed with great interest all these memorials. The royal party then proceeded to the dining-room, where fruits, ices, and other refreshments had been prepared, but her Majesty partook only of a cup of tea and ' Selkirk bannock.' When the Queen was passing through ' Sir Walter's library,' some photographic views of Abbotsford, which had been taken recently by Mr. Horsburgh of Edinburgh, attracted her attention, and she graciously acceded to the request of Mr. Hope-Scott that her Majesty might be pleased to accept of a set of the photographs. Her Majesty expressed to Mr. Hope-Scott the great pleasure she had experienced in visiting what had been the residence of Sir Walter Scott. The Queen and suite then entered their carriages, and left Abbotsford about seven o'clock. The day was not so bright as the preceding one; but the little rain which fell, just as her Majesty had got under the shelter of the historical roof, did not spoil the holiday which some thousands of people from Galashiels, Hawick, Kelso, Berwick, and Edinburgh had been bent on making.

Mr. Hope-Scott, in a letter to Mr. Badeley of August 23, 1867, gives a brief description of the Queen's visit, concluding as follows :—

' Throughout her visit, her Majesty was most gracious and kind, and her conduct to Mamo was quite touching.

She showed a great deal of interest in the place and the
principal curiosities, looked remarkably well and active,
and, I am told, is much pleased with the reception she
has met with on the Border.'

The political aspects of Mr. Hope-Scott's character,
on which it is now time that we should enter, do not
require any very extended discussion. His opinions
and feelings were Conservative in the constitutional
sense, and in his early years seem to have gone a good
deal further. It is perhaps scarcely fair to bring evidence from the correspondence of youths of nineteen,
but Mr. Leader tells him (November 3, 1831): 'The
latter part of your letter is an admirable specimen of
Tory liberality and Tory argument. . . . What! are all
Radicals fools or knaves, and all Conservatives honest
or intelligent? . . . *Absint hæ ineptiæ pæne aniles.*' A
few years later the Thun correspondence, though only
affording incidental references to Mr. Hope's own letters,
shows clearly that, like 'young Oxford' of that date and
long afterwards, he adopted Tory views as deductions
from Scripture, and as the political side of religion.
Thus Count Leo Thun, writing to Mr. Hope on December 14, 1834, says: 'We both agree in the first
principles; I copy your own words: "Everything we
do is to be done in the name of the Lord : admitting
this, it is evident that the *principle* on which we are to
act with regard to politics is to be derived from the
Scriptures." ' The future Austrian statesman, however,
declares that he cannot find in the Scriptures 'that
blind and passive obedience' which his friend requires,
and enters at considerable length into the question, con-

troverting the application which the latter had made of certain passages. Again pass on a few years, and we find Mr. Hope writing to Mr. Badeley (it is the first letter in that collection), January 12, 1838 : 'I have managed to read Pusey's sermon, in which there is nothing that I am disposed to quarrel with. The origin of civil government used long ago to be a favourite subject of inquiry with me ; and I had long been convinced of the absurdity of any but the patriarchal scheme. Aristotle, the most sensible man, perhaps, who ever lived, came to the same conclusion without the aid of revelation.'

These views sustained practically some modification as time went on. Toryism, in its *historical* sense, could never be the political creed of a mind on which the Church of England had lost its hold. This begins to appear in a speech made by him at an early date, without preparation indeed, but not carelessly spoken. On the occasion of the ceremony of turning the first sod for the Sheffield and Huddersfield Railway, at Penistone (August 29, 1845), Mr. Hope said :—

If you lived under a despotic government, you would have lines made without reference to your local wants, and perhaps from visionary views of public advantage, but without reference to your private interests. It would be the same if a democratic body were to govern. In the one case you would be subject to the dictates of the imperial office ; in the other, to the votes of a turbulent assemblage ; but in neither case would there be that mixed regard to public justice and private interests which are combined in our efficient system. I dare say we [railway lawyers] are troublesome, but we belong to a system which has in it great elements of constitutional principle, which combines a regard for the public interest, and for private rights, with that free spirit which enterprises of this nature require in a great commercial country.[1]

In the letter to Mr. Gladstone, of December 9, 1847 (quoted p. 86), we perceive an uncertain, sea-sick tone, the sadness natural to a mind not yet sure of its course. Very different is the buoyancy that breathes in Mr. Hope-Scott's remarks, ten years later, on the rivalry between Manchester and Liverpool, in his speech on the Mersey Conservancy and Docks Bill (quoted p. 124), though that, perhaps, is too rhetorical for us to found an argument upon. It will be more to the purpose here if I give an extract from a letter which he had written that same year, as an Irish proprietor, on the eve of a contested election, to the agent for his estates in co. Mayo, Joseph J. Blake, Esq., at Castlebar. It will show the wise and kindly spirit in which he dealt with his people, as well as the reference to the interests of Catholicity which now governed his politics :—

As to the election for the county of Mayo, I am in considerable ignorance about the state of parties and the opinions of the candidates in that particular part of Ireland. I may state, however, that I should myself prefer the candidate who is the most sincere friend of the Catholic Church, and most disposed to take a calm and careful view of the questions which most affect the interests of the Irish people—say Tenant Right, for instance, in which I think something should be done, but perhaps not so much as the more noisy promoters of it insist on. I do not, however, wish to influence my tenants more decidedly than by letting them know my general feelings on these subjects. (March 25, 1857.)

The question here involved, which has very recently

[1] *Sheffield and Rotherham Independent*, August 30, 1845.

ripened into difficulties so formidable as far as regards Ireland, also affected at the time, as it still affects, the state of property in the Western Highlands, where it seems to have interfered a good deal with Mr. Hope-Scott's efforts to raise the condition of his tenantry. He urged on them the necessity of cultivating more of the waste land which stretched for miles before their doors, but they never took kindly to this task. No rent was to be demanded for the reclaimed lands, and they were promised compensation if called upon to give them up at any future year. They were perfectly convinced of Mr. Hope-Scott's sincerity, but were unwilling to enter into these schemes of amelioration without the security of possession guaranteed by leases.[2] My office not being that of the political economist, it is unnecessary to enlarge on the subject, especially as the following important letter of Mr. Hope-Scott himself will enable the reader to judge of the reasons upon which he acted :—

J. R. Hope-Scott, Esq. Q.C. to the Right Hon. W. E.
Gladstone, M.P.

(*Private.*)   Abbotsford : Oct. 28, 1868.

Dear Gladstone,—As you are kind enough to care for my political ideas, I will try to describe them.

Born and bred a Tory and a Protestant, I have discarded both the creeds of my youth. But with this difference in the result : in religion I have found sure anchorage ; in politics I am still adrift.

Had the followers of Sir Robert Peel been able to found a

---

[2] Further details of Mr. Hope-Scott's relations with his Highland tenants will be found in chap. xxvi. See also chap. xxiv. pp. 181, 182 in this vol. as affording some indirect illustration.

permanent party, my case would probably have been different. But death took many of them, and the rest are scattered.

Of the two great parties now forming on the ruins of the old ones, that which you lead has a claim upon me for the work of justice [disestablishment of the Irish Church] which it has undertaken, and which the other seeks to frustrate. But, nevertheless, this work is to me no test of the abiding principles of the party. In you I acknowledge the promotion of it to be a sign of honesty and courage which few can better appreciate than myself; and I know that you mean it as a pledge of steady advancement in the same path. But amongst those who act with you there are many minds of a very different stamp.

A few words will bring out my views.

Speaking logically, justice to the Catholic people of Ireland means, if it means anything, the undoing of the Reformation, the replacing of the Church of the great majority in the position from which it has been unjustly removed.

But had you proposed this, or anything savouring of this, you know that your followers would have been few indeed; and that you have been able wholly to avoid such a danger for yourself, and even to turn it against your political opponents, has arisen chiefly from the moderation and wisdom of the Catholic clergy.

By their acquiescence in mere disestablishment you got so far rid of the fear of Popery as to give scope to the voluntary principles of ultra-Protestantism, and, as a consequence, many now support you upon grounds so wholly different from your own, that, when the assault is over, and the stronghold taken, half your forces may disappear from the field, or remain only to rebel against your next movement.

This, then, is the reason why, seeking for a party, I cannot accept the present action against the Irish establishment as materially affecting my choice; but I must add that the Church question does not, in point of statesmanship, appear to me to be either the most important or the most difficult of the Irish questions.

That of Land Tenure exercises a wider influence among the people, and calls for a higher science of government.

Now, upon this most difficult and most delicate subject, there are prominent men among your supporters who have put forth views which I am forced to call in the highest degree crude, if not extravagant.

The law of demand and supply renders one class dependent upon another to an extent little short of slavery, not only in contracts for land in Ireland, but in all questions which, in free countries, turn upon the possession by one man of what another cannot or will not do without. The scale of wages of the agricultural labourers in some counties in England, and the rates paid for the worst lodgings by the poorest classes in our large towns, are full of the same meaning as the difficulties of the Irish tenant farmer.

But, more than this, the Irish land question itself is not exclusively Irish. It is to be found also, smaller of course in extent, but identical in its main features and in some of its worst consequences, in the West Highlands of Scotland ; and I, who am a proprietor in both countries, can hardly be expected to put much trust in the political physicians who, to cure a disease in Mayo or Galway, propound remedies the first principles of which they would deem inapplicable to the same disorder in Argyle or Inverness.

That I am hopeless of any reasonable mode of relief being found, I will not say ; but, if it is to be safe, it certainly cannot be speedy ; and if it is to be permanent, it must depend upon a change in the habits of a race rather than upon a new distribution of landed property by Parliament.

And now, turning from Irish to general policy, I profess that I accept your principles of finance and commerce with entire satisfaction, and with a confidence in your power of applying them which I give to no other man.

I enter heartily also into your schemes for the material improvement of the labouring classes, and admire the wisdom as well as the kindness of what you have done.

With regard to the Franchise, I have no fear of Household

Suffrage, and I prefer it to the more limited measure which
you formerly advocated, because it brings into play a greater
variety of interests; and, if it is liable to the objection that it
gives votes to the ignorant and the profligate, I answer that
your bill would have bestowed still greater, because more exclusive and more concentrated power, upon a class which com-
prises not only the Lancashire operative, but the Sheffield
rattener.

Moreover, I believe that all which is worth defending in
our social and political state in England and Scotland has
better guarantees in the spirit of the people than in any pro-
vision of the law. When Talleyrand said that England was
the most aristocratic country in the world, because there was
scarcely any one in it who did not look down on somebody else,
he touched the keystone of our society. I have already met
with amusing instances of the effect on Scotch middle-class
Liberals of the recent enfranchisement of those below them;
and my conviction is, that the more you widen the base, the
more closely will you bind the superstructure together.

What I fear more than democracy is the strife between
capital and skilled labour. This appears to me to be among
the most pressing questions of the day, and I shall think well
of the statesman, whoever he may be, who, with a just but
firm hand, shall regulate the relations of these forces.

On Education I hope we are agreed; at any rate, I feel
sure that you will not intentionally divorce it from religion;
but I have yet to learn what measure your party would
support.

There remains one subject of home policy which with me
is paramount. At the time when I became a Catholic the so-
called Papal Aggression was the great topic of the day; and
while the ignorance and violence of the majority, both in and
out of Parliament, greatly assisted my conversion, the steady
reason and justice of Lord Aberdeen, and of those who, like
yourself, acted with him, drew from me a greater feeling of
respect than I have ever been sensible of on any other political
occasion, or towards any other political men. I felt that they

were determined honestly to carry out the principles of Catholic emancipation, amidst great popular excitement, and without reference even to their personal prejudices, far less to their political interests, and I honoured them with no stinted honour.

In the same direction much still remains to be done, and I wonder to myself whether you will ever head a party which will venture its political power in a contest with county magistrates and parish vestries on behalf of the Catholic poor.

I wonder too sometimes, but with less of hope, whether yours will be a party which will be content to forego that political propagandism which seems chiefly favoured in England when applied to the weaker countries which profess the Catholic faith, and which, in those countries, seems to impair religion much more than it increases temporal prosperity ; and, lastly, whether it will have enough moderation to admit that the protection of the public law of Europe ought not to be denied to the States of the Church, merely because a neighbouring power demands them in the name of Italian Unity.

Such, my dear Gladstone, are the thoughts of a somewhat indolent, but not indifferent observer of what is going on around him. They are put before you neither to elicit opinions nor to provoke controversy, but to explain how it is that an old friend, who loves and admires you, should withhold his support, insignificant as it is, at the very moment when, as the leader of a party, you might be thought to have justly earned it.

Yours aff^{ly},
JAMES R. HOPE-SCOTT.

The Right Honble W. E. Gladstone, &c. &c. &c.

The Right Hon. W. E. Gladstone, M.P. to J. R. Hope-Scott,
Esq. Q.C.

Hawarden, N.W.: Nov. 1, '68.

My dear Hope-Scott,—Everything in your handwriting is
pleasant to read, and I thank you sincerely for your letter.

When I come to the *gros* of your letter touching politics, I
own it appears to me that we have a moral title to your serious
and even strenuous aid.

I hope you will not think my writing to say so a bad compliment, for, as far as the value of the aid is concerned, even
such as yours, I assure you I cannot afford to buy it at the
present moment by personal appeals in writing.

But you praise *justly* the ' moderation and wisdom' of the
R. C. clergy on the question of the hour—why do you not
imitate them ?

Simply because you cannot trust those who are acting with
me in the *paulo post futurum.* Is that a sound rule of
political action ? You think much, as I do, of the importance
of the Land Question. You see a great evil—you do not see
any other man with a remedy—you hold off from us who made
a very moderate proposal in 1866, because eminent men
among our supporters have made proposals which you think
extravagant or crude, and to which we have never given any
countenance.

Now I will not indulge myself here by going over the
many and weighty matters in which we are wholly at one; all
that you say on them gives me lively satisfaction.

I will only, therefore, touch the one other subject on which
you anticipate difficulty as possible—that of political propagandism, meaning the temporal power of the Pope : for I do not
suppose you mean to censure English pleas for civil rights of the
United Greeks in Poland against the Emperor of Russia,
though touching their religion.

I have at all times contended that the Pope as prince
ought to have the full benefit of the public law of Europe, and
have often denied the right of the Italian Government to

absorb him.   But you must know that extraordinary doctrines, wholly unknown to public law, have been held and acted on for the purpose of maintaining the temporal power.   If you keep to public law, we *can* have no differences.   If you do not, we may : with Abp. Manning I have little doubt we should.   But that question is and has been for years out of view, and is very unlikely to come into it within any short period.   Rational co-operation in politics would be at an end if no two men might act together until they had satisfied themselves that in no possible circumstances could they be divided.   Q.E.D.

There in brief is my case, based on yours, and I would submit it to any committee you ever spoke before, provided you were not there to bewilder them with music of the Sirens.

Now pray think about it.   I shall bother you no more. I wish I had time to write about the Life of Scott.   I may be wrong, but I am vaguely under the impression that it has never had a really wide circulation.   If so, it is the saddest pity; and I should greatly like (without any censure on its present length) to see published an abbreviation of it.

With my wife's kindest regards,

Always aff^{tely} yours,

W. E. GLADSTONE.

J. R. Hope-Scott, Esq. Q.C.

Mr. Hope-Scott, in replying to the above letter of Mr. Gladstone's (under date ' Abbotsford, November 4, 1868 '), says :—

I fully acknowledge the compliment which you have paid me in writing at such length at such a time, and there are some things in your letter which I am glad to have had from yourself.   But your main argument for action fails to convince me.   I cannot put ' paulo post futurum ' into my pocket, and march to the poll.   For the present, then, I cannot enlist with you in politics, but I can do so heartily in any attempt to extend a knowledge of Walter Scott.

The following letters, of the same year, will further

illustrate Mr. Hope-Scott's view of the Irish disestablishment question, and the independent line of politics
which he adopted in his closing years :—

J. R. Hope-Scott, Esq. Q.C. to the Lord Henry Kerr.

Norfolk House, St. James's Square :
March 22, '68.

Dear Henry,—[The Archbishop] thinks that if Gladstone is
serious (which he and I both believe him to be) about the Irish
establishment, he will carry his motion, although it seems
probable that Disraeli will make it a rallying-point, and may
even dissolve Parliament if beat. How he is to manage the
latter operation in the present condition of the Reform Question
I hardly see. . . .

It is astonishing to find on all sides such proof of the
progress of opinion in Irish, and I think generally, in Catholic
matters. The Fenian blister has certainly worked well ; but
besides that, Ireland and the Catholic religion offer the best
field for the Liberals, as a party to recover the ground which
Disraeli last year ousted them from. Hence it is that my two
months' absence from England seems to count as years on this
point. Indeed, Gladstone's great declaration on Monday last is
supposed to be due to the rapid progress of a few weeks, or
even days. . . .

Yrs affᵗˡʸ,
JAMES R. HOPE-SCOTT.

The Same to the Same.

Dorlin, Strontian : Sept. 16, '68.

Dear Henry,— . . . In politics I have taken my line, and
have told Curle and Erskine that, as at present advised, I
do not intend to meddle in the Roxburgh or any other
election. I trust neither party enough to identify myself with
either ; and while I do not think that the demolition of the
Irish establishment is enough of a religious question to make
me support the Liberals, I think it sufficiently so to prevent
my siding with the Conservatives. On the other matters
which you mention, members of both political parties seem to

be at present free to follow their own consciences or interests, but their leaders may at any moment require obedience, and in that case I would rather trust the necessary tendency of the Liberals than that of the Conservatives on all home questions ; and foreign policy seems, by accord of all parties, to have now settled into non-interference. . . .

Y^{rs} aff^{ly},
JAMES R. HOPE-SCOTT.

The Lord Henry Kerr.

In a speech at Arundel, January 5, 1869, perhaps the last Mr. Hope-Scott made on a public occasion, he remarked that he did not think the wisest thing had been done in remodelling the constituency by simply numbering heads. By depriving Arundel of its member, a large interest had been left unrepresented—that is, the Catholic interest. An intimate friend of his, possessing excellent means of information and judgment, said to me : ' Hope-Scott, in his latter years, was not political—not a party man in any sense. Indeed, he got into a scrape with the Whigs when the Duke of Norfolk voted with the Tories. This much mortified the Whigs, and they complained to Hope-Scott of the Duke's line : he said he wished him to be of no party. This was his line as a Catholic. Every lawyer, in fact, is Conservative. Revolution is against all their theories of government.' This, however, so far as it relates to the personal influence exercised by Mr. Hope Scott, must be balanced by the evidence of another friend, also very intimate with him, to whom the *late* Duke of Norfolk, while still traditionally a Liberal, had remarked that he thought Conservatives would do more for Catholics, and that nothing was to be expected from the Liberals.

CHAPTER XXVI.

1851–1873.

THE reader has now been enabled to form an opinion
of Mr. Hope-Scott's character and actions in various
aspects. The most important of all—his religious life,
his services to the Church, and his charities during his
Catholic period—remain to be reviewed; and that
interval appears the most natural for making such a
survey, which comes just before the time when he was
visibly approaching the end of his career.

The path by which Mr. Hope-Scott was led to Catholicity has been made sufficiently apparent. We have seen that he was principally influenced by two reasons, affecting, on the one hand, Church order, and on the other, dogma : the Jerusalem Bishópric, which was set up by Anglicans and Lutherans together ; and the Gorham judgment, which rejected an article of the Creed. These reasons were, as he acknowledged, *clenched* by his disgust at the outcry raised against the exercise of Papal authority in the institution of the Catholic hierarchy in England ; and perhaps the greater stress ought to be laid upon this last, as it might have been the less expected, because his early ecclesiastical studies, and early contact with Catholic society, were certainly not such as could have led him to views usually classed as ' ultramontane.' On this head it may be sufficient simply to state that, when the time of its promulgation arrived, he rendered, without reservation, the homage of his intellect to the exalted dogma of Infallibility, which in our days has been welcomed by the whole Catholic world from the voice of its Chief Pastor. It is, further, only necessary to refer to his political letter to Mr. Gladstone (p. 195) to see that he endeavoured to make his influence (often so much more effective than any outward agitation) available towards the recovery of the temporal power and the rights of the Holy See.

As to his religious habits as a Catholic, every page of this memoir shows, or might show, that he was a man of great faith, great earnestness, and the most sincere intention to obey the will of God. Yet it must be remembered that his duty called him into the very thick of the battle of life from morning till night : whilst so engaged (and it was the case during half the year) it was by no means in his power either to attend daily mass or to be a frequent communicant, though, at Abbotsford, he would communicate two or three times a week.   But a little anecdote will serve to prove that he took care to place himself in the presence of God in the midst of the busy world in which he moved. He told his friend Serjeant Bellasis that he found he was just able to say the *Angelus* in the time he took to mount the stairs of the committee-rooms at Westminster. At home he regularly said the *Angelus* ; as was noticed by persons who accidentally entered his room at the hours assigned to it, and used to find him standing to say it.

The one absorbing devotion of his Catholic life was undoubtedly the adoration of our blessed Lord in the Sacrament of the altar.   Few who have seen him in prayer before the Tabernacle could forget his look of intense reverence and recollection, the consequence of his strong faith in the Real Presence.   After the Blessed Virgin and St. Joseph, St. Michael was his favourite saint ; his favourite books of devotion the *Missal* and the *New Testament* ; and, among religious orders, he was personally most attracted by the *Society of Jesus*, with members of which Order we have already seen that he was on terms of friendship, even before his reception into the Church.

His admiration for the Society lasted throughout his life ; and for more than twenty years together, until

the end, I believe that for the direction of his conscience it was to the Jesuit Fathers that he always had
recourse.   In private conversations, when expressing
the great satisfaction he felt at seeing the Society established in Roxburghshire and the Highlands, he often
said that the Jesuits seemed to him ' like the backbone of
religion.' Yet this love for the Society never led to any
want of hearty apprehension of the merits of other Orders,
or of the Seculars.   Thus he hoped, at one time, to see
the Dominicans at Galashiels, and showed the greatest
regard for the Oblate Fathers of Mary Immaculate, who
were for nine years in charge of the mission there,
while, both in London, and at Abbotsford and Dorlin,
the Fathers of the Oratory and the Secular clergy were
welcome and honoured guests.   The high value he set
upon the Rev. P. Taggart (whom he used to call ' the
Patriarch of the Border '), and on the hard-worked
Highland priests, is well remembered.   I am here, however, partly anticipating another branch of the subject,
and shall conclude what I have to say about the personally religious aspect of his character by the following
letter, from a friend who knew him well, and which
contains one or two fine illustrations of it, and some
very interesting general recollections also :—

Mrs. Bellasis to the Hon. Mrs. Maxwell-Scott.

Villa Ste Cécile : Dec. 31, 1880.

My dear Friend,—You ask me [for] some of those impressions which memory gives me of the kindest friend we ever
possessed—your excellent father.

Years have rolled on, and yet the intercourse with so
striking a person has left a remembrance not to be deadened

by lapse of time. The noble form—that beautiful, intellectual
countenance—the kindly tone of voice, so encouraging in difficulty, so sympathetic in sorrow, so persuasive in advice—who
that knew James Hope-Scott could ever forget?

He had a peculiar way of listening, with the head a little
bent on one side, to the most trivial subject broached by a
friend in conversation, as if it was of the deepest importance,
which pleased you with its unintentional flattery. With true
Christian politeness he never interrupted you, but, if the
subject was an important one, he would come down with some
unanswerable view which at once approved itself to the listener
as *the* course to be followed: 'Hope thinks so-and-so'—and it
always proved the right thing.

With regard to his generosity, it was his nature to be generous—he had learned the pleasure of giving; and, when any
principle was involved in a gift, there was no stint. As an
illustration of this, I remember on one occasion a friend—not
rich—known to us both, had given me a picture to dispose of,
as she did not care for it: it was small, and out of condition,
and of an objectionable subject, though we had not perceived
its closely veiled viciousness. I failed in persuading a picture
dealer to purchase it, and, having to return home by my husband's chambers, I there found Mr. Hope-Scott. I mentioned
my want of success, and your father at once said, ' Let us see
it.' It was fetched up from the carriage, and after looking at
it attentively—' Well,' he said, ' Mrs. Bellasis, I think you must
leave this with me.' I did so, and learnt afterwards that on
my leaving the room he crushed the painting with his heel,
put it on the fire, and sent me a cheque for my friend for 30*l.*

His faculty for languages was very great, and when in the
south of France, rambling daily over the pretty property he
possessed at Hyères, I used to be amazed at the fluent way in
which he talked with the workmen; whether it was the car-
penter, the plasterer, mason, or gardener, he talked with each
in the terms of their respective occupations and trades, quite
unhesitatingly. Provençal talk is certainly puzzling, but he
seemed as if born to it; and the French gentlemen told me he

spoke exactly all the niceties of their language, whether in repartee or in illustration.

How profoundly Catholic he was those near and dear to him must know far better than outsiders. No consideration ever closed the purse or the lips where the interests or the honour of Holy Church were concerned. There was no parade of piety in him; and yet, if he thought he could say the word in season, he spoke *unreservedly*. I recollect on one occasion a very distinguished member of the Parliamentary bar, who was, in common parlance, a man of the world—long gone to his rest—met my husband and your father walking together in Piccadilly. Mr. X. stopped them, exclaiming, ' Well, you two black Papists, how are you ? ' ' Come, come,' replied Mr. Hope-Scott, ' don't you think it is time *you* should be looking into your accounts ? ' ' Oh, I'm all right *now*,' was the reply, half jocularly. ' Well,' said Mr. Hope-Scott, ' but how about those *past* pages—eh ? ' Mr. X., taking no offence, drew himself up and said, with great gravity, ' I tell you what it is, Hope : I am thoroughly, intellectually convinced; but ' (he added, striking his breast) ' my heart is not touched ! ' and thereupon the three parted. Had he been a Catholic, he would have used, I suppose, the term ' will ' for ' heart.' [1]

All that Mr. Hope-Scott did in religious observances was done so naturally, so simply—whether it was in going down to the committees with my husband, he would pull out his rosary in the cab, and so occupy his thoughts through the busy streets; or when, in mounting the stairs at Westminster to reach the committee-rooms, he would repeat, *sotto voce*, with my husband, some slight invocatory prayers, or verse of a Psalm—such things were only known to the extreme intimacy of long friendship. Such was the hidden, deeply pious life of one who, for many years at least, though certainly in the world, was yet not of it. I might say he was *above* it; for who, more

---

[1] This courage in giving religious admonition where he saw it was needed, is a trait which I have occasionally observed appearing in his correspondence, and quite in keeping with his favourite expression, ' *Liberavi animam meam.*' —R. O.

than our dear friend, saw through, and so thoroughly despised its shams, its allurements, its ambition, and modes of thought?

There is one other remembrance which is a very bright one : I allude to his ever-ready wit. When he was in good health, and *well*, before he was threatened with the coming malady, how amusing he was—such a cheery companion! I have often thought, when we left his company, that I would put down his clever, witty rejoinders—they were legion! and never a spark of ill-nature. I never remember his saying an unkind word of any one.   E. J. B.

The services rendered by Mr. Hope-Scott to the cause of Catholicity may be grouped in three great divisions :—1. The giving advice, at no small cost of time and trouble, either on great questions affecting the interests of the Church, or on those of a more local and personal description. 2. Pecuniary charities. 3. The foundation of churches and missions. I will endeavour to give some idea of each of these, though of course the very nature of charity, but still more that of *counsel*, involves so much of secrecy, that particulars which remain on record, and can be given to the world, we may safely assume to be only specimens of many more which must remain untold.

1. The first division includes, as we shall see, many of the great questions affecting the Catholic Church in these countries during his active career as a Catholic. But his services were chiefly those of a wise and trusted adviser behind the scenes, for he never entered Parliament, and rarely took part in public meetings. That he thus kept at a distance from a sphere of action for which his powers so eminently fitted him, was a subject of regret even outside of Catholic society, as will appear from a letter

of Lord Blachford's to Mr. E. S. Hope, already cited, in which his lordship remarks :—

I have sometimes been disappointed that in joining the Church of Rome [Mr. Hope-Scott] was not led by circumstances to adopt in England the task so brilliantly, but so differently performed in France by M. de Montalembert—that of asserting for English R. Catholics that political and Parliamentary status to which their education and importance entitle them. It would have been an advantage for all parties.

And, earlier in the same letter :—

Given a constituency, he united almost every qualification for public life. He seized instantly the point of a matter in hand, and was equally capable of giving it words at a moment's notice, or of working it out thoroughly and at leisure, and that either by himself or, what is as important, through others. He would have made no enemies, and multitudes of friends ; and his quiet tact and flexible persuasiveness, grafted on a clear grasp of leading principles, would have made him invaluable in council.

It would be useless to speculate on the motives of this abstinence, or on the part which he might have played in Parliamentary life in the years when the too brief career of Mr. Lucas was drawing to its close, and a great opportunity seemed to offer itself for a leader to step forward who should unite, in a degree equal to his, faith and devotedness with eloquence, and a rare talent for the conduct and marshalling of affairs. However, among the transactions affecting Catholic interests in which Mr. Hope-Scott's knowledge and experience were turned to account, may be named the following :—

(1) *The Catholic University of Ireland*, which has since shown such struggling yet persistent vitality, had

been in contemplation as far back as 1847. Serious
steps were being taken towards its foundation in 1851,
when Mr. Hope's advice was immediately sought by
Archbishop (afterwards Cardinal) Cullen: he said, 'Get
Newman for your Rector;' and from him the Archbishop
came straight to Birmingham. There is a letter of Archbishop Cullen's to Mr. Hope (dated Drogheda, October
28, 1851), in which, after thanking him for valuable
advice regarding the University, his Grace says: ' I
think we shall be guided by what you have suggested.
For my part, I adopt your views altogether. . . . If we
once had Dr. Newman engaged as President, I would
fear for nothing ; and I trust that this point will soon be
gained. After that, everything else will be easy.' From
a letter of Mr. Allies to Mr. Hope (August 19, 1851) it
appears that Dr. Newman regarded it as of the highest
importance for those charged with the construction of
the new University to obtain information from Mr. Hope
as to the course of studies pursued in the Catholic
universities abroad ; and in another letter (August 30)
Mr. Allies proposes to Mr. Hope a long string of questions as to university legislation. What Mr. Hope
looked upon as of the most consequence may be
gathered from a postscript to that letter, marked
' private :' ' J. H. N. showed me your letter, with which
he entirely agrees ; and I need not say that I feel myself
all the force of what you say. All paper rules and con-
stitutions are nothing in comparison to there being a
good selection of men, and a perfect unity and subordination in the governing and teaching body. If this
is to succeed, my belief is that the only way is to

appoint J. H. N. head, with the *fullest powers*, both for the selection of coadjutors and the working into shape.' Mr. Allies (with the Very Rev. Dr. Leahy, afterwards Archbishop of Cashel, and Mr. Myles O'Reilly) was, at the time, engaged with Dr. Newman in drawing up a report on the organisation of the University, after consulting a certain number of persons, among whom was Mr. Hope.

In 1855 Mr. Hope-Scott presented to the new institution one of his splendid gifts—a library of books on civil and canon law. ' Your books '(writes Dr. Newman to him, August 1) ' will be the cream of our library.' In the difficulties of later years, when Dr. Newman felt his duty as Rector of the University and that as Father-Superior of the Oratory pulling him in different directions, the congregation, not from any one's fault, but from the nature of the case, being unable to get on without him, it was to the same faithful counsellor he turned. I may here mention that Mr. Hope-Scott warmly took up the idea of founding an oratory at Oxford (January 1867), and gave 1,000*l.* towards this object, which he refused to take back when the design was laid aside. In a conversation on the subject of this memoir, which Cardinal Newman condescended to hold with me, his Eminence said, ' Hope-Scott was a truly good friend—no more effectual friend—from his character and power of advice.' He had stood by him all through as a good friend and adviser in the difficulties of the Oratory connected with his rectorship, and so in another critical moment relating to other affairs. I venture to transcribe the eloquent words in which the Cardinal has placed on record the value he had for his friendship, in the dedication to his ' University Sketches : '—

'To JAMES R. HOPE-SCOTT, ESQ., Q.C., &c. &c., a name ever to be had in honour when universities are mentioned, for the zeal of his early researches, and the munificence of his later deeds, this volume is inscribed, a tardy and unworthy memorial, on the part of its author, of the love and admiration of many eventful years.—Dublin, October 28, 1856.'

(2) The assistance rendered by Mr. Hope-Scott to Dr. Newman under the anxieties of the *Achilli Trial* has already been briefly alluded to (p. 151). The first meeting of Dr. Newman's friends to hold consultation in the affair was a scene, as I have heard it described, which brought out in a striking manner Mr. Hope-Scott's talents for ruling and advising those in perplexity. At first all was confusion, but order began to appear the moment that he entered the room ; he seemed to have a just claim to take the lead, and placed everything in the right point of view. I find him writing to Mr. Badeley (from Abbotsford, November 15, 1852), to ask whether it would be *professionally* correct for him to appear at Dr. Newman's side on the day of sentence, adding : ' I need hardly say that I should much like to show him any signs of respect and affection. There are, indeed, few towards whom I feel more warmly.' This, it seems, would not have been etiquette if he had appeared in wig and gown ; and Mr. Badeley (who was one of Dr. Newman's counsel) suggested his sitting with Sir A. Cockburn, to assist, if not to speak. However, a motion for a new trial was made, and on

January 31, 1853, judgment was given discharging the rule on technical grounds, and imposing a nominal fine. There is a very interesting account of this in the Badeley correspondence, part of which I am tempted to subjoin. So important an event affecting Newman can scarcely be considered foreign to Hope-Scott, and it affords also a specimen of Mr. Badeley's familiar letters to his friend, which entered into the daily life I have endeavoured to describe.

Edward Badeley, Esq. Q.C. to J. R. Hope-Scott, Esq. Q.C.

Temple: Feb. 1, 1853.

My dear Hope,— . . . Newman has been here, and seems well satisfied with the result, and I think he has reason to be so. The judges paid him great respect, and though Coleridge preached him an immensely long Puseyite sermon, much of which he might as well have spared, full credit was given for Newman's belief of the truth of his charges, and for proper motives. You will see a tolerably correct report of it in the 'Times,' but the best report of *the judgment* is in the 'Morning Post.' The speeches of counsel are *execrably* given both in that and in the other papers. My speech is *very incorrect*, but I have been gratified by very kind expressions about it, particularly from my legal brethren: it was not long, but it seemed to produce some sensation, particularly as I started by avowing my friendship for Newman. My conclusion, as well as I remember it, was as follows:—

'There may be some, my Lords, who seek in Dr. Newman's conviction a malignant triumph, and who would gladly avail themselves of the sentence of this Court, to crush the man whose writings have been their dread, as his life has been their shame. The cry of party prejudice and of religious bigotry may be raised in other places, and its echo may perhaps be heard even within these walls; but your Lordships, I am confident, will disregard it, and in the exercise of your sacred

functions you will be guided only by the dictates of wisdom
and of justice ; you will respect the high character of Dr. Newman, his genius, his learning, his piety, his zeal, the purity of
his motives, the sanctity of his life ; you will remember the
anxiety he has undergone, the expense which he has incurred,
the facts which he has proved ; and bearing these in mind, you
cannot pass upon him any sentence of severity, you can but
inflict a nominal punishment. 'Vestrum est hoc, Judices,
vestræ dignitatis, vestræ clementiæ : recte hoc repetitur a vobis,
ut virum optimum atque innocentissimum, plurimisque mortal-
ibus carum atque jucundissimum, his aliquando calamitatibus
liberetis, ut omnes intelligant in concionibus esse invidiæ
locum, in judiciis veritati.' [2]

There was some applause when I sat down, and all seemed
highly delighted with my quotation. . . . The small amount of
the fine is regarded by the *Myrmidons* (Achilli's followers) as
a heavy blow to them, and all regard it as a triumph for us.
One of the most satisfactory things, however, is the declaration
of the Court that they are not satisfied with the finding of the
jury upon the facts, and that if the question as to a new trial
had rested solely on that finding, they would have felt themselves bound to send the case to another jury. And so ends
this important case. I think we may congratulate ourselves.
Newman is gone home to-day, and means to write to you to-
morrow or next day. He was very tired yesterday, but seems
quite alive again now, and in excellent spirits. The crowd in
and about the Court was immense ; . . . Newman was well
attended by a numerous party of friends, and cheered as he
left the Court.   Ever believe me

Yours most affect[ly],

E. BADELEY.

(3) *Charitable Bequests, &c.*—In a letter of the Very
Rev. Dr. (since Cardinal) Manning to Mr. Hope-Scott,
dated ' Rome, March 3, 1854,' and marked ' private and
confidential,' occurs the following passage : ' I am

[2 Cic. 'Pro Cluent.' 71.]

rejoiced to hear that you have been invited to communicate with Government on the Charitable Bequests. And I think you will be glad to know that this fact has given, as I know, great satisfaction to the Cardinal. In conversation he had often named you to me, and I feel sure that he would have selected you on his own part for such a purpose.'

I quote the following lines from a long and interesting letter of Dr. Manning's to Mr. Hope-Scott, dated ' 78 S[outh] A[udley] St., January 28, 1856 : ' ' Do you remember a conversation, the summer of 1854, one Sunday evening, at 22 Charles St., on the good which might be done by four or five men living together and preaching statedly at different places, on courses of solid subjects? The thought has long been in my mind both before and since our conversation, and it has been coming to a point under an increased sense of the need.'

Correspondence of this kind, which I can merely notice, would, of course, illustrate Mr. Hope-Scott's position as a leading Catholic layman of his time, in the confidence of the heads of the Church.

(4) *The Repeal of the Ecclesiastical Titles Act* is an event too familiar in recent Church history to require much comment. The Government in 1851, having, in compliance with popular clamour, passed a bill by which Catholic prelates were prohibited, under many penalties, from assuming territorial titles of sees, found itself, from the very first, obliged to treat this enactment as a dead letter, in consequence of the legal difficulties and complications which arose from it. Common sense suggested its removal from the statute-book. This

was not effected without considerable effort to escape from that necessity by some less humiliating alternative. Mr. Hope-Scott gave evidence, lasting for two days (July 9 and 16), before the Select Committee appointed in 1867 to report on the operation of the Ecclesiastical Titles Act ; and to that evidence, showing all the luminous clearness and completeness which was so characteristic of him, but especially to an admirable *Statement* on the whole case which he submitted to the committee [see *infra*, p. 218], there can, I think, be no doubt that the final adoption (in 1871) of the only satisfactory remedy—a total repeal of the Act—was mainly due.

A letter of the London correspondent of a Dublin newspaper of the day, relating to Mr. Hope-Scott's examination before the Select Committee above mentioned, contains, in the lively manner of a journalist, some particulars worth preserving :—

It used to be said of Mr. Hope-Scott in the great days of railway committees, ere the London, Chatham, and Dover had made its *scandalum magnatum*, that his briefs were worth 15,000*l*. a year ; but that if he could forget some slight knowledge of the common law that he had acquired in his youth, there was no reason why they might not mount up to 25,000*l*. The story is only worth relating as an instance of the professional lawyer's ingrained contempt for such a tribunal as a committee composed of five or more ordinary members of the House of Commons. But to-day [July 16, 1867] it so happened that when Mr. Hope-Scott for the first time in his life had to sit in a chair and be examined and cross-examined before such a committee, his Common Law stood him in good stead. There is something extremely impressive in the complete simplicity of this eminent lawyer's appearance. A great natural superiority of intellect, an apt and complete study of his subject, ample readiness and subtlety of statement, these you expect; but not a certain direct and cogent candour, which appears to be, and which indeed is, utterly unaffected. The success of Mr. Hope-Scott with Parliamentary committees is, I have always thought, due to the fact that he unites the qualities of a great lawyer with the qualities that make a man a great member of Parliament. . . . His evidence was limited to the substantiation and illustration of the legal positions laid down in the document drawn up by him [see page 218], and of the whole case he was evidently master to its most minute points. Mr. Walpole and Mr. Chatterton both essayed what we may call cross-examination—it cannot be said successfully.[3]

The following letters on this subject appear to merit preservation; it will be seen that not all Catholic politicians of the day had so clear a view of the case as Mr. Hope-Scott :—

J. R. Hope-Scott, Esq. Q.C. to the Right Hon. Spencer H. Walpole, M.P.

[Draft Copy.]   Norfolk House, St. James's Square :
Confidential.   June 15, '67.

Dear Walpole,—I wrote to Mr. M'Evoy from Arundel to request that he would make an appointment with you on the subject of the Eccl. Titles Act, but, as I have received no reply, I presume that he is still out of town.

My object, however, may be as well, perhaps better, attained if you will read the memorandum which I enclose, and in which I have endeavoured to state the case against the Act, in the manner in which it *must* be stated to the Commons' committee, should the proposed inquiry take place.

You will gather from the memorandum that R. Catholics owe a great deal to the forbearance of the Government and the judges, and I can assure you that they are far from desirous to requite such treatment by pointing out the infractions of the law by which it has been accompanied.

<hr />

[3] *Irish Times,* July 18, 1867.

Moreover, in the event of the Act not being repealed, it is evident that they would greatly endanger their present immunity by showing how easily it might be destroyed.

Under these circumstances, if I had to choose between acquiescence in the retention of this Act, and a Parliamentary inquiry of certain inconvenience and of doubtful result, I should naturally prefer the former; but the question has apparently advanced too far to be now set aside, and I therefore venture to suggest to you, and through you to the Government, that the most just, and to all concerned the most convenient course, would be, that the Ministry should supersede further inquiry by an avowal that the action of the Public Departments is impeded by the Act, and should introduce a Government bill to repeal it.

I have marked this letter and the memorandum ' Confidential ' for reasons which you will understand ; but I do not mean to limit the use of them in any case where you think that they may assist. the consideration of my suggestion.

Believe me, &c. &c.,

J. R. H.-S.

The Right Honble Spencer H. Walpole, &c. &c. &c.

His Grace the Duke of Norfolk, E.M. to J. R. Hope-Scott, Esq. Q.C.

House of Lords: July 28, 1870.

My dear Mr. Hope,—Monsell, into whose hands I put the affair of the Ecc. Titles Bill, and to whom I gave your papers on the subject, says that both O'Hagan and Sherlock see no objection in the bill. He says that he will try and get some one to protest against the language of the preamble, but he does not feel sure that anybody will even do that. I believe O'Hagan says that, though Papal instruments are declared void, in a court of law such instruments are not called for to prove such facts as divisions of dioceses, &c. What had we better do?

Yours affec^{ly},

NORFOLK.

J. R. Hope-Scott, Esq. Q. C. to his Grace the Duke of Norfolk, E.M.

Bedford Hotel, Brighton : March 5, '71.

Dear Henry,—[After mentioning the enclosure of a rough draft of memorandum made in 1870, and of the clause he had proposed to Mr. Gladstone[4] with reference to the Eccl. Titles Bill :—]

These I now send you, and, with them, a letter which you wrote to me last July showing how the matter then stood. In connection with this letter, I send you likewise a print of my statement made and circulated before the committee met in 1867, and given in evidence by me before that committee. A reference to it will show that the view which your letter attributes to Lord O'Hagan is certainly not correct as regards England, though there are some circumstances in Ireland which make it more applicable there. As the bill is now to go to a Select Committee of the Commons, there seems a fair chance of getting a favourable alteration, and it is certainly well worth the attempt. As I wrote to you last summer, the *clause* I proposed would be of the greatest practical value, and might save some amount of feeling among Protestants by letting them fire away at the Papal authority; but if it cannot be got, the words 'and all assumption, &c., is wholly void' should either go out, or the whole of that recital be qualified so as to mean *legal and coercive*, not merely spiritual, jurisdiction, &c.

I am sorry to add to the number of your labours for the Church, but at present I am not able to take the field myself;

---

[4] In 1870 Mr. Hope-Scott had proposed to Mr. Gladstone the following *clause* with reference to the Ecclesiastical Titles Act :—

'Before all courts, in all questions affecting the rights or property of any religious body not established by law, or of the members of the same, as such, it shall be sufficient to prove the existence 'de facto' of any ecclesiastical arrangement material to the inquiry, and no evidence shall be required of the manner in which, or of the persons by whom, such arrangement may have been originally made.'

and as you are at any rate to be in London this week, you may take the opportunity of moving in the matter.

Y^{rs} aff^{ly},

JAMES R. HOPE-SCOTT.

Remember J. V. Harting in case of need.

IIis Grace the Duke of Norfolk, E.M.

The whole subject has belonged to the domain of history since the Repeal passed under Mr. Gladstone's administration in 1871. Still, I am unwilling to dismiss it without quoting the wise and powerful words with which Mr. Hope-Scott concludes the 'Statement' of 1867, several times referred to :—

No Act of Parliament can cause direct hardship to the subject while the Ministers of the Crown, the judges, the magistrates, and the public concur in disregarding it; but it is one thing to be secure by the law, and another to be secure only by a general contempt of the law. In the latter case a gust of popular excitement, such as occurred in 1850–1, or the interest or prejudice of an individual, or the scruples of a single official, or of a single judge, might at any time turn this dormant Act into a real instrument of oppression ; and therefore the grievance of the Roman Catholics is this, and it is essentially a practical one, that, whatever their present immunity may be, they are not, and, as the law stands, they never can be, secure of its continuance. From this it follows, that in all matters to which the Act may be applied, Roman Catholics find it necessary to take the same precautions, and resort to the same expedients, as if its application were certain. In short, they are under the constant sense that a penal statute is at the door, and that it depends upon little more than accident whether it shall come in or not : and thus, if the apprehension of evil be, as it certainly is, an evil in itself, the mere existence of the Act is a practical hardship, and there can be no remedy short of its repeal.[5]

[5] *Minutes of Evidence* (J. R. Hope-Scott, Esq., Q.C.), p. 26.

(5) It appears from Mr. Hope-Scott's papers that, in May 1869, he was giving his weight to the opposition against the *Scottish Education Bill*, as a measure, in its original form, based on the principle of Presbyterian ascendency, and was advocating a denominational system in the interests of Catholicity.

(6) The Parliamentary committee on *Conventual and Monastic Institutions* (originally designed by its mover, Mr. Newdegate, to inquire into the ' *existence, characters, and increase*' of those institutions, but restricted, on a motion of Mr. Gladstone's, to inquire into ' *the state of the law*' respecting them) held its sittings May 17 to July 25, 1870, and Mr. Hope-Scott's attention seems to have been much occupied with the subject. During the earlier stages of the affair he was at Hyères, but his correspondence shows how carefully he was kept informed of what passed. A letter to him from the Duke of Norfolk (dated Norfolk House, April 21, 1870) gives an idea of the line Mr. Hope-Scott had taken : ' I was very glad to receive your letter ' (the Duke writes). ' It had great weight with our committee to-day, and we decided to ask Government for nothing, but to resist inquiry in any form.'

(7) To services like these, in which he was the trusted counsellor of those who were acting for Catholicity in general, might be added illustrations of the many instances in which Mr. Hope-Scott's legal knowledge and experience were applied to the business affairs of priests on the missions, or of convents, if such cases were not, from their own nature, uninteresting except to those immediately concerned, and implying also the same

confidence that belongs to other privileged communications. The words of a valuable letter, from which I have more than once quoted, are here in point: [6] ' What I always admired in him was his patient charity —not so much the alms he gave, considerable as they were, but the manner in which, busy as he was, and often exhausted by his professional labours, he gave time and attention to all sorts of cases of distress and perplexity, or of importance to religion. " Consult Mr. Hope," was the advice given to numberless persons who had no claim whatever upon him but that of needing what no one else could so well give. One of the titles of our Blessed Lady, " Auxilium Christianorum," might in one sense have been applied to him.' Under this head of charity may well be included his undertaking, at the cost of time so serious to himself, the guardianships of bereaved families, of which a list has been given in a former chapter (p. 139).

2. Of Mr. Hope-Scott's pecuniary charities in England (in the Catholic part of his life) I am not able to give a special account; but I may mention one characteristic trait, that he felt it his duty to do more for Westminster than other places, because it was there that he earned his money; following the excellent principle of helping, in the first instance, the locality in which Almighty God has placed one. Accordingly, at Westminster he gave ground for Catholic *Poor Schools*, with property endowment of 50*l*. per annum; and gave great assistance to the *Filles de Marie*, a community of religious ladies so employed in the Horseferry Road, in the same district.

[6] Lady Georgiana Fullerton to Lady H. K., May 5 (1881).

A large proportion of his private benefactions seem to have been of a description especially in keeping with his tender and thoughtful mind, such as giving a mother the means of going to visit a daughter whom she had reluctantly allowed to enter a convent; enabling sick priests to go abroad for their health; setting up a poor schoolmistress with the means of purchasing a school; paying the expenses of a funeral; and so on.

Like all men either wealthy or reputed to be so, he was continually importuned with petitions for pecuniary aid, sometimes asked for by way of gift, sometimes as loans. To particularise such in any recognisable manner would of course be impossible, for fear of wounding the feelings of persons who were the objects of his kindness; but, avoiding this as well as I can, I may say that there were instances in which Mr. Hope-Scott cleared people out of overwhelming difficulties by gifts of lavish generosity—hundreds of pounds, and in some cases as much as 1,000*l.* I could produce an example of the former in which the prompt liberality shown was only equalled by the delicacy and forbearance; for it may easily be supposed that the difficulties thus relieved were not always free from blame on the part of those involved in them. Seldom, perhaps, can it be otherwise; but what would happen if all charity were measured by the deserts of the recipient?

What may have been the actual amount of Mr. Hope-Scott's charities during his life it would be very hard to conjecture; but this much I can state, on the testimony of one who knew the fact from his own personal knowledge, that in twelve or thirteen years (from

1859 or thereabouts) he gave away, in charity of some form or other, not less than 40,000*l.* It is right to observe that, quite towards the close, as he was retiring from his profession, there was a great diminution in his charitable expenditure; for, instead of the ample, though merely professional, income he had enjoyed for a great part of his life, he had become, relatively speaking, a person with very limited means. Believing it still to be his duty to provide for his 'son and heir,' and for his other children, of course he had no longer the power of doing all that he had done under circumstances altogether different.

MISSIONS ON THE BORDER: GALASHIELS, KELSO, &c.

Mr. Hope-Scott's zeal for the support of Catholicity was naturally felt most by places near him in the Highlands or on the Border, where he built churches and schools, and aided struggling missions. Of those on the Border, the most important was the Church of Our Lady and St. Andrew at *Galashiels*, which, as a manufacturing town, has a large Catholic population. True to his organising genius, he intended it should be a centre for smaller out-missions around it, as *Selkirk*, *Jedburgh*, *Kelso*, &c. It was completed gradually, and the following extract from a letter of his to Father Newman (dated Abbotsford, December 30, 1857) shows, in a pleasing and simple manner, the heart which Mr. Hope-Scott threw into the work he was offering to Almighty God :—

I hope that ten days or so will render [the church] fit for use in a rough way; and I hope it will be so used, and that I shall not be hurried in the decorative part, which I cannot afford to do handsomely at present, and which I think will be done better when we have become used to the interior, and have observed what is to be brought out and what concealed. The shell I am well pleased with. It is massive and lofty, no side aisles, but chapels between buttresses—and no altar-screen— more like a good college chapel than a parish church. The whole plan, however, has not been carried out, so the proportions cannot be fairly judged of. Some day perhaps I may finish it, or some one else instead; and to keep us in mind that more is to do, we have a rough temporary work at the west end (not really west), with square sash windows of a repulsive aspect.[7]

Mr. Hope-Scott lived to finish it, and the work, I have heard, can hardly have cost him less than 10,000*l.* He also gave to the Jesuit Fathers at Galashiels a library of books, chiefly on civil and canon law, in value about 500*l.* The last cheque he signed with his failing hand was one for 900*l.* in discharge of the last debt on Galashiels Church. The mission at Galashiels was held at first by the Oblate Fathers, but from the end of July 1863 by the Jesuits.[8] The following letter (worthy of preservation also because of the writer) will show that Mr. Hope-Scott had wished, almost immediately on finding himself a Catholic, to have a Jesuit Father at *Abbotsford* :—

---

[7] There are readers who will be glad of the preservation of the following dates connected with Galashiels Church. The plans were completed July 1, 1856; first payment, November 1856; last account rendered, February 1858; the church was opened on Candlemas Day, February 2, 1858, by Bishop Gillis; finished finally in 1872, and opened in August 1873.

[8] There is a letter of Father Jos. Johnson, Provincial S.J., to Mr. Hope-Scott, dated February 24, 1859, from which it appears that the Society, in consequence of the many demands upon them, were unable to accept the mission of Galashiels at that time.

The Père de Ravignan, S.J. to J. R. Hope, Esq. Q.C.

Voici, Monsieur, ce que le T. R. P. Général, m'écrit de sa main de Rome le 10 Juin :

' Je désire bien que M. Hope sache combien j'ai été consolé à la bonne nouvelle.—Jamais je ne l'avois oublié—il m'avoit inspiré tant d'intérêt ! '

Pour ne point l'oublier non plus, je vous demande la permission de vous dire ici que le R. P. Provincial d'Angleterre, a accueilli, avec le plus grand désir de vous satisfaire, la prière que vous avez bien voulu me communiquer, d'établir un de nos Pères chez vous en Écosse. Le P. Etheridge, provincial actuel, doit arriver demain à Londres.

Ce matin nous étions tous heureux près de cet autel. Bénissons le Seigneur de tant de grâces.

Veuillez agréer toutes mes tendres et profondes sympathies in X^{to} Jesu.

X. DE RAVIGNAN, S.J.

Londres : 16 Juin 1851.

Mr. Hope-Scott built the Church at *Selkirk*, dedicated to Our Lady and St. Joseph.

The mission of *Kelso*, where he built the Church of the Immaculate Conception, would furnish many instructive pages for a history of the re-settlement of the Catholic Church in those very desolate regions. A letter of the Rev. Patrick Taggart [9] to Mr. Hope-Scott, dated Hawick, September 3, 1853, contains some details which, in connection with later events at Kelso, are full of interest. They show how deeply felt is the spiritual isolation of such localities, and how unexpectedly great is the number of Catholics often to be found in them, left to themselves. Father Taggart first speaks of the great kindness which he had received from

[9] Compare page 203 of this volume.

Sir George and Lady Douglas, of Springwood Park, near Kelso, and then goes on to say :—

Lady Douglas is a genuine Catholic, just as a daughter of old Catholic Spain should be. Her sister is staying with her just now. . . . I think they do not like the idea of attending Divine service in a public hall. I told them that Father Cooke would be delighted to afford them any assistance in his power under present circumstances. I also told them that I thought that, if possible, a small church would be built at Kelso in the meantime ; and that the time was not far distant when perhaps the Bishop would be able to give to Kelso a resident priest. This news so delighted them that they could not find words to express their joy. . . . I do not know of any part of this district that is at present more destitute of the ministrations of a priest than Kelso and its environs. The mission extends twenty miles north-east of Kelso—that is, forty miles from Galashiels and from Hawick ; and there is not a village in that, I might almost say, immense tract of country that does not contain its ten and twenty poor Irish Catholics. I attended Kelso, once in the month, for nearly five years, and I am the first priest who offered up the Holy Sacrifice of the Mass at Kelso since the days of the so-called Reformation. I therefore know its geography and its wants. . . .

PATRICK TAGGART.

Accordingly, a church was built for Kelso at the expense of Mr. Hope-Scott. It could hardly have been finished more than a year or two, when, on the night of August 6–7, 1856, it was attacked by a Protestant mob, set fire to, and burned to the ground, with the schoolhouse and dwelling-house adjoining, including books, vestments, and furniture, the property of Mr. Hope-Scott. Four of the ringleaders were put on their trial on November 10. In charging the jury, otherwise fairly enough, ' the Lord Justice-Clerk remarked that, as to whether it were necessary that Mr. Hope-Scott should build the Roman Catholic chapel at Kelso or not, the jury might have very considerable doubts, as it appeared that the priest did not live there, but some miles distant at Jedburgh ; but that was a matter which the prisoners had nothing to do with, as every one was at liberty to build such a place of worship if he chose ; neither did it matter whether the attack upon the chapel was made in consequence of any attempts to proselytise Protestants to the Catholic faith.   In going over the evidence, his lordship said he could have wished that Mrs. Byrne, the schoolmistress, had given timely notice to the police of what she had heard as to the resolution to fire the chapel, as that would have been a better course than quitting the chapel.   However, they could not blame the poor woman ; and *perhaps, being a Catholic, she might not like to make an appeal to the police.'*   (Quoted from the report in the ' Scottish Press,' November 11, 1856.[1])

The jury's verdict would surprise any unprejudiced reader who studies the evidence.   They found the charge of wilful fire-raising not proven against the prisoners, but found three of them guilty of mobbing and rioting, but, in respect of their previous good conduct, recommended them to mercy.   The three got off with eighteen months' imprisonment and hard labour.   I quote the following remarks on the affair generally, and on the Lord Justice-Clerk's charge, from an article in

---

[1] I italicise the last sentence, which at first sight gives a curious idea of the practical equality of legal protection existing for Catholics at the time ; though probably all that was intended to be conveyed is the strange impression that Catholics might entertain a scruple about appealing to the police. —R. O.

the 'Scotsman,' republished by the 'Northern Times' of November 15, 1856 : [2]—

In the town of Kelso there is, it seems, a more or less considerable colony of Irish; and it needs scarcely be said that the mixture of that element with the border material does not work together for the promotion of harmony and good order. At St. James's Fair, held at Kelso on 5th August last, a Scotch butcher-boy quarrelled and fought with an Irish mugger. Scotch and Irish rallied round these champions of the two countries, and in the *mêlée* which ensued, a young Scotchman was unhappily and barbarously killed. The Kelso crowd, in very natural rage, burned the muggers' camp, threw their carts into the Tweed, and drove them from the neighbourhood of the town. But there remained the resident Irish of the town, and it seems to have been deemed fitting to hold them guilty as art and part. It is not clear that any of them were in the fight—at least, no person among them was charged with the murder; but there is a short cut through all these difficulties. Most Irishmen are Roman Catholics—Kelso has a Roman Catholic chapel—let it be burned. Accordingly, after considerable talk and preparation (which seems to have included getting drunk), a mob assembled the next evening, and did burn the chapel with perfect ease and effect. . . .

Some mystery may dwell in readers' minds as to how such an affair could be arranged and completed without any one but the rioters themselves having any voice thereanent. And the mystery is not quite cleared away by the evidence. The woman that lived under the chapel heard, on the day of the fair and the fight (i.e. the day before the incendiarism), that the chapel was to be burned, and slept out of her house, so as not to be in the way; coming back the next day she heard the same rumour, and left again at night—when it happened as she had been foretold. But though other witnesses, some of whom had witnessed the burning, testified that the design had been

---

[2] I have not met with any *letter* of Mr. Hope-Scott's to the *Scotsman*, but this article is probably from his pen.—R. O.

talked about in the town all day, the chief magistrate mentions
in his evidence that he ' had not had the slightest expectation
of a disturbance ; ' the superintendent of police was in the same
state of information, and the police constable ' had not taken
any alarm.'   All this, however, is of little consequence, seeing
that when the alarm was taken, there was no result but
that of disturbing two or three people who might as well
have gone to bed.   The guardianship of the town is confided
to one county policeman, who must be a tumultuous sort of
person himself, since he seems to require a ' superintendent ' to
keep him in order.   The said superintendent, when he did
know what was going on, first tried a little moral suasion, with
the result usual in such cases : ' I cautioned them against
proceedings of that kind, and advised them to go to their
homes—they disregarded me.'   His disposable force, condensed
in the person of ' the police constable,' took the same course.
' We warned them '—the answer was a volley of stones.   ' We
retired, and went to call the magistrates.'   ' By the time we
got back the chapel was completely destroyed.'   It would be
unreasonable to blame the superintendent and his ' force ' for not
successfully fighting several hundred men, although we do think
they might have done more as to identifying the ringleaders:
the real blame lies with the authorities, who appear to have
failed to provide decently adequate means for preserving the
public peace.   The use of a local police force must be measured,
not by what it detects and punishes, but by what it prevents,
or may reasonably be supposed to prevent. . . .

So wide-spread is [the feeling that Roman Catholic chapels
are somehow an intrusion and an offence] that it would almost
appear as if the very bench were not placed above its influence.
The Lord Justice-Clerk made some very sound and strong
remarks on the nature of the outrage ; but he added : ' Whether
it was necessary on the part of Mr. Hope-Scott to build this
chapel—which it scarcely seemed to be, seeing the priest did
not live there, but at Jedburgh—or whether it was a prudent
proceeding to attempt, by the erection of this chapel, to win
converts to the Roman Catholic faith—was of no importance
here.'   Since it was of no importance, the expressed doubt and

the implied censure had, we very humbly think, have been better avoided. . . . Though there had not been a single Roman Catholic in or near Jedburgh, Mr. Hope-Scott had a perfect moral as well as legal right to spend his money in building a chapel, without either having it burned down by a mob, or himself pointed at from the bench. As a matter of fact, however, there does appear to have been a congregation as well as a chapel. The Lord Justice-Clerk was pleased to add that the Roman Catholic school attached to the chapel 'could not but have been of the utmost use;' and we could thence infer that, Roman Catholic children having parents, there must have been use also for the chapel. The fact relied on, of the priest 'living at Jedburgh,' is evidence, we should think, not of a want of hearers, but of a want of funds to pay two priests. But look where we should be landed, on this hand or on that, if others than those that choose to provide the money are to decide where church-building is ' necessary ' or is ' prudent.' The extreme chapel-attendance of Episcopalians in the county of Roxburgh was shown by the census to be 454; and for the accommodation of that number the county contains five chapels. Four of them might be pronounced not ' necessary,' and all of them not ' prudent.' Or, to go from the country of the rioters to that of the rioted upon. In our humble opinion, seven-eighths of the churches belonging to the Establishment in Ireland are utterly unnecessary, and every one of them very imprudent. Such, too, is notoriously the opinion of all but a fraction of the population among whom, and out of whose funds, these churches are built and maintained. The late lamented Roman Catholic chapel at Kelso was immeasurably less unnecessary and offensive than these; for not only had it a congregation, but was paid for only by those that used it or approved of it. Of course, the Lord Justice-Clerk did not mean that his opinion or that of any other man as to the chapel being unnecessary was any justification of the outrage—his lordship said the contrary very impressively; but his remark, though not what is called a fortunate one, is useful as indicating, in however faint and refined shape and degree, the feeling which on such topics is apt to lead us all more or less astray.

MISSIONS IN THE WESTERN HIGHLANDS : MOIDART.

The purchase by Mr. Hope-Scott of the estate at Lochshiel, in the wilds of Moidart, his 'Highland Paraguay,' as Cardinal Manning calls it, in an old letter to him (January 28, 1856), was attended, as I have already hinted (p. 160), by some noteworthy circumstances. In the first place, the condition of the Catholic remnant in the Highlands is, perhaps, little known even to Catholic readers. An interesting letter to Mr. Hope-Scott, dated October 12, 1854, from the Rev. D. Macdonald, in charge of the mission of Fortwilliam, furnishes a statistical table, from which it appears that in 1851, in the Highlands and insular districts within the range of his knowledge, there was but one single school, where, to do justice, considering the scattered population, there ought to have been twenty-six. The people were so miserably poor, that out of thirteen missions, only two could afford their priest 50l. per annum ; one, 35l. ; three, 30l. ; and the rest, ranging from 25l. down to as low as 12l. per annum. Of course the priests could not subsist on these incomes without some other aid, and this was obtained by taking small farms, from which they endeavoured to eke out a living.

'In Moidart' (I here copy from another well-informed correspondent) 'a severe crisis had just passed over the people. The cruel treatment which has depopulated the greater portion of the Highlands, and converted large tracts of country into sheep-farms and deer-forests, had overtaken them. Dozens of unfortunate families occupying the more fertile portions of the estate were

ruthlessly torn from their homes, and shipped away to
Australia and America. Their good old priest, the Rev.
Ranald Rankin, broken-hearted at the desolation which
had come over his flock, accompanied the larger portion
of these wanderers to the shores of Australia. His impression at the time was, that the whole of the country,
sooner or later, would share the same unhappy fate;
for in bidding farewell to his Bishop, the late Dr.
Murdoch, Vicar-Apostolic of the Western District, he
assured his lordship, who felt at a loss how to supply
his place, that it was a matter of little or no consequence, as the mission was practically ruined already.
The Bishop's reply was characteristic : "Moidart has
always been a Catholic district ; and so long as there
remains one Catholic family in it, for the sake of its old
steadfastness, I shall not leave it unprovided." '

In the meantime, Mr. Hope-Scott, having already
become a landed proprietor in Ireland, in the county
Mayo, much wished to possess also a Highland property.
Lochshiel was offered to him ; but, after consideration,
he decided against taking it. In 1855 the estate was
again in the market, but Mr. Hope-Scott had not heard
of it. The owner, Macdonald of Lochshiel, was a
Catholic, and, it may be presumed, a devout one, since
he had the Blessed Sacrament and a priest in his house.
He had been obliged to sell, and the property had been
bought by a brother-in-law of his, named Macdonell,
who added to the house. He, too, found himself
obliged to sell, and this time the estate was on the
point of passing into the hands of people from London
who would have rooted out the Catholic population

from the land. Hearing that it had been actually sold
to Protestants, two old ladies of the same family, living
at Portobello, went to the lawyer, and asked him, if
possible, to postpone the signature of the deeds for nine
or ten days, to give another purchaser a chance. He
agreed to do so. They then commenced a *novena* that a
Catholic might buy it. (I ought perhaps to explain, for
the benefit of some of my readers, that Catholics have
great faith in the efficacy of prayer persevered in for
nine days when there is some important object to be
gained.) The ninth day came, and Mr. Hope-Scott pur-
chased the property, for the sum of 24,000*l.*, without
even having seen it. His attention had been drawn to
it by the late Mrs. Colonel Hutchison, of Edinburgh, a
lady well known among Scotch Catholics for her shrewd
good sense and innumerable good works. He certainly
was induced to purchase by the fact that Lochshiel
had never been out of Catholic hands, and that all the
population were Catholic, with the personal motive, however, of providing his wife with a quiet and pleasant
change of residence.

'On his arrival, the character of the people, and the
wild and glorious scenery of the place, made a favourable and lasting impression on his mind ;[3] but the state
of the country might have appeared to him as little more
advanced than it was under the earlier Clanranald chiefs
three or four centuries ago. The peasants generally
were in a state of great poverty. Their cottages were

---

[3] How deeply the Highland scenery impressed his imagination may be
seen from the beautiful verses, 'Low Tide at Sunset on the Highland Coast,'
which will be found in Appendix IV.

miserable turf cabins, black and smoky ; agriculture was imperfectly understood among them, and the small patches of moorland upon which they tried to raise crops of oats and potatoes were inadequate to the maintenance of themselves and their families. There was no demand or employment of labour. There was no school upon the estate. The principal building assigned to religious worship, and which served as the central chapel for Moidart, was a miserable thatched edifice, destitute of everything befitting the service of religion. The want of good roads was severely felt. It was difficult to get into " the *Rough Bounds*," as this part of the Highlands was aptly styled by the more favoured districts, and, once in, it was more difficult still to get out.

'Mr. Hope-Scott lost no time in trying to improve matters. It was a fundamental maxim with him that, in a neglected estate like this, no improvement was more sensible, or paid better, than the construction of good roads. These occupied his attention for several years and gave most beneficial employment to the tenant . The cost in some instances was very great ; for, in constructing the present beautiful carriage drive from Sheil Bridge to Dorlin House, hundreds of yards of solid rock had to be blasted ; part of the river Sheil had to be embanked ; huge boulders between the cliffs and the sea-shore had to be cleared away, while a considerable line of breastwork had to be erected as a protection against the waves of the Atlantic, which, in a south-west gale, beat with great fury against the coast. The other roads were carried to those parts of the estate where the tenants were principally clustered, and were a great boon.

[These road-making operations in the Highlands were evidently in Mr. Hope-Scott's mind in one of his last letters to his dear friend Dr. Newman. The great Oratorian, then busy with the 'Grammar of Assent,' writes to him on January 2, 1870 : 'My dear Hope-Scott,—A happy new year to you and all yours—and to Bellasis and all his. . . . I am engaged, as Bellasis knows, in cutting across the Isthmus of Suez ; and though I have got so far as to let the water into the canal, there is an awkward rock in mid-channel near the mouth which takes a great deal of picking and blasting, and no man-of-war will be able to pass through till I get rid of it. Thus I can't name a day for the opening. Ever yours affectionately,—JOHN H. NEWMAN.'

Mr. Hope-Scott's reply is—' Hôtel d'Orient, Hyères (Var), France, January 12, 1870.—Dear F. Newman,— [After giving an account of Serjeant Bellasis's health, then seriously ill, and anxiously asking for masses and prayers for him,] That rocky point in your enterprise is a nuisance—more especially as rocks lie in beds, and this may be but the " crop " of some large stratum. As a road-maker, I know what it is to have to come back upon my work, and to strike a new level to get rid of some seemingly small but hard obstacle. . . . Yours ever affectionately,—JAMES R. HOPE-SCOTT.']

' The improvement of the tenants' own condition was a subject of serious consideration. It was impossible to build new houses for every one ; but great facilities were offered by the proprietor to such as were willing to build for themselves. Wood and lime were placed at their disposal free of charge, and a sum of 10*l.* or 12*l.* was added to help in defraying the expenses of the mason-work. A few cottages of a superior kind were built at the entire expense of the proprietor ; but the cost was out of all proportion with the rental of the estate, and this attempt had to be abandoned for a time. Mr. Hope-Scott's kindness towards the smaller tenants was very marked. Besides helping them to better houses, he frequently assisted them with considerable sums of money towards increasing their stock of cattle, or towards repairing losses from accidents and disease. In some cases his generosity extended to the poorer tenants on neighbouring estates, when, for instance, they felt themselves at a loss for means to purchase a new boat or to provide themselves with fishing-nets.[4] To encourage a spirit of independence among them, he used to grant sums of money on *loan* ; but when, at the end of a successful season, the borrowers came back with the money, he invariably refused to accept it, or he would give instructions to have it passed on to some other poor person in difficulties.' His efforts to induce them to extend cultivation have been elsewhere noticed (p. 191). 'He never left the country towards the end of autumn without leaving a few pounds for distribution among the poorer classes. The clergyman of the district had always strict injunctions to report any case of hardship, or illness, or distress, and to draw upon

---

[4] Mr. Hope-Scott had formed schemes for the employment of the people in working the salmon fisheries, and, when the salmon was out of season, the deep-sea fishing, and enabling them to dispose of their fish.

his purse for what was required. The habits of the
people soon showed signs of real improvement. A more
orderly or respectable class of tenants are not to be
found in any other part of the Highlands. From the
day of his coming among them until now the rents
have remained the same, greatly to the prosperity of the
tenants. With the rest of the proprietors residing in
and near Moidart he was very popular. His relations
with them were invariably pleasant and happy.

'In 1859, Mr. Hope-Scott commenced the erection of
a school at Mingarry, with ample accommodation for
scholars and teacher. It was completed in 1860. This
was an improvement very acceptable to the tenants.
Hitherto the Catholic children had to cross over to a
neighbouring estate, where the Society for the Propagation of Christian Knowledge had established a schoolhouse and teacher, or they had to frequent another
school, often very irregularly, in Ardnamurchan. The
secular teaching in both of these schools was excellent
of its kind. But, although the most cordial relations
have, for generations past, existed between the Catholics
on the north and the Presbyterians on the south side
of the river Sheil, it was always a subject of regret
among the former that they had no means of educating
their children nearer home, and under Catholic teachers.
After the school was successfully opened, Mr. Hope-
Scott supplied funds to defray the teacher's salary.

'In 1862, he erected, at a cost of about 2,600*l.*, the
present church and presbytery at Mingarry, within a
few hundred yards of the school ; but, to his grief, this
was the least satisfactory of all his undertakings, from

one cause or another, neither church nor presbytery
coming up to his expectations; and the former was for
years a continual source of trouble and expenditure.'
He built also another, at Glenuig, mentioned already.

To complete the history of Dorlin, so far as it is
connected with Mr. Hope-Scott: when, towards the
close of his life, he had completely given up practice, he
made up his mind to part with it, great as he acknowledged the wrench was—but to a Catholic purchaser—
and sold it to Lord Howard of Glossop, the present
proprietor, who worthily carries out the admirable
example bequeathed him by his predecessor.[5]

The missions of *Oban*, and, on the other side of
Scotland, *St. Andrews*,[6] must also be named as either
created or largely assisted by Mr. Hope-Scott; and,
among Scottish religious houses, lastly, but not least,
St. Margaret's convent at *Edinburgh* (the Ursulines of
Jesus), as a cherished object of his benefactions, and
kind counsel and help.

Mr. Hope-Scott's Irish Tenantry.

Of Mr. Hope-Scott's dealings, as a Catholic proprietor, with his Irish estates (co. Mayo), what has
appeared in a former chapter (p. 190) gives a pleasing
idea, quite borne out by other letters that have come

---

[5] Lord Howard of Glossop died as these sheets were passing through
the press, December 1, 1883. R. I. P.

[6] He had been otherwise interested in St. Andrews, during the years
1846–51, when associated with Sir John Gladstone (father of the Premier)
in a scheme for developing that town as a bathing-place, building houses, &c.
This, however, was a speculation on which it would be needless to enlarge,
even if I had the details. In a letter to Miss Hope-Scott (May 25, 1867)
he observes, 'St. Andrews is the best sea quarter in Scotland, I believe
(and you know I have property there, which proves it).'

before me. The Rev. James Browne, writing to him on June 12, 1856, to acknowledge a donation for the chapel and school of *Killavalla*, says of his tenantry there: ' They all look upon it as a blessing from God that they have got a Catholic landlord, who has the same religious sympathies that they have themselves.' Thirteen years later (May 9, 1869) the same priest writes : ' I have been holding stations of confession among your people at Balliburke, Gortbane, and Killadier. I was glad to find them happy and contented, the houses neat, and the people most comfortable.'

CHARITIES AT HYÈRES.

At Hyères I can say from my own knowledge that Mr. Hope-Scott's support of a chaplain is to be numbered among his charitable and fruitful deeds. The arrangement was made with all his usual thoughtfulness ; it enabled a most excellent priest, who was in a slow decline, but could still hear confessions and do much good, to spend a few winters in a warm climate. The Rev. Edward Dunne acted also as confessor to the little English colony at Hyères, as well as to the family of Mr. Hope-Scott. It often happens that, in such a watering-place, strangers whose case is hopeless come for a last chance of life. Sometimes they are Catholics, or needing instruction, and willing to receive it ; sometimes they are in distressed circumstances. Father Dunne's great prudence and charity well fitted him for these ministrations, and he was equally beloved by Catholics and Protestants. The good which such a priest does is shared by the benefactor who places him in the position where he has the means of doing it. The following passage from a letter of Father Dunne's to Mr. Hope-Scott (May 26, 1869), which must have been one of his last, will interest the reader as an example :—

You will be glad to know that my being at Hyères was a great blessing to a poor young man who died there towards the end of April. He had been at sea, and was for years without receiving the sacraments. His poor mother, a very pious woman, was in the greatest anxiety about him. He could not speak French, and it would have been impossible for him to make his confession if I, or some other English-speaking priest, was not there. I mention this, as I know it will be a consolation to you to know that your charity and benevolence were, under God, the means of saving a poor soul, and will secure for you the prayers of a bereaved mother, and three holy nuns, aunts of the poor young man.

CHAPTER XXVII.

1868–1873.

Mr. Hope-Scott's Speech on Termination of Guardianship to the Duke of
Norfolk—Failure in Mr. Hope-Scott's Health—Exhaustion after a Day's
Pleading—His Neglect of Exercise—Death of Mr. Badeley—Letter of
Dr. Newman—Last Correspondence of Mr. Hope and the Bishop of
Salisbury (Hamilton)—Dr. Newman's Friendship for Mr. Hope-Scott and
Serjeant Bellasis—Mr. Hope-Scott proposes to retire—Birth of James
Fitzalan Hope—Death of Lady Victoria Hope-Scott—Mr. Hope-Scott
retires from his Profession—Edits Abridgment of Lockhart, which he
dedicates to Mr. Gladstone—Dr. Newman on Sir Walter Scott—Visit of
Dr. Newman to Abbotsford in 1872—Mr. Hope-Scott's Last Illness—
His Faith and Resignation—His Death—Benediction of the Holy
Father—Requiem Mass for Mr. Hope-Scott at the Jesuit Church, Farm
Street — Funeral Ceremonies at St. Margaret's, Edinburgh — Cardinal
Newman and Mr. Gladstone on Mr. Hope-Scott.

MR. HOPE-SCOTT's duties as trustee and guardian of the
Duke of Norfolk had lasted altogether eight years, when
they terminated of course on the Duke's attaining his
majority, on December 27, 1868. The speech made by
Mr. Hope-Scott, at the banquet given by the Duke in
the Baron's Hall at Arundel Castle, to the Mayor and
Corporation of Arundel, on the following day, was a
striking and beautiful one. I copy a few lines of it
from the summary given in the 'Tablet' of January 16,
1869 :—

Mr. Hope-Scott paid a well-merited tribute to the virtues
of the Duchess when he said that if they observed in the
Duke earnestness and yet gentleness, strict justice and yet
most liberal and charitable feelings, neglect of himself and
attention to the wants of all around him, let them remember

that his mother brought him up. The guardianship being now over, the ward must go forward on the battle-field of life, depending not upon his rank or property, but upon his own prudence, his own courage, but above all, his fidelity to God. It was true that his path was strewn with the broken weapons and defaced armour of many who had gone forth amidst acclamations as loud and promises as bright, but the groundworks of hope in his case were the nobility of his father's character, the prayers of his mother, the strong domestic affections which belong to pure and single-minded youths, great powers of observation, great vigour of will, and the daily and habitual influence under which he knew that he lived, of well-reasoned and well-regulated religion.

The celebrations at Arundel were, I believe, the last occasion, unconnected with his profession, at which Mr. Hope-Scott ever spoke in public. He had already, for some years, showed signs of failing health. It used to be supposed, as has been previously mentioned, from the facility of his manner in pleading, that he got through his work with little trouble. People little knew what commonly happened when he reached home, after the day's pleading was over. Such was his state of lassitude, that he would drop, like a load, upon the first chair he found, and instantly fall into a profound sleep : sometimes he was half carried, thus unconscious, to bed, or sometimes placed at table, and made to swallow a little food. Even when the prostration was not so overpowering, the chances were that he would fall fast asleep, at dinner or at dessert, in the middle of a sentence. All this resembles very closely what Thiers related of himself to Mr. Senior. The French statesman, after a day of Parliamentary battle, had often to be carried to his bed by his servants, as motionless and helpless as a corpse. This strange torpor, after extreme intellectual exertion, seems to have been observed in Mr. Hope-Scott from a very early stage in his career, during the great railway excitement of 1845. It was probably connected with the shock given to his constitution, in his childhood, by the fever at Florence. There was always a kind of struggle going on in his system. Unfortunately, throughout his professional life he never took proper exercise. It was, however, in vain to advise him on this point. He said he could not *both* work hard and take exercise also, or would playfully insist that he had sufficient exercise in pleading. 'Why don't you go out?' asked a friend. 'Don't you think,' replied Mr. Hope-Scott, 'that the work in committee gives a man sufficient exercise? Cicero considered making a speech was exercise.'[1] This great mistake was the more to be wondered at in Mr. Hope-Scott, as he had had the advantage of an early initiation into field sports. At Arundel, indeed, he sometimes went out shooting, but these were exceptional occasions. His chief active amusements, gardening and architecture, were insufficient to compensate the depression caused by the tremendous strain of half the year at Westminster.

In the year 1856 he was exceedingly unwell, and the failure in his health became very appreciable, his physician telling him that he had 'the heart of an overworked brain.' Within two years after this, the violence of his grief at Mrs. Hope-Scott's death further disordered him. He had an illness in 1865, and again a

[1] There is proof, however, in an interesting passage (Cic. ad Q. Fr. III. iii. 1) that Cicero did reserve time for walking exercise, even in his busiest days.

scrious one in 1867, which, however, he got over, and
went on as usual, but became much stouter, and suffered much from impeded circulation.

It happened also, soon after this, that the breaking
up of some very dear associations, or sure signs of it,
began to give warning that the end of all things was at
hand.   On March 29, 1868, rather suddenly, died Mr.
Badeley, the most affectionate and faithful friend of so
many years.   On hearing of his illness Mr. Hope-Scott
had hastened home from Hyères to assist him, and was
with him each day till the last.   Dr. Newman wrote the
following letter on this occasion :—

The Very Rev. Dr. Newman to J. R. Hope-Scott, Esq. Q.C.

Rednall : March 31, 1868.

My dear Hope-Scott,—What a heavy, sudden, unexpected
blow!   I shall not see him now till I cross the stream which
he has crossed.   How dense is our ignorance of the future ! a
darkness which can be felt, and the keenest consequence and
token of the Fall.   Till we remind ourselves of what we are—
in a state of punishment—such surprises make us impatient,
and almost angry, alas !

But my blow is nothing to yours, though you had the great
consolation of sitting by his side and being with him to the last.
What a fulness of affection he poured out on you and yours!
and how he must have rejoiced to have your faithful presence
with him while he was going !   This is your joy and your pain.

Now he has the recompense for that steady, well-ordered,
perpetual course of devotion and obedience which I ever
admired in him, and felt to be so much above anything that I
could reach.   All or most of us have said mass for him, I am
sure, this morning ; certainly we two have who are here.

I did not write to you during the past fortnight, thinking it
would only bother you, and knowing I should hear if there was
anything to tell.   But you have been as much surprised as

R 2

any one at his sudden summons. I knew it was the beginning
of the end, but thought it was only the beginning. How was
it his medical men did not know better?

I suppose the funeral is on Saturday. God bless and keep
and sustain you.

Ever yours most affectionately,
John H. Newman.

The year had not yet come round when the last
correspondence passed between Mr. Hope-Scott and
another dear friend, Dr. Hamilton, Bishop of Salisbury,
his brother-Fellow at Merton so many years before.

J. R. Hope-Scott, Esq. Q.C. to the Right Rev. Dr. Hamilton
(Bishop of Salisbury).

Hyères: March 10, 1869.

My dear Friend,—I have watched the papers with anxiety,
and learnt all I could from home about your health, but have
been unwilling to trouble you with a letter. However, Manning
has just been here, and we naturally spoke with our old affection of you, and joined in hopes for your welfare ; and I thought
you might like to know that two of your oldest friends have
been so engaged. Hence these few lines. May God keep
you !   Yours ever affect^ly,

James R. Hope-Scott.

The Right Rev. Dr. Hamilton (Bishop of Salisbury) to
J. R. Hope-Scott, Esq. Q.C.

33 Grosvenor Street : March 13, 1869.

My dearly loved Friend,—I have received your note, *non
sine multis lachrymis,* and though I am too weak to write an
answer myself, I must dictate a few words of thankfulness to it.
Few trials of my life I have felt with such keenness as my
separation from two such friends, from whom I have learnt so
much, and whom I have loved and love so dearly as Manning
and yourself. Perhaps this feeling for you both has helped to
prevent my doing that which it has been my daily aim not to

do, namely, to hinder either by word or deed that object which I venture to say is as dear to me as to you—the reunion of Christendom. May GOD forgive me anything which has led me to lose sight of this in all my ministrations! Nothing, however, would tend more to forward this than a just and charitable estimate of the claims of the Church of England on the part of the authorities of your communion. I have dictated these few words, and my chaplain, Liddon, has written them exactly as I have dictated them, and I beg you to receive them as a legacy of affection and deep respect from your old brother-Fellow,

W. K. SARUM.

J. R. Hope-Scott, Esq. Q.C. to the Rev. Canon Liddon.

Villa Favart, Hyères: March 17, 1869.

My dear Sir,—Accept my grateful thanks for the letter which you added to that of my very dear friend the Bishop. To him I do not write, for it is plain that he should make no exertion that can be avoided; but I trust to your kindness to assure him that I was indeed deeply moved—more than I can well say—both by his love for me and by his sufferings, and that my prayers, and those of others far more worthy than myself, are offered to GOD for him.

Yours very truly,

JAMES R. HOPE-SCOTT.

And another twelvemonth had not been completed before Mr. Hope-Scott's attached friend and familiar neighbour of many years (both in London and at Hyères), Serjeant Bellasis, was visibly nearing his departure.[2] The

[2] With Mr. Serjeant Bellasis, who had been received into the Church about the same time with himself, Mr. Hope-Scott lived upon terms of fraternal intimacy, sharing chambers with him, both in Parliament Street and Victoria Street (see Vol. I. p. 102). Their professional pursuits at the Parliamentary Bar (of which the Serjeant also was a distinguished member), with many winters spent together at Hyères, had thrown them greatly into each other's society; and as co-executors to the will of Bertram, Earl of Shrewsbury, the friends had become still more closely united by the anxious years of suspense and litigation of which it was the occasion. Mr. Serjeant Bellasis died January 24, 1873.

following letters witness, in a most touching manner, to their mutual affection, and to that of Dr. Newman for them both :—

The Very Rev. Dr. Newman to J. R. Hope-Scott, Esq. Q.C.

The Oratory : March 3, '70.

My dear Hope-Scott,—After writing a conversational letter to Bellasis yesterday, I heard at night so sad an account, which I had not anticipated, of his pain and his weakness and want of sleep, that I not only was distressed that it had gone, but felt that it would even harass him to receive a second letter so soon, and, as he would anticipate, as unseasonable as the former. Therefore I enclose with this a few lines to him, which you can let him have when you think right.

I do not undervalue the seriousness of your first letter about him, and have had him constantly in my mind ; but I did not contemplate his pain, or his sudden decline. I thought it would be a long business, but now I find that the complaint is making its way.

What a severe blow it must be to you! but to me, in my own way, it is very great too, though in a different way; for, though I am not in his constant society as you are, he has long been *pars magna* of this place, and he has, by his various acts of friendship through a succession of years, created for himself a presence in my thoughts, so that the thought of being without him carries with it the sense of a void, to which it is difficult to assign a limit. Three æquales I shall have lost— Badeley, H. Bowden, and Bellasis ; and such losses seem to say that I have no business here myself. It is the penalty of living to lose the great props of life. What a melancholy prospect for his poor boys ! When you have an opportunity, say everything kind from me to Mrs. Bellasis. I shall, I trust, say two masses a week for him. He is on our prayer lists. What a vanity is life ! how it crumbles under one's touch !

I hope you are getting strong, and that this does not weigh too heavily on you. . . .   Ever y^{rs} aff^{ly},

JOHN H. NEWMAN.

J. R. Hope-Scott, Esq. Q.C. to the Very Rev. Dr. Newman.

Hôtel d'Orient, Hyères, Var, France :
March 6, '70.

Dear F. Newman,—I received yours yesterday evening, but withhold the enclosure for Bellasis, as I think it might do him harm. [After giving a somewhat better account of his friend's health :]

Masses and prayers I am sure he has many, and I know how grateful he is for your deep interest in him. . . . Should he be able to get out, I hope for more progress : but, with slight exceptions, he has now been confined to the house for weeks. However, his patience helps him greatly, and when, as lately he has often been, free from pain, his cheerfulness revives, and with it his interest in the works he has undertaken, and the subjects which have long interested him.

I am sure that the dedication of your new work [the 'Grammar of Assent'] to him affects him, as that of your poems did Badeley, in a very soothing way. Few have such extensive means of testifying to their friendships as you have.

Y^{rs} aff^{ly},

JAMES R. HOPE-SCOTT.

Repeated griefs of this kind would not be without their effect on Mr. Hope-Scott's own already failing health. By 1870 the physicians pronounced that there was functional, though not organic, disease of the heart, the valve losing its power to close. He spoke of this himself to a near relative at the time, adding that he had immediately asked whether he might expect the end to come suddenly ; but had been told that in all probability it would not, and that he would have warning of its approach. He now began to talk of retiring, and did take the first step, by giving up a certain number of causes. But he said to a professional

friend : ' I own I dread giving up ; it is almost like the
excitement of racing, and the reaction would be so
strong, life so flat, when such an interest is lost, and the
stimulus over.'   Before this happened, meeting another
friend in the street, who had wisely retreated in time,
Mr. Hope-Scott asked him how he got on ?   ' Oh, very
well ; I fall back on my old classics—don't you do
the same ? '   ' Oh no,' replied Mr. Hope-Scott ; ' when I
go to the country, I find it indispensable to allow my
mind to lie entirely fallow.   I live in the open air, go
on planting, and do no mental work whatever.'

This was the state of things when he had suddenly
to meet a new sorrow, and the last.   A son, indeed
(James Fitzalan), was born to him on December 11,
1870, thus replacing the long wished-for blessing which
had been given and withdrawn ; but Lady Victoria's
health had for years been enfeebled, a fever came on,
and, after lingering for a time between life and death,
she expired at Norfolk House on December 20, aged
only thirty, leaving three little girls, besides the newly
born babe.   It happened on this occasion, as so often
in Mr. Hope-Scott's life, that he had persuaded himself
that things would be as he wished they should.   He
never believed that Lady Victoria was dying, though
she was in her agony, and had been senseless for ten
days ; nay, he could hardly be made to think it, even
at the last moment ; and this time he never recovered
the shock.   The morning after the funeral [3] he said that
he considered he had had a warning that night —

---

[3] Lady Victoria Hope-Scott was laid beside her father and her two infant
children in the vault at Arundel Castle.

the disease had made a *stride*. He had never contemplated surviving his wife, and had made all arrangements on the supposition that he was to die before her. On the very night that followed he altered his will. He sent for his confidential clerk, destroyed quantities of papers, and, in short, evidently considered himself a dying man. He now definitively retired from his profession, and, though he survived for more than two years, what remains to be told is little more than the story of a last illness.

The years 1871 and 1872, indeed, passed tranquilly enough, as if there was a lull and a silence after the storm. Mr. Hope-Scott resided chiefly at Abbotsford, and devoted part of his leisure in the first year to preparing an edition (the Centenary) of the Abridgment of Lockhart's ' Life of Scott.' [4] He also thought that it was time for the larger 'Life' to be revised, and the extracts from letters to be compared with the originals, &c., and actually began the task after the republication of the Abridgment, but, I believe, very soon gave it up. He dedicated the Abridgment to Mr. Gladstone, whose letter in reply to his proposal to do so is subjoined :—

The Right Hon. W. E. Gladstone, M.P. to
J. R. Hope-Scott, Esq. Q.C.

11 Carlton House Terrace, S.W. :
March 25, '71.

My dear Hope-Scott,— . . . I learn with pleasure that you now find yourself able to make the effort necessary for applying yourself to what I trust you will find a healthful and genial employment.

---

[4] *The Life of Sir Walter Scott, Bart., abridged from the larger work,* by J. G. Lockhart, with a Prefatory Letter by James R. Hope-Scott, Esq., Q.C. Edinburgh : Adam & Charles Black, 1871.

You offer me a double temptation, to which I yield with but too much readiness. I am glad of anything which associates my name with yours; and I feel it a great honour to be marked out in the public view by your selection of me as a loyal admirer of Scott, towards whom, both as writer and as man, I cannot help entertaining feelings, perhaps (though this is saying much) even bordering upon excess.

Honesty binds me to wish you would do better for your purpose, but if you do not think any other plan desirable, I accept your proposal with thanks. Believe me

Aff^{tely} yours,

W. E. GLADSTONE.

J. R. Hope-Scott, Esq., Q.C.

From the letter of dedication, which I should have been glad, if space had permitted, to give as a whole, I subjoin the opening and closing paragraphs, with notices (inclusive of some critical remarks) of the deeply interesting pages which intervene :—

J. R. Hope-Scott, Esq. Q.C. to the Right Hon.
W. E. Gladstone, M.P.

Arundel Castle : April 10, 1871.

My dear Gladstone,—Although our friendship has endured for many years, and has survived great changes, it is not on account of my affection for you that I have desired to connect these pages with your name. It is because from you, more than from any one else who is now alive, I have received assurances of that strong and deep admiration of Walter Scott, both as an author and as a man, which I have long felt myself, and which I heartily agree with you in wishing to extend and perpetuate. On my part, such a desire might on other grounds be natural ; on yours it can only spring from the conviction, which I know you to entertain, that both the writings and the personal history of that extraordinary man, while affording entertainment of the purest kind, and supplying stores of information which can nowhere else be so pleasantly acquired, have in them a great deal which no student of human nature ought to neglect, and much also which those who engage in the struggle of life with high purposes—men who are prepared to work earnestly and endure nobly—cannot pass without loss.

[After quoting passages from Mr. Gladstone's letters to himself, showing the hold which Walter Scott had over his friend's mind, Mr. Hope-Scott states his reasons for abandoning his original idea of having a new Life written, and for preferring to publish an Abridgment of it, and the Abridgment by Lockhart himself:—]

A work of art in writing is subject to the same rules as one in painting or in architecture. Those who seek to represent it in a reduced form must, above all things, study its proportions, and make their reduction equal over all its parts. But, in the case of written compositions, there are no mechanical appliances as there are in painting and architecture, for varying the scale; and there is, moreover, a greater difficulty in catching the leading principle of the design, and thus establishing the starting point for the process which is to follow. Hence, an abridgment by the author himself must necessarily be the best —indeed, the only true abridgment of what he has intended in his larger work; and I deem it very fortunate that Cadell's influence overcame Lockhart's repugnance to the task. . . .

There is [however] an abiding reason why Scott's personal history should not be too freely generalised, and an abstract notion be substituted for the real man. . . . In Scott, if in any man, what was remarkable was the sustained and continuous power of his character. It is to be traced in the smallest things as well as in the greatest; in his daily habits as much as in his public actions; in his fancies and follies as well as in his best and wisest doings. Everywhere we find the same power of imagination, and the same energy of will; and though it has been said that no man is a hero to his *valet-de chambre*, I am satisfied that Scott's most familiar attendants never doubted his greatness, or looked upon him with less respect than those who judged him as he stood forth amidst the homage of the world. In dealing with such a character, it is hardly necessary to say that the omission of details becomes, after a certain point, a serious injury to the truth of the whole portrait; and if any man should object that this volume is not short enough, I should be tempted to answer, that if he reads by foot-rule, he had better not think of studying, in any shape, the life of Walter Scott.

[In what follows, Mr. Hope-Scott speaks of 'the depth and tenderness of feeling which Lockhart, in daily life, so often hid under an almost fierce reserve,' and regards it as matter of thankfulness that he was spared the suffering he would have felt in the death of his only daughter, ' whose singular likeness to her mother must have continually recalled to him both the features and the character of her of whom he wrote ' those touching words in the original Life which Mr. Hope-Scott quotes, with evident application to his own bereavement, to which he makes a short and sad reference. He concludes :—]

And now, my dear Gladstone, *vive valeque.* You have already earned a noble place in the history of your country, and though there is one great subject on which we differ, I am able heartily to desire that your future career may be as distinguished as your past. But since it is only too certain that the highest honours of statesmanship can neither be won nor held without exertions which are full of danger to those who make them, I will add the further wish, that you may long retain, as safe-guards to your health, your happiness, and your usefulness, that fresh and versatile spirit, and that strong sense of the true and beautiful, which have caused you to be addressed on this occasion by   Your affectionate friend,

JAMES R. HOPE-SCOTT.

The Right Hon. W. E. Gladstone.

Dr. Newman's letter, on receiving from Mr. Hope-Scott a copy of the Abridgment, is full of interest :—

The Very Rev. Dr. Newman to J. R. Hope-Scott, Esq. Q.C.

The Oratory: May 14, 1871.

My dear Hope-Scott,—Thank you for your book.   In one sense I deserve it ; I have ever had such a devotion, I may call it, to Walter Scott.   As a boy, in the early summer mornings I read 'Waverley' and 'Guy Mannering' in bed, when they first came out, before it was time to get up ; and long before that, I think, when I was eight years old, I listened eagerly to the 'Lay of the Last Minstrel,' which my mother and aunt were reading aloud.   When he was dying I was continually thinking of him, with Keble's words—'If ever floating from faint earthly lyre,' &c. (Sixth after Trin.).[5]

It has been a trouble to me that his works seemed to be so forgotten now.   Our boys know very little about them.   I think F. Ambrose had to give a prize for getting up 'Kenilworth.'   Your letter to Gladstone sadly confirms it.   I wonder whether there will ever be a crisis and correction of the evil ? It arises from the facilities of publication.   Every season bears its own crop of books, and every fresh season ousts the foregoing.   Books are all annuals ; and, to revive Scott, you must annihilate the existing generation of writers, which is legion. If it so fares with Scott, still more does it so fare with Johnson, Addison, Pope, and Shakespeare.   Perhaps the competitive examinations may come to the aid.   You should get Gladstone to bring about a list of classics, and force them upon candidates. I do not see any other way of mending matters.   I wish I heard a better account of you.

Ever y^{rs} aff^{ly},

JOHN H. NEWMAN.

During all this time Mr. Hope-Scott's health continued steadily to fail ; yet he suffered rather from

---

[5] Compare a letter of Dr. Newman's to J. R. Hope in 1852.   See *ante*, p. 153.

malaise than from any acute symptoms. Now and then there were gleams in which he seemed better for a space, but they were but as the flickerings of the flame in the socket. In March 1872 Bournemouth was tried. In the summer of that year he was in Scotland, and in July had the great happiness of receiving a visit of about a fortnight from Dr. Newman at Abbotsford, which revived the memories of twenty years—for so long was the interval since his former visit. This, I suppose, was the last occasion of Mr. Hope-Scott's entertaining guests. He was able to move about quietly; old times were gently talked over, and there was nothing to show that the great separation was very imminent. It was even possible, the doctors had told him when the disease was first apparent, to linger under it for twenty years. Thus the last days at Abbotsford looked as if lit up by the setting sun. He fell off, however, a day or two after Dr. Newman left; went first to Luffness, and in October, whilst staying in Edinburgh, the heart affection becoming worse, he seemed, for a time, in immediate danger; yet rallied, and removed to London by easy stages, halting first at Newcastle and then at Peterborough. Owing to the thoughtful kindness of Mr. H. Hope, of Luffness, he was accompanied by Dr. Howden, the family physician at Luffness. It was, however, a most anxious journey, and it often seemed doubtful whether he would reach his destination alive. Soon after his arrival in London he had a dangerous attack, and received the last sacraments, with the Holy Father's blessing. This was at No. 7 Hyde Park Place, the house of his widowed sister-in-law, the Hon. Mrs. G. W. Hope; and here, under her affectionate care, and that of his daughter, Mary Monica, Mr. Hope-Scott spent the few months that remained to him.

Miss Hope-Scott (now the Hon. Mrs. Maxwell Scott), during those months, kept a diary, commencing March 13, 1873, of all that passed, which she has kindly placed in my hands. At first the entries were usually of ' a good night,' and ' tired,' or ' very tired,' during the day, though he is occasionally able to go into the library, to talk a little with his younger children in their turns, and to see near relatives from time to time. Soon the nights get less good, the days more languid, and he is seldom able to leave his room. For about a fortnight (April 4–17) there seemed a slight improvement, but this did not last, and on April 28 there was a great change for the worse. Sir W. Jenner, Sir W. Gull, and Mr. Sims held a consultation, and pronounced very unfavourably. Father Clare, S.J., brought the Blessed Sacrament, and spent the night in the house. The following morning, Tuesday, April 29, he heard his confession, and gave him Holy Communion. It was the morning on which he usually received. The two physicians hesitated about Extreme Unction being administered, for fear of causing excitement. But, on the priest's asking him what he wished, the reply at once was, ' Dear Father, give me all you can, and all the helps which Holy Church can bestow.' During the administration of the sacrament he answered all the prayers himself; and the physicians, on leaving the room, said there had not been the least excitement. I

take these particulars from a letter of Father Clare's to
the Hon. Mrs. Maxwell Scott, in which he also says :
'During the whole of his illness I never knew him
to show the slightest impatience, I never heard one
murmur ; but in all our conversation there was *invariably* a cheerful resignation to the holy will of our
good God. His lively faith and wonderful fervour in
receiving Holy Communion, which was at least twice a
week, I have never seen surpassed.'

The Duke of Norfolk was telegraphed for from
Arundel. He arrived about 2 P.M. Mr. Hope-Scott
was able to see him, spoke of the blessing which his
church would bring on him (the splendid church of
St. Philip's, Arundel, just completed by the Duke), and
promised to pray for him the next day, when it was
to be opened. Sir William Gull now left hardly any
hope. The ceremony of the opening of the church was
deferred, and all the Arundel party arrived that night.
The following is the last paragraph in the diary :—

'In the afternoon, dear papa, after taking something, said out aloud his favourite prayer, "*Fiat,
laudetur.*" [6] Then, looking at me, he said, "God's will be
done," and asked me to say some prayers. I said the
Angelus, in which he joined, and the "Offering." Father
Clare comes about five, and goes out, to return about
seven, meaning to spend the night again. A little
before seven I was in the library with Aunt Lucy and
Uncle Henry. Aunt Car. suddenly called me, and we
all went in. I gave dearest papa the crucifix to kiss,

---

[6] This prayer is as follows : *Fiat, laudetur, atque in æternum superexal-
letur, justissima, altissima, et amabilissima voluntas Dei in omnibus. Amen.*

and Uncle Henry read the prayers. Edward[1] was there too, Mr. Dunn, &c.

'He died very peacefully and calmly, about seven.'

To this is only to be added that there was conveyed to Mr. Hope-Scott on his death-bed the special blessing of his Holiness Pope Pius IX.

Shortly after death, the body having been laid out, according to Catholic custom, with lights round the bed and flowers upon it, a sudden change was observed to have come over the face of the deceased, which assumed a totally different expression. All signs of sickness or pain seemed to vanish, and in one minute he had become like what he used to be in very early years. Readers who may perhaps have witnessed a change of the kind, which is not unfrequent, will understand the striking remark made by a friend on this occasion : ' It is sometimes given to the dead to reveal their blessedness to the living.'

The following particulars of the Requiem Mass for Mr. Hope-Scott, and of the funeral, are taken, with alterations and omissions, from newspapers of the day (the ' Tablet ' of May 10 ; ' Scotsman,' May 6 and 8 ; and ' Edinburgh Courant,' May 8, 1873.)

The Requiem Mass for the repose of the soul of the late Mr. Hope-Scott, Q.C., took place at the Church of the Immaculate Conception, Farm Street, on Monday, May 5, at eleven o'clock. The coffin was removed, on

---

[1] The persons mentioned by their Christian names in this paragraph of the diary are—Lady Henry Kerr, Lord Henry Kerr, the Hon. Mrs. G. W. Hope, and her son, Mr. Edward Stanley Hope, nephew to Mr. Hope-Scott, and now (1883) one of the Charity Commissioners for England and Wales.

the previous evening, from Hyde Park Place, and laid
on a splendid catafalque in the church.   The mass was
celebrated by the Very Rev. Fr. Whitty, Provincial of
the Jesuits, *coram Archiepiscopo* ; and the sermon was
preached by the Very Rev. Father (now his Eminence
Cardinal) Newman (by whose kind permission it is
placed in the Appendix to this volume).   Cherubini's
Second Requiem in D minor, for male voices only, was
used.   Weak with old age and sorrow, Father Newman
had almost to be led to the pulpit, but the simple
vigour of language and the lucidity of style so peculiarly
his own remained what they had ever been.   When,
towards the conclusion of his discourse, he came to
speak of the last hours of the deceased, Father Newman
almost broke down, and for a moment it seemed that
his feelings would prevent him from finishing.   The
solemnity of the occasion — the church draped in
black, the old man come so far purposely to pay the
last offices to his friend—produced such an impression
on those who witnessed it as they are not likely to
forget.

Among the clergy and laity present were—Mgr.
Weld, the Hon. and Rev. Dr. Talbot, Revs. R. G. Mac-
mullen, C. B. Garside, Father Fitzsimon, S.J., Father
Clare, and the Fathers, S.J., of Mount Street ; Father
Coleridge, S.J., Father Amherst, S.J., Father Christie,
S.J., Father Dalgairns, of the Oratory, the Duke of
Norfolk, the Duke and Duchess of Buccleuch, the Mar-
quis and Marchioness of Lothian, Cecil, Marchioness
Dowager of Lothian, the Marchioness of Bute, Lord
and Lady Howard of Glossop, Lord Henry Kerr, Mr.

Hope of Luffness, Mr. Edward S. Hope, Mr. Herbert Hope, Field-Marshal Sir William Gomm and Lady Gomm, Lord Edmund Howard, the Earl of Denbigh, Lady Herbert of Lea, Lady Georgiana Fullerton, Mr. Allies, Mr. Langdale, &c.

The Dowager Duchess of Norfolk and the Ladies Howard, Mr. Hope-Scott's daughters, the Hon. Mrs. George W. Hope and Misses Hope, and Lady Henry Kerr, occupied a separate tribune.

On Wednesday, May 7, the remains of Mr. Hope-Scott, Q.C., were interred in the vaults of St. Margaret's Convent, Bruntsfield, Edinburgh. The coffin had been conveyed from London on Tuesday, and was placed on ・a catafalque within the choir of the chapel, where several sisters of the community (Ursulines of Jesus) watched until the morning. The catafalque was draped in black, surrounded by massive silver candlesticks hung with crape, and lit up with numerous wax candles. The altar, sanctuary, organ, and choir gallery were hung with black cloth. The east aisle of the chapel was occupied by the relatives and friends of the deceased; the west aisle by the young ladies of the convent school, about fifty in number, dressed in white, and with white veils, and the household servants from Abbotsford; whilst at the south were persons who had received special invitations. In the stalls of the choir were the clergy, and the sisters of the convent in their accustomed places.

The ceremonies commenced at eleven o'clock, when a procession, consisting of the cross-bearer and acolytes, the clergy in attendance, and the Right Rev. Dr. Strain, Bishop of Abila, V.A. of the Eastern District of Scotland, entered the chapel at the great south door, and marched slowly up the centre of the choir to the sanctuary, the organ sounding whilst the bell was heard tolling in the distance. The Bishop was attended by the Rev. George Rigg, St. Mary's, and the Rev Mr. Clapperton. The Rev. W. Turner acted as master of the ceremonies; the Rev. Father Foxwell, S.J., said the Mass, which, by the express desire of the deceased, was a Low Mass, although accompanied by music (Father Foxwell, stationed at Galashiels, frequently said Mass at Abbotsford). During the Mass, among other exquisite music sung by the choir, was the *Dies Iræ*. The . Rev. W. J. Amherst, S.J., Norwich, a great personal friend of Mr. Hope-Scott's, preached the sermon (which, by his kind permission, is placed in the Appendix to this volume).

Bishop Strain then read the Burial Service in front of the bier, and concluded by giving the absolution. The procession was then formed, and during the singing of the *Dies Iræ* emerged from the church, and walked to the vault, in the following order :—cross-bearer and acolytes, the young ladies of the convent school, the *religieuses* of the community of St. Margaret's, the clergy and Bishop, then the coffin, borne shoulder-high, and attended by the pall-bearers, the Duke of Norfolk, Lord Henry Kerr, Mr. H. W. Hope of Luffness, and Dr. Lockhart of Milton Lockhart. The ladies who followed the coffin were Miss Hope-Scott, the Hon. Mrs. G. W. Hope, Lady Henry Kerr, and Mrs. Francis Kerr. Then followed the relatives and friends, servants, and tenant-farmers of Abbotsford.

The procession marched slowly from the quadrangle in front of the chapel northwards to the entrance to the vaults, the sisters of the community chanting the psalm *Miserere.* It opened up at the mortuary door, and the coffin was borne into the vault, and placed in the recess assigned to it beside the coffin of his first wife, and under those of his two children. A short service here took place, the *Benedictus* was sung, and the funeral service terminated.

The outer coffin, which was of richly polished oak, bound with brass ornaments, had a beautiful crucifix on the lid, and beneath, a shield bearing the following inscription :—

'JAMES ROBERT HOPE-SCOTT, THIRD SON OF GENERAL SIR ALEXANDER HOPE, OF LUFFNESS AND RAN-KEILLOUR. BORN JULY 15, 1812. DIED APRIL 29, 1873. MAY HE REST IN PEACE.'

I have now placed before the reader the materials from which he will be enabled in some measure to judge what Mr. Hope-Scott was, and how he appeared to those around him. But to all beauty of character there belongs a lustre, outside of and beyond it, which genius alone can portray. This task has fortunately been performed by two of his most intimate friends of whose genius it is needless to say a word—Cardinal Newman and Mr. Gladstone—by whose kind permission their respective papers on his life will be appended to this volume. With reference to certain expressions on religious subjects in Mr. Gladstone's Letter, it will be remembered that it here appears as a biographical and historical document, and therefore without omissions —a remark which I feel assured that the illustrious writer will not misinterpret, and that both will accept the gratitude and admiration due from all surviving friends of Mr. Hope-Scott, for the splendid tribute which each of them has given to a memory so dear.

APPENDIX I.

Funeral Sermon by his Eminence Cardinal Newman, preached at the Requiem Mass for Mr. Hope-Scott, at the Church of the Immaculate Conception, Farm Street, May 5, 1873.

I HAVE been asked by those whose wish at such a moment is a command, to say a few words on the subject of the sorrowful, the joyful solemnity which has this morning brought us together. A few words are all that is necessary, all that is possible; just so many as are sufficient to unite the separate thoughts, the separate memories, the separate stirrings of affection, which are awakened in us by the presence, in our midst, of what remains on earth of the dear friend, of the great soul, whom we have lost,—sufficient to open a communication and create a sympathy between mind and mind, and to be a sort of testimony of one to another in behalf of feelings which each of us has in common with all.

Yet how am I the fit person even for as much as this? I can do no more than touch upon some of those many points which the thought of him suggests to me; and, whatever I may know of him and say of him, how can this be taken as the measure of one whose mind had so many aspects, and who must, in consequence, have made such distinct impressions, and exercised such various claims, on the hearts of those who came near him?

It is plain, without my saying it, that there are those who knew him far better than I could know him. How can I be the interpreter of their knowledge or their feelings? How can I hope by any words of mine to do a service to those who knew so well the depths of his rare excellence by a continuous daily intercourse with him, and by the recurring special opportunities given to them of its manifestation ?

I only know what he was to me. I only know what his loss is to me. I only know that he is one of those whose departure hence has made the heavens dark to me. But I have never lived with him, or travelled with him ; I have seen him from time to time; I have visited him; I have corresponded with him ; I have had mutual confidences with him. Our lines of duty have lain in very different directions. I have known him as a friend knows friend in the tumult and the hurry of life. I have known him well enough to know how much more there was to know in him ; and to look forward, alas! in vain, to a time when, in the evening and towards the close of life, I might know him more. I have known him enough to love him very much, and to sorrow very much that here I shall not see him again. But then I reflect, if I, who did not know him as he might be known, suffer as I do, what must be their sufferings who knew him so well ?

1. I knew him first, I suppose, in 1837 or 1838, thirty-five or six years ago, a few years after he had become Fellow of Merton College. He expressed a wish to know me. How our friendship grew I cannot tell ; I must soon have been intimate with him, from the recollection I have of letters which passed between us; and by 1841 I had recourse to him, as a sort of natural adviser, when I was in difficulty. From that time I ever had recourse to him, when I needed advice, down to his last illness. On my first intimacy with him he had not reached the age of thirty. I was many years older; yet he had that about him, even when a young man, which invited and inspired confidence. It was difficult to resist his very presence. True, indeed, I can fancy those who saw him but once and at a distance, surprised and perplexed by that lofty fastidiousness and keen wit which were natural to him ; but such a misapprehension of him would vanish forthwith when they drew near to him, and had actual trial of him ; especially, as I have said,

when they had to consult him, and had experience of the sim
plicity, seriousness, and (I can use no other word) the sweetness of his manner, as he threw himself at once into their
ideas and feelings, listened patiently to them, and spoke out
the clear judgment which he formed of the matters which they
had put before him.

This is the first and the broad view I am led to take of
him. He was, emphatically, a friend in need. And this same
considerateness and sympathy with which he met those who
asked the benefit of his opinion in matters of importance was,
I believe, his characteristic in many other ways in his intercourse with those towards whom he stood in various relations.
He was always prompt, clear, decided, and disinterested. He
entered into their pursuits, though dissimilar to his own ; he
took an interest in their objects ; he adapted himself to their
dispositions and tastes ; he brought a strong and calm good
sense to bear upon their present or their future ; he aided and
furthered them in their doings by his co-operation. Thus he
drew men around him ; and when some grave question or undertaking was in agitation, and there was, as is wont, a gathering
of those interested in it, then, on his making his appearance
among them, all present were seen to give to him the foremost
place, as if he had a claim to it by right ; and he, on his part,
was seen gracefully, and without effort, to accept what was conceded to him, and to take up the subject under consideration ;
throwing light upon it, and, as it were, locating it, pointing out
what was of primary importance in it, what was to be aimed at,
and what steps were to be taken in it. I am told that, in like
manner, when residing on his property in France, he was there
too made a centre for advice and direction on the part of his
neighbours, who leant upon him and trusted him in their own
concerns, as if he had been one of themselves. It was his un-
selfishness, as well as his practical good sense, which won upon
them.

Such a man, when, young and ardent, with his advantages
of birth and position, he entered upon the public world as it
displays itself upon its noblest and most splendid stage at

Westminster, might be expected to act a great part, and to rise
to eminence in the profession which he had chosen. Not for
certain ; for the refinement of mind, which was one of his
most observable traits, is in some cases fatal to a man's success
in public life. There are those who cannot mix freely with
their fellows, especially not with those who are below their own
level in mental cultivation. They are too sensitive for a
struggle with rivals, and shrink from the chances which it
involves. Or they have a shyness, or reserve, or pride, or
self-consciousness, which restrains them from lavishing their
powers on a mixed company, and is a hindrance to their doing
their best if they try. Thus their public exhibition falls short
of their private promise. Now, if there was a man who was
the light and the delight of his own intimates, it was he of
whom I am speaking ; and he loved as tenderly as he was
beloved, so that he seemed made for domestic life.

Again, there are various departments in his profession, in
which the particular talents which I have been assigning to
him might have had full play, and have led to authority and
influence, without any need or any opportunity for those more
brilliant endowments by which popular admiration and high
distinction are attained. It was by the display of talents of an
order distinct from clearness of mind, acuteness, and judgment,
that he was carried forward at once, as an advocate, to that
general recognition of his powers, which was the response
that greeted his first great speech, delivered in a serious cause
before an august assembly. I think I am right in saying that
it was in behalf of the Anglican Chapters, threatened by the
reforming spirit of the day, that he then addressed the House
of Lords ; and the occasion called for the exercise, not only of
the talents which I have already dwelt upon, but for those
which are more directly oratorical. And these were not wanting. I never heard him speak ; but I believe he had, in
addition to that readiness and fluency of language, or eloquence, without which oratory cannot be, those higher gifts
which give to oratory its power and its persuasiveness. I can
well understand, from what I knew of him in private, what

these were in his instance. His mien, his manner, the expression of his countenance, his youthfulness—I do not mean his youth merely, but his youthfulness of mind, which he never lost to the last,—his joyous energy, his reasonings so masterly, yet so prompt, his tact in disposing of them for his purpose, the light he threw upon obscure, and the interest with which he invested dull subjects, his humour, his ready resource of mind in emergencies; gifts such as these, so rare, yet so popular, were necessary for his success, and he had them at command. On that occasion of his handselling them to which I have referred, it was the common talk of Oxford, how the most distinguished lawyer of the day, a literary man and a critic, on hearing the speech in question, pronounced his prompt verdict upon him in the words, 'That young man's fortune is made.' And, indeed, it was plain, to those who were in a position to forecast the future, that there was no prize, as it is called, of public life, to which that young man might not have aspired, if only he had had the will.

2. This, then, is what occurs to me to say in the first place, concerning the dear friend of whom we are now taking leave. Such as I have described were the prospects which opened upon him on his start in life. But now, secondly, by way of contrast, what came of them? He might, as time went on, almost have put out his hand and taken what he would of the honours and rewards of the world. Whether in Parliament, or in the Law, or in the branches of the Executive, he had a right to consider no station, no power, absolutely beyond his reach. His contemporaries and friends, who fill, or have filled, the highest offices in the State, are, in the splendour of their several careers, the illustration of his capabilities and his promise. But, strange as it may appear at first sight, his indifference to the prizes of life was as marked as his qualifications for carrying them off. He was singularly void of ambition. To succeed in life is almost a universal passion. If it does not often show itself in the high form of ambition, this is because few men have an encouragement in themselves or in

their circumstances to indulge in dreams of greatness. But that a young man of bold, large, enterprising mind, of popular talents, of conscious power, with initial successes, with great opportunities, one who carried with him the good-will and expectation of bystanders, and was cheered on by them to a great future, that he should be dead to his own manifest interests, that he should be unequal to the occasion, that he should be so false to his destiny, that his ethical nature should be so little in keeping with his gifts of mind, may easily be represented, not only as strange, but as a positive defect, or even a fault. Why are talents given at all, it may be asked, but for use? What are great gifts but the correlatives of great work? We are not born for ourselves, but for our kind, for our neighbours, for our country: it is but selfishness, indolence, a perverse fastidiousness, an unmanliness, and no virtue or praise, to bury our talent in a napkin, and to return it to the Almighty Giver just as we received it.

This is what may be said, and it is scarcely more than a truism to say it; for, undoubtedly, who will deny it? Certainly we owe very much to those who devote themselves to public life, whether in the direct service of the State or in the prosecution of great national or social undertakings. They live laborious days, of which we individually reap the benefit; nevertheless, admitting this fully, surely there are other ways of being useful to our generation still. It must be recollected, that in public life a man of elevated mind does not make his own self tell upon others simply and entirely. He is obliged to move in a groove. He must act with other men; he cannot select his objects, or pursue them by means unadulterated by the methods and practices of minds less elevated than his own. He can only do what he feels to be second-best. He proceeds on the condition of compromise; and he labours at a venture, prosecuting measures so large or so complicated that their ultimate issue is uncertain.

Nor of course can I omit here the religious aspect of this question. As Christians, we cannot forget how Scripture speaks of the world, and all that appertains to it. Human society, indeed, is an ordinance of God, to which He gives His sanction and His authority; but from the first an enemy has been busy in its depravation. Hence it is that, while in its substance it is divine, in its circumstances, tendencies, and results it has much of evil. Never do men come together in considerable numbers, but the passion, self-will, pride, and unbelief, which may be more or less dormant in them one and one, bursts into a flame, and becomes a constituent of their union. Even when faith exists in the whole people, even when religious men combine for religious purposes, still, when they form into a body, they evidence in no long time the innate debility of human nature, and in their spirit and con-duct, in their avowals and proceedings, they are in grave contrast to Christian simplicity and straightforwardness. This is what the sacred writers mean by ' the world,' and why they warn us against it; and their description of it applies in its degree to all collections and parties of men, high and low, national and professional, lay and ecclesiastical.

It would be hard, then, if men of great talent and of special opportunities were bound to devote themselves to an ambitious life, whether they would or not, at the hazard of being accused of loving their own ease, when their reluctance to do so may possibly arise from a refinement and unworldliness of moral character. Surely they may prefer more direct ways of serving God and man ; they may aim at doing good of a nature more distinctly religious, at works, safely and surely and beyond all mistake meritorious; at offices of kindness, benevolence, and considerateness, personal and particular; at labours of love and self-denying exertions, in which their right hand knows nothing that is done by their left. As to our dear friend, I have already spoken of the influence which he exercised on all around him, on friends or strangers with whom he was con-nected in any way. Here was a large field for his active goodness, on which he did not neglect to exert himself. He gave others without grudging his thoughts, time, and trouble. He was their support and stay. When wealth came to him, he was free in his use of it. He was one of those rare men who

do not merely give a tithe of their increase to their God ; he
was a fount of generosity ever flowing ; it poured out on every
side ; in religious offerings, in presents, in donations, in works
upon his estates, in care of his people, in almsdeeds. I have
been told of his extraordinary care of families left in distress, of
his aid in educating them and putting them out in the world,
of his acts of kindness to poor converts, to single women, and
to sick priests ; and I can well understand the solicitous and
persevering tenderness with which he followed up such bene-
volences towards them from what I have seen in him myself.
He had a very retentive memory for their troubles and their
needs.   It was his largeness of mind which made him thus
open-hearted. As all his plans were on a large scale, so were
his private charities.   And when an object was public and
required the support of many, then he led the way by a
munificent contribution himself. He built one church on his
property at Lochshiel ; and another at Galashiels, which he
had intended to be the centre of a group of smaller ones round
about ; and he succeeded in actually planting one of these at
Selkirk.   Nor did he confine himself to money gifts : it is
often more difficult to surrender what we have made our own
personally, than what has never come actually into our tangible
possession. He bought books freely, theological, historical, and
of general literature ; but his love of giving was greater than
his love of collecting.   He could not keep them ; he gave them
away again ; he may be said to have given away whole libraries.
Little means has any one of determining the limits of his
generosity.   I have heard of his giving or offering for great
objects sums so surprising, that I am afraid to name them.
He alone knows the full measure of his bounties, who inspired,
and will reward it.   I do not think he knew it himself.   I am
led to think he did not keep a strict account of what he
gave away.   Certainly I know one case in which he had given
to a friend many hundreds, and yet seemed to have forgotten
it, and was obliged to ask him when it was that he had
done so.

I should trust that, in what I am saying, I have not given

any one the impression that he was inconsiderate and indiscriminate in giving. To have done this would have been to contradict my experience of him and my intention. As far as my opportunities of observing him extended, large as were his bounties and charities, as remarkable was the conscientious care with which he inquired into the nature and circumstances of the cases for which his aid was solicited. He felt he was but the steward of Him who had given him what he gave away.

He gave away as the steward of One to whom he must give account. There are at this time many philanthropic and benevolent men who think of man only, not of God, in their acts of liberality. I have already said enough to show that he was not one of these. I have implied the presence in him of that sense of religion, or religiousness, which was in fact his intimate and true life. And, indeed, liberality such as his, so incessant and minute, so well ordered, and directed too towards religious objects, almost of itself evidences its supernatural origin. But I insist on it, not only for its own sake, but also because it has a bearing upon that absence of ambition which, in a man so energetic, so influential, is a very remarkable point of character. Viewed in itself, it might be, even though not an Epicurean selfishness, still a natural temper, the temper of a magnanimous mind, such as might be found in ancient Greece or Rome, as well as in modern times. But, in truth, in him it was much more than a gift of nature ; it was a fruit and token of that religious sensitiveness which had been bestowed on him from above. If it really was the fact that his mind and heart were fixed upon divine objects, this at once accounts for what was so strange, so paradoxical in him in the world's judgment, his distaste for the honours and the pageants of earth ; and fixed, assuredly they were, upon the invisible and eternal. It was a lesson to all who witnessed it, in contrast with the appearance of the outward man, so keen and self-possessed amid the heat and dust of the world, to see his real inner secret self from time to time gleam forth from beneath the working-day dress in which his secular occupations enveloped him.

I cannot do justice by my words to the impression which in this respect he made on me. He had a tender conscience, but I mean something more than that—I mean the emotion of a heart always alive and awake at the thought of God. When a religious question came up suddenly in conversation, he had no longer the manner and the voice of a man of the world. There was a simplicity, earnestness, gravity in his look and in his words, which one could not forget. It seemed to me to speak of a loving desire to please God, a single-minded preference for His service over every service of man, a resolve to approach Him by the ways which He had appointed. It was no taking for granted that to follow one's own best opinion was all one with obeying His will; no easy persuasion that a vague, obscure sincerity in our conclusions about Him and our worship of Him was all that was required of us, whether those conclusions belonged to this school of doctrine or that. That is, he had deep within him that gift which St. Paul and St. John speak of, when they enlarge upon the characteristics of faith. It was the gift of faith, of a living, loving faith, such as ' overcomes the world' by seeking 'a better country, that is, a heavenly.' This it was that kept him so.' unspotted from the world' in the midst of worldly engagements and pursuits.

No wonder, then, that a man thus minded should gradually have been led on into the Catholic Church. Judging as we do from the event, we thankfully recognise in him an elect soul, for whom, in the decrees of Omnipotent Love, a seat in heaven has been prepared from all eternity—whose name is engraven on the palms of those Hands which were graciously pierced for his salvation. Such eager, reverential thoughts of God as his, prior to his recognising the Mother of Saints, are surely but the first tokens of a predestination which terminates in heaven. That straightforward, clear, good sense which he showed in secular matters did not fail him in religious inquiry. There are those who are practical and sensible in all things save in religion; but he was consistent; he instinctively turned from bye-ways and cross-paths, into which the inquiry might be diverted, and took a broad, intelligible view of its issues. And,

after he had been brought within the Fold, I do not think I
can exaggerate the solicitude which he all along showed, the
reasonable and prudent solicitude, to conform himself in all
things to the enunciations and the decisions of Holy Church;
nor, again, the undoubted conviction he has had of her super-
human authority, the comfort he has found in her sacraments,
and the satisfaction and trust with which he betook himself
to the intercession of the Blessed Virgin, to the glorious St.
Michael, to St. Margaret, and all saints.

3. I will make one remark more. I have spoken, first, of
his high natural gifts, of his various advantages for starting in
life, and of his secular prospects. Next in contrast with this
first view of him, I have insisted on his singular freedom from
ambition, and have traced it to that religiousness of mind
which was so specially his; to his intimate sense of the vanity
of all secular distinction, and his supreme devotion to Him
who alone is 'Faithful and True.' And now, when I am
brought to the third special feature of his life, as it presents
itself to me, I find myself close to a sacred subject, which I
cannot even touch upon without great reverence and something
of fear.

We might have been led to think that a man already
severed in spirit, resolve, and acts from the world in which he
lived, would have been granted by his Lord and Saviour to go
forward in his course freely, without any unusual trials, such as
are necessary in the case of common men for their perseverance
in the narrow way of life. But those, for whom God has a
love more than ordinary, He watches over with no ordinary
jealousy; and if the world smiles on them, He sends them
crosses and penances so much the more. He is not content
that they should be by any common title His; and, because
they are so dear and near to Him, He provides for them
afflictions to bring them nearer still. I hope it is not presumptuous thus to speak of the inscrutable providences of
God. I know that He has His own wise and special dealings

with every one of us, and that what He determines for one is no rule for another. I am contemplating, and, if so be, interpreting, His loving ways and purposes only towards the very man before us.

Now, so it was, there was just one aspect of this lower world which he might innocently love ; just one, in which life had charms for a heart as affectionate as it was religious. I mean that assemblage of objects which are included under the dear name of Home. If there was rest and solace to be found on earth, he found it there. Is it not remarkable, then, that in this, his sole earthly sanctuary, He who loved him with so infinite a love met him, visited him, not once or twice, but again and again, with a stern rod of chastisement. Stroke after stroke, blow after blow, stab after stab, was dealt against his very heart. 'Great and wonderful are Thy works, O Lord God Almighty ; just and true are Thy ways, O King of ages. Who shall not fear Thee, O Lord, and magnify Thy name ? for Thou only art holy.' I may speak with more vivid knowledge of him here than in other respects, for I was one of the confidants of his extreme suffering under the succession of terrible inflictions which left wounds never to be healed. They ended only with his life ; for the complaint, which eventually mastered him, was brought into activity by his final bereavement. Nay, I must not consider even that great bereavement his final one ; his call to go hence was itself the final agony of that tender, loving heart. He who had in time past been left desolate by others, was now to leave others desolate. He was to be torn away, as if before his time, from those who, to speak humanly, needed him so exceedingly. He was called upon to surrender them in faith to Him who had given them. It was about two hours before his death, with this great sacrifice, as we may suppose, this solemn summons of his Supreme Lord confronting him, that he said, with a loud voice, ' Thy will be done ;' adding his favourite prayer, so well known to us all : ' Fiat, laudetur, atque in æternum superexaltetur, sanctissima, altissima, amabilissima voluntas Dei in omnibus.' They were almost his last words.

We too must say, after him, ' Thy will be done.' Let us
be sure that those whom God loves He takes away, each of
them, one by one, at the very time best for their eternal
interests. What can we, in sober earnest, wish, save that very
will of God? Is He not wiser and more loving than we are?
Could we wish him back whom we have lost? Who is there
of us who loves him most but would feel the cruelty of recalling
to this tumultuous life, with its spiritual perils and its dark
future, a soul who is already rejoicing in the end and issue of
his trial, in salvation secured, and heaven begun in him?
Rather, who would not wish to have lived his life, and to have
died his death? How well for him that he lived, not for man
only, but for God! What are all the interests, pleasures,
successes, glories of this world, when we come to die? What
can irreligious virtue, what can innocent family affection do for
us, when we are going before the Judge, whom to know and
love is life eternal, whom not to know and not to love is eternal
death?

O happy soul, who hast loved neither the world nor the
things of the world apart from God! Happy soul, who, amid
the world's toil, hast chosen the one thing needful, that better
part which can never be taken away! Happy soul, who, being
the counsellor and guide, the stay, the light and joy, the
benefactor of so many, yet hast ever depended simply, as a
little child, on the grace of thy God and the merits and strength
of thy Redeemer! Happy soul, who hast so thrown thyself
into the views and interests of other men, so prosecuted their
ends and associated thyself in their labours, as never to forget
there is one Holy Catholic Roman Church, one Fold of Christ
and Ark of salvation, and never to neglect her ordinances or to
trifle with her word! Happy soul, who, as we believe, by thy
continual almsdeeds, offerings, and bounties, hast blotted out
such remains of daily recurring sin and infirmity as the sacraments have not reached! Happy soul, who, by thy assiduous
preparation for death, and the long penance of sickness, weariness, and delay, hast, as we trust, discharged the debt that lay

T 2

against thee, and art already passing from penal purification to the light and liberty of heaven above !

And so farewell, but not farewell for ever, dear James Robert Hope-Scott! He is gone from us, but only gone before us. We then must look forward, not backward. We shall meet him again, if we are worthy, in 'Mount Sion, and the heavenly Jerusalem,' in 'the company of many thousands of angels, the Church of the firstborn who are written in the heavens,' with 'God, the Judge of all, and the spirits of the just made perfect, and Jesus, the Mediator of the New Testament, and the blood which speaketh better things than that of Abel.'

J. H. N.

APPENDIX II.

Words spoken in the Chapel of the Ursulines of Jesus, St. Margaret's Convent, Edinburgh, on the 7th day of May, 1873, at the Funeral of James Robert Hope-Scott, Q.C. By the Rev. William J. Amherst, S.J.

A. M. D. G.

MY DEAR BRETHREN,—In complying with the request which has been made to me, to say a few words on this solemn occasion about one who was so immeasurably my superior in everything, I feel as a child would when suddenly asked to give an opinion on some abstruse question which it could not comprehend. But when asked to address you, however sensible I might have been of my own inferiority, I could not, even in thought, entertain a reluctance; I could not show the slightest hesitation to speak the praises of one whom I admired so much, to ask your prayers for one whom I so much loved.

Scotland is blessed in giving a resting-place to one of her noblest sons; and this religious community is doubly blessed in providing the holy spot where his body shall repose. I need not enter into all the particulars of his life. Those which I should naturally think of to-day are sufficiently known to you all. But if I do not enter into any details, it is not that they are without a very strong interest. They might well be recorded as the history of a great and noble character, as an example to the young men of our own day, and as possessing, from his family connections, more than ordinary value for every one. But I must speak of his character in general, and single out those points which I consider deserving of especial praise. We must praise the dear deceased. It is our duty to do so. What are our desires now? What is our great wish? That God may have mercy on his soul. God will hear us when we appeal to Him by the good works which His servant has done. We should all praise him, that we may be so many witnesses before God of the things which we know must entitle him to mercy from his Father who is in heaven.

When I first heard that he was dead—especially when I was asked to speak about him—I began to think of his character in a more careful manner than I had ever done before. Besides my own thoughts about him, I have heard what they say of him who were most closely allied to him. I have listened to those who, though not related to him, were his most intimate friends and acquaintance. I know what is thought of him by those who knew him well. I have seen letters written since his death from many different persons; from those who knew him in early days, those who knew him in middle life, and again, those who knew him in later days. I have read letters from some who knew him during the whole of his and their lives. There is a unanimity in the thoughts of all about him which is most striking. The thoughts and words of every one seem to form one beautiful melody, one harmonious song. They all testify to the same great intellectual qualities, the same goodness of heart, the same excellence of demeanour. They speak of him as being one who was more fit for the foremost places in the State than some who have actually attained them. They speak of him in such terms as these, 'the loveable,' 'the amiable,' 'the beautiful.' Besides having talents of the highest order, the dear deceased possessed a nature peculiarly susceptible of good impressions. And he seems to have opened his whole heart to receive the dew of heaven; and the grace of God produced a hundredfold in his soul. To have known a man such as he was, who possessed such power of mind combined with such high attainments, such soundness of principle with such rectitude in practice, such independence of thought, and such submission to conscience and lawful authority; to have known him—to have been, I may say, on terms of friendship and intimacy with him—will be amongst the most pleasing

and the saddest recollections of my life. I have said his submission to conscience. It seems almost like presumption in
me, standing as I do in the midst of those who knew him so
much better than myself, to single out any one distinguishing
characteristic; but it always struck me that a great conscientiousness was that which showed itself the most, and shone
most brilliantly to those who had the happiness of knowing
him. The voice of conscience seemed to have a magic effect
upon him. The call was no sooner heard than it was obeyed,
and without any apparent hesitation of the will. It was this
delicacy of conscience, and his good-will to act upon it, combined with his most perfect demeanour, which gave him that
authority over others which was so beautifully spoken of by his
venerable friend on Monday last, when I and many of you, my
dear brethren, had the happiness of being present. For it was
this conscientiousness which purified, consolidated, and gave
direction to all the great qualities of his soul. To this influence which he had over others I am myself a willing witness.
I felt the force of it myself. And in saying this, my dear
brethren, I speak most sincerely what I believe to be true. I
should deem it an irreverence on an occasion like this to say a
word which I did not believe. Though by no means a young
man myself when I first had the happiness of making acquaintance with the dear deceased, during the few years that I knew
him he exercised an influence over me, for the effects of which
I now thank God, and hope that I shall thank Him for all
eternity.

It was, my dear brethren, to this great gift of conscientiousness, aided by the grace of God, that he who has left us owed
the greatest blessing of his life—his submission to the one
holy Catholic and Apostolic Church. The obstacles which
stood in the way of his entering the Church must have been
great. The old French saying does not stand good when one
who is not a Catholic is thinking of entering the Church. It
is not the first step towards the Church which, in this country
at least, costs the sacrifice. The first step costs little; it
most frequently costs nothing. It is generally a pleasant step

to take. Many have taken that step; but few have persevered
in their onward march. The step which costs the sacrifice is
that which crosses the threshold when the door has been
arrived at. For on one side stands that powerful tempter,
human respect, whose baneful influence has sent back hundreds,
perhaps thousands, into the dreary waste. On the other side
stands ambition, with noble and captivating mien. I need not
speculate here as to what ambition may say to others; but I
will imagine what ambition may have said to our departed
friend. It may have addressed him in some such words as
these: ' You are conscious, innocently conscious, of possessing
great talents. You cannot have associated as you have done
with men of great intellect, with the first men of the day,
without having in some degree measured yourself with them,
without knowing something of your own great power. You
are, perhaps, desirous yourself of advancing in the highest
paths. You may have a praiseworthy ambition of using the
gifts you have received for the good of others, and to make a
return to God for all that He has bestowed upon you. You
cannot but know that from your family connections, and the
position you hold in society, you have as fine an opening as
was ever presented to a young man. Enter the Catholic
Church, and all such knowledge will be useless; all such
thoughts may be cast aside.' There is no use, my dear
brethren, in blinding ourselves to the truth in this matter.
We know it, and it is well that we should recognise it. In
this country, which boasts so much of its religious liberty, the
influence—the persecution I must call it—of public opinion is
such, that when a man enters the Church, he deprives himself
of all chance of progress in the high walks of life. It may be
said that in the line in which he had hitherto walked he
succeeded as well after he entered the Church as he had done
before. It is true that he reached the highest point of eminence as an advocate, and his religion was no obstacle in the
way; but if it was so, it was because it was the interest of
suitors to make use of his power. But if he ever entertained
any idea of attaining to the highest offices in the State· and he

may well have done so—the fact of his having entered the
Catholic Church would, in all probability, have proved a bar to
his advance. He resisted the tempters ; he despised human
respect, and he thrust aside ambition. Having walked up to
the open door of the Church, he did what conscience told him
he ought to do, and, passing the threshold, he went in. My
dear brethren, there can be no doubt that the life which he led
before this time had prepared him for the step which he took.
He had a great devotion to the will of God. His favourite
prayer was those well-known words : ' May the most just, the
most high, and the most amiable will of God be done, praised,
and eternally exalted in all things ! ' And though before he
became a Catholic his thoughts may not have been put into
that particular formula, yet no doubt the substance of those
words had been his prayer through life. As the will of God
had been his guiding star, so, and as a consequence, he always
had a great love for Jesus Christ our Redeemer. I cannot,
indeed, state this as a positive fact on my own personal knowledge, but it could not have been otherwise ; and you, my dear
brethren, who knew him so much better than I did, will, I
think, agree with me in this respect. When he became a
Catholic, Jesus Christ was the object of his continually increasing love. By the means which God provided for him in
the Church, his faith in his Redeemer, his hope in his Redeemer, and his love for his Redeemer, grew stronger, and
went on increasing to his dying day.[1] As he loved Jesus all
his life, pray, my dear brethren, that his merciful Lord may
show mercy to him now.

Some amongst you, my dear brethren, have already heard
from the lips of one as much my superior as the subject of my
discourse was, that a distinguishing feature of the departed
was the intensity of his domestic affection. And the venerable
preacher observed that the great trial of him who has left us
was to receive a succession of terrible wounds in the tenderest

---

[1] The last words which he heard on earth whilst the crucifix was pressed
to his lips, and they were spoken by those lips which here he loved the most,
were these : ' You know that you have loved Jesus all your life.'

part of his noble nature. You will remember his words. He
said that God had repeatedly struck him ; that He had stabbed
him. It was so, indeed ; and yet, my dear brethren, at the
same time that a merciful God so severely tried His servant, it
was through those same domestic affections that He gave to
him the greatest comfort, next to a good conscience, that a
man can have on his death-bed. For to him who had always
been so kind and gentle with others, and anticipated all their
wants, was given during the many long months of his illness
all that help and comfort which the most tender, filial, and
sisterly love could give. As God blessed him in making him
the object of such strong and persevering affection, so He has
blessed those also who were the willing instruments of His
mercy.

Pray, my dear brethren, that he may rest in peace. We all
owe a great deal to him, more than we can ever repay during
life. Generosity was a remarkable feature in the dear deceased.
His generosity was of a noble kind. It was not confined to
generosity with his worldly means. He was generous in his
sympathies. He sympathised with all who had any relations
with him. No one was ever with him who did not feel this.
He was generous with his worldly means ; he was generous with
his counsel and advice. He was ready and willing to help any
one in any way he could. I feel that I owe him much myself.
I have already alluded to the obligations which I am under to
him. And who is there amongst you, my dear brethren, who
does not, in some respect, owe him much ? As he was
generous to others, let us be generous to him. Let us pray,
and continually pray, to God for him. If any of you may be
inclined to relax in your prayers for his soul, because you think
that his good works were such that we have reason to hope that
he is even now enjoying the sight of God, I do not quarrel
with you for so thinking—I may think so myself ; but still I
urge you to pray. Pray as if you thought it were not so. Do
not let your hope lessen the effect of your love. Pray for him
as you would wish him and others to pray for you if you were
dead.

And here, my dear brethren, I might finish my discourse. But who is there who knew the dear departed, who does not feel an irresistible impulse to turn from the dead to the living? This influence may have been felt on other occasions by others. For my part, I have never so deeply felt how impossible it is to separate the one who has gone from those whom he has left behind. Pray for the father; and pray also for the children. Pray for those whose future must be a matter of interest to you all. And you may pray with a firm hope of being heard. For it would seem that there is a special providence over them, for already those children have found a home—homes, I may say—which a Guardian Angel might have chosen for them. Pray that God would ratify and confirm all those blessings which that fond parent had bestowed upon his own, especially those blessings which, with increased earnestness, he must have desired when he saw that, at a critical moment in life, the hand which had guided was to make sign no more. Pray, my dear brethren, that those two honoured names which he bore, and which for so many years have been allied to all that is best and of sterling worth, to all that is great and noble, may long continue the ornament and the pride of Scotland. Once more, let me turn from the living to the dead; and I will conclude with the prayer of the Church—' Eternal rest give to him, O Lord; and may a perpetual light shine upon him! May he rest in peace!'

APPENDIX III.

The Right Hon. W. E. Gladstone, M.P. to Miss Hope-Scott [*now the Hon. Mrs. Maxwell Scott*].

Hawarden: Sept. 13, 1873.

MY DEAR MISS HOPE-SCOTT,—I found awaiting me, through your kindness, on my return from Scotland, Dr. Newman's Address on your much-loved father's death. I need not say that one of my first acts was to read it. It does not discourage me from attempting to put on paper my recollections of him, as my free intervals of time may permit. It is well that a character of such extraordinary grace as his should have been portrayed by one who could scarcely, I think, even if he tried, compose a sentence that would not be 'a thing of beauty.' His means and materials for undertaking that labour of love were as superior to mine as his power of performing it. I will only say that I countersign, with full assent, to the best of my knowledge, the several traits which Dr. Newman has given. He must have much more to say. I shall at once lay before you all my little store of knowledge, in addition to that worthier tribute of your father's own letters, to which you are not less welcome. Lights upon his mental history my memory may, I hope, serve here and there to throw; but these will be principally for the period antecedent to what he himself described as 'the great change of his life.'

Few men, perhaps, have had a wider contact with their generation, or a more varied experience of personal friendships, than myself. Among the large numbers of estimable and remarkable people whom I have known, and who have now passed away, there is in my memory an inner circle, and within it are the forms of those who were marked off from the comparative crowd even of the estimable and the remarkable by the peculiarity and privilege of their type. Of these very few, some four or five I think only, your father was one : and with regard to them it always seemed to me as if the type in each case was that of the individual exclusively, and as if there could be but one such person in our world at a time. After the early death of Arthur Hallam, I used to regard your father distinctly as at the head of all his contemporaries in the brightness and beauty of his gifts.

We were at Eton at the same time, but he was considerably my junior, so that we were not in the way of being drawn together. At Christ Church we were again contemporaries, but acquaintances only, scarcely friends. I find he did not belong to the ' Oxford Essay Club,' in which I took an active part, and which included not only several of his friends, but one with whom, unless my memory deceives me, he was most intimate— I mean Mr. Leader. And yet I have to record our partnership on two occasions in a proceeding which in Oxford was at that time, and perhaps would have been at any time, singular enough. At the hazard of severe notice, and perhaps punishment, we went together to the Baptist chapel of the place, once to hear Dr. Chalmers, and the other time to hear Mr. Rowland Hill. I had myself been brought up in what may be termed an atmosphere of Low Church ; and, though I cannot positively say why, I believe this to have been the case with him ; and questions of communion or conformity at that date presented themselves to us not unnaturally as questions of academic discipline, so that we did not, I imagine, enter upon any inquiry whether we in any degree compromised our religious position by the act, or by any intention with which it was done.

After Oxford (which I quitted in December 1831) the next occasion on which I remember to have seen him was in his sitting-room at Chelsea Hospital. There must, however, have been some shortly preceding contact, or I should not have gone there to visit him. I found him among folios and books of grave appearance. It must have been about the year 1836.

He opened a conversation on the controversies which were then
agitated in the Church of England, and which had Oxford for
their centre.   I do not think I had paid them much attention ;
but I was an ardent student of Dante, and likewise of Saint
Augustine ; both of them had acted powerfully upon my mind ;
and this was in truth the best preparation I had for anything
like mental communion with a person of his elevation.   He
then told me that he had been seriously studying the controversy, and that in his opinion the Oxford authors were right.
He spoke not only with seriousness, but with solemnity, as if
this was for him a great epoch ; not merely the adoption of a
speculative opinion, but the reception of a profound and powerful religious impulse.   Very strongly do I feel the force of
Dr. Newman's statements (pp. 271, 272) as to the religious
character of his mind.   It is difficult in retrospect to conceive
of this, except as growing up with him from infancy.   But it
appeared to me as if at this period, in some very special manner,
his attention had been seized, his intellect exercised and
enlarged in a new field ; and as if the idea of the Church of
Christ had then once for all dawned upon him as the power
which, under whatever form, was from thenceforward to be
the central object of his affections, in subordination only to
Christ Himself, and as His continuing representative.

From that time I only knew of his career as one of un-
wearied religious activity, pursued with an entire abnegation of
self, with a deep enthusiasm under a calm exterior, and with a
grace and gentleness of manner, which, joined to the force of
his inward motives, made him, I think, without doubt the most
winning person of his day.   It was for about fifteen years, from
that time onwards, that he and I lived in close, though latterly
rarer intercourse.   Yet this was due, on my side, not to any
faculty of attraction, but to the circumstance that my seat in
Parliament, and my rather close attention to business, put me
in the way of dealing with many questions relating to the
Church and the Universities and Colleges, on which he desired
freely to expand his energies and his time.

I will here insert two notices which illustrate the opposite

sides of his character. It was in or about 1837 that I came
to know well his sister-in-law, Lady F. Hope, then already a
widow. I remember very clearly her speaking to me about the
manner in which he had ministered to her sorrow. It was not
merely kindness, or merely assiduity, or any particular act of
which she spoke. She seemed to speak of him as endowed with
some special gift, as if he had, like one of old, been ' surnamed
Barnabas, which is, being interpreted, the Son of Consolation.'

I now pass to the other pole of his mind, his relish for
all fun, humour, and originality of character. In one of his
tranquil years he told me with immense amusement an anecdote
he had brought from Oxford. He was in company with two
men, Mr. Palmer, commonly called Deacon Palmer, and Arthur
Kinnaird, of whom the one was not more certain to supply the
material of paradox, than the other to draw it out. The deacon
had been enlarging in lofty strain on the powers and position of
the clergy. ' Then I suppose,' said Kinnaird, ' you would hold
that the most depraved and irreligious priest has a much higher
standing in the sight of God than any layman ? ' ' Of course,'
was the immediate reply.[1]

His correspondence with me, beginning in February 1837,
truly exhibits the character of our friendship, as one founded in
common interests, of a kind that gradually commanded more
and more of the public attention, but that with him were
absolutely paramount. The moving power was principally on
his side. The main subjects on which it turned, and which also
formed the basis of our general intercourse, were as follows :
First, a missionary organisation for the province of Upper
Canada. Then the question of the Relations of Church and
State, forced into prominence at that time by a variety of
causes, and among them not least by a series of Lectures,
which Dr. Chalmers delivered in the Hanover Square Rooms,

[1 Of course, Mr. Palmer, who was clear-headed, knew what he was
saying, and meant that, in comparing an irreligious priest with a religious
layman, the priest, *as such*, belongs to a higher spiritual order than the
layman *as such*, just as it is a mere truism to say that a fallen angel, as
regards his degree in the order of creation, is superior to a saint.—ED.]

to distinguished audiences, with a profuse eloquence, and with
a noble and almost irresistible fervour. Those Lectures drove
me upon the hazardous enterprise of handling the same subject
upon what I thought a sounder basis. Your father warmly
entered into this design ; and bestowed upon a careful and
prolonged examination of this work in MS., and upon a searching
yet most tender criticism of its details, an amount of thought
and labour which it would, I am persuaded, have been intolerable to any man to supply, except for one for whom each and
every day as it arose was a new and an entire sacrifice to duty.
As in the year 1838, when the manuscript was ready, I had to
go abroad on account mainly of some overstrain upon the eyes,
he undertook the whole labour of carrying the work through
the press ; and he even commended me, as you will see from
the letters, because I did not show an ungovernable impatience
of his aid.[2]

The general frame of his mind at this time, in October
1838, will be pretty clearly gathered from a letter of that
month, No. 24 in the series, written when he had completed
that portion of his labours.[3] He had full, unbroken faith in
the Church of England, as a true portion of the Catholic
Church ; to her he had vowed the service of his life ; all his
desire was to uphold the framework of her institutions, and to
renovate their vitality. He pushed her claims, you may find
from the letters, further than I did ; but the difference of
opinion between us was not such as to prevent our cordial
co-operation then and for years afterwards ; though in using
such a term I seem to myself guilty of conceit and irreverence
to the Dead, for I well know that he served her from an immeasurably higher level.

If I have not yet referred to his main occupation, it is
because I desire to speak specially of what I know specially.
It was, however, without doubt, in his Fellowship at Merton
that he found at this period the peculiar work of his life. A
wonderful combination of fertility with solidity always struck

[2 J. R. Hope to Mr. Gladstone, August 29, 1838, in ch. ix. vol. i. p. 170.]
[3 Ibid., October 11, 1838, ch. ix. vol. i. p. 173.]

me as one of his most marked mental characteristics. Only
by that facility could he have accumulated and digested the
learning which he acquired in relation to Church, and especially
to College History and College Law. In mastering these systems
how deeply he had drunk of the essential spirit of the times
which built them up, may be seen from a very striking letter
(No. 9) respecting Walter de Merton.⁴ He gave the world
some idea of the extent and fruitfulness of these labours in
connection with the next subject on which we had much communication together, the subject of what was termed in 1840
Cathedral Reform. My part was superficial, and was performed in
the House of Commons. His was of a very different character.

As a hearer, and a rapt hearer, I can say that Dr. Newman
(p. 266) has not exaggerated the description of the speech which
he delivered, as counsel for the Chapters (I think) before the
House of Lords in 1840.⁵ I need not say that, during the last
forty years, I have heard many speeches, and many, too, in
which I had reason to take interest, and yet never one which,
by its solid as well as by its winning qualities, more powerfully impressed me. At this period he had (I think never or)
rarely spoken in public, and he had not touched thirty years
of age.

I cannot now say who was the prime mover in the next
matter of interest which we pursued in common. It was the
foundation of Trinity College, Glenalmond. We drew into our
partnership the deceased Dean Ramsay, one of the very few
men known to me who might, perhaps, compete even with
your father in attracting affection, though very different in
powers of mind. The Dean worked with us usefully and
loyally, although, as was to a certain extent his nature, sometimes in fear and trembling.

The early prosecution of this enterprise was left for a time
mainly to me, while your father paid his visit to Italy in 1840,
in company with Mr. Rogers, now Lord Blachford, from whom

[⁴ J. R. Hope to Mr. Gladstone, dated 'Rochester: Sunday, July 29,
1838,' in ch. viii. vol. i. p. 153.]
[⁵ See ch. xi. vol. i. p. 204.]

I hope you may obtain memorials of it far better worth your having than any which I could supply, even had I been his companion. I remember that I wrote for him in bad Italian a letter of introduction to Manzoni, of whom, and of whose religious standing-ground, he gives (No. 32)[6] a remarkable account. I wish I could recover now that letter, on account of the person for whom, and the person to whom, it was written.

I think it was shortly before or shortly after this tour, that your father one day spoke to me—I well remember the spot where he stood—about his state and course of life. He had taken a resolution, with a view to the increase of his means, to apply some part of his time to the ordinary duties of his profession; whether he then said that it would be at the Parliamentary Bar or not, I am not able to say. He, on this occasion, told me that he did not intend to marry; that, giving a part of his time in the direction I have just mentioned, he meant to reserve all the rest for the Church and its institutions; and of these two several employments he said, 'I regard the first as my kitchen-garden, but the second as my flower-garden.'[7] And so it was that, almost without a rival in social attractions, and in the springtide of his youth and promise, he laid with a cheerful heart the offering of his life upon the altar of his God.

It was, I think, the undertaking to found Trinity College which gave rise to another friendship, that it gave me the greatest pleasure to witness—between him and my father. In 1840 my father was moving on towards fourscore years, but 'his eye was not dim, nor his natural force abated;' he was full of bodily and mental vigour; 'whatsoever his hand found to do, he did it with his might;' he could not understand or tolerate those who, perceiving an object to be good, did not at once and actively pursue it: and with all this energy he joined a corresponding warmth and, so to speak, eagerness of affection, a keen appreciation of humour, in which he found a rest, and

[6 See ch. xiii. vol. i. p. 248, Mr. Hope to Mr. Gladstone (Milan: November 18, 1840).]

[7 Compare letter of J. R. Hope to Mr. Gladstone, quoted in ch. xxii. vol. ii. p. 102.]

an indescribable frankness and simplicity of character, which, crowning his other qualities, made him, I think (and I strive to think impartially), nearly or quite the most interesting old man I have ever known. Nearly half a century of years separated the two; but your father, I think, appreciated mine more than I could have supposed possible, and always appeared to be lifted to a higher level of life and spirits by the contact. On one occasion we three set out on a posting expedition, to examine several sites in the midland counties of Scotland, which had been proposed for the new College. As we rolled along, wedged into one of the post-chaises of those days, through various kinds of country, and especially through the mountains between Dunkeld and Crieff, it was a perpetual play, I might almost say roar, of fun and laughter. The result of this tour, after the consideration of various sites near Perth, Dunkeld, and Dunblane, was the selection of the spot on which the College now stands. I am ashamed to recollect that we were, I do not say assisted in reaching this conclusion, but cheered up in fastening on it, by a luncheon, which Mr. Patton, the proprietor, gave us, of grouse newly killed, roasted by an apparatus for the purpose on the moment, and bedewed with what I think is called partridge-eye champagne.

Your father's influence operated materially in procuring a preference for this beautiful but somewhat isolated site on the banks of the Almoud. The general plan of the buildings was, I think, conceived by Mr. Dyce—another rare specimen of the human being—a master of Art and Thought in every form, and one whose mind was stocked to repletion with images of Beauty. I need not tell you what was your father's estimate of him. As to the site, the introduction of Railways, which did not then exist for Scotland, has essentially altered the scale of relative advantage for all situations, in proportion as they are near to or removed from these channels of communication, and has caused us, in estimating remoteness from centres, to think of a mile as much as we should formerly have thought of ten. But I ought to record that, in all questions relating to the college, your father's mind instinctively leaned to what may be

called the ecclesiastical side; and though the idea of a great
school was incorporated in the plan, his desire was that even
this should not be too near any considerable town. I remember also his saying to me, with reference to Glenalmond, and
the opportunities which the college chapel would afford, 'You
know it will plant the Church in a new district.'

He laboured much for the college; and had, if my memory
serves, a great hand in framing the Constitution, with respect
to which his academic learning gave him a just authority.
He laboured for it at first in love and enthusiasm, afterwards in
duty, at last perhaps in honour : but after a few years it necessarily vanished from his thoughts, and he became unable to
share in facing the difficulties through which it had to pass.
Events were now impending which profoundly agitated, not
only what is termed the religious world, but the general mind
of the country. I need not here refer to the unwise proceedings of great and ardent Churchmen, which darkened the skies
over their heads, and brought their cause from calm and peaceful progress to storm, and in some senses to shipwreck. I do
not think that, with his solid judgment, he was a party to any
of those proceedings. They seem to have gradually brought
about an opinion on the part of the ruling authorities of the
English Church that some effort should be made to counteract
the excesses of the party, and to confront the tendencies, or
supposed tendencies, now first disclosed, towards the Church of
Rome, by presenting to the public mind a telling idea of
Catholicity under some other form. I am now construing
events, not relating them ; but they are events which will be
a prime duty of the future historian to study, for they have
(I think) sensibly affected in its religious aspects the history of
this country, nay, even the history of Western Christendom.

About this time Baron Bunsen became the representative
of Prussia at the British Court. I remember that your father
used to strike me by his suspicions and apprehensions of particular persons ; and Bunsen, if I recollect right, was among
them. That distinguished person felt an intense interest in
England ; he was of a pious and enthusiastic mind, a mind of

almost preternatural activity, vivacity, and rapidity, a bright imagination, and a wide rather than a deep range of knowledge. He was in the strongest sympathy, both personal and ecclesiastical, with the then reigning King of Prussia, who visited England in the autumn, I think, of 1841. Sir Robert Peel, however loyal to the *entente* with France, had a strong desire for close relations of friendship with Germany ; and the marriage of the Queen, then recent, told in the same sense. All these circumstances opened the way for the singular project of the Anglican Bishopric of Jerusalem, which I believe to have been the child of Bunsen's fertile and energetic brain, and which received at that particular juncture a welcome due, I think, to special circumstances such as those which I have enumerated.

Wide as was the range of Bunsen's subsequent changes, he at this time represented the opinions of the Evangelical German Church, with the strong leaning of an *amateur* towards the Episcopate as a form of Government, not as the vehicle of the continuous, corporate, and visible life of the Christian Church. He had, beyond all men I ever knew, the faculty of persuading himself that he had reconciled opposites ; and this persuasion he entertained with such fervour that it became contagious. From some of these letters (in accordance with my recollections) it would appear that in the early stages of this really fantastic plan (see No. 48) [8] your father's aid had been enlisted. I must not conceal that my own was somewhat longer continued. The accompanying correspondence amply shows his speedy and strong dissatisfaction and even disgust.

I do not know whether the one personal influence, which alone, I think, ever seriously affected his career, was brought to bear upon him at this time. But the movement of his mind, from this juncture onwards, was traceably parallel to, though at a certain distance from, that of Dr. Newman. My opinion is (I put it no higher) that the Jerusalem Bishopric snapped the link which bound Dr. Newman to the English Church. I have a conviction that it cut away the ground on

[8 See ch. xvi. (vol. i. p. 319), J. R. Hope to Mr. Gladstone, November 19, 1841.]

which your father had hitherto most firmly and undoubtingly
stood. Assuredly, from 1841 or 1842 onwards, his most fond,
most faithful, most ideal love progressively decayed, and
doubt nestled and gnawed in his soul. He was, however, of a
nature in which levity could find no place. Without question
he estimated highly, as it deserves to be estimated, the tremendous nature of a change of religious profession, as between
the Church of England and the Church of Rome; a change
dividing asunder bone and marrow. Nearly ten years passed, I
think, from 1841, during which he never wrote or spoke to me
a *positive* word indicating the possibility of this great transition.
Long he harboured his misgivings in silence, and ruminated
upon them. They even, it seemed to me, weighed heavily
upon his bodily health. I remember that in 1843 I wrote an
article in a review (mentioned in the correspondence) which
referred to the remarkable words of Archbishop Laud respecting
the Church of Rome as it was; and applied to the case those
other remarkable words of Lord Chatham respecting America,
' Never, never, never.' He said to me, half playfully (for the
article took some hold upon his sympathies), ' What, Gladstone,
never, never, never? '

It must have been about this time that I had another conversation with him about religion, of which, again, I exactly
recollect the spot. Regarding (forgive me) the adoption of the
Roman religion by members of the Church of England as nearly
the greatest calamity that could befall Christian faith in this
country, I rapidly became alarmed when these changes began ;
and very long before the great luminary, Dr. Newman, drew
after him, it may well be said, ' the third part of the stars of
heaven.' This alarm I naturally and freely expressed to the
man upon whom I most relied, your father. On the occasion to
which I refer he replied to me with some admission that they
were calamitous; ' but,' he said, ' pray remember an important
compensation, in the influence which the English mind will
bring to bear upon the Church of Rome itself. Should there
be in this country any considerable amount of secession to that
Church, it cannot fail to operate sensibly in mitigating what-

ever gives most offence in its practices or temper.' I do not pretend to give the exact words, but their spirit and effect I never can forget. I then thought there was great force in them.

When I learned that he was to be married, my opinion was that he had only allowed his thoughts to turn in the direction of the bright and pure attachment he had formed, because the object to which they had first been pledged had vanished or been hidden from his view. I think that his feelings underwent a rally, rather, perhaps, than his understanding, when I was first put forward as a candidate for the University of Oxford in 1847. At least, I recollect his speaking with a real zest and interest at that time of my wife, as a skilful canvasser, hard to resist.

I have just spoken of your father as the man on whom I most relied; and so it was. I relied on one other, also a remarkable man, who took the same course, at nearly the same time; but on him most, from my opinion of his sagacity. From the correspondence of 1838 you might suppose that he relied upon me, that he had almost given himself to me. But whatever expressions his warm feelings combined with his humility may have prompted, it really was not so; nor ought it to have been so, for I always felt and knew my own position beside him to be one of mental as well as moral inferiority. I cannot remember any occasion on which I exercised an influence over him. I remember many on which I tried; and especially when I saw his mind shaken, and, so to speak, on the slide. But these attempts (of which you may possibly have some written record) completely failed, and drove him into reserve. Never, on any one occasion, would he enter freely into the question with me. I think the fault lay much on my side. My touch was not fine enough for his delicate spirit. But I do not conceal from you that I think there was a certain amount of fault on his side also. Notwithstanding what I have said of his humility, notwithstanding what Dr. Newman has most truly said of his self-renouncing turn, and total freedom from ambition, there was in him, I think, a subtle form of self-will, which led him, where he had a foregone conclusion or a latent tendency, to indulge it, and to refuse to throw his mind into free partnership with others upon questions of doubt and difficulty. Yet I must after all admit his right to be silent, unless where he thought he was to receive real aid ; and of this he alone could be the judge.

Indeed, his own intellectual calibre was too large to allow him to be other than fastidious in his judgment of the capacities of other men. He had a great opinion of the solidity and tact of Denison, Bishop of Salisbury. He thought also very highly of Lord Blachford. When Archbishop (then Archdeacon) Manning produced his work on the ' Unity of the Church,' he must, I think, have seen it before the world saw it ; for I remember his saying to me, ' That is going to be a great book,' or what would have been not less emphatic, ' That is going to be a book.' Again, he was struck with Mr. W. Palmer's work on the Church, to which also testimony has been borne by Dr. Newman in his ' Apologia.' But I do not recollect that he had an unreserved admiration at once of character and intellect in any case except one—that of Dr. Newman himself.

Whatever may have been the precise causes of the reticence to which I have referred (and it is possible that physical weakness was among them), the character of our friendship had during these later years completely changed. It was originally formed in common and very absorbing interests. He was not of those shallow souls which think, or persuade themselves they think, that such a relation can continue in vigour and in fruitfulness when its daily bread has been taken away. The feeling of it indeed remained on both sides, as you will see. On my side, I may say that it became more intense ; but only according to that perversity, or infirmity, of human nature, according to which we seem to love truly only when we lose. My affection for him, during those later years before his change, was, I may almost say, intense ; and there was hardly anything, I think, which he could have asked me to do, and which I would not have done. But as I saw more and more through the dim light what was to happen, it became more and more like the affection which is felt for one departed.

As far as narrative is concerned, I am now at the close. In 1850 came the discussions and alarms connected with the Gorham judgment; and came also the last flickering of the flame of his attachment to the Church of England. Thereafter I never found myself able to turn to account as an opening any word he spoke or wrote to me. The year had been, for my wife and me, one of sorrow and anxiety, and I was obliged to spend the winter in Italy. In the spring of 1851 I dined at his brother's and met him. He spoke a few words indicative of his state of mind, but fell back immediately into silence. I was engaged at the time in opposing with great zeal the Ecclesiastical Titles Bill, but not even this circumstance led him to give me his confidence. The crisis had come. I am bound to say that relief soon became visible in its effect upon his bodily health. His road and mine were now definitively parted. After the change had taken place, it happened to me to be once, and once only, brought into contact with him in the course of his ordinary professional employment. I had been giving evidence in a committee-room on behalf of a railway. He was the opposing counsel, and had to put some questions to me in cross-examination. His manner in performing this usually harsh office was as engaging as in ordinary social intercourse; and though I have no doubt he did his duty by his clients, I thought he seemed to handle me with a peculiar tenderness.

On June 18, 1851, he wrote to me the beautiful letter, No. 95.[9] It was the epitaph of our friendship, which continued to live, but only, or almost only, as it lives between those who inhabit separate worlds. On no day since that date, I think, was he absent, however, from my thoughts; and now I can scarcely tear myself from the fascination of writing about him.

And so, too, you will feel the fascination of reading about him; and it will serve to relieve the weariness with which

[⁹ See ch. xxi. (vol. ii. p. 95), where this letter is given.]

otherwise you would have toiled through so long a letter. I hope it is really about *him*, and that egotism has not slily crept into the space which was meant to be devoted to him. It notices slighter as well as graver matters ; for the slight touches make their contribution to the exhibition of every finely shaded character. If anything which it contains has hurt you, recollect the chasm which separates our points of view ; recollect that what came to him as light and blessing and emancipation, had never offered itself to me otherwise than as a temptation and a sin ; recollect that when he found what he held his 'pearl of great price,' his discovery was to me beyond what I could describe, not only a shock and a grief, but a danger too. I having given you my engagement, you having accepted it, I have felt that I must above all things be true, and that I could only be true by telling you everything. If I have traversed some of the ground in sadness, I now turn to the brighter thought of his present light and peace and progress ; may they be his more and more abundantly, in that world where the shadows that our sins and follies cast no longer darken the aspect and glory of the truth ; and may God ever bless you, the daughter of my friend !

Believe me always and warmly yours,

W. E. GLADSTONE.

Miss Hope-Scott.

APPENDIX IV.

VERSES BY J. R. HOPE-SCOTT.

FEAST OF THE CIRCUMCISION, 1859 (THE BIRTHDAY OF C. H. S.).

NEW Year's Day returns again,
Does it bring us joy or pain ?
Does it teach us to rely
On the world, or pass it by ?
Will it be like seasons gone,
Or undo what they have done ?
Shall we trust the future more
Than the time we've spent before ?
Is it hope, or is it fear
That attends our new-born year ?

Childhood, busy with its toys,
Answers, it expects new joys ;
Youth, untaught by pleasures past,
Thinks to find some that will last ;
Manhood counts its honours o'er,
And resolves to gather more ;
While old age sits idly by,
Only hoping not to die.

Thus the world—now, Christian, say
What for me means New Year's Day.

New Year's Day is but a name,
While our hearts remain the same ;
All our years are old and few,
Christ alone can make them new.

Around Him our seasons move,
Each made fruitful by His love.
Summer's heat and winter's snow
May unheeded come and go;
What He suffered, what He taught,
Makes the year of Christian thought.

Then to know thy gain or loss,
From the cradle towards the Cross
Follow Him, and on the way
Thou wilt find His New Year's Day.
Advent, summoning thy heart
In His coming to take part,
Warned thee of its double kind,
Mercy first, but wrath behind ;
Bade thee hope the Incarnate Word,
Bade thee fear the avenging Lord.
Christmas next, with cheerful voice,
Called upon thee to rejoice ;
But, while yet the Blessed Child
Sweetly on thy homage smiled,
Lo ! beside His peaceful bed
Stephen laid a martyr's head.
Next a day of joy was won
For thee by our dear Saint John :
But its sun had scarcely set
When the earth with blood was wet :
Rachel, weeping for her slain,
Would not raise her heart again ;
And St. Thomas, bowing down,
Grasped in death his jewelled crown.

Thus the old year taught thee : say,
Thinkest thou that New Year's Day
Will these lessons sweep away ?
Foolish thought ! the opening year
Claims a sacrifice more dear

Than the martyrdom of saints,
Or the blood of innocents.
Christ Himself doth now begin,
Sinless, to atone for sin ;
Welcomes suffering for our good,
Takes His Saviour's name in blood,
And by Circumcision's pain
Makes the old year new again.

Then, with Him to keep the Feast,
Bring thy dearest and thy best ;
Common gifts will not suffice
To attend His sacrifice.
Jesus chose His mother's part,
And she brought a piercèd heart.
But what Christ for Mary chose,
Doth His utmost love disclose ;
Bid her not unkind to be,
But to share that choice with thee.
Ask her sufferings, ask yet more,
Ask for those thy Saviour bore ;
Upon earth hath never been
Sorrow like His sorrow seen ;
He exhausted man's distress,
Pain, and shame, and loneliness.
Ask to feel His thorny crown,
Ask to make His wounds thine own ;
With His mother claim to be
Partner in His agony.
This obtain, and thou wilt care
Little what thy New Years are ;
There can thee no grief befall
Which the Cross did not forestall ;
Joy in this world there is none
Like that which the Cross hath won.
Grasp it, and the year begin
With no fear, except of sin ;

Love it, and, in turning o'er
All the gifts in hope's bright store,
Choose but one—to love it more.

Low Tide at Sunset on the Highland Coast.

Ye dark wild sands, o'er which th' impatient eye
Travels in haste to watch the evening sky,
When last I gazed, how nobly heaved your breast,
In purple waves and scattered sunbeams drest!
Then o'er you shouted many a gallant crew,
And in gay bands the sea-fowl circling flew;
In your embrace you held the restless tide,
And shared awhile great Ocean's power and pride.
But now how sad, how dreary is the scene
In which so much of life hath lately been!
Your barren wastes untraversed by a sail,
Your only voice the curlew's distant wail;
With rocky limbs and furrowed brow you lie
Like some lone corpse by living things passed by;
Till Night in mercy spreads her clouded pall,
And rising winds mourn at your funeral.
Yes, you are changed, but not more changed than he
Who lately stood beside that smiling sea;
For whom each bark which hastened to the shore
Some welcome freight of love or honour bore;
Who saw reflected in the peaceful flood
His home made happy by the bright and good.
Gladly he looked upon you; now, apart,
He veils his brow and hides his desolate heart;
From him life's joys have quickly ebbed away,
Leaving the rocks, the sands, and the declining day.
To-morrow's tide again the shore will lave,
To-morrow's sun will gild the crested wave;

New ships will launch and speed across the main,
And the wild sea-fowl ply their sport again ;
But for the broken-hearted there is none
To gather back the spoils which Death hath won.
   None, did I say? O foolish, impious thought,
In one whom God hath made, and Christ hath bought !
Thou who dost hold the ocean in Thy hand,
And the sun's courses guide by Thy command,
Hast Thou no morrow for the darkened soul,
No tide returning o'er its sands to roll ?
Must its deep bays, once emptied of their sea,
For ever waste, for ever silent be ?
   Not such Thy counsels—not for this the Cross
Stretched its wide arms, and saved a world from loss !
When life's great waters are by sorrow dried,
Then gush new fountains from Christ's wounded side ;
The Ark is there to gather in our love,
The Spirit, dove-like, o'er the stream to move.
   Then look again, and mirrored in thy breast
Behold the home in which thy dear ones rest ;
See forms which lately vanished from thy sight,
Shine back with crowns, and palms, and robes of light !
See richer freights than ever ocean bore
Guided by angel pilots to the shore !
In faith, in penitence, in hope shall be
Thy traffic on that bright and changeless sea.

On Resuming his Profession.

Mourner, arise ! this busy fretful life
Calls thee again to share its toils and strife ;
The pause conceded to thy grief is o'er,
And the world's march can stay for thee no more.
Then dry thy tears, and with a steadfast mien
Resume thy station in the troubled scene ;

Sad, but resolved, thy wonted vigour prove,
Nor let men deem thee weak from sorrowing love.
The wakeful bed, the sullen sharp distress,
The still recurring void of loneliness ;
The urgent prayer, the hope, the humble fear,
Which seek beyond the grave that soul so dear,—
These yet are thine, but thine to tell no more,
Hide, then, from careless hearts thy sad but precious
          store.
And if life's struggle should thy thoughts beguile,
Quicken the pulse, and tempt the cheerful smile,
Should worldly shadows cross that form unseen,
And duty claim a place where grief hath been,
Spurn not the balm by toil o'er suffering shed,
Nor fear to be disloyal to the dead.
     'Twas nature bade thee grieve, and for thy grief
The Lord of nature now ordains relief.
Like iron molten by the founder's art,
To fierce affliction yields the stubborn heart.
The fiery blast its ancient form destroys,
And bids it flow released from base alloys ;
But the kind God, who doth the flames control,
Wills to re-cast, not to consume, the soul :
Hence tempering breezes, hence the lessened pain,
That the vexed heart may rest and form again.
Then be it so—but, ere that heart grows cold,
See that its later be its nobler mould.
See that, by pain made new, and purged from dross,
It bear, in sharp relief, the image of the Cross.

TABLE OF LETTERS, ETC.

Page	Writer	Date	Subject
	A		
	Abcken. See *Inglis*		
i. 279	Adams (Rev. W.) to J.	Dec. 15, 1846	Merton Coll. Re'orm
ii. 42	R. H.		
ii 208	Allies (T. W.) ,,	Aug. 19 and 30, 1851	Cath. Univ., Ireland
App. II.	Amherst, S.J. (Rev. W. J.)	—	Funeral Sermon
ii. 106	Austin, Q.C. (Chas.), to Mr. E. S Hope	May 6, 1873	High qualities of J. R. H -S.
	B		
	BADELEY (E. L.):		
ii. 189	J. R. H. to Mr Badeley	Jan. 12, 1838	Origin of Civil Govt.
i. 140	Mr. Badeley to J. R. H.	Nov. 5, 1837 ?	Mr. Hope's wish to give up the Law
i. 207	,, to Hon. Lady Hope	July 24, 1840	Mr. Hope's speech before the Lords
i. 223	Mr. Hope to Mr. Badeley	Sept. 14, ,,	Installation at Salisbury
i. 258	,, ,,	Dec. 24, ,,	Visit to Rome
i. 259	,, ,,	Dec. 29, ,,	,, ,,
i. 266	,, ,,	April 1, 1841	,, ,,
i. 279	,, ,,	,, ,,	Merton College
ii. 44	,, ,,	Feb. 28, 1843	The 'Pupilla Oculi'
ii. 46	,, ,,	Sept. 28, ,,	Researches at York
ii. 23	Mr. Badeley to J. R. H. .	Jan. 6, 1844 .	Speech for Macmullen
ii. 41	,, ,,	Oct. 26, ,,	Ward's 'Ideal'
ii. 50	,, ,,	Sept. 22, ,, .	Oxford affairs
,,	J. R. H. to Mr. B. . .	,, ,, .	Dr. Döllinger
ii. 55	,, ,, . .	Nov. 7, ,, .	Interview with Metternich
ii. 41	Mr. B. to J. R. H. . .	Nov. 8, ,, .	Ward's 'Ideal'
ii. 60	J. R. H. to Mr. B. . .	Dec. 19, ,, .	Visit to Rome—Sir W. Follett
i. 284	Mr. B. to J. R. H. . .	Sept. 12, 1846	Scotch College
ii. 62	J. R. H. to Mr. Badeley .	Oct 16, 1847 .	Impression of Rome
ii. 86	,, ,,	Jan. 16, 1848 .	Hampden affair
ii. 108	,, ,,	Feb. 23, 1849	Oath of Supremacy
ii. 99	,, ,,	Oct. 25, 1851	Argument for conversion
ii. 150	,, ,,	Jan. 21, 1852	Visit to Luffness

[1] The numbers refer to the originals in Mr. Gladstone's possession.

Page	Writer	Date	Subject
i. 150	J. R. H. to Mr. Gladstone (No. 6)	July 26, 1838	Relations of Ch. and State (his work on)
i. 151	Mr. Gladstone to J. R. H.	,, ,,	,, ,,
,,	J. R. H. to Mr. Gladstone (No. 7)	,, ,,	,, ,,
i. 152	,, ,, (No. 8)	July 28, ,,	,, ,,
i. 153	,, ,, (No. 9)	July 29, ,,	Pilgrimage to the tomb of Walter de Merton
i. 155	Mr. Gladstone to J. R. H.	July 30, ,,	His book on Ch. and State
i. 155–159	J. R. H. to Mr Gladstone (No. 10)	July 31, ,,	,, ,,
,,	,, ,, (No. 11)	,, ,,	,, ,,
i. 160–167	,, ,, (No. 12)	Aug. 2, ,,	,, ,,
,,	,, ,, (No. 16)	Aug. 4, ,,	,, ,,
i. 168	,, ,, (No. 23)	Aug. 29, ,,	Rev. B. Harrison's appt. Ch. and State— Work on ' Colleges'
i. 171	Mr. Gladstone to J. R. H.	Sept. 7, ,,	Ch. and State
,,	J. R. H. to Mr. Gladstone (No. 24)	Oct. 11, ,,	,,
i. 175	Mr. Gladstone to J. R. H.	Jan. 11, 1839	,,
i. 215	J. R. H. to Mr. Gladstone (No. 42)	Sept. 6, 1840	Scotch College
i. 219	Mr. Gladstone to J. R. H.	Sept. 8, ,,	,,
i. 248	J. R. H. to Mr. Gladstone (No. 32)	Nov. 18, ,,	Scotch College—Manzoni—the Jesuits
i. 281	,, ,, (No. 33)	Jan. 5, 1841 .	Scotch College
ii. 102	,, ,, (No. 36)	June 25, 1841	' Cabbage-garden and flower-garden '
i. 282	,, ,, (No. 39)	Aug. 3, ,, .	Scotch College
,,	Mr. Gladstone to J. R. H.	Aug. 6, ,, .	,,
i. 308	,, ,,	Nov. 6, ,, .	Value for Mr. Hope's advice
i. 209	,, ,,	,, ,, .	Jerusalem Bishopric
i. 328	,, ,,	Nov. 20, ,, .	,, ,,
i. 319	J. R. H. to Mr. Gladstone (No. 48)	Nov. 19, ,, .	,, ,,
i. 329	,, ,, (No. 49)	Nov. 24, ,, .	,, ,,
ii. 36	Mr. Gladstone to J. R. H.	Nov. 23, 1843	About a Refuge for the Destitute
,,	,, ,,	Dec. 14, ,,	Same subject
,,	J. R. H. to Mr. Gladstone (No. 60)	Dec. 18, ,,	,, and Newman's sermons
ii. 37	,, ,, (No. 61)	Feb. 5, 1844 .	Eccl. Courts Bill
ii. 38	Mr. Gladstone to J. R. H.	Aug. 12, ,,	,,
,,	J. R. H. to Mr. Gladstone (No. 62)	Aug. 16, ,,	Sir R. Peel and Mr. Gladstone
ii. 39	Mr. Gladstone to J. R. H.	Aug. 20, ,,	His own political career
ii. 42	Memorandum : J. R. H. (with W. E. G. and Mr. Manning)	Feb. 11, 1845	The attempted censure of Tract 90
ii. 66	J. R. H. to Mr. Gladstone (No. 65)	Mar. 10, ,,	The Oakeley case
,,	Mr. Gladstone to J. R. H.	,, ,,	,, ,,

[2] Messrs. Adam & Charles Black, publishers, Edinburgh.

Page	Writer	Date	Subject
i. 94	J. R. H. to Lady H. Kerr	Mar. 15, 1836	Legal studies
i. 177	„ „	Mar. 4, 1839 .	Hard work on committees
i. 335	„ „	Dec. 18, 1841	Religious position
ii. 143	„ „	July 23, 1847	Engagement to C. H. J. L.
i. 98	Miss—H. to Lady H. Kerr	April 6, 1873 .	Filial dutifulness, &c., of J. R. H.

L

Page	Writer	Date	Subject
i. 34	Leader (J. T.) to J. R. H.	Aug. 1, 1831 .	J. R. H.'s spirits
	„ „	Sept. 5, „	„ „
ii. 188	„ „	Nov. 3, „	Toryism
i. 35	„ „	Jan. 20, 1832	The time coming
i. 38	„ „	Mar. 19, 1833	His regard for J. R. H.
i. 69	„ „	June 6, 1834 .	About their tour
i. 76	„ „	Nov. 11, 1834	J. R. H.'s change of profession
ii. 100	Lewis (D.) to J. R. H.-S.	May 15, 1851	Conversion of J. R. H.-S.
	Liddon. See *Hope*		
ii. 155	LOCKHART (correspondence described):		
ii. 148	Lockhart(J. G.) to J. R. H.	April 8, 1851 .	J. R. H.'s conversion
ii. 173	„ to Mrs. Hope-Scott	Aug. 29, 1850	J. R. H.'s portrait

M

Page	Writer	Date	Subject
ii. 230	Macdonald (Rev. D.) to J. R. H.-S.	Oct. 12 1854	Highland Missions
	MANNING (H.E. CARDINAL):		
ii. 11	The Ven. Archdeacon Manning to J. R. H.	Dec. 30, 1841	Pamphlet on Jer. Bishopric
ii. 103	„ „	Dec. 9, 1842 .	Advises relaxation
ii. 42	„ „ (memorandum)	Feb. 11, 1845	The proposed censure on No. 90
ii. 89	Rev. H. E. Manning to J. R. H.	Nov. 23, 1850	Resignation of office
ii. 91	„ „ (private)	Dec. 11, „	Sympathy in movement towards conversion
ii. 92	„ „	April 7, 1851 .	Their conversions
ii. 93	„ „	Oct. 21, 1851 .	„ „
ii. 212	„ „	Mar. 17, 1852	„ „
ii. 213	„ „	Mar. 3, 1854 .	Charitable bequests
ii. 230	„ „	Jan. 28, 1856	Preaching communities
ii. 58	Manzoni (Alessandro) to J. R. H.	May 8, 1845 .	'Highland Paraguay'
i. 136	Merton Coll. Reforms, Report of J. R. H. on	Oct. 1838 ? .	Friendship for J. R. H. and for Mr. Gladstone
i. 210	Montagu (Right Hon. Lady) to Hon. Lady H.	July 25, 1840	J. R. H.'s speech before the Lords
i. 120	Murray (T. B.) to J. R. H. (referred to)	Dec. 31, 1838	The S. P. C. K.

THE END.

LONDON : PRINTED BY
SPOTTISWOODE AND CO., NEW-STREET SQUARE
AND PARLIAMENT STREET

www.ingramcontent.com/pod-product-compliance
Lightning Source LLC
Chambersburg PA
CBHW060516030726
47498CB00004B/969